Swing Hammer Swing!

Jeff Torrington

Swing Hammer Swing!

HARCOURT BRACE & COMPANY

New York   San Diego   London

First published in Great Britain
in 1992 by Martin Secker & Warburg Limited
Copyright © Jeff Torrington 1992

Requests for permission to make copies
of any part of the work should be mailed to:
Permissions Department, Harcourt Brace & Company
6277 Sea Harbor Drive, Orlando, Florida 32887-6777.

Library of Congress Cataloging-in-Publication Data
Torrington, Jeff, 1935–
Swing hammer swing!/Jeff Torrington.—1st American ed.
p.   cm.
ISBN 0-15-187427-1
1. Novelists, Scottish—Scotland—Glasgow—Fiction.
2. Unemployed—Scotland—Glasgow—Fiction.
3. Marriage—Scotland—Glasgow—Fiction.
4. Glasgow (Scotland)—Fiction.
I. Title.
PR6070.0685S95   1994
823'.914—dc20   93-47299

Printed in the United States of America

First American edition, 1994
A B C D E

For my Mother
My wife Margaret
And Family

Now, the buildings they go up
Just as high as the sky
But me, I'm feelin low enough
Like I could die.
They say they're building this city
Fresh from the start
But there's a demolition party
Working down in my heart.

I'm a man to pity
Got the blues, south city:
Nothin to gain
Nothin to lose
That's how it is with them
South City Blues.

1

Something really weird was happening in the Gorbals – from the battered hulk of the Planet Cinema in Scobie Street, a deepsea diver was emerging. He hesitated, bamboozled maybe by the shimmering fathoms of light, the towering rockfaces of the snow-coraled tenements. After a few moments the diver allowed the vestibule door to swing closed behind him then, taking small steps, he came out onto the pavement which in the area sheltered by the sagging canopy bore only a thin felting of snow. Up the centre of this quiet little grave for privileged snowflakes desecrating feet had trudged a pathway which shone with a seal-like lustre. One person though – a young girl, to judge from the footprints – had ignored the conventional route, and skipped off into the untrodden snow where she'd left the steps of an unknown dance sparkling in her wake.

The diver's gear was from Laughsville: it consisted of a heavy grey plastic boilersuit which was studded all over with fake rivets. The chest area was cluttered by a harness of entwining pipes and pseudo valves, fanciful apparatus which, had it been translated into reality, would've rendered the suit's occupant woad-blue and windless before his boots had so much as dipped into the briny. It also gave the impression, this suit, of having recently passed through the business-end of a shark or some other multi-toothed predator; so badly holed was it, that a string vest would by comparison have looked watertight. The helmet, apart from offering a cramped but nevertheless very private place to drown in, provided zero protection; the thing had a gashed brow and had been all but eaten out by a virulent strain of galloping paint cancer. The diver's feet were stuffed into patched gumboots and, to complete his submarine ensemble, he wore on his tiny hands a pair of ladies' Fair Isle patterned mittens.

The diver's identity wasn't hard to crack. Like a clue slipped within brackets his bandy legs gave the game away. Sensing rather than seeing me – the faceplate was completely misted over – the diver stopped, turned quickly in his tracks, then scuttled back in the direction of the vestibule's grotto-like gloom. Before he'd reached it, though, I'd caught'm by the elbow. From within the helmet there sounded a muffled sigh, then his hand rose to unlatch the faceplate. As it swung open with a thin squeal, a pungent aroma of peppermint confirmed that the suit's occupant was indeed Matt Lucas, the chief operator of the Planet Cinema. Lucas was a mint imperial junky; totally hooked on 'Granny's Windbreakers' he was. Only during mealtimes or sleep itself was his luckless tongue spared the chore of lobbing one of these flavoured pebbles around his dentures. No conversation with Lucas was possible that wasn't accompanied by the clack-clacking sound of the world's most boring sweetie.

'Lo, Matt.'

'Aye, hullo Tommy.'

'You're a wee bit late for Halloween, eh?'

The helmet waggled. 'Ach, it's a stunt Mr Burnett's dreamed up.'

From the bundle of handouts he had wedged under his arm he tugged a sheet out and passed it to me. I studied it.

2

BEETLES BEETLES BEETLES BEETLES
THE YELLOW SUBMARINE
DIVE   DIVE   DIVE   DIVE
TO THE
PLANET CINEMA
FOR FATHOMS OF FANTASTIC FUN
Forget the telly,
Forget the Bingo,
We've got:
JOHN PAUL GEORGE & RINGO!
THE DAB FOUR

'I've to go round handing them out,' Lucas explained.

'You'd be as well chucking them in a midden.'

'The boss's coming wae me.'

'Did Paddy trap this morning?' I asked him.

He nodded. 'Aye, but I don't know what for: heaviest thing he lifted was an aspirin.'

'Got a nippy turnip, has he?'

'Did the sun rise in the east the day?'

Come Judgement Day the prosecution would exhibit the damning evidence of Paddy Cullen's liver – a drink-maimed organ which not even his good qualities, like his sense of humour or his generosity, would gainsay. Paddy would spend Eternity chasing a mobile pub barefooted across a jagged terrain of smashed whisky bottles. My own skull was gowping, the outcome of pigging the booze alongside Cullen in the Dog, followed by an after-hours session in the Moderation Bar. After that the shape of Thursday had become fluid, very fluid: glints and glimmers of glasses half-recalled; faces, and from the holes in them, long idiotic conversations. Later Paddy and me had pissed steamy shadows on a brick wall. The sky had been littered with smashed tumblers.

Cullen had spewed a perfect map of Africa – complete with Madagascar. Even when he's bevvied that boyo shows talent.

From the Planet Cinema, its proprietor, Oswald J. Burnett, now emerged. 'The Zombie in the Crombie' Cullen called him and with good reason. Ever since the death of his manager, Rinty O'Dowd, Burnett had been a man motoring on air. But unlike many film exhibitors of the sixties who'd gone running off to Bingoland as fast as their legs-eleven could carry them, Burnett had remained loyally behind to nurse fatigued films from this choked Hollywood conduit. But even he'd to concede that the Planet was well into its last reel of existence and that the Hammer epic to beat them all was fast approaching. Today Burnett was wearing his Gestapo outfit: shades, Cossack mink-fur hat, leather coat and overshoes. As he loomed closer I found myself wondering, not for the first time, how many animals had perished that his vast coat might live. It'd probably something to do with all those Nazi movies I'd sat through, but the coat seemed to bestow on its wearer a sort of sinister sheen, a sartorial threat of interrogation. Burnett was a real lard-bucket, shifting sixteen maybe seventeen stones. As usual his face was full of amiable little pleats and tucks. A man slow to anger was Burnett, but when he did get aroused the Mussolini with a migraine would by comparison have looked sweet'n sapsy.

As he limped towards Lucas and me, a cigar stump was reeking at a corner of his mouth. He dumped his bundle of yellow handouts into my hands. 'Hold these a minute, Tom. That's it. Ta.' His hands were free now to adjust the maroon scarf he'd wound about his neck. This done he jettisoned the cigar butt, tossing it out onto the slushy street, 'God's forgotten to shut his fridge door again Thomas, eh?' I nodded and gave'm back his handouts. Burnett patted Lucas's shoulder. 'What d'you make of this? Came across it in the Rectifier Room. Left over from some salty saga. Can't recall which. But, no matter.'

I figured he was referring to the diving gear and not to the hapless Lucas. Burnett flicked the faceplate shut and then knuckled the helmet's crown, 'Off you toddle, Matthew. I'll catch you up. Just keep a lookout for sharks.'

We watched Lucas as he ventured beyond the canopy's cover, his gumboots crackling through the crisp scrolls of shovelled snow outside Nelly Kemp's fag'n paper shop. A conger eel with toothache would've drowned laughing if such a figure had come stomping past its home reef. Burnett sighed. 'Is it not terrible what's to be done to turn a coin these days?' I was sure the auld goat was referring to himself and not to Lucas. The fact that his employee might feel a right eejit inside that suicidal suit wouldn't have occurred to'm: Fathoms too deep, it was.

It's really mind-blowing how quickly we can accommodate even the most outlandish spectacle, taking it in our visual stride: 'Look – a deepsea diver!... Where?... ower yonder, plodding through that urban snowdrift. See'm . . . Yeah, I've got'm. A diver, right enough. Imagine that . . . ho hum . . . yawn yawn . . . It might well be that senility disturbs our shockproofing, attacks the mind's defensive cladding in much the same way that deserted villas shrug off their roof tiles to admit the elements. Certainly the kneecreaker in the doorway of Nelly Kemp's fag'n paper shop had been stricken motionless by the sheer novelty of meeting up with a deepsea diver instead of her usual street encounters with dogs, moggies and tenuous life-wisps like herself.

Burnett stretched around me to thrust a handout into the shaking paw of a passing greybeard. The old guy stared in seeming amazement at the piece of paper that'd so suddenly bloomed on his palm. But as he continued on his way the yellow page detached itself from his palsied hand and drifted into a corner of the snowy rectangle where it adhered like a postage stamp. Meanwhile Lucas was trying to deliver a handout to a lamp-post.

'What the devil's he doing?' Burnett muttered.

'His faceplate's steamed up,' I explained, then suggested a method of overcoming the problem.

'Shit'n it!' No wonder Burnett looked incredulous.

'Naw – spit'n it,' I said. You must've seen scuba divers doing it?'

Burnett seemed to find the idea distasteful. 'I believe a smear of liquid soap is equally effective,' he informed me.

Two guys standing in the snow outside a doomed cinema discussing the most efficacious method of preventing a deepsea diver from trying to deliver handouts to lamp-posts! Who, aware that such an absurd conversation was not only possible but had actually taken place, could haughtily discount other so-called improbabilities? Eddie Carlyle, my pious brother'n law, for instance, might one day be confirmed in his naive belief that Heaven is a sort of Butlins with room-service. Well, why not? Jesus himself could turn out to be a lanky, likeable bloke, a Red Coat in fact, with a straw hat tilted rakishly on his head – so much more chummy looking than that luminous doughnut sentimental artists seem to insist on.

Burnett was admiring his handout. 'Decent little job, eh? Got Madge to run'm off on the Gestetner. Wish I'd thought of it a whole lot sooner.'

I nodded. 'Only a couple of things wrong as far as I can see.'

He looked a bit miffed. 'Wrong?'

'You've got The Dab Four,' I said.

'So?'

'Should be "The Fab Four"!'

'Dab, Fab, Crab – what's the difference? Anyway, "dab" sounds better than "fab", whatever that's supposed to mean.'

'Fabulous.'

'Good, so we're agreed?' He looked pleased with himself. 'What's the other thing then?'

'Oh, nothing much – a spelling mistake, that's all. You've got Beatles with two ees when it should be ee-ay.'

He shook his head emphatically. 'I think not, Thomas. Always has been two ees, always will be. Look it up, there's the fellow.'

Again he adjusted his scarf, gave me a farewell salute then went off in the wake of submariner Lucas who, after his difficulty with the lamp-post, was encountering even stiffer resistance from an electrical junction box which despite the lure of a night on the Sticks watching the Dab Four just didn't want to know.

2

Our car, a Volkswagen Beetle, was fairly buzzing along, so zippily in fact that twice within a minute we'd overtaken the same hobbling greybeard. 'You're fond of first gear, aren't you, Eddie?' I said to the driver, and old Father Time lolling there on the rear cushions like a musical coffin tinkled out a series of chimes which I suppose is as near to human laughter as any mechanical contrivance can get. Eddie, my brother'n-law, made one of his hrrumphing noises. Wouldn't it be a pity if after a lifetime of hairshirting, hymnifying, and hallelujahing, St Pete slammed the pearly portal in Eddie's face just because on a few occasions he'd indulged in the odd hrrumph.

It had stopped snowing but now and then bright flurries of the stuff fell from humpy window ledges where maybe a bird had newly settled. Pigeons, beaten to a fine lead by hunger, flickered amongst the rusted girders of the railway bridge. Over there, still standing but only just, was the Brandon Snooker Hall. Dampness had laid a green baize on its bricked-up windows. Where were they now, those gallus geometricians whose wordless lectures on the properties and projections of the moving sphere had us leaning on the smoke in awe? Cuts Colquhoun, Spider Sampson,

Skinner Murphy: gone, all of them – potted by Time, the fastest cue in town.

Fires fuelled by wooden beams burned in cleared sites. Rubble was being trucked from busted gable ends and demolishers worked in a fume of dust and smoke. You would've thought that the Ruskies had finally lobbed over one of their big megaton jobs: streets wiped out, landscapes pulverised. On a gutted site near a fire that drizzled sparks on him, a greybeard sat in a lopsided armchair, placidly smoking his pipe. I nudged Eddie and pointed to the old guy. He spared the greybeard a cold glance then returned his attention to the windscreen through which could be seen advancing streets shorn of their pavements by the snow, and of their buildings by the Hammer. It was inaccurate to call them 'streets' anymore for they looked like a series of bleak airstrips.

Most of the old Gorbals had been levelled by now. Housing Planners had taken up their slum-erasers and rubbed out the people who'd lived there. Some original specks still clung to the Redevelopment blueprints but these would be blown away shortly. In Scobie Street, for instance, a few commercial concerns continued to function: there was Nelly Kemp's fag'n paper shop; Joe Fiducci's barbering joint; The Salty Dog Saloon (my local watering hole); and Shug Wylie's public lavatory (Men Only) which stood out in the middle of the street almost directly opposite the Planet Cinema. The movie house was bracketed by the defunct O'Leary's betting shop and the derelict Blue Pacific Cafe, mention of which is made in local bard John Scobie's 'Ode to a Flea Ranch', where he described the kinema as being 'A crackit planet betwixt the deil and the deep blue sea . . .'

As the car continued on its way the bulky typewriter lodged in my lap dug deeper and deeper grooves into my thighs. Eddie Carlyle just sat there, his gloved hands on the gloved steering wheel. Bugs of melted snow glistened on his dark sombre overcoat, and his tight shirt collar, as hard as cuttle bone, creaked with his every neck movement. Eddie reminded me of yon defensive guy in Chekhov's 'Man in a Shell'. Even his aftershave lotion had a camphorish pong to it, which is appropriate for someone who'd mothballed his life, who'd deprived himself of pleasure down here all the better to enjoy it in the sweet bye-and-bye.

The Beetle crawled into the crevice of a sidestreet. To our left shuttered warehouses and abandoned workshops began to pass while on our right a padlocked adventure playground could be seen. Within it on a sagging gallows a piebald tyre hung in a perfect lack of motion.

We came now to a thoroughfare that blitzed the senses with its sudden buzz and uproar. Here, there were many shops doing business: bakers, fruitshops, fishmongers; banks, dairies, butchers. Above these thronged premises there were dental surgeries which shared their common stairs with tenanted flats from between the curtains of which faces could now and then be glimpsed. On the pavements, shoppers' feet churned the slush to a fine black mud. It was as if Cumberland Street had returned in all of its commercial glory. But, alas, it hadn't. This was in fact Crown Street, what remained of it, a barrier already collapsing before the Hammer's onslaught. There'd be no gainsaying it – soon from the sky there would fall a hard pelting of slates.

'That's it!'

I pointed to a battered-looking shop on an equally battered corner where old election posters hung in a dismal rash of unfulfilled promises. (Come back Alice Cullen – we need you now!) Eddie brought the car to a crackling halt in the gutter. He switched off the engine. Bright sparks of snow drifted by. In a shop window an xmas tree stood bathed in its sentimental fires.

Cradling a polythene-wrapped giant teddy bear a man lurched past. He was doing the Boozer's Bolero – three steps forward on tippytoes, two back heavily on heels. Potent stuff this xmas spirit. Eddie, being such a switched-off cat, made a nipple of his mouth and milked titsing noises from it. A real Paradise put-down is Eddie. Imagine arriving up there, sporting your new wings and your 'Be A Harp Hotshot in Just Two Weeks!' booklet, only to find the place stiff with Eddies!

I raised the typewriter from my lap a little and MacDougall (the self-raising flower), who'd obviously been beset by castration fears, pulsed with gratitude as my manly blood revisited him. 'He lives! Praise the Lord – he lives!' C'mon now, show some respect. A most poignant moment in my life has arrived. I patted my old Imperial Fictionmaster. Sorry pal, hate doing this, but I need the bread. I wasn't coming the con either. The jingling mitt of xmas had me by the throat. 'C'mon you tight bastard, buy your wife a decent pressy for a change. How many wee bottles of eau-de-Cologne d'you think a woman needs?'

'We've still the pram, remember,' Eddie said.

We've-still-the-pram-remember . . . Now, where's that coming from? What can it mean? Just a mess in a dixie, is that it? No, not at all. What we have here is a variation on those egghead puzzles where you're required to identify a concealed geometrical shape by coordinating the variant spaces. There's no lid-of-the-box-solution here, everything's down to the manipulator's geometrical know-how. Likewise to interlock the voids in Eddie's remark depends on a shared pool of familial knowledge. Given this info, everything soon clicks into place. Thus *We've-still-the-pram-remember* unpacks to read: 'We'd best step on it for we've still got that pram to uplift!' What pram? The one being offered to Rhona and myself by Rhona's sister, Phyllis, and her husband Jack too, of course. I was to uplift it from their place this very afternoon.

At the moment Rhona is in the Maternity Hospital, prematurely as it happens, due to an elevated blood-pressure condition . . . Decoding of message complete.

'C'mon,' Eddie now urged, 'move yourself!'

It's amazing how contact with his Nazi steering wheel – gloved or not – turns Eddie into an insufferable little Volkswagenführer. It's like he's hooked a jump-lead into a super ego-booster. Ex auto, of course, he lives a vapid existence, snailing along at the heels of his mother Letitia Dalrymple Carlyle. When he's not doing this then he's slaving away in a textile warehouse in the despatch room of which he prepares for consignment parcels of cambric, organdie, buckram and tarlatan.

'Right,' I responded, 'get your arse roon here and haud the door. This thing's a ton weight.'

Bugged by my tone, not to mention my language, he snapped. 'This could've waited. I'm not a flippin taxi service. You do realise that I'd to get – '

' – time from your work? Aye, I think you mentioned it a couple hunner times.' I shrugged my shoulders. 'Anyway, I don't see what all this hurry-hurry's about: Rhona's no due tae February.'

He caught me adrift at the nets with a moralistic backhand volley, 'It'd never cross your mind of course, that since her hyster – her operation, Phyllis might get depressed by the very sight of that pram.'

'Heavy, man.'

His shirt collar crackled, at least I think it was his collar though it might well've been his indignant soul stretching its astral muscles. How godalmighty powerful he looked all of a sudden – like a thrush unzipping a worm.

'"Heavy, man,"' he mimicked me. 'What's that supposed to mean? Why can't you speak normally instead of . . . of . . .'

normal words failed him. I got a Zen buzz: 'Man who rides on Beetle should refrain from stamping his foot . . .'

'Eddie,' I said, 'get the door, will you – before my bastard'n legs drop off!'

3

The shop was crammed floor-to-ceiling with junk. Every nook and cranny had been utilised to accommodate the domestic fall-out which had resulted from that most disastrous of community explosions – the dinging doon of the Gorbals. Leaving in their wake the chattels of an outmoded way of living, whole tribes of Tenementers had gone off to the Reservations of Castlemilk and Toryglen or, like the bulk of those who'd remained, had ascended into Basil Spence's 'Big Stone Wigwam in the Sky'. To be found in this shop with its pervasive stink of Time-rot were their old zinc tubs, their steamie prams, their wringers and their scrub-boards, their quaint old wirelesses, wind-up gramophones, dusty piles of 78s, EPs and LPs, twelve-inch tellies, wallydugs, wag-at-the-wa's, brass fenders, fire-irons, fretworked pipe-racks, marquetry pieces, box cameras and speckled photographs scattered as far and wide as no doubt were the people they depicted, cartons stuffed with picture postcards, old music sheets and books, hundreds and hundreds of books, every domestic prop you could think of, aye, and including not one but at least half a dozen kitchen sinks.

Into this shop too, like so many stale pizzas, had tumbled wall plaques which showed every sentimentalised rural scene imaginable. Ours had been 'The Watermill', though its stream had been diverted after Da Clay'd vented his spleen on it with a flying boot (a great spleen-venter was my old man). The leader of the 'Ducks in Flight' had winged on for many a year with a broken neck caused by – who else? – Vic Rudge, when he'd taken a potshot at it with his Webley air pistol. Those selfsame ducks might very well be here as might also my old bike, a royal-blue'n white Argyle with a wee kiltie on the handlebar stalk. With some rummaging I might even be able to howk out those stookie ornaments Ma Clay'd been so fond of: Boy with Cherries, for instance. Poor bugger, he was always getting his conk knocked off before he'd a chance to sample the fruit. 'Tantalus' I'd nicknamed him, being at that time a raggedy-arsed kid who mainlined on bookprint.

'Don't put it there – you'll scratch it!'

The typewriter, about to mate with its dim reflection on a dust-streaked table was hastily transferred to the lid of a travel-weary trunk. The shop's owner, a crabbit wee nyaff came over now and, looking aggrieved, rubbed a finger across the table's stourie surface. If I'd scratched it I'd make good the damage, he warned me, which was really rich considering the tabletop already had more scrapes and blemishes on it than there were on my Jimmie Rodgers record collection. Muttering under his breath he fixed his querulous glance on me. 'You, is it? And what rubbish are you trying to unload this time?'

The old yap bent to give the machine the once-over. He poked at it with a finger, mainly in the area of the ribbon spools but never once pressed a key which was about as nutty as buying a car solely on the design of its ashtrays. He straightened. When he spoke his voice was loused up with catarrh and a crack ran through all of his words.

'What's this, then?'

When I told'm he snapped. 'Aye, I didnae think it was for sweepin carpets! But what'm I supposed to do wae it?' Again I told'm. 'Buy it?' he squawked. 'I thought maybe you wanted it rebuilt.'

'It's a fine auld machine,' I assured him, then slipped in a quick commercial which glossed over the typewriter's crucial lack of the letter I. 'I'll give you a wee demo if you like.' Adjusting the creased sheet of paper I knelt beside the chest and briskly typed: 'The fast brown dog jumps over the lazy fox . . . Now's the hour to come to the help of the party . . .'

'There, how's that?'

He shrugged his skinny shoulders. 'Hanged if I know. Havnae got on ma readin specs.' He tugged now from his pants pocket a hankie, so clatty it would've been the talk of the steamie. Raising the pestilent rag he proceeded to snort his brains into it. When the messy job was done and his sight had been partially restored he looked cross to find me still there. 'Better chance of sellin a cracked chantie. Who'd want a typewriter aroon these parts?'

What a question. A blizzard of authors was sweeping through Glasgow. To get into the boozers you'd to plod through drifts of Hemingways and Mailers. Kerouacs by the dozen could be found lipping the Lanny on Glesca Green. Myriads of Ginsbergs were to be heard howling mantras down empty night tunnels.

'I thought maybe a ten-spot,' I said, as in the classical manner I assumed the stance of the black-belted Haggler.

'Ten bob for that rubbish! You're off your trolley, sonny.'

My Haggle-Master wouldn't be chuffed with me. Recklessly I'd exposed myself to the Haggler's prime foe – the non-Haggler. Mindless of tradition, ignorant of the rules of engagement, the subtle testing of balance until the fulcrum of compromise had been attained, the auld bugger'd simply waded in and fetched me a boot in the cheenies. Turning now he peered into the backshop gloom then shouted, 'Alice, come ben a minute.'

After a few moments a peely-wally lassie of around fourteen, a comic in one hand, a half-gnawed apple in the other slouched into our presence. She wore a skimpy mauve dress and a nasty line in facial acne. There was a blue slyness to the eyes that slid from me to my 'fine example of British craftmanship . . .'

'What d'you want, Gramps?' she asked through a gobful of mushed apple.

'You say you get typing at school? Right, have a bash at this thing, then.'

She wasn't overkeen (me even less so) but Gramps insisted. The girl sighed then placed the half-chewed apple on Biffo the Bear and kneeled before the machine. Very self-consciously she adjusted her skinny fingers on the guide keys. I leaned over her. 'If it helps just copy what I've typed.' But with a nervous gulp she began to rap out something entirely different:

'Of all the f shes n the sea the merma d s the one for me.'

She tried again with identical results. Next, with a glance up at me, she struck a rapid tattoo on the i key: the amputated leg kicked impotently.

'Well?' her grandfather queried.

The girl rose. 'It's alright, I suppose, considering its age.' Her mouth sappy once more with pulped apple she turned mocking blue eyes on me.

'A pound,' the junkman offered.

'A fiver, surely.'

'Thirty bob.'

'Four pounds, then?'

'Two, no more.'

I sighed. 'Okay, but it's daylight robbery.'

The old man, still grumbling under his breath, creaked off into the backshop where presumably he stashed his loot. His granddaughter grinned at me then, pausing only to spit out an apple seed, said, 'You'd better give me five bob or I'll tell'm . . .'

4

Underway again, if beetling along at walking pace could be called that, I'd to grin to myself at the recollection of Little Nell and her Grandfather. Smart kids around these days, real bright buttons. The backdrop depicting the High Court seemed to have jammed but with a supreme heave the scene-shifters got it on the move and replaced it with a solemn view of the City Mortuary. We came, appropriately enough, to a dead halt beside it.

'What's that ticking noise?' Eddie asked.

I glanced over my shoulder. The Grandfather clock lay as before on the rear seat, its white face glimmering and, the embalmer's touch, a long-ago midnight or noon caught in its clasped hands. It was a gonner all right, had well'n truly popped its cogs. Family tradition has it that it stopped short, never to go again, the very night its maker, Granda Gibson had taken a turn for the better and was soon on his way to a sprightly recovery in the Victoria Infirmary.

Eddie was shaking his head. 'You surely don't imagine that it's coming from that thing?'

I shrugged. 'Why not?'

'Grow up. A box of junk, that's all it amounts to. Mother won't let it in the house. Don't say you weren't warned.'

'How no?'

Eddie, bravely, and completely without an anaesthetic, studied his own reflection in the rear-view mirror. He plucked at his flat overlip, drawing it up to examine one of his yellow incisors. They looked like old piano keys his choppers did. Mercifully, he dropped the lid on them. 'I'll tell you why not – because that chiming orange-box is riddled with dry rot. If it's ticking then it can only be a deathwatch beetle.'

'Garbage.'

'Agreed. And the same goes for some of that other junk you've foisted on us. Take that wardrobe for a start . . .'

'Dartholes. How many times have I . . .'

'Who'd hang a dartboard on a wardrobe.'

'We didnae. Some of my pals were hellish aimers. Take Potsie Green for starters: compared wae him Mr McGoo had twenty-twenty vision. I'll tell you another thing . . . Bless you!'

'I wasn't sneezing, I was going shhhh . . .'

'Shhhhh?'

'Shut up. I can still hear it.'

'What?'

'Ticking.'

His gaze swivelled suspiciously in my direction then homed in on the bump in my Marine combat jacket. 'What've you got in there?'

'A bomb.'

From beneath the jacket I produced an alarm clock. It was a blue malevolent-looking job, the destroyer of a thousand sleeps: the thing had leapt unasked onto my person as I'd left the shop.

'Vicious looking bugger, eh? A double-action rouser. If you don't hit the rug after the first bell it pishes on you.'

'For any favour!' A look of sufferance creased his lugubrious face. What was it with this creep? Wasn't this proof positive that I

20

was going to change my ways? Hadn't I dumped the very machine that'd threatened to turn his sister's life into a fiction? Not only that, I'd replaced it with a clock – the symbol of regularity and responsibility. Come Monday next I fully intended to cease being Dr Munn's catspaw in his attempt to sabotage the National Health Service system by choking it with paper, lots and lots of paper. Sick lines by the shovelful; first, intermediary then, with much reluctance, final certificates; rambling letters to hospital consultants about rambling patients; X-rays which often not only failed to match the afflicted part but also the afflicted patient; and overprescribing on a scale so mega it must've been keeping at least a couple of pill barons in pink caddies.

My illness – a nomadic back pain (the malingerer's mate) eluded Dr Munn's perfunctory attempts to pin it down, but the Health Board, really concerned about my welfare, summoned me to the cave of their resident shaman, a Dr Sword, who while he was no great shakes with a scalpel was blessed with a magic fountain pen which in about as long as it takes to write 'Fit for work' could 'cure' even the most tenacious illnesses on the spot. His steely gaze had soon focused on the source of my ailment. 'About as classic a case of self-induced narcolepsy as I've come across,' he told his assistant, a Dr Butler (this duo became the infamous 'Sword'n Buckler', the very utterance of whose names sent foreboding shivers through the sub-world of means-testees, tribunalees, and appeals-panelees).

The first painlets of my affliction were sown the day I'd been doing some mental grazing in my dictionary and came across the word 'sabbatical'. It seems that there's this racket pros and parsons are into which allows them to sod off from the state gallery for a year or so. This is so that their mental and physical batteries can be recharged while they enjoy a little exotic nookying, surfing, or hang-gliding. Fair enough. Nowt wrong

21

with that. But worrabout the wurkers? Nuffink doing; they were to ramain unsabbied. Bloody liberty. Was I, the son of a dead Clydesider going to stand for it? No way, Comrade! So, with the aid of that rascally old anarchist, Doc Munn, who willingly covered my trail with sick lines, I sabbied forth from my workplace (at that time I was a fireman on the railways) to give my braincogs a good airing.

Instead of indulging in some mild eccentricity like, for instance, trying to construct an atomic mousetrap or designing a navel-fluff remover for blind persons, I decided to fulfil a long-cherished ambition – the writing of a novel. And why not? I'd writing talent, bags of it. Hadn't my English teacher, Mr Ironsides, said so? No, as a matter of fact he hadn't. Ironsides saw himself in the role of a literary shepherd. He stood on the mound of his ego, ever vigilant to preserve us from grammatical howlers. Using specialised signals, he sent his dogs into the heart of a paragraph to snap at the heels of woolly adjectives, sniffing out ellipses and split infinitives, before urging them to drive the word-flocks into tight, pedantic pens where the casualty rate from suffocation was often high. Ironsides deprecated what he called my 'lone wolfishness' and he harped on about my vulgarities in matter of style: 'I asked for an essay, boy – not a billposter.'

At last the traffic lamp close by the mortuary gave us the come on and the snow-mottled traffic, with a grinding of gears, began to surge towards Glasgow Cross. From the verdigrised rim of the alarm clock a tiny bug, a molecule on legs, had emerged. I studied it as it began an epic journey from twelve to six, its polar opposite. A time-beastie? No. Time-beetle, then? Nope. How about a clockroach? Bingo! Aye, a clockroach, a wee time-beastie that lives in a nine to five universe. I felt chuffed. It seemed that I was still on the Muse's mailing list. I glanced from the window as the

VW chuntered up the High Street, the vestigial spine of ancient Glasgow. In a shop window a nude male mannequin was to be seen staring up at a silvery tree from the branches of which handbags and gloves dangled like mutated fruits. I must sort that away for the future use of. Aye, despite the loss of my I-less pal (I could still feel its tactile phantom pressuring my thighs), I would soldier on at the writing game. Those goons who urged me to be sensible and not to strain my working-class braincells beyond their inherited capacity, hadn't they heard of a jotter'n pen – the only tools required by a writer? A tannery jotter with all the arithmetic tables printed on the back cover, not forgetting yon stotting word – avoirdupois! 'Open your jotters and leaving a margin begin: There was once this deepsea diver who discovered a tenement building on the floor of the ocean. He went through one of its closes and found himself in a backcourt where the calm corpses of housewives with carpet beaters in their hands floated around. Also to be seen was King Neptune himself, having forty winks in a lopsided armchair.'

Swinging to'n fro on the windscreen was a tiny plastic skeleton, one of those keyring curios. Eddie probably hung it there as a 'memento mori', though one glance in the mirror at his corpsy face would've served the same purpose. Mentally I saluted the grinning effigy. 'Lo there, Morto – this Hereafter biz, it's a bit of a giggle then, isn't it?'

The car braked as another traffic lamp ripened.

'Big night at the Tent Halls, Saturday, eh?'

Eddie ignored my remark, still sore, I suppose about the time I'd taken in the junk shop. Or maybe he was too absorbed in watching for a wave from Jesus, out there on the slushy pavement. Could be that he was receiving divine Morse through the juddering gearstick. Must be dead comforting to know you've got it all buttoned up on the Other Side, to sit here in a crummy

Beetle completely at ease with the shuddersome prospect of Eternal Life. In my Father's Garage there are many Jags. But also one or two Minis for the agnostics.

Passing now on our left was the Sighthill Cemetery which provided a much more potent memento-mori for the residents of the Fountainwell Road High Flats. Nifty location, when you thought about it; from the mossy gravestones you'd get a renewed zest for living. 'You down there, and me up here, you can't smoke fags and you can't drink beer!'

Eventually we'd shaken off Springburn and after a while were skittering through the tight streets of Crabton. It was the kind of place you'd only visit if your plane crash-landed there. Its architectural theme was anonymity and this had been so faithfully subscribed to that even though it'd a graveyard bang at the heart of its main thoroughfare you'd've been hard pushed to locate it.

Having shaken off Crabton, an Arctic landscape began to impose itself, a slow unpleating of fields like a luminous fan that eventually wagged me to sleep. When I awoke from this doze we were already in the environs of the recently built Nat Smollet Estate. What a groovy Winter Wonderland. Even the snow hereabouts had a luxurious sheen to it, a golden lustre derived from a plenitude of sodium-vapour lighting. Rolling past on either side I could see chunky, snow-capped mortgages and also many a lofty foreclosure with xmas trees chained in their windows. It was here in Fat Wallet, as I called it, that those star-favoured creatures Mr and Mrs Jack Sherman, had their abode.

5

If JPS is right and Hell is other people then, presumably, Purgatory is where they kennel their dogs. Phyllis Sherman had more or less to dig me out from under an avalanche of salivating beef and bad breath called Faraday, a St Bernard who wore a ketchup bottle where you'd expect to find the traditional brandy keg. Phyllis fetched the brute clouts which would've amounted to aggravated assault had they been directed at a human. '*Far-a-day* (punch punch) STOP IT! (punch punch) Ouf, you brute. Who put this stupid bottle on you? Jason . . . Jason, come through here at once!' But young Jason, who'd been awaiting Alpine rescue under a pile of 'snow' in the linen cupboard, wisely decided to lie doggoe and let Faraday take his lumps. The St Bernard was eventually condemned to cool it in the cellar for a while though even from there his baying was powerful enough to suggest that he'd the backing of half the Kennel Club. His heavy headbutts on the door threatened an imminent outburst of mangled hinges, flying screwnails, and instant sawdust. Phyllis stormed to the vibrating door then in a high but controlled voice, she cried: 'Just keep that up, boy, and you'll be on pound food for the rest of your *very short* life!' Faraday clammed. Right there'n then he shut down on the barking, the panel beating, the works. I don't know what they put in that pound grub but one thing's for sure – it must be helluva hard on canine tastebuds.

'Sorry about that,' Phyllis apologised, 'but yesterday an old tramp mouthed off at'm outside the supermarket. Maybe seeing you he . . . well, never mind, he's quiet enough now.'

Jeezuz, they took no prisoners in this house. First they set the dog on you then obliquely let you know you're a ringer for some festering old dosser! Phyllis returned to the interrupted ritual of receiving her visitors' coats, an effete, diddleclass custom. Scobie Street folks didn't go in for that kind of thing, they could shuck their own duds except maybe when they were partying, in which case an appointed household urchin or urchins would see to their removal and the garments would eventually fetch up on the host's bed in a wild, incestuous tangle. When I knocked back Phyllis's invite to remove my combat jacket her ruthlessly cropped eyebrows arched a millimetre or so, just enough to indicate her indelible contempt for my shirtless origins and my shiftless ways. Although Phyllis, like her sister Rhona, had been Gorbals-born, the Carlyle family through some unspecified windfall had come into money and soon after they'd shaken the slum dust from their shoes and headed for the far more salubrious district of Kings Park, where Mr Carlyle set himself up in business as a locksmith. Their new home had been a first-class sandstone tenement which was tiled from entrance to topdeck and had, for goshsakes, lino on all of its landings and flowering pot plants along its window ledges.

At the time of the Carlyle departure Rhona had been around ten or eleven and I was considered to be 'going with her' as they said in those days. When I put in an appearance at their new home Mrs Carlyle was far from pleased to see me. In fact, she gave me a long finger-wagging lecture about my need to keep away from her daughter in the middle of which she lost all control of herself, seized me by the shirt collar and dragged me down the stairs, along the close, then pitched me out onto the pavement. As I rose shakily to my feet and she was dusting her hands she screamed at me: 'Get back to the Scabby where you belong – you and your guttersnipe family. And if I see you so much as within a mile of my daughter I'll have the police on you, d'you hear?'

Of course Rhona and me had gone on seeing each other – there were parks in plenty thereabouts to serve our purpose. I sometimes wonder if the Carlyles hadn't flitted whether Rhona and I would've continued 'going with each other' or if our childhood crush, despite the spice of forbidden kisses, would've petered out in the usual way of juvenile romances. In fact, we'd begun to see less'n less of each other and eventually a whole week might pass without a meeting. One day I saw her with a gawky-looking lad who'd a face like a well-scrubbed kneecap and a Stan Laurel haircut. He wore these posh school togs and god help us was carrying Rhona's books. The next time I saw Rhona I was half-cut and in the company of gangsters like Vic Rudge, Hatchet Hannah, Chibber Freeland, and Kinch O'Kane. Over the Glasgow Green it was, when the carnival had turned up for the Fair Holidays. And thereby, as they used to say, hangs a tale.

Phyllis was smirking at me, amused by my reluctance to part with my jacket.

'What's up Patton?' she asked. 'Scared they'll start World War Three without you?' This was a stray bullet from an old battle between us. Phyllis ridiculed me whenever the opportunity presented itself. 'A walking contradiction,' she'd called me to my face. As someone who proclaimed pacifism yet wore a CND button on a Yankee combat jacket, I suppose she had a point. If only I'd thought to quote old Walt Whitman's gentle put-down: 'Do I contradict myself? Very well then, I contradict myself.'

27

Instead I'd come out with some juvenile crap about 'being at war with society'. No wonder she'd given that the horse laugh, this shrew with the armour-plated name.

She continued to hold out her hostess-white hands, making a sort of give-it-me gesture that somehow seemed playful, big-sisterly even. 'Playful?' 'Big Sisterly?' Take me to Rubberland! If Phyllis here ever got to be 'playful' or 'big sisterly' then the cobra's a cupcake and all bets are off. No way was I about to shuck my jacket for her. She might get the notion that I was fixing to stay longer than the time it would take to lash the totmobile to the roof of the VW, and be on our way with it to Mother Dragon's lair in Kings Park. In its current state of isolation my pad in Scobie Street was becoming too vulnerable to burglary for the pram to be stored there so, for the time being, it would join the rest of our stuff that'd already been stored in Rhona's childhood nest. The pram arrangement also allowed for oblique deference to the superstition against being over-prepared for the babe's arrival, lest the Lord smiteth the presumptuous womb or some such guff. Another reason why my jacket was staying put was the post-moth condition of the sweater beneath it . . .

Eddie too dawdled over the doffing of his overcoat. 'Hadn't we best see to the business first?' he suggested in exactly the tones you'd expect from the bloke with the measuring tape and the eternal life equipment when he called to take charge of the remains. Phyllis was getting stroppy about this dithering. 'What kept you, anyway?' she asked her brother as she hauled his coat off and all but skewered it on a peg. 'Mum's been up to high-doh. On that blasted phone every five minutes.'

Eddie hooked a thumb in my direction. 'His fault. Spent forever in a junkshop. I think he'd a job convincing its owner that he wasn't part of the stock.'

My, my, a rare funny from Bleakchops. It's your turn, sis.

Don't let me down. Phyllis smirked at me. 'A junkshop? Started your Christmas shopping at last have we Patton?'

Fine teeth this classy croc had – and such a lot of them! Her smile snapped shut. She tightened the cap of the ketchup bottle she'd removed from Faraday during our epic struggle in the hall, then she began to holler her son's name. 'I'll warm your botty if you don't come here this instant.' Not much of an offer: the lad stayed put in his Alpine retreat. I saw now that Phyllis had lost a good deal of weight since her operation. It suited her though. She wore a plum coloured sweater with what I think they call a cowl neckline, and a pair of slimline slax. Her hair was piled up in a style I approved of in Rhona though she seldom adopted it, claiming that it gave her headaches. Both sisters shared the same hair colouring, intensely black and plentiful with a rooky blue sheen to it. They also had in common a certain air of haughtiness, maybe even snootiness, which was integral with the slant of their cheekbones and the way they seemed to have of looking down their noses at you. I reckon Rhona had the edge in looks but Phyllis was definitely ahead in the bum-stakes. Too bad though she'd opted to haul on the pantie-girdle, its visible ridges marred the smooth flowline of her buttocks.

'Donald's dropped in,' Phyllis told her brother as we followed her like a pair of greasy meter-readers down the hall. With every yielding footstep the carpet reminded us that we were treading a multi-bucks tapis into which its purchaser, Jack Sherman, had woven long tiring days and short sleepless nights. Eddie acknowledged Phyllis's remark with a nod. 'He's into a Minx now, I see. Never did like that Zephyr, did he?' Hrrumph . . .'

Aye, 'Hrrumph', indeed! What would the intrepid mountaineer, hiding up there in his snug cave, make of such verbal drizzle? If later in life when he was able to find his way around a dictionary, he tried to reconstruct this confab between his mother and his Uncle Eddie, it would appear that one year, just before Christmas, a man called Donald had dropped into something (though what the 'something' was hadn't been defined). After that the man had changed into a flirty lady who for some reason had a spite against the wind. As if the planet of infancy wasn't far enough away without adults lousing up communications with such static.

In my plebeian way I'd expected that the statuses of a textile warehouseman and unemployed drifter would at the most rate Eddie and I a mug of coffee and a biscuit à la cuisine in the garrulous company of Florrie Monks, a diligent domestic toy Phyllis had picked up at some Renta Drudge Agency. But, gee-whizz, wasn't the Lady of the Manor actually leading us towards the Shermans' most holy of holies – The Peacock Throne Room itself? By jings aye she was!

When you entered the lounge you could immediately see what good money and bad taste could achieve between them. This walled contrivance was a strategy of furnishings, fabrics and mural decor which had been intended to suggest artistic reticence but had ended up being little more than visual muggery. With a pilgrim's awed stoop, my eyes blinking rapidly as if to imply bedazzlement in the treasurehouse of tackiness, I took in the porcelain, the ivory knick-knacks, the fishtank in one corner, the TV set in another, the horse-mobile, a tinkling herd that circled on the ceiling, the glass galleon with the tiny wooden bottle rammed up its gimcrack asshole, the xmas cards in a star-shaped arrangement on one wall and with a burgeoning astral twin arising on the facing one. And the christmas tree! We mustn't forget the christmas tree – a green furry brute, wrenched from a colossal socket in a northern forest and dragged down here to be humiliated by such prissy lowland gew-gaws . . .

Close by the nancyfied spruce, sitting on the throne of the master himself, was a merry little jackanapes with a face as red and as hearty as a good-going stove and with such a cherubic smile, not to mention an abundance of white hair, that he could've passed for Santa in civvies. I'm all too well aware that the daily grind of money-making can put years on a person but not even for a fleeting moment was I diddled into thinking that this festive goblin could be Jack Sherman newly returned from a hard day's night at the mintmill. No, Sherman was never as a rule home this time of day. It was more usual for him to come creeping in from his passionate affair with money hours after we sluggards had begun bending the straw. How, lacking such heroes, could capitalism (and cardiac consultants) flourish? Sherman was a kind of finance plumber. On call twenty-four hours a day, it was his job to ensure that capital was free to flow within its prescribed circuits: a bunged-up merger, the fracture of a feduciary joint; the overflowal of a Swiss Bank account – Jack was the lad to turn to. Money from money – it was wily pitching!

It turned out that wee Santa in the armchair was a retired triple-ball-merchant. All of his spare time was now pledged to the Supreme Pawnbroker, who'd proclaimed that all souls were redeemable even if you'd lost your ticket on an astral suit that was out at the elbows.

'Tom,' says Phyllis with all the tenderness of a Venus fly-trap. 'This is a good friend of ours – Donald Strang.' She flicked a tentacle to indicate to her visitor that I (audible sigh) was her brother-in-law, Tom Clay. As it happened I knew this man by repute: Rhona had done a good PR job on'm back in those days when she'd been naive enough – and brave enough – to accept on the strength of a single dream that her chief mission in life was to be the 'saving' of my soul. At that time, I'd been an eastern mishmashist, a sucker for all the curry-flavoured come-ons. My enthusiasm began to wane though the day I saw on the telly a renowned mystic, Swami Narwalagee, I think his handle was, losing his cool at an airport because they couldn't fix'm up with a seat on a homebound flight. Now, this was the very turkey who'd claimed in one of his books to be able to transport his physical body to any spot on the planet by occult means. But to be honest, I don't think I ever got over the newspaper exposé which revealed that T. Lobsang Rampa, whose stuff on Tibetan lore I'd devoured, was really a plumber from London. I've nothing against tradesmen, especially not plumbers, but I have to admit that after this revelation my mystical ballcock was never quite so buoyant.

But where was I? Yeah, Rhona, and her attempts to get me to tune into the Good News which, she claimed, radiated from every page of the NT. She reinforced this claim by slipping biblical tracts and scriptural leaflets into books I was currently reading, thus I could end up using as a page marker in Kierkegaard's angst-ridden *Either/Or*, a jolly little message with a headline like: 'Getting Into God's Good Books'. No thanks, I told my domestic apostle, I much preferred auld Nick's bad yins. Many of these tracts had come from the pen of the man now shaking my mitt. At that time Strang had been an active backcourt bible-basher. Kids with hardly a backside to their troosers would be encouraged by Strang to 'Count Your Many Blessings', and not only that, they were to name them one by one; after which they were expected to 'Climb, Climb, up Sunshine Mountain, faces all aglow . . .' Strang claimed that he'd saved many a soul and, God willing, would save many more. To test'm the Lord had visited on his pawnbroking servant hypertension, arthritis and growing deafness.

Strang, looking as if he meant it, said that he was indeed delighted to make my acquaintance. This assurance was spoken with that sonic boom which can sometimes be the mark of the hard-of-hearing – either that or they're whispering like spies in a corner. But as we pressed flesh I sensed that the puckish ex-pawnbroker was more curious than he was delighted to meet me. It was obvious that he was comparing two Clays – the wraith who'd preceded me here from gossip's shallow grave; and the so-called 'real' me, that conjurer's cabinet of sliding mirrors, drawstrings, and secret compartments. 'So this,' his subvoice was probably saying, 'is the rogue who all but broke Letitia Carlyle's heart! Here was the very devil who'd lassoed her younger daughter's affections then dragged her back to the evil stews of the slums from which good fortune had freed her. Aye, it's a fact, there's more to the human handshake than a mere mingling of sweat.

The introduction over we all sat down and had tea. It was not, alas, served by yon wee treasure, Florrie Monks, who despite valiant efforts had failed to overcome cancelled bus services and sidewalk snowdrifting in order to be here. Anyway, Florrie usually did for the Shermans in the mornings although now and again if she was free from her prison visits (her sons were Monks by name but not nature – one of the wee gem's jokes, god bless'r!) she'd toss in the extra hour or so and maybe even do some babysitting. It was left to Phyllis to be 'mother' and she poured tea so pale my old man would've slung it down the sink, muttering in disgust as he did so, 'Ants' piss, that's what this is. Ants' piss!'

Strang, his rosy cheeks dishing out the smiles even when he was cramming a scone into that hole in his beard, began to tattle about some sort of Jesus Jamboree which was taking place the next evening at the Tent Hall, an evangelic nerve-centre not far from Glasgow Cross. I'd been made vaguely aware of its imminence from whispering in the Carlyle camp, gossip about the important personages who'd be attending, real pulse-jerking stuff.

Stuck in the room's coldest corner, right next to the goldfish tank, I gazed in at the torpid creatures as they drifted around in their chilled green world. Immortality for shubumpkins? Why not! Creatures far less worthy and not so brawly vested, have been granted divine status. There's your scarab beetle for a start; those dynasts from the Delta, the sharp lads with the pointy tombs, they weren't so uppity that they wouldn't hinge a knee to auld SCARABAEUS SACER. So, why shouldn't – Beg your pardon? You want to know the nature, dimension and location of the Shubumpkin soul? Jeez, that's a tough yin. Let's just say that it's a wee fart of foreverness which is akin to a bubble in a spirit level and is lodged in the creature's thorax.

In a corner a Grandfather clock coughed discreetly before ushering in the hour. 'Grandfather' bugger all! Grandfakir was more like it for the thing was no more than five years old. Simulated antiquity, that's all, like the mane of the immortal pawnbroker, breaking metaphysical wind on Sherman's armchair. 'I shake my bleached locks at the runaway pun . . .' (Sorry, Walt.) On a bookshelf amidst jade and ivory knick-knacks another timepiece, Sir Gulliver Newton, stood knee-deep in Chinese peasantry and told the hour with a series of metallic burps, as if Time gave it heartburn then, abruptly, resumed stolid Presbyterian ticking.

The elect trio in the lounge, knowing that they'd never die but would go on and on forever, gabbed in that nonchalant manner such self-delusion tends to engender. But his nibs in the corner there, he could feel it all right, the inner jag of his mortality, the certainty that he was for the all-time off. It made no difference whether he went raging 'against the dying of the light' just to please Taffy Thomas, or strolled off whistling Colonel Bogie – his personal extinction was assured.

'And can we expect you, Mr Grey?'

The question had been sprung on me by Strang of the Three Balls.

'Clay,' I corrected him. 'The name's Clay.' Although going by Phyllis's scowl 'Mud' might've been more apt.

'I'm sorry, Mr Clay. I was wondering if you'd be going to the Tent Hall on Saturday evening.'

Before I could come on with some softly-pedalled response, Eddie had intervened. 'He's an atheist,' he said, his face souring as if he'd caught a whiff of his own personality. 'He doesn't believe in anything.'

'Well, if he's an atheist he believes in that,' Strang said trickily. 'But let'm speak for himself. He has a tongue, hasn't he?'

A strategy surfaced: lose heavily here; take a right good verbal gubbing. Such humiliation might soften Phyllis some, make her more amenable to the grief I was going to lay on her about my acute shortage of the readies. Would she be willing to delay receipt of the pram money (£7) until I'd got fixed up in Toilville? But of course she would, just so long as I was prepared to pay the required pride-poundage, be willing to do a little metaphorical shoe-licking. At that moment though Strang was checking my Pearly Gate credentials. No, I told'm, I've never been to the Tent Halls. Yes, I no longer attended church. No, I did not believe in the existence of God.

'What about prayer?' he asked.

'What about it?'

'Do you?'

'Do I what?'

'Ever pray.'

'Never.'

'Not even in a crisis?'

'I said "never".'

In my brathood I'd done a whole mess of praying: 'This night as

35

I lie down to sleep, I pray Thee Lord my soul to keep. If I should die before I wake – then geeza nudge for goodness sake!' This was Da Clay's jokey version and there were ructions in the auld homestead when Ma heard me lipping it. Skint though we always were in those days, Ma Clay made sure I'd a penny to rattle into God's rainy-day box (only, as I recall, it was really a velvet bag). Uncollectable now, of course, those donations; a closed account which no longer attracted interest. The George Bleaker Memorial Church: who was this guy Bleaker that they'd seen fit to pile grey stone upon grey stone in his memory? The holy gloom of that place did for my fledgeling soul, that's for sure. The Reverend Humphrey Weaver had merely acted as its embalmer with his needling attacks on its sinworn state. Angels disguised as house spiders, he told us openmouthed goslings, watched from nooks in our bedrooms to see what we got up to. Every time you committed a sin, according to Revd Weaver, a knot was tied in your sin-thread; when the time came for you to present yourself at the Pearly Gates, St Peter would demand to see your sin-thread; if your knots exceeded a certain amount he'd snap at you: 'Go away – you're far too knotty to get in here!' Maybe this was the reason for the high mortality rate of the leggy beasties in and around the Scabby! The stink of the Bleaker Memorial still clings to its roofless ruin to this day although not with the same potency, of course. A unique guff it had been, a gagging odour of newly-raked bones and corpse-ash, a stink of rotted bibles and regret. Aye, and what had we to regret if not our poverty? 'Much more!' Weaver would cry. 'You should regret drawing a breath if you have not thanked the Lord for it!' We should also regret bemoaning the need to toil, to sweat and to grieve. Had not Providence made each and every one of us spiritual millionaires? Old John Scobie, the conchy bard, had hit the coffin-nail on the head when he'd penned his 'Weaver's Tale':

Yon kirk's an awfu guff aboot it,
of Satan's oxters, I don't doot it.
A stench of roasted flesh'n shit:
Waur than Calvin birlin oan Hell's spit!

The Bleaker Memorial Church reminds me of one of those fairground arcade machines where the dropping of a coin animates some dusty drama, usually of a haunted house or an execution. You dropped your penny into 'God's Purse', a prissy velveteen bag dangled before you on the end of a pole by a soor-faced elder then, much like the mannikin priest in the amusements machine who was to be seen jerkily rising to read scripture to the condemned man, the Reverend Weaver would pop up in his pulpit, rock to'n fro for a few moments before his mouth began to flap and the 'Word of Nod' (another of Da Clay's sardonic amendments) fell upon the congregation like a shower of dead ashes.

My mouth had gone ahead of me, always a dodgy procedure. What had it been on about so far? Ach, yon 'suffer the weans' stuff. You would've thought by now it would've tired tugging at that stale udder. What a repertoire of frowns Her Haughtiness could muster. Eddie looked equally aggrieved; his round barometer of a face warned of stormy times to come. Both Carlyles of course recalled that there was a trapdoor for the unwary concealed in the gab-structure I was erecting. You could see the pair of them flinching when the rubicund gnome stomped around on the planking of my argument, testing the soundness of it. And, as he'd been intended to, he soon found the major flaw in the joinery. Aware of this I kept rumbling on like the Bleaker Memorial's organ.

Long after the yellow fingers of Auld Warnock had quit its equally yellow keys – he'd held up his hands to prove his lack of complicity – it'd growled on, composing a hymn of fiendish complexity, much to the frustration of the Reverend Weaver who'd already risen, his as-yet unhurled thunderbolts cooling the longer he'd been delayed. Talking about that kist o' whussles, we kids used to think that it was haunted and – but, I'll have to give way . . . Santa seems keen to insert his clause.

'Good heavens, lad, is that the best you can do? I've heard better from a junior bible class.' He dug his forefinger into the chair's cushioned arm and it was as if he'd pressed a button and sent a surge of power coursing through his theological machinery. 'To start with, Calvin was French, not Swiss. You're probably getting confused by the lengthy time he spent in Geneva, having fled there from the wrath of administration for his pro-Protestant activities. Getting his nationality wrong is bad enough, but to compound this error by associating Calvin's doctrine of Predestination with the frail grammar of a Sunday School teacher you once had, well, that's absolute claptrap. You say this youth – I take it he was a young person? – yes, you say that he made the mistake of believing that Jesus said: "Suffer little children to come unto me", instead of "Suffer THE little Children to come unto me", and as a consequence he misinterpreted "suffer" to mean the "endurance of pain" instead of "to allow" or "to permit" which is, of course, the archaic meaning of the word. Be that as it may, to go on from there to make the ludicrous insinuation that Calvin was under a similar delusion and that this bred in him a sort of Inquisitional lust for the destruction of all heretics be they children or adults – it's just plain daft.' He hitched forward on the armchair. 'In fact, Mr Clay, I'd go as far as to say that your notions of Calvinism are dafter still.' He laughed and skiffed his palms against each other. 'It's my belief that you wouldn't recognise Calvinist Predestination if it alighted on your nose and read aloud the Institutes from cover to cover. Allow me,' the hobgoblin continued, 'to unravel that ball of wool and thistles you've presented as an argument. Far from being a "baby burner" – your own crude and thoroughly malicious phrase – Calvin based his beliefs on the following principles: one, as a result of Adam's fall, Man has become totally depraved; two, the power of God's will is absolutely unchallengeable . . .'

As Strang continued to rub my nose in it Phyllis got to her feet and began unobstrusively to transfer the tea things to a hostess trolley. Unlike her brother who was openly gloating, her face remained expressionless. But no doubt she was relishing the sight of me being verbally taken apart. Eddie had actually stuck his head above the rim of that slit trench in which for a lifetime he'd been crouching, hiding from the world's alarms. His smirk deepened as Strang's dialectic artillery pounded my fortifications to rubble. 'Gentlemen, let's synchronise our watches!' Eddie compared the time on his wrist-gizmo with that of the Grand Fakir clock in the corner.

'. . . And since man has no will of his own the superiority of faith to do good works is self-evident; three, there is no salvation by an act of man's will but only through the given grace of God . . .'

Phyllis guided the tinkling trolley from the room. Ostensibly taking up the cudgels on my own behalf I managed to slow the Calvinist express and to come on at him with some existentialist stuff. Let's see how he could handle a Sartrean special en route between Nothingness and Nowhere-to-Go. He listened to my spiel politely enough but obviously without much interest. Eventually I ran out of steam and came to a halt.

Strang sighed. 'It's an odd thing,' he remarked, 'but so many young men these days seem to be talking about Nothing.'

I surveyed my opponent over the wreckage of my opening gambit and faced the paradox of inviting defeat without too much loss of face. Eddie's peripheral smirks were getting through to me. My initial thrusts, so confident of finding the soft underbelly of christianity, had snapped on an unexpectedly tough shield.

'This Devil you talk about?' I queried, 'Where d'you accommodate him in the scheme of things?'

Strang shrugged his shoulders. 'As a Christian it is my duty NOT to accommodate him. On the contrary, I must always try to make him as uncomfortable as possible. "In the scheme of things", as you put it, the Devil is nothing more than God's shadow, a dark mimic created by its exclusion from light. Lacking God it would have no shape and, but for we sinners, it would certainly have no substance. The Devil, in fact, is nothing more than our guile for defeating our own ends.'

'C'mon,' I chivvied, 'that's like a bloke shaving off his remaining hair to cover his baldness.'

Strang laughed. He seemed to be enjoying himself. 'Need I remind you Mr Clay, that man's mind teems with error? He is swarming with falsity, a hive of indiscretions, ever busy making the bitter honey of sin.' He laid both of his arms along the chair's broad ledges. What an old ham he was! 'I can see in you so much resembling myself at a similar age . . .'

The windbag's rhetorical sigh dutifully followed.

'Yes, how busily I flitted from one book to the next, ransacking the treasures of the Garden of Knowledge, gathering up the intellectual pollen, winging home at the day's end with my mixed bag of "scientific certitudes"?' The appeal seemed to be addressed to an invisible audience which, judging by the direction of his gaze, had hidden itself behind the xmas tree. 'You loot one mind, and then another.' (A languid hand-wave here.) 'And so it goes on. Busy doing nothing . . .' He shook his bleached locks. 'There's lots of sunshine about in youth, Mr Clay. But it gets dark all·too soon, believe me. Then what d'you find, eh?' Behind the garish spruce the audience was holding its collective breath. 'You find that all of those gaudy minds, so open and alluring, have curled up into themselves and are feeding on nothing but their own separate darknesses.' The gestural cliché of beard-stroking now occurred. 'And you can be sure that every one of those shrivelled blooms is now parasitical with doubt, is host to a million bugs of dread.'

Thrusting suddenly into the lounge as if an over-dramatic director had given her an almighty push, there entered in haste a mother with a bloodstreaked child in her arms. 'Look what I found in the linen cupboard,' she declared then, in mock rage, wagged a fist in the gory but grinning boy's face. 'He's got ketchup everywhere.' She gave him a little shake. 'I'll shoot the boots off you, m'lad.'

Catching me, so to speak, between faces, one registering fading shock, the other growing relief, the boy held out both arms to me. 'Uncle Tommy, when did you come?' His evident delight at seeing myself, while giving me a charge, seemed to make his parent cross. Although Jason tried to wiggle free, he was held tightly in a mother-fast lock. How insultingly wary she looked. 'Uncle Tommy,' the boy now asked, 'are you still taking me to the Garralies?'

Phyllis corrected him, 'The Kelvingrove Art Gallery.'

'Are you?' Jason appealed directly to me but before I could say yeah or nay, mummy jabbed in. 'It all depends on the weather.'

Aye, whether she could come up with an excuse to wreck the outing! The kid was loose with live matches in a gunpowder store and didn't know it. 'C'mon, scamp,' Mother Sherman said, 'it's an early bath for you.'

'But it isn't night yet,' the saucy smout declared. 'Sleepy Sam won't be for ages yet?'

Phyllis frowned, 'Sleepy who?'

The boy laughed. 'Sleepy Sam. He comes and biffs you with a bag of soot. Doesn't he Uncle Tom?'

Phyllis gave me that look which meant, 'Filling his head with rubbish again, were you?'

Jason was still straining towards me. 'Uncle Tommy, are there really men-in-armour at the Ga – '

'The museum?' I nodded. 'That's right, kiddo, horses too.'

'Speaking of which,' Strang said as he slid down off the slopes of the financial giant's bumrest. 'I'd better get the ones under my bonnet on the move.' Catching the boy's mystified gaze, he chuckled. 'I'm talking about the horses under my car bonnet, laddie.' He raised a hand to ruffle his grizzled thatch. 'Did you think I stabled them up here?' He was allowed to chuck the boy under the chin, even to pat his head and, with only the mildest of ritual disapproval which usually attend such proceedings, he was even permitted to slip a silvery coin into Jason's grasp. The last time I'd tried to do something avuncular like that I'd been on the receiving end of a stern put-down by Phyllis. 'How's he expected to know the difference between you and some old pervert trying to ply him with money in the street?' had been her astounding and, I admit it, wounding condemnation.

'I'll get your coat,' Phyllis said to Strang then bore Jason away so quickly from the sight and sound of me that the closing door nipped off the tail-end of the lad's 'Goodnight, Uncle Tommy.' Uncle Eddie, whom the boy always ignored, because Uncle Eddie found such small fry too big to handle, stood with his back to us apparently very interested in the xmas cards whose sugary sentiments glued fragmenting friendships together for yet another annum. What a lonely bugger he was, but as miserable as sin with it. The archetypal mean man, Eddie was; he who as old Walt once observed, 'Walks to his own funeral dressed in his shroud'. With a pang I suddenly recalled my own Uncle Norman who always seemed able to pluck from his pocket a florin he'd been roasting on his thigh all the day to give to his favourite and only nephew. 'Well, that's another Clay gone to clay,' my old man had said as we plodded from the muddy glumness of that wee Dumfries cemetery.

Turning in my direction Strang advanced into the relative chilliness of Shubumpkin Corner to extend his hand towards me. I rose to shake it. 'Nice to've met you, Mr Clay. Very interesting. You should pop along to the Tent Halls one Saturday. Such a cheery crowd. And happiness, if you'll suffer me to say so, isn't a treasure the world is over-endowed with, is it?' Smiling at the crafty way he'd inserted 'suffer' into his homily I also found myself nodding for some reason. As our hands dropped away he sprang a curious question on me. 'D'you ever go hill-climbing Mr Clay?' When I shook my head he briskly nodded his own. 'Good, good. My advice to you is never to do so. You understand – never!' With a farewell hand salute he moved towards the door. 'Good-day to you also, Edward, God willing it we'll meet tomorrow evening.'

The lounge door closed behind him. Before I was fully aware of what I'd done a lighted cigarette was burning between my fingers, the thing seemed to've self-ignited at the heart of my musings. I was puzzled, aye, even a wee bit intrigued, by the ex-pawnbroker's warning against any notion I might have to go climbing. It wasn't very likely – I can get dizzy standing on the edge of a pavement; you'll never catch yours truly spikebooting it up Ben Nevis, yon chittery place where Englishmen head by the coachload in order to fling themselves from its icy ledges. By the way, I'm talking about the mountain here, and not the Ben Nevis Bar up the Calton. Aye, it can be a right cauld shop but I'd rope myself to its gantry anytime.

With all the outrage on his waxy chops of a priest finding a couple canoodling in the Confessional, Eddie strode up to me and would've struck the fag from my lips if I hadn't got to it first.

'No smoking allowed in here!' he hissed.

I nodded, but helped myself to several deep puffs before nipping the fag and burying it in the moist compost of a nearby houseplant. I wagged a hand through the smoke.

'There, wisnae that loud, was it?'

6

I'd this dream once which began with me being stretchered into
the Salty Dog Saloon. My carriers were a pair of Jewish lads from
my secondary school, Bauxenbaum and Yaffie. With a carelessness wakened life would've censured them for they couped me
onto a table and left me there to my own goyish devices. I lay on
my back, broken and bloodied as an ant newly-spat from the
grassy jaws of a palpitating mower. I began to call for water but
the word for some reason came out in German: 'Wasser . . .
Wasser . . .' I've no idea why this was, unless the dream-director
wanted to exploit the word's sibilance, its suggestiveness of a
puncturing tyre or lung: certainly, the springy consonant of the
English equivalent would've contradicted the tone of collapse
thus far established by the dream.

I could've 'wassered' away there until closing time for all the
interest the barstaff took in me which, considering they were
family, was a real put-down. The fact that they were dead and not
merely dying might have had some bearing on their indifference
but you would've thought Ma Clay at least could've spared me a
word of comfort or even a consoling glance. But no, with cloth
and cleaning fluid she remained completely absorbed in the
erasure of a stain from the polished counter. (Out, damned spot!)

Da Clay, a pencil stub behind his ear, was fine-combing a racing paper, still on his eternal search for winners, while Granda Gibson stood near the end of the counter, his attention enmeshed in the shrouding of a model sailing ship. The only one doing what barstaff should be doing, namely the pouring and selling of booze was Uncle Norman. His customer was his former boss, Farmer Irwin. Two children capered up and down the Saloon. One of them was my young brother Martin, who died aged seven during the meningitis scourge which swept the Scabby in the late forties. He was skimming beer mats at a baby who wobbled around in her rubbers and nappy making cooing noises. Like an infant Atlas she bore on her puny shoulders a grotesquely huge head. A greybeard came hobbling into the shop. He looked as if he'd been in a fire: threads of smoke were still unravelling from the seams of his scorched cardigan and on his charred face blisters were quickening.

This weird wee dream popped up for reappraisal as I stormed the counter of the Salty Dog and elbowed my way into the two-line crush of boozers to claim my usual spot. 'Hey, Sammy,' I shouted as I tugged the alarm clock from my pocket, 'your pub's ten minutes fast again.'

Aye, there's no doubt about it – living's a fine thing to be doing: people are forced to respond; they can't just ignore you in the cavalier fashion of dreams. Sammy's the exception, of course. Not a blind bit of notice did he take of me. But then he was watching the till wasn't he? And believe me, with so many poor mouths pressing around him, that till took all the watching it could get. I stuck the clock on the counter in front of me, then skiffed a bright confetti of snow over Auld Andy Spowart who'd been trying to nurse a cure for rheumatics from a glassful of thin red wine. 'Sorry, Andy,' I apologised as he bubbled up like a fart in bathwater, 'but you will stand in the daftest places!'

It took me a while to get an order. There was no sign of Paddy Cullen in the heaving ranks. Paddy was the second projectionist at the Planet. A grand wee picture house. A great place for Fleas' Conventions. What was yon saying again? Aye: 'Ye go into the Planet wae a coat and come oot wearing a jaiket.' Like the cinema, this very boozer was for the kibosh. It was galling to think of it becoming a rancid patch of waste ground. The Salty Dog Saloon, the best wee boozer bar none. Hands fluttered over foam-topped pints and nuggets of whisky gleamed everywhere. Clinks of glasses, clack of the doms, the rapid thwock-thwock-thwock of darts biting the board. Paper decorations were strung across the ceiling and in cottonwool lettering the gantry mirror wished everyone the compliments of the season. Freddy Green, who did a little bartendering on the side, had a group of drinkers straining towards him as he told another one from his Bumper Fun Book: the fuse of the story was well lit and soon burned to its mirthful explosion. The area behind the bar served as Freddy's stage. There he clowned, did tricks and pattered up the boozers. Sad Sam Murney, the chargehand, of whom it was rumoured that he pissed into a leg-catheter rather than desert his till, was forever chiding Freddy when he got out of order, whereupon the comic would offer his time-honoured response: 'Get a smash at that coupon! He disnae know whether tae part wae it or fart wae it!'

'Can you no buy a watch like everybody else?' Millie, the weekend lassie (some lassie!) asked as she shoved a pint of lager towards me. I patted the clock. 'Got it from Alky Anon. Soon as it rings I'm off my mark.'

Millie was big, blonde and brassy. She lifted the clock and jammed it to her ear. 'Bloody thing's no workin!'

I nodded. 'Well, as they say, Millie – nothin's perfect.'

'Aye, you're right there Tommy lad, so you are,' a voice said moistly into my left ear. 'Nothing's perfect, but it could be a damned sight better.'

I frowned and lifted my pint. Just my luck to get lumbered with Talky Sloan. Talky was an old socialist hack, one of the greybeards who gave capitalism laldy in the area of the pub known as 'Commie Corner'. In his youth Talky had come across that fat slug of a word 'bourgeoisie' and had hungrily sank his socialist fangs into it. Thereafter he became addicted to its decadent juices, a dependancy so chronic that he could scarcely string a few political sentences together without reference to the archaic class beastie. He held out a vibrating hand (for a glad moment I thought he was saying ta-ta!) then he tilted his fingers down sharply. 'That's whits wrang wae this country, son – nae balance – ower much gold at the English end. Ask yersel, go on, why should a Londoner get three sheets mair'n a Glesca punter? Aye, for doing the same job? I'll tell ye for why – coz that's how your boorjwazee get to rule – by division. Aye, your auld "divide'n conquer" tactic . . .'

As he rambled on Talky was casually parting with a ten bob note for the pint that'd been shoved across to'm. All round me the underpaid Glesca boozers were lashing out good loot for their medicine, aye'n maybe needing just that wee drappie more than their English counterparts. Talky dropped some of his change and as he bent to pick it up I did a conjuring trick so knackily that they should've been giving me a Magic Circle membership, instead of trying to push a pub raffle ticket on me. I dismissed my chance of a prize – it was rumoured to be a 'wee swing on Big Millie's garters' – then as Talky continued to yammer politics, boorjwa-zeeing for all his worth I switched on my mental scrambler and tuned into a really ludicrous sight – that of a Volkswagen Beetle with a Silvercross pram mounted on its roof. What an eyepopper! It was a wonder somebody hadn't come out and flung a bucket of water over them. For a start the Beetle was never designed to accommodate a roof-rack and certainly not to handle a pram that looked like it'd been made for export to Brobdingnag. I'd suggested to Eddie that we'd be better mounting the car on the pram but the joke hadn't gone down too well. An accident seemed inevitable but, surprisingly, we'd got as far as humping the baby-truck up Ma Carlyle's stairs before one happened: I nudged against a pot plant on the stairhead window ledge and down it crashed.

Three doors opened simultaneously; three harpies appeared on the upper landing; three grim and slippered harridans descended with scolding tongues – Letitia Carlyle to the fore. Had these cauldron carlins been armed with clubs I've no doubt they would've pulped me on the spot. The plant itself, a fungoid wee leaf-dropper, lay on the linoleumed landing amidst the shards of its pot and the spilled earth, its tuft of roots sticking up like the paws of a dead moggie. Loud were the lamentations of the Macbeth Sisters, louder still their condemnations: 'clumsy', 'stupid', 'careless' – these were three of the milder adjectives Ma Carlyle spat waspishly into my face.

Collectively they seemed to be insinuating that this had been no accident, that, in fact, it had been a cold, calculated act of vegicide. 'Ladies and gentlemen of the jury, this was by no means the first time that the accused had topped a houseplant. I bring to your attention the case of the Blitzed Begonia! When he was no more than ten years old the fiend who stands there in the dock, this ice-hearted chlorophyll-killer, deliberately and most wantonly smashed to bits with a brick the beloved begonia plant of Mrs Lizzie Ferguson, a peaceable old lady who had innocently put her plant, her pride and joy, out into the backcourt so that it might catch a sup or so of rain. It was then that this monster struck!

Aye, it was true enough, I had indeed offed Granny Ferguson's begonia. I'd no choice, for it was the task I'd drawn from the Scobie Hatchet's Dare-Box. What a hullabuloo that caused. I ice one cruddy little plant and suddenly I'm Public Enemy No. 1. Hatchet Hannah, who'd turned over Blind Geordie's cane, was forgiven quicker than I was. Even months later I overheard Mrs Dawson say to a new neighbour, 'See that yin there? A right bad wee bugger. Put a brick through Granny Ferguson's pot plant after the auld sowl put it oot for a wee drink of rain . . .'

Harry Moffat, known snidily as Harry the Hump because of an unfortunate addition to his shoulders, poked his head from the opened trapdoor of the cellar. He'd a wee keek up Millie's skirt as he did so but who could blame'm for that? A sinbad with bad sins burdened. Might've become my stepfather, Harry, if fate had taken it up its humph. He'd had a fancy for Ma back'n the old days when she'd skivvied in the Dog on Mondays – her day off from Sammy Stein's Snapshot Parlour where she'd worked as a printer/developer. Little jokes and shared confidences. Harry came to Ma's funeral and in his nervousness had dropped his hat into the grave as the coffin was being lowered. The gravediggers had presumed that this was an eccentric departure from the earth-throwing custom and made no move to retrieve the hat. Harry had just stood there, pink with embarrassment as the rain had thrashed his bald napper. The hat would still be there yet, crushed against the rotten lid, squashed wreath of a dream. Harry was for his jotters when the Dog shut up shop. He would not be going with Proprietor Peacock to the new premises, soon for opening elsewhere in the city. It seemed a hunchback would not fit in with the snazzy decor. Millie'd be okay though, her hump was on the socially-approved side.

'What the bloody hell!'

Talky Sloan, having gulped over some stout, hastily dumped

the glass back on the counter. He plucked something from his drink and tossed it down into the beer swill. The frothy shroud cleared to reveal a wee plastic skeleton, the very one I nicked from Eddie Carlyle's Beetle with the intention of hanging it in the family cupboard.

'Hey, Sanny, get yoursel ower here a minute!'

Sanny Stirrat, the bestower of headaches, loused-up stomachs and broken homes, refused to accept responsibility for the presence of a skeleton in Talky's bevvy. As if he kept a special eye open for such novelties, he claimed in that dead-pan way of his that the stout had been skeleton-free when the pouring'd been completed. He looked real cheesed-off at the barrage of quips that was now let loose from boozy mouths: 'Hey, Sanny, is that the new drink! Cemetery Shandy?'

'Talky, it looks like somebody's a bone to pick with you!'

'Canny say noo your stout's no got "body" in it!'

I clapped his shoulder. 'If I was you I'd steer clear of the horses ramorra. Helluva unlucky a thing like that.'

The pub door opened and in came Cullen. At times Paddy could make the inmates of a dosshouse look elegant; Cullen had outdone himself this evening. As usual he wore the heavy, lint-flecked overcoat which senile moths nostalgically referred to as 'the good old days'; a suit that was out of date when Burton was a boy; a dinner-speckled tie with matching shirt; but, unbelievably, tonight he was wearing a pair of needle-toed shoes that'd certainly 'Hound Dogged' to Presley way back when. He ducked into the ruck of drinkers and had soon barged his way to my side.

'What's with the winklepickers?' I asked.

He barked out an order then speaking from the side of his mouth he said: 'Nora planked my shoes tae stop me from hitting the bookies. Had tae stick these on. I've no been hame yet.'

His order arrived and he snatched greedily at the whisky. He had a good bead on him, more than plenty considering he'd a stint to perform in the Planet in less than an hour.

'You seen that wee shitpot Killoch?' he asked. 'Don't feel like trapping the night.' He held out his tremoring hands. 'Would you look at that, eh. Time I jacked in the pneumatic-drill.'

'Got the shakes?'

'Aye, the snakes as well.'

The whisky went over in a single throw. 'See yon Yankee pish you put us ontae last night. Whassit called again?' I told him. 'Aye, that's it.' He shook his head, 'Fuckaw comfortin aboot it – neither north nor south. Then that Mick's Blood on tappy it. Up half the night shittin shamrocks and shillelaghs. Tongue like a toad's arse this morning and Nora going on at me like the Recordin Angel.' Nora was Paddy's sister with whom he got what he called 'board and lashings'.

He was a short man, Cullen, blighted with a 'Dublin Pot' through his addiction to stout. His brown hair was beginning to peter out on the foreslope of his skull and his fingers habitually settled on this spot as if he entertained hope of a miraculous resprouting.

'We shifted some last night, eh?' he said as he drew his pint of stout towards him. 'Last I remember was the rammy in the Mod after you slipped yon double-six intae the dom school.'

I shook my head. 'You're away off course, Paddy – that was last week, in here. Sure you know Gus Hagen disnae allow the doms after hours.'

Continuity had a tendency to snap for Paddy these days, leaving him to scrabble around, trying to pick up the dropped hours like they were scattered beads. One morning he woke up to find himself lying on a manky mattress in a backcourt; on his chest there was a frying pan and in the pan a dead budgie; Paddy had never been able to figure that one out. I signalled to Milly but

Paddy intervened. 'Naw, this one's on me.' From his inside pocket he produced a healthy spread of banknotes. 'Who says the Irish nags fill the bookies' bags now, eh?'

'You knocked it off?'

He nodded happily and peeled a couple of quid from the wad. 'Here, they're still wet wae McGarvie's tears.' I made a show of rejection but Cullen pressed them on me. 'Take'm, you've a face on ye like somebody that's shat himself in a stuck lift.'

'Ta, Paddy, what's the score now – ten, twelve?'

'Fifteen, but who's countin? Don't leave the country, that's all.'

He lifted the clock, and looked at it curiously. 'Yours?'

I nodded.

'How come?'

'I turned into a clockroach the day,' I could've said, but didn't. Cullen's apt to banjo you for coming stuff like that.

Meanwhile, Talky Sloan was saying: 'Well, the bloody thing didnae jump in there by itself . . .'

7

When Nelly Kemp was a sprightly lass of no more than sixty years of age, she kept a caged parrot on the counter of her fag'n paper shop in Scobie Street. The parrot was called Jacob, a right vicious auld bugger with a beak on'm that could've snapped truck axles. Since such an opportunity never came his way he contented himself with snapping at the customers – in German, strangely enough, although to earn his corn he'd throw in the odd English phrase like: 'No tick here, chum! . . . Hullo, Sailor . . . How's your bum for spots? . . . Thanks for coming – come again! . . .' What exactly Jacob was saying in German remains unknown but the Scabby legend has it that one day, Solly Singer – the last Jew in Scobie Street – on hearing the bird's Teutonic prattling, clapped his hands to his ears and fled the shop never to be seen on the premises again.

The wretched squawkbag first roosted in my awareness around the time Herr Hitler was becoming bunkered behind his collapsing fronts. Consequently my memory of Jacob owes more to mental taxidermy than to accurate recall, a mock-up filched from other parrots seen and glimpsed in life, books, or films; a compound which produced a very oddly speckled bird. I vaguely recall though the whispering net of gossip which settled over

Nelly's shop because of Jacob. It was a time of ultra suspicion, when walls were said to've ears and 'keeping mum' was a national safeguard. Jacob's Goebbels-sounding phraseology had not, it seemed, been well received by those customers whose loved ones were away 'doing their bit' to see off the Hun.

'There's more to Nelly Kemp than meets the eye,' Ma Clay said one day to Mrs Muirhead (later taken by Death while seated on the stairhead lavvy pan doing – as was her custom – a bit of knitting: 'Cast off while casting on!' said Da Clay when told of it.) Mrs M. had nodded; 'Aye, she's worth a watching that yin!'

At the time this exchange was less comprehensible to me than Da Clay's letters 'from the War' were proving to be. The writings of a lunatic they looked like, bent and twisted words like an orchard through which a hurricane was racing, scattering the fruit of meaning. Now'n again though, a ripe phrase would accidentally plop into Ma's hand and she'd shine up yon wee glasses of hers the better to see her windfall and triumphantly declare: 'Your Da's feet've broke oot again!' I remember how even Fagan, the street's bookie, used to kick up a fuss about Da Clay's 'prescriptions'. In fact, he refused to accept them unless they were printed out. No way was he going to 'blind' himself trying to crack the code of Da's ten cross roll-ups. But, as I was saying, sometimes Ma Clay'd come out with really weird wee statements which would be communicated with those knowing glances through which parents and other grown-ups semaphored covert information, stuff that 'wisnae for weans' ears . . .' When I was sent from the room because grown-ups' talk was to take place, I naturally jammed my ear to the cracked door panel. There, I heard such a jumble of nonsense I'd have been as well listening to the Nazified Jacob's Germanic diatribes. It seemed that 'yon rid-heided wee besom, her wae the snooty neb that worked in the Empire Dairy' had a bun in the oven and wisnae sure of the baker. That she'd 'do away with it' was on the cards . . . There followed some static about constant baths in boiling hot gin and something unthinkable that was to be done with a knitting needle. Aye, strange times right enough! As for Jacob, he's said to've snuffed it on VE night, overcome by the smoke from the street bonfires. It sounds a touch too convenient but it doesn't pay to knock a neat ending.

The bell of Nelly's shop gave a foggy croak as I shoved open the door. Nelly came with lots of sighs and rheumaticky creakings from her living-room through the back where, no doubt, she'd been pouring over maps of Brazil and Paraguay in the company of Martin Borman and some other grizzle-haired Gestapo merchants. A black shawl covered the crone's bent and wasted shoulders and spikes of frosty hair stuck out from under her hat, a squashed felt cabbage of a thing. Her face had its usual 'gone to lunch' look about it, as if all life had fled its dusty planes to leave only a repertoire of twitches and frowns. Her slippered feet scuffed along the worn waxcloth as she came to position herself behind the counter. For donkeys' years she'd stood there dispensing Scobie Street's needs. Here we kids had come with our burning pennies to buy the trashy treasures of childhood: the buttermilk dainties; the soor plooms; hard cakes of toffee; chunks of tablet, marzipan potatoes and all the other sugary muck that've made synonyms of prosperity and dentistry.

Here too could be bought caps for our toy pistols; kites, peeries and dabbities; clay pipes for bubble blowing; and you could have a shot at winning a prize by pushing a number from the Fortune Board with a 'key' that looked like a sardine-can opener. In those days the shop was a wellhead of gossip: thousands of character assasinations had taken place in that narrow area between the counter and the bunched sticks and bleach bottles. Granda

Gibson used to claim that 'the knives're busier in that shop than in Tough's the Butchers'.

Nelly had news for me. Somebody had been enquiring after my good self. 'Aye, a wee fella wae a stripy bunnet and a leather jaicket,' she told me as her arthritic hand swung over like one of those fairground cranes to drop a packet of cigs before me.

'Was he maybe from the Pools?' I suggested.

She made a face at me. 'A debt collector more likely.'

'What'd he want to know?'

'Everything.'

'Such as?'

'A right nosey wee bugger.'

'What'd you tell'm?'

She sighed, 'Oh, the usual.' Nelly got out her battered tick book and began to flap through its debt-scarred pages. 'I said you'd done a moonlight and left me debt enough to prove I'm daft.'

'Never catch me doing that, Nelly.'

'Aye, so another hunner names in here told me.' Nelly sniffed as her locked fingers clamped themselves to a page. 'They pile their stuff onto the back of a lorry and that's the last you see of them. Saft heart goes wae soft heid, right enough.'

'You're the saint of Scobie Street, Nelly,' I assured her. 'I cross myself everytime I pass your shop.'

'Aye, cross the road's more like it. High time that wife of yours was hame. She'd soon square your tail.' Her dusty face puckered in sympathy. 'How is the poor sowl, then?'

'No bad, Nelly. A bit browned off at times, that's all.'

She nodded. 'Aye, it's a funny business this new-fangled blood-pressure thing. Had nothing like that in the auld days.'

Nelly peered closer at the tick book, her lips working silently as she totted up the debt. I gave a familiar cough. 'Eh, Nelly, how

aboot sticking this week back in the fridge? You know how it is
. . . Christmas and that.'

She shook her head, then with a sigh looked around her dusty
hole of a shop, at its sagging shelves along which were lined
cardboard boxes; at the piled-up sweetie jars, the festive spread of
comics and magazines on the counter. 'I'd be as well turning this
into a dampt soup kitchen and be done with it,' she lamented.

'I've an insurance policy about due, Nelly.'

She sniffed again. 'Aye, you're well covered Tommy Clay – jist
like the Titanic.' She crooked her only mobile finger. 'Half of it
then, c'mon.'

'Give's a break, Nelly, eh?'

She was not for budging. 'I promised that wee Mammy of
yours, God rest'r, that I'd keep an eye on you. No managing very
well, am I? C'mon laddie, let's be having it.'

The auld bugger made me fork up. Half the tick was down to
ciggies. I could've reminded her that she'd encouraged my
smoking habit with her two-fags-and-a-match policy back in the
days when I'd been weaned off the cinnamon sticks by the
fearsome Vic Rudge who made it a rule that all members of the
Scobie Hatchet had to be smokers. The fly bastard had made ten
Woodbines the obligatory membership fee, the tribute to be kept
by him, of course, in the gang's 'cough box'.

'When you moving to Bearsden, Nelly?' I asked her while
pocketing my change and the twenty smokes.

'Bearsden!' she yelped. 'It's a single-end in the cemetery's my
next stop.' She slammed the tick book shut on all of those names,
the owners of which had undoubtedly been vocal and sincere-
sounding in their promises to settle their outstanding accounts. I
suppose if they hadn't welshed on their commitments she'd have
been able to go on a world cruise. Must have plenty squirrelled
away but the bulk of it was destined for her dodgy nephew who

did her banking business. Her natural bent for nosiness now asserted itself. 'Have you no had word of a new hoose yet, Tommy?'

I shook my head. 'I think they're waiting till the wife's by, just'n case she has quads.'

'God forgive you, Tommy Clay.' She thumped the tick book into a drawer. 'Did you hear about the Wotherspoons then?'

'What about'm?'

'Just two points short of a back'n front in wan of the good bits up by.'

I shrugged. 'Christ, I think I'd them down for a home win, tae!'

'Whut?'

'Nothing, Nelly.' I made for the door. A man couldn't spare the time to hang around spitberrying with a Nazi sympathiser. There were important things to be done. A man must be about his adult affairs, see to his heavy responsibilities. I suddenly remembered something and returned to the counter. 'I'll have that,' I said, pointing to a comic.

'*The Beano*, you mean?'

I nodded, 'And a packet of Jelly Babies.'

8

Snow rasped under my tread as I made my way down Scobie Street. I passed Greasy Tam's knackered fish'n chip shop. The place hissed with fractured water pipes and although it was too dark to see I knew that the big salmon that'd swum above the frying pans lay now in a shatter of blue scales on the floor. Tam'd kicked the bucket shortly after he'd clinched the padlock on his premises. Rumour has it that he died from a 'sudden bath' though this isn't very likely. He'll be down in Hell right now peeling totties for Heaven's endless round of purveys. It was odds-on too that he still hadn't changed his apron.

I stepped into a closemouth to light a fag. Cyclops, a black one-eyed cat, came and plonked himself dispiritedly down on his bum. Its long whiskers fankled in the shrewd breeze. It stared up at me, seemed to be dumbly imploring me to tell it why there were no fishheads or meatscraps to be found in the middens anymore – those cat restaurants where moggies met to talk pussy and exchange fleas. Cyclops should've taken notice of the Great Scabby Exodus when the squeal had gone out in the rodent world and the rats had come scuttering from their verminous nooks, from cellars, attics, backcourt washhouses, not forgetting the dunnies, squeaking out into the open, furring the street and pavements as they squirmed off like a pestilent grey snake while adults and teenagers clubbed and stoned them in an orgy of slaughter. House-rats desert kaput tenements just as surely as their marine mates quitted sinking ships – but try telling that to an empty-bellied one-eyed moggy!

As I moved on again I passed Bucky Lyons' dead dream where it stood snow-webbed in the gutter. A black Singer Gazelle, it'd been picked clean by the auto vultures. Flex dangled from its looted lamps but nothing of value remained: stripped from boot to bumper. I recalled the sunny day Bucky'd come puttering home in it, so proud of his fifty quid prize. 'She's auld, but reliable Tam,' he informed me, no doubt echoing the salesman's spiel. Gleaming there in the sunlight it hadn't looked too bad at that. 'Just the job for wee runs doon the coast, eh?'

In fact, the 'runs' had gone no further than around the block, and the running had been done by a bunch of corner fellas who pushed from behind while Bucky at the wheel shouted excitedly, 'The slope, lads – she'll start on the slope!' It soon became evident that the slope existed more in Bucky's head than in reality. Still, it made for a good Sunday afternoon's entertainment. The Scobie Street folk would line their elbows along their cushioned window sills and call good-naturedly to one another while they waited for the 'show' to begin. And begin it would with a cry of 'Here they're noo!' and Bucky's banger'd come slowly around the corner propelled by leg-power, lung-power, and sheer willpower, its petrol sloshing uselessly around in its tank. Bucky's wife and glum weans watched from their window, their briny dreams of cockleshells and crabs fading Sunday by Sunday until the pantomime was over and the Gazelle had been mounted on bricks and Bucky had taken to living under it so that his bootsoles soon became more familiar than his face.

It stopped, my body did, seized up without my say-so. Sensing disaster it immediately identified that condition so distressing to us humans – the loss of light. The street-lamp that had stood opposite my close, old faithful with his attendant gang of shadows, had been extinguished. I saw the image of the engineer's bulbous index finger as it skimmed down a column of names, pausing at Scobie Street where the fresh spoor of an asterisk indicated the footnote: 'Cleared for Demolition'. But this Mr Snuffit will effect no drastic eclipse but will compassionately proceed with a diminution of light, a lid slowly closing on a civic coffin; but darkness all too soon, my friends – hurry!

Tactile almost, this blackness, a clingy nothingness such as was daily endured by Old Salter, a Salty Dog regular who suffered the triple deprivation of sight, hearing and speech. I plunge into it, wade my way towards the close where a canary hops jauntily within its glass cage. What friendly chirrups of light! Keep singing, whatever you do. Don't stop! Safe on dry land I turn to help my shadow ashore. I grin at my funk. Jumpy as spit on a hob.

Something white blazed past my head and glissaded along the close wall, undoing itself as it went, before disintegrating with a crystalline explosion. A snowball, a banal, kneaded-by-human-hand snowball. I turned, easily catching up with my grin which was so anxious to prove how amused it was by the prank. Nothing to be seen out there of course except the dark inner lid of the dead street. Another snowball was pitched. It flew in from the dark with a precision that lacked all jollity and pinned a white tag over my heart. I brushed the cold fragments from my chest and turned, heading for the reassuring light. Reassurance against what? A couple of snawballs for heaven's sake, lobbed at me no doubt by a passing schoolboy, an urchin's way of wishing me a festive howdy. As I went up the stairs two at a time to stretch my legs, I heard a third snowball spending itself uselessly against the close's rear wall.

Silence and dust upon the stairs and the welcoming glimmer of a gas mantle on each landing; kept burning night'n day for fear auld Wattie Mullens or myself should fall and break our necks – but wishing we would elsewhere. Doors closed on their last slams and sheets of corrugated iron nailed over most of them. An empty screwtap'n a doll's head on the landing where wee 'Creepy' Crawley had made his last stand against the 'Tallymen' by sticking up a notice board which bore the legend: 'Dept of Housing. WARNING! Proceed no further – property dangerous beyond this point: Master of Works.' I'd helped Creepy with his spelling but otherwise steered clear of him. Just as well, for they'd come for him, those sharks who don't know the meaning of danger. I'd re-erected the notice after Creepy had been taken to the Victoria Infirmary for re-assembly; it just might give pause to any predator who was on my trail for one reason or another. But someone had stolen it. That wee punter in Nelly Kemp's shop for instance, him of the stripy head. What species of piranha was he? Surely Gas Board meter-collectors weren't buggering around in zebra bunnets and leather jackets these days?

My brave whistling ceased as I stepped onto my half-landing. The stairhead cludgie door was ajar, which it hadn't been when I'd left. Not that I kept it locked, of course, since I went along with the thievish logic of 'what's secured means most insured', though I doubt if lead-lifters apply such logic. I took out my lighter and poked its jittery flame into the dark closet. I relaxed. The catch of the wee window had worked itself free and the draught must have been strong enough to shove open the door. The lighter flame blew out as I secured the catch. But I flicked it on again and shielded it with my hand. On the floor a Jiffy bleach bottle had gathered a few snowflakes about its dull shoulders, giving itself a festive air.

Fourteen bums from a single landing had shared this wally

throne; the Muirheads and the Finnegans, the Wilsons, not forgetting the Sanquhars and the Clays too, of course. Big Paddy Finnegan, a docker, used to stink the place out with his Saturday gut of stout. Sometimes when I was in here, maybe doing a bit of hand-gliding over a picture of Esther Williams in a one-piece bathing suit, Finnegan would storm down to fist the door and bawl through its cracks: 'C'mon, get your proddy arse off that mantrap – there's some serious shiting to be done here!' Up 37 Scobie Street only three apartments remained occupied: in the close, Auld Granny Ferguson and her company of spooks; Rhona and me, two up on the right; and directly above us – worse luck – Wattie Mullens, coalheaver, retired.

From the moment I looked into the cludgie something had been trying to grab my attention. I finally got a fix on what it was: wedged between the rusted claws of the bumpaper holder was a copy of the London *Times*. Now the fact that this upperclass rag had a sales demand in the Gorbals on par with the purchasing ratio of gumboots and brollies in the Sahara, made its presence in my cludgie all the more bizarre. What was even more mind-blowing was the fact that it bore today's date: December 20th. The image of a dapper, bowler-hatted gent sitting on the edge of the biffy doing the crossword (it was all but completed) kept trying to assert itself but reason refuted this. It was just conceivable that a London *Times* reader might've had some reason to venture into the Gorbals, but that he should penetrate to the very heart of the Scabby itself scarcely seemed credible. Yet, somebody had done so. Here was the proof in black'n white. Who then? An ace gumshoe hired by Ma Carlyle or Phyllis Sherman to rake some dirt up on me, anything that'd serve as a wedge to split myself and Rhona apart? Naw, that was a load of balls. What about the wee leatherback then? Could've been him right enough.

An agent from the Futility Furnishing Company, here in the flesh to express his client's concern about not having heard from me in such a long suspicious time. Since the bleach bottle refused to confirm or deny my conjectures on the grounds that it might incriminate itself, I left the cludgie and 'ascended to my nest in the fissure of the cliff'.

Home sweet home consisted of a couple of rooms linked by a lobby where the electric meter munched amps and the floorboards crackled like a pensioners' prayer meeting. The kitchen looked into the backcourt, the bedroom into the street. Dampness was a way of life: shoes left under the bed turned blue and given fifty or so more years the Scabby would've bred the first domestic water rat.

I stuck the kettle under the tap and let a thread of water unwind into it. Our geyser was knackered. Curdie Frame, the bloke I'd got in to fix it, claimed it needed some kind of hard-to-find gadget and had gone off to look for it in Sumatra or Afghanistan. I don't really expect to see Curdie, the gizmo, or my two quid, surfacing this side of eternity. If they do then I'll stick the bread on Thistle to win the League. When I'd accumulated enough Loch K. to brew a mug of coffee I set the kettle on a ring of the gas cooker and put a light under it. Pressure was low. I went out to the lobby meter and worked the lobba-bob routine. The meter's cashbox had been jemmied and its contents returned to general circulation. Theoretically unlimited gas supplies could now be tapped by clanking the same shilling through the meter's guts as often as required. I say 'theoretically' because the gas supply was almost neglible. One of these days, very soon now, I would have to report the theft from the meter's cashbox. Luckily I'd a good description of the therm-thief: he was a man in his mid-to-late twenties, around five-eleven in height; lean of build; ten, maybe eleven stones; long, dirty fair hair, nothing special in the looks department; a blue-eyed post-hippie mess with scuffed suede boots and faded jeans; Marine combat jacket, and threadbare sweater; he affects no jewellery whatsoever, his sole concession to ornamentation being a CND button.

The meter thief had no moral qualms about busting the bob-box, none whatsoever. In his opinion the Gas Board had reneged on their end of the deal – namely, to provide him, the consumer, with a continuous and adequate supply of energy. But on the contrary they'd blown down their pervasive and scandalously expensive tubing the equivalent of an industrial raspberry. So weak and so spasmodic had their supply been that Peggy Sampson, next close to his, having popped her old and worried head into the proverbial oven, had, to her utter disgust, wakened to find herself completely undead though suffering from a splitter of a headache. Since the GBH (Gas Board Heavies) frowned on meter break-ins, the orbit of the 'crime' would have to be widened to include other knock-likely items. There'd be no use telling even the dimmest of Defective Constables that the only thing taken was the meter's contents. Even his ponderous neurons would get around to thinking. 'Wot we've got here is an inside job, that's wot . . .' Fortunately most items of any real value had long since been removed to Ma Carlyle's place to be stored there until that joyous day when a Corporation billet could be found for them. To pre-empt a genuine break-in I'd been forced to boot in my own front door which would mean replacing the busted lock. No problem there, plenty of locks to be found all about me. Keys might be harder to locate. Billy Sanquhar, an erstwhile neighbour of mine, on the day of his departure, as his wife'n weans sat peaceably in their covered wagon before riding off into the sunrise that was Castlemilk, had defiantly hurled his keys into his gutted living-room and exclaimed triumphantly:

'That's me, Tam – oota fuckin jile at last!' Unhappily for Billy things hadn't worked out for I hear that he's now to be found in a place of confinement to the east of the city famous for its porridge and its absolute mania, bordering on paranoia, for locks'n keys.

I chucked some sticks into the grate. The fire had burned down to a few pale sparks. With some paraffin I kept in a ginger bottle I soon had a good blaze going. Splay-thighed I crouched there, toasting my chestnuts until enough was enough and I'd to back off some. There was plenty of fuel to be had. At the moment I was burning my way through the Finnegans' old dresser, the one that'd collapsed and died during their flitting. So too had auld Granny Finnegan. Maybe her ghost was glaring indignantly at me from some corner. 'In the name of jayziz, would you be lookin' at that – yon godless proddy chopping up my good furniture and not a bolt of lightning's come near'm!'

Sitting by a cheery fire in my rent-free slum, eating a piece'n jam and slurping down a mug of coffee, I'd a wee swatch at *The Beano*, just to see how my old chums were faring in their timeless world of chortles, japes and tee-hees. Sad to report they all looked a mite jaded, their laughter just a bit hollow for comfort, their wheezes a whole stab crueller. Old jinks in new inks. Somehow the mix didn't pay off. It was as painful as watching your granny trying to rock'n roll. I took a drawing pin and tacked the comic to a wall so's I'd remember to take it over to young Jason, should I be granted the privilege of seeing him come Sunday.

A wee gander at the London *Times* now, the grown-ups' 'comic' with its dangerous, if not immoral, endorsement of the thrills to be had from monetary speculation. Page after page of jobbers and robbers. Assessment of today's fancied runners by experts in the financial paddock: 'Falling Sterling looks capable of outrunning Diving Dollar in the Stock-Exchange Stakes.' The

mysterious reader of this snob-job had left a clue: 14 across –
something puzzling about transport: Starts R blank, blank, U,
blank . . . a mere moment and yours truly, his mental edge honed
to perfection by the Scottish Educational System which enables
him to simultaneously operate a lathe, whistle Dixie, and scratch
his bum, sees that the answer can only be 'rebus', a puzzle game in
which a succession of letters and drawings conspire to conceal a
word. The real puzzle here was how someone who was capable of
fishing from his lexicographical lagoon such exotica as 'glossec-
tomy', 'primagravida', and 'furfuraceous' should have failed to
hook in a torpid trout like 'rebus'.

'Not only that,' says Jeremiah who has appointed himself
chairman of a committee, hastily recruited from my worry
centres, 'what about the snowballs?'

'Well, what aboot them?'

'A thrown snowball implies a thrower, does it not?'

'Granted. But do three thrown snowballs necessarily indicate a
trio of pitchers?'

'That's not the point – you were targeted by an unknown
assailant or assailants.'

'That's right, go on.'

'Well, what if it's a knife next time? A gun, even a rifle?'

'Why should anyone throw a gun or a rifle at me?'

'The question you should be asking yourself is – '

The door got chapped.

I knew before I'd opened it who'd be out there. Wattie
Mullens. On the scrounge again. Scarcely a day went by that
didn't find'm on my doorstep begging like a sly old monk. Mostly
what he was after was company, but since he was such a boring
old fart he got only a modicum of my fraternal feelings. Rhona
was always willing to while away a half 'n hour or so with'm; she'd
spend even longer with Granny Ferguson, although it was plain

for all to see that the half-blind old kneecreaker was no longer the full shilling. I've seen her having an animated chat with an empty chair; every day invisible callers crowd into her living-room to keep her company. Rhona was always nipping down with a bowl of soup, a slice of cake, and whatnot. I did what I could for the auld yin but she stubbornly refused to update my image, so that I remained the snottery-nosed tyke of my early days, the begonia-batterer, the very sight of whom made her froth up like a pan of boiling milk.

'Just a wee tate sugar, Tommy, lad.'

Between his coarse mitts Wattie extended to me the sugar bowl. He wore the usual crap: baggy pants, stained grey cardigan, and a collarless shirt fastened at its neck by a safety-pin. His face, with its bonal trickery, would've delighted a woodcarver. The auld midden was beginning to smell like something that'd been left to rot in a drawer. These days he was looking more like one of those flayed punters who'd staggered from the Nazi deathcamps. He seemed to subsist on a diet of baked beans, cream crackers, and a potent fortified wine. Rhona'd put him in contact with a social worker but more often than not by the time she called he'd be off on one of his jaunts, his favoured places being the Glasgow Green and Richmond Park where I saw him once arguing the toss with a hissing swan at the Ducksy. He was also said to have a liking for hanging around the lassies' school playground, especially when they were playing netball in their navy blue knickers and white blouses – randy old devil! In his cheeky way he slippered in at my back. 'Have you been burgled, then?' he asked.

'Burgled?'

He nodded as he looked around the place which, I'll be first to admit, was in a state of some disorder. He nodded. 'Aye, gave you a right turning ower, eh?' His gaze raked across the kitchen table with its mess of typewritten sheets, journals, notebooks, maps, mags, and what-not scattered over it, 'Away wae your tipper-tapper as well, eh?' He sneezed twice, so violently you could almost hear his bones chiming. 'Is the wife no in then?'

'Aye, there she is – hanging on the pulley,' I said as I knelt at the food cupboard.

Wattie jiggled about at my back. 'Forgetting she was in by . . . Is that salmon you have there? My, it's been a long while since I had a peck of salmon, and semolina in cans noo! Whatever next?'

I gave'm the filled sugar bowl but the fly old devil wasn't for returning to his flat right away. He mouthed the familiar drivel about what a comfort it was to be blessed with such a good neighbour, then he pottered over to the sink and keeked through the window. 'They're making a right hole ower there, eh?' he said, his weepy eyes staring out into the blackness in which a semi-demolished tenement was definitely not visible. He nodded. 'Tough old buggers they buildings but. No like the eggboxes they're stickin up noo. Aye, wan shout'll be enough to bring them doon, so it will.'

He came over and planted himself in Rhona's armchair. 'See you've got a good bleezer on.' He stretched his hands out to the crackling flames. 'Cannae thole a black grate these days. Ma bones're stapped wae ice, so they are. Plenty of kinneling to be got but.' He scratched his scrawny chest, causing panic in the colony, no doubt. 'And the price of coal! God love us, we'll soon be queueing up at the jewellers for it.' He shook his head. 'And tae think I must've lugged a thoosand tons of the stuff on my back tae. Maggie, god rest're, never had tae hinge her back tae mend oor fire – bunker aye full tae the gunnels, so it was.'

He stared into the heaped sugar bowl as if it was a crystal in which he could see shapes from the past arising. 'Ach, the days of the auld hairy engine is finished so they are. Nineteen forty-seven it was, hellish winter yon. Cauld enough tae make a polar bear

70

greet; snaw never aff the grun. Big Troy, as fine a Clydesdale as ever champed oats, slipped and snapped his leg . . .'

As the old man's memory began to slide down the slope of that legendary winter I tossed him a fag which he eagerly lighted, although its immediate effect was to double him over in a fit of coughing so powerful and so prolonged I expected to see his lungs flop onto the carpet. He gradually recovered, clambering onto each breath like an old turtle onto a rock. He left shortly afterwards, some ciggies and the tin of semolina he'd coveted the richer. But before I'd got the door shut on'm, he said: 'Oh aye, Tommy, I meant to tell ye, there was a bloke lookin for you the day.'

'A wee guy, striped bunnet, leather jacket?'

He nodded. 'That's'm.'

'Say what he was after, did he?'

'Naw, just a lot of daft blether.'

'What aboot?'

'Wish-washy kin o'stuff. Cannae remember. Was he wan of they bampots fae the papers aboot your burglary, then?'

'Aye – Pat Roller himself. Be seeing you, Wattie.'

With Wattie gone the worry committee, led by Jeremiah, trudged in once more, but I lighted a fag and chased them. Sure, there was plenty to be thinking about: the snowball pitcher(s): the London *Times*' mystery man (or woman – it doesn't pay to have mind-set); the snooping leatherback. Something seemed to be coming down and I'd the notion I wouldn't know what until it had ricocheted from my turnip. I was proved right almost immediately – something did in fact come down, namely *The Beano* I'd tacked to the wall. Granny Finnegan's ghost strikes again!

Later, sitting by the fire's garrulous flames with wan images leaking from my fourteen-inch telly, I wrote up the day's events so far in my current journal. Granda Gibson had been the instigator of what had become a lifelong habit for me. I was around twelve or thirteen at the time. I remember how exasperated he'd become as he guddled in a box of snapshots for a particular photo he wanted to show me. As he let pour from his hand a little cascade of sepia images he muttered, 'What this family needs is a historian, somebody to put its days into order. Right there'n then I'd volunteered for the job and, what's more, had stuck to it. Around twenty or so volumes, starting with modest jotters, but as my powers of expression increased so too did the journals in size'n girth.

On the TV a deepsea diver was to be seen wagging a penknife at a shark that looked about as long and twice as powerful as an American locomotive. I grinned. 'Go on wee Matt Lucas! I'll have it wae chips.' The shark who didn't have his brain millions of years for nothing, neatly, with his fabled choppers, snipped a yard or so from the diver's airline then backed away in brute astonishment as its victim gave an overwrought impression of a washing machine gone manic.

'That's that, Matt!'

9

Maternities have a fine tang of life to them, an invigorating ozone quite unlike those fetid airs which haunt the paindoms of infirmaries. The visitors who'd flocked here before me had left a scattering of imprints on the rubber floor-tiling; by now these early birds would've found their apportioned twigs on the great tree of birth and would be well into chit-chat about nest building and grublore. I entered a long corridor which was vibrant with the calls, cries, and mewlings of fledgeling days. Everywhere I glanced my eyes were strobed by gleam and glint, the shimmering of festive foils, fairy lamps, and paper bunting.

I'd brought Rhona some tangerines. How very xmassy they looked in their foil jackets as they nestled there at the base of the red netbag. I'd also brought her a magazine which had drained vatfuls of ink to recount the marital leapfrogging of a lightweight actress who'd acquired a large following, not to mention a large behind, and achieved apotheosis after playing a royal asp-licker in Tony and Cleo.

A nurse trotted past, followed a few paces later by a pair of glum-looking porters. I gave them a friendly nod but in return got a severe scowling. Aye, quite right, too: friendly nods won't put milk in a wean's belly nor will they put coal in the grate. Never mind your widow's mite, mate – just try living on the porters' pittance, see how much bread that'll butter. For starters, you'll have to forego fripperies like glossy mags and tangafucknrines.

A consultant, well, a guy in a white coat with a stethoscope coiled like an asp in one of its pockets and the air of a baby-boffin about'm, went by. From his consultative lips there came birding Acker Bilk's 'Stranger on the Shore', a tune which for some reason lays a hex on me. The corridor went on and on. Radiators sweated and grumbled. A wall crack which secretly fed on darkness and human indolence had stolen yet another inch towards its anarchic dream of downfall and rubble. I passed an xmas tree and saw myriads of tiny clays marooned on the shiny contours of appleglass planets.

Do Maternities have mortuaries? The question was prompted by the sight of a porter who approached me pushing a trolley upon which lay a sheet-swaddled form. The porter was a swaggering lout with a napperful of blazing red hair and a beard of the same colour burning along his jawbones, which were set in the whistle-mode so that his lips could trill some tum-tiddily-tum-tum lug-sickener from Gilb and Sullv. The figure on the trolley wasn't completely swaddled – its feet bared their soles to me and starkly semaphored that they'd have no further need for shoes and socks. Some poor woman taken in labour? No, definitely not! I'd've laid a sawbuck to a cent that this pair of peds belonged to a man!

Rhona's ward sister had an apt name for one of her profession – Pulham. As soon as I heard it I felt the pressure begin to mount in that spare lobe my brain uses as a neural trashcan, a coup for the mind's ordures, the psychic equivalents of sapped teabags, fishheads, and veg. peelings. Inevitably, the trashcan popped its lid and out leapt this cankerous doggerel:

Thrust, mother, thrust
From your natal cord unspool'm.
Thrust, mother thrust!
And as you push – I'll Pulham!'

I've some cheek coming that snash. Pain is no joke – especially
birth pain. The very thought of giving birth makes my eyeballs
sweat. Imagine serving as the escape tunnel for a nine-pounder
from Wombsville as it, all jaggy knees and elbows, goes for broke
after its prime breath! I remember watching TV this day and an
old dame came on. I figured from her genteel appearance that we
were about to learn how to make crêpe suzette using only
digestive biscuits, or how to construct a deluxe bumpaper holder,
using platinum paperclips and a handful of rubies. But instead,
doesn't she start to rabbit about what giving birth really felt like.
Quoth she: 'With the fingers of both hands take a firm grip of
your upper lip. Now, keeping a tight hold on it, peel your lip from
your gum then in one continuous movement yank it up over your
nose, brow and bonce, securing it with a knot behind the
ears . . .'

No, I'm not into such grief. When it comes to pain, hurt, ache,
twinge, sting or spasm, I'm kin to the goofer who got manhandled
from the Stoic's Club for complaining that its chairs were too
hard. Talk about windy? Just call me Chicago! Show yours truly
an injection kit, dental pliers, or a suture needle, and I'll show you
a fainting on a scale that would bring a sneer to the lips of even the
most squeamish of Victorian lady novelists.

About as comforting as would be the sight of a burning petrol
station to a roadweary driver riding a tankful of echoes was the
view ahead of me: Sister Pulham, the Maternity Medusa stood
guard at the entrance to Rhona's ward, waiting with her
petrifying glare to turn late-arriving hubbies into Mr Frosties.

Although she'd her back to me she wasn't any easier on the eye –
that rear of hers, for instance, could've roosted a colony of
gannets. Although I was fully twenty feet or so from her I could
feel the animosity coming off her like heat from a foxhole, I mean,
a stokehole. The handle of the netbag had wound itself tightly
about my forefinger and I'd to pause to let it unwind. This proved
to be fortunate for while I was rubbing at my corpsy digit, trying
to entice it back into my bloodflow, doesn't this bloke with a tan
Fedora on his loaf and a flash camel-haired coat hung around his
shoulders (two humps – one to either shoulder which made'm
look like a Yankee linebacker who'd been chopped off at the
knees) come stepping in a fancy pair of pavement prancers from
Rhona's ward and without seeming to consider the enormity of
his actions went bouncily up to Sister P. and, eyelevelling her
stony globes, began to lay some grief on her. This guy deserved
either a medal for bravery or rubber cutlery for lunacy. The
Sister's response was painfully predictable: before Fedora Fred
knew what was coming down he was all but bundled into the
Sister's office, the door of which closed with a glassy smack.
There he was, bottled up like a lab rat in a maze. And just as that
rodent gets a volt-jolt across its raisins every time it touches the
wrong button, so the now bewildered-looking flatbelly got
smacked down on a move he'd intended to be conciliatory: 'Mr
Hoxton, try to remember that we're running a maternity hospital
here – not a holiday camp.'

He nodded. 'Yes, I accept that, nurse, but surely we . . .'

He'd done it now – banged his snitch against that most
sensitive of levers, the one marked 'status'.

Sister Pulham, as if she'd been hooked into a Force Ten Gale,
seemed to inflate at a tremendous rate. 'Nurse? Did you call me
"nurse"? I think we mean SISTER, do we not?'

The Tangerine Man flitted quickly past the office outside of which, at a file-strewn table, a couple of Nightingales were straining to hear what was being so nastily mouthed by their superior. On entering Rhona's ward I immediately saw that changes had been made since my last visit: Big Agnes Coulter, who'd occupied the bed to Rhona's right, had gone. Her bed had been stripped to the bolster and her usual pigsty of a locker looked startlingly bare. The bed to Rhona's left contained a new occupant – a teary-eyed brunette who in her grey/blue bed-jacket looked like a beached whale. Her husband, a flattish-looking guy who wore what looked like industrial glasses, steel-rimmed things which seemed to be acting as a brace for the overhang of his brow, was gripping his spouse's hand so tightly I got the impression he was terrified that she might suddenly, with rude noises issuing from her backside, go on a wrecking sortie amongst the ceiling decorations. It was too bad that big Agnes was away. Dead cheery she'd been, though her humour had been a bit on the blue side for Rhona's taste.

The novel in which Rhona was rather pettily pretending to be so absorbed that she hadn't yet become aware of my presence, was, surprisingly enough, a James Bond one. I'd never known her to read such stuff. Quite shocking really; like going into Granny's purse and finding a condom. Not even the scraping of the chair legs on the polished parquet tiling diverted her from the improbable doings of Fleming's cynical robot. I seated myself and slung the laden netbag onto her bed. Eventually – it seemed like minutes, but was probably only ten seconds or so – Rhona, the book still unlowered from her face, asked, 'Well, gave her a good ticking-off, did we?' Her voice sounded husk – no, not huskier. Alien? Uh-uh. Hollower, then? Nope. Phoney? Aye, that's it – phoney. A vocal forgery, somebody else trying to pass counterfeit verbals in Rhona's name. With no thanks due to either Mr Fleming nor his callous plaything, the novel itself literally provided a dramatic twist by dipping to reveal its reader's face. A shockwave that would've taken the Richter Scale needle clean off the dial hit me. Jeezuz! What'd they done to my Rhona? Her face . . . her features had been put through a blender – every familiar quirk and line had been erased so that nothing recognisable remained, only a pink puddinglike mass, a maxfactored melange upon which wobbled the red O of a mouth. As words began to wriggle from this creepy orifice I was already on my feet and grabbing at the netbag. Patients and visitors alike turned to stare in amazement as I fled the ward.

The pair of nurses were still monitoring the fate of Fedora Fred, their ears trained like radar dishes on the office. By the sound of it, the contest was over – I could picture him lying on the floor with his feet in the air while the Medusa zapped his twitching corpse with a last round of mouth-ammo. As I approached them the nurses eyed me as if I'd no right to be this side of the skirting board. Where, I demanded to know, had they stashed my wife this time? On the roof maybe? In the attic? Was I getting warm? How about the basement . . . Trained to deal with visitors' sarcasm they didn't respond for a long time then one of them condescended to consult a register and I was given a ward number, purely as a favour I should understand. From the same charity bag came terse directions: lift; turn left; Mrs Clay's new ward was to be found at the far end of the corridor.

The lift was in Australia when I pressed its come-hither button. Once those abbos had her fully wound up she rose as gracefully as a cow with a gutful of pig-iron. The gate crashed open, then crashed shut again. There followed a massive shudder throughout its mechanism then it slowly sank back to Australia. I should've done some stair-stomping but got mulish. Never give in to gadgets. Once these gizmos get to know you're a soft touch they're into their own thing: the tranny, for instance'll start tuning itself into Jimmy Shand and the cutlery drawer'll take to pitching steak-knives at you.

I began to massage the bell-stud. A longish time later the lift capitulated and came to me with an ominous crrrrch-crrrrch-crrrrrrrching sound, like two major components were intent on erasing each other. The gate staggered open in much the same way as the Planet's curtain used to before Burnett retired it and left it to rot in the wings. A porter, one of the pair who'd scowled at me in the corridor, was the clanking box's sole passenger. If anything, he seemed even more scunnered with me than before. Half-man, half-walrus, he looked like an escapee from Doc Moreau's Island.

'Whatja keep ringing that bell for?' he growled. 'Fuck'n thing dirling in ma ears . . .'

I stepped into the lift and stood alongside him.

The machine, making more bedlam than a fire drill on Noah's Ark, began to lift off. I decided to ask the walman about the barefooted cadaver; if anybody knew why a male stiff should be getting hurled around a Hatchery during the visiting hour, he seemed the most likely. The business niggled me. There had to be a rational explanation. Such as? Well, supposing this wino – let's call'm Charlie – had a premonition that he's 'on the last go round' as Woody G. puts it. Charlie, not wanting to peg out, al fresco, on a crummy street bench, creeps into the Maternity and hides himself in the warmth of its boiler-room. In a way he's returned to the womb, gone back to Mammy. Aye, could've been something along these lines. A bit of a longshot, but at least Charlie had acquired some history which, I suppose, is preferable to being laid out on a slab with a John Doe ticket tied to your toe.

The porterish half of the walrus, far from being interested in my questions, seemed more concerned with our ascending machine's iron grumblings, so much so that he stepped to one side and pressed his ear to the wall and listened intently, as if he was conversant with the language of inanimate complaint. Supposing he should hear some crisis point declaring itself, what'd he do – jump clear? I repeated my question but we'd already arrived at my floor and the gate was well into its stop-go routine before he responded.

'What corpse?'

I stepped from the lift and turned to face him, 'The one I saw being wheeled somewhere – the mortuary, I suppose, by one of your muckers. Big fellow, bright red hair, beard . . .'

His cobwebby moustache stirred in the faint breeze of his reply. 'Naw, nae rid-heided porters work here, mack, especially no deid yins . . .'

With a gasping, squealing sound the gate shunted itself shut then, harnessing all of its antique energies, the lift bore its demi-human skywards.

On entering Rhona's new ward I was told by a nurse that I'd find her in the Day Room. I went there, Rhona was watching television while she worked her nails over with a slim manicure file. One other couple shared the room with us, a giggly twosome who seemed to be treating the solemn business of approaching parenthood with undue levity: the poor mite in her womb would feel it'd been caught up in a mirthquake. Demonstrating the proper decorum, Rhona, never once raising her voice, even managing to throw in decoy smiles from time to time, gave me a right good sand-bagging, a bawling-out done entirely in whispers. Keeping her head so close to mine that any passerby would've thought that we were exchanging endearments, she hissingly informed me that I was the giddy limit. The use of 'giddy' was the closest Rhona ever got to swearing, a euphemism which although puerile was at least more honest than her brother's hrrumphing. With a smile only the possessor of flawless ivories would risk she choppily announced in my left lughole that, no, she didn't want to hear my excuses since all of my lies were as unimaginative as they were repetitive. She was, she further informed me, sick to the perfect back teeth of my feeble fictions which usually involved old women falling off buses; stuck lifts; a meeting with someone I'd long presumed dead; transport fated to break down the moment I'd purchased my fare ticket. No, please, she didn't want to hear a single word concerning my ability to arrive twenty minutes into the visiting period. I suppose it was lucky she'd forestalled me for I'd been about to tell her the unvarnished truth for a change. It hadn't been a woman who'd been involved in a transport accident this time, in fact, it'd been a tipsy greybeard who, in the whimsical way of the drunk had decided to come down the bus stairs the same way he'd gone up them, namely, headfirst. He'd landed on his beak and – but what's the use of going on? She didn't want to know what hazards had attended my journey here. Liars fully deserve the cuts and bruises they get when reality catches up with them. Even if I'd walked in here with an honestly-acquired broken nose she'd soon enough have twisted out of shape my account of how I'd come by it.

Rhona's attention had now tilted to a higher plane where life could be relied upon to be free of long-haired latecomers, where the tedium of waiting is edited out, and zones of mistrust can be crossed in the winking of a heroic eye. Yes, the wonderful world of 'Disney Exist' where dreams really do come true.

Rhona sawed away at her fingernails with such vigour and flashing of the file you would've thought it was an attempt at self-erasure. Her eyes remained fixed on the telly-screen. Beneath the imperious mantle of her purple housecoat she was wearing the quaint-looking nightdress I jokingly refer to as her 'nun's negligee'. I glanced at her as a commercial for a chocolate bar filled the screen. 'Bite a Delite Tonite!' the voice-over ordered, and presumably if we did then everything would turn out rite.

The movie was the usual eye-fodder: the romance between the heroine and the son of an autocratic millionaire was on the verge of exposure. The lovelorn pair sat now in his car which overlooked a small industrial town – every brick'n stick of which belongs to dollar-driven Daddy. The son began now to philosophise which was signalled by the thoughtful way he raised his left eyebrow. 'Pop'll just have to shake the notion that the world's his auction room and the future his by merely raising a finger . . .' Now steady on, Junior, Pop might've bugged your dash. Anyway, what's this future jazz? Aint no such thing to be found on our half-assed planet. Take that TV set for instance, it makes with a whole batch of buttons that're wired to nowhere. They await, you see, an advance in electronic know-how that's not going to be around in the buzz-box's lifetime. Symbolic buttons, then – good for damn all. A touch of swank, that's what it amounts to. Most of us front our lives in the same way – twiddle-twiddling, trying to tune in to non-existent signals.

'How did you manage to smash Mum's pot plant?' Rhona asked.

I frowned. 'On the news was it? "Cops hunt aspidistra-slayer!" '

'I phoned her before you got here – seeing as I'd plenty of time on my hands.'

Into the Day Room there came a Sikh with his swollen wife. He escorted her to a chair and helped her to lower her baggy body into it. His amber turban and green transport livery gave'm a sort of 'ready-to-go' air. He looked a bit cheesed-off, fed-up, scunnered.

'You tell'm it's none of his business,' he said to her. 'If you don't tell'm then I bliddy tell'm.'

Rhona put her nail file into its pouch and pressed the stud closed with a faint plocking sound. 'I hear you took yon old Grandfather clock to mother's?'

I nodded.

'Why?' she asked.

I got a little wiggy. 'Because.'

'Call that an answer?'

'It'll have to do.'

Rhona sighed. It was becoming a habit this sighing business. We didn't have visits anymore – we had sigh-ins. She'd forced me to become fluent in Sighamese. So much so that I can intuit meaning from the merest breath of disgruntlement. This latest sigh, for instance, was a carry-over from my refusal on my last visit to agree to attend a simple little service in honour of Dad Carlyle, the second anniversary of whose death would be this coming Sunday. 'It's not even a service,' Rhona had told me. 'Just a few prayers and some readings from Dad's favourite passages. Surely that's not a lot to ask?'

How smugly dismissive of the atheist's viewpoint some salvationists can be. Because I'd found no evidence to support the notion that our ball of mud and stones has a celestial gaffer looking after it, having found not so much as a divine thumbprint or a button from his cloudy coat, I was judged to be some kind of moronic cyberman whose solenoids were incapable of experiencing that sensitivity which is the hallmark of your true Christian. I'd turned her down flat then and if she asked once more I'd do the same. I had proposed, however, that I'd take young Jason to the Kelvingrove Museum so that Phyllis and Jack Sherman would be able to attend the anniversary of the laid-low locksmith.

Rhona began now to drill me about my financial outgoings. Had I paid this, had I paid that? Well, that's what Friday nights at the maternity were all about, why they're called 'husbands preferably' visits so that the expectant couples can be alone with their debts and to plan for the wifeless week ahead. My tongue clacked away like a calculator. Yes, I'd contacted the Gas Board about emptying the meter. Yes, I'd made a payment to the Futility Furnishing Company. Soon I hadn't a debt in the world. Talk about relieved. Phew! as Pansy Potter would say. It was great to feel so unburdened. Free and floating. It was best not to come up too fast or you could get the marital bends, a most painful affliction, I'm told. Its victims literally laugh themselves to death. From hilarity Rhona was in no danger whatsoever. But now as she continued to speak I thought I detected a lighter tone developing in her voice.

'Tom, can I ask you something?'

'Fire away.'

'Would you . . . well, would you be fussy about what it was?'

'I'd prefer a white yin if you can manage it.'

'Eh?'

'You know, un enfant blanc – a white wean.'

She smiled (yeah, read all about it – Rhona smiled!) I'm talking about a job, stupid. Would you be fussy about what it was?'

'Take a stab at anything, me: brain surgery, chastity belt fitting; helping Kim Novak on with her bra. You name it.'

Again that chronic sigh of hers. 'Be serious. Just for once, stop acting the goat.' The smile had fled; in fact she now looked on the verge of tears. More levity juiced my tongue but I stifled it. She was right, it was high time I tossed away my dog-eared script with its quips and repartee for all occasions. Time, too, for me to cut out that harlequin prancing around her emotions, the verbal skipping from one corner of a lie to another, calling her in only to trip her up, confounding with a glee that was almost malicious her grey-eyed appeal for a truce, a pause between puns. Something extremely important was happening to us – we were becoming parents. From now on it was incumbent upon me to come clean, to meet her beyond the rhinestones and the rhetoric.

'You'd do anything? D'you really mean that?'

A sinister blip had appeared on my internal radar screen. Anxious personnel were crowding around. 'What the hell's this, then? Something's in the air and heading our way, folks!' From a pocket in her housecoat Rhona fished out an envelope and from this envelope she removed a letter. A gasp filled the control room: 'My God! – this is for real!'

'I got a letter from Uncle Billy this morning,' she told me. 'You remember him?'

'Wooden leg; walks with his worries to one side?'

'Stop acting it. Dad's brother – lives in Townhead.' She thrust the letter at me. 'Here, read it for yourself.'

I conned the pedantic writing which covered two pages: 'Hope you are well . . . blah, blah, blah . . . I visited your mother the other day' (I bet you hit six boozers on the trot after that Billy, boy!) 'She tells me that your Tom's still not got work. I'm sure this must be a worry to you, especially since you're hoping for a new house. I was wondering if I could be of some help.' (All communications lost as Clayville suffered a direct hit!) 'A vacancy has turned up in our warehouse for a packer. The wages are reasonable and the work is fairly light. Perhaps you could mention this to Tom and, if he's agreeable, he could maybe pop in to see me for a chat . . .'

I now demonstrated so much aversion to the letter you would've thought its pages were infested with anthrax. 'Well?' Rhona's gaze had all the warmth and compassion of a Nazi Stormtrooper with his Luger pistol jammed up your nostril.

'Uncle Billy,' I said manfully, 'he's in bananas – right?'

She nodded. 'Been in the same warehouse for the past ten years.'

'Well, he should be about ripe by now.'

'What?'

'Rhona, I don't relate to bananas. Can't stand the frigging things.'

'Mind your language.' She indicated the letter. 'His address's on the top. Go, see'm.'

'When?'

'Tomorrow afternoon; he's never out.'

'I'm taking the Cub Pack to Ben Nevis, Saturday . . .' (Strang's weird remark about keeping clear of high places returned to me. What'd he been getting at?) Rhona's brow had darkened again. I nodded. 'Okay, okay, I'll go see the man, but I'm not making any promises. Right?'

She nodded. The film resumed. The multibucks boyfriend was now showing his gal from the boondocks some impressive-looking real estate. It was one of those colonnaded mansions which tend to be populated, in the movies, that is, by manic Southern belles; the house and adjoining ranch sat in lush grassland which was only slightly smaller than Texas. 'Hell, no dear,' he growled, whacking his riding boot with his stetson, 'wouldn't roost chickens in tharrr. Place I kinda had in mind'll use up two and a half mountains of prime stone . . .'

Follow that, Mr Clay!

'Tom.'

'What?'

'Tom, I wish things could be . . . well, you know – normal.'

Of course I knew what she meant. Knew only too well. Yet despite myself, there was my bowtie becoming luminous, beginning to twirl and, in my buttonhole, the plastic carnation was readying itself to squirt comic acid. 'There's a lot of static on the line,' I said. 'What's "normal"?'

86

'You know – regular.' Her voice dropped. 'See that lassie over there?'

'Minnie-Ha-Ha, you mean?'

'Shhh, she'll hear you.' Rhona moved closer to me so that her mouth was almost touching my ear. 'She's having her own house built in Bishopbriggs.'

'Is that the lum she's got stuck up'r goonie, then?'

She became huffy again. 'No use talking to you.'

A new tactic: the clown inverts his gaudy mouth; tears pulse from dry eyes; a tale of great personal sacrifice he would unfold, of how, that very afternoon he'd cashed in his tipper-tapper, a castastrophe on the scale of Rudolph Nury-what's-it surrendering his legs to a surgeon.

'But why? Surely you weren't that stuck that you'd to . . .'

'It was an auld machine, Rhona – knackered.'

'What'd you need the money for?'

'Well, there's yon joker that comes doon the lum for a start.'

'I'm in a Club for young Jason, remember?'

'Too right! The Stork Club – membership expanding!'

She seemed in much better fettle now. An old joke between us surfaced.

'Tom, don't go daft and get me that flank musquash coat you promised me ages ago.'

'I've my eyes on something even better,' I said. 'I've put down a deposit on a new cord for your iron. How about that?'

Her soaring spirits were plain to see. The fact that I'd dumped my typewriter had restored buoyancy to her dream balloon. Already she was airborne. By the time the visiting period was over she was all but out of sight, and I was little more than a humble dung-beetle nosing its ball of spittle and planetary dust up that mythical slope called the future . . .

10

The Planet Picture House was, in reality, a big dud neon sign with a bit of crumbling cinema attached to it. Old folks out for a wee daunder might, through force of habit, find themselves wandering into this kinematic museum to watch the breakdowns and odd snippets of film. During the forties someone had hurled a dagger through the screen and the rough repair work had resulted in a big L-shaped scar that flawed the close-ups of such modern stars as Don Ameche and Alice Faye. The Planet was well into its last reel of existence, a fact mourned by its faithful patrons as they sat at home glued to their TV sets.

'Hurry up, Tam – the fleas are hungry!' shouted Big Snowy Callaghan, the doorman-cum-bouncer, as I came into the vestibule. He was a huge punter with a mane of white hair and a face he'd charitably donated to most of the city's infirmaries for needlework practice. Snowy was proud of his scars and when drunk he'd give you a conducted tour of them. 'This long wan here's Tam Padden's work – could fairly handle a malky, yon bastard. Big Durkin fae the Toonheid gave me this twelve-stitcher but you should've seen his coupon – butcher's windae stuff. This fella was done wae a sheath-knife, Billy Higgins fae the Calton. He was found wae the point of an anchor up his arse in the KGV back'n the fifties.'

'Lo, Snowy,' I said, pausing by him, 'how's business?'

Folding the *Evening Citizen* he'd been reading, he jerked a thumb towards the pile of coins old Maude, the cashier, had accumulated. 'Soon have enough to post a letter. That right, Maude?' Knitting what might be a balaclava for one of the boys on the Somme, she didn't answer. Maude's age was legendary. Whenever folk started to conjecture what it might be, the expression, 'She was here long afore the angels', was bound to be heard. This meant that she predated the angels which during the Planet's one and only refurbishment had been painted on the auditorium's ceiling by a man called Seamus O'Toole. O'Toole's efforts to emulate Michaelangelo had, alas, fallen far short of the mark: his sun, moon and stars weren't all that bad but his angels were diabolical – a hard jawed squadron with muscles like stevedores who wielded harps that looked like swatches of railings that'd been swiped from Scobie Street backcourts during the war. The angels were still up there but years of smoke had done for them and a thick coat of nicotine gunge now mercifully concealed their bolloxed artistry. As for O'Toole, who'd risked life and limb to perform his sub-Sistine miracle, he'd been killed in a freak accident in a cheese store when a wheel of the finest yellow fell on him from a height. Hard Cheddar, as the expression has it.

I chaffed to Snowy for a few minutes, mainly about the cuddies, then I went upstairs, heading for the operating box. On my way there I bumped into Nessie Maxwell, who was burdened in life by an alcoholic husband and, at present, by a trayful of ice-cream tubs, crisps, nuts, drinks and popcorn. (It was rumoured that Paddy Cullen got his nuts from her for nothing but the fat man vigorously denied this.)

'Bloody Eskimo pictures,' Nessie grumbled. 'Fat chance I've got of selling ice-cream!'

'Cheer up, Nessie,' I said, 'we're due any day now for the return of Bogie in *Sahara*.'

'Well, he'd better come on a fast camel or he'll find the door bolted,' Nessie said as she tottered off towards the balcony to see if any punters were to be found on its frozen slope.

The lounge had definitely fallen on hard times. On one famous occasion a chunk of its ceiling had fallen and nearly brained a wee rogue from Devon Street while he was hacking a generous swatch from the treasured Templeton carpet with a lino knife, 'Jist for a wee souvenir,' as he'd explained to the sheriff. This much admired tapis was now but a shadow of its former glory; in recent times it'd taken to weaving for itself a manic-looking fungal design, an activity which you could feel nibbling at the soles of your shoes if you stood overlong on any one spot. It had to be conceded that a heavy dose of sledgehammering was just what the place needed. Depressing it was to see the old bumweary couches mouldering in dark corners, a stench of finito plagued the nostrils; let's face it, there're fewer smells more poignant than the stink of plush going to pot.

I went through a doorway on the brow of which the title 'Manager' had been perfunctorily stencilled. A duplicate green painted door at my elbow repeated the title but this time it was inscribed in the loops and swoops of the signwriter's art. What was happening behind the green door? Not much, seemingly for Burnett was making with the heavy zees. Holding down two jobs was proving tiring for him for since the sudden passing of Rinty O'Dowd, he'd been functioning in the dual role of Proprietor/ Manager. With the Hammer all but poised over the Planet's roof there seemed little point in hiring a replacement for O'Dowd –

not that such a person was likely to be found anyway. O'Dowd had been a one-off; a showbiz manqué who'd done a stint 'on the boards' in his youth, he could always be depended upon to keep a queue from wearying with his impersonations, tap-dancing and comic patter. He'd made his exit in fine style. 'Aye,' says Freddy Greene, 'he gets his usual fistful of Islay Mist, gives a shuffle – you know, yon fankly thing he'd do wae his legs – raises his glass, says "Cirrhosis", cocks his heid yon wey of his, then puts ower a gubful. It couldna've got past his tonsils before his heid hit the sawdust . . .'

Apart from seeing to the nightly receipts – this didn't take long – or, when needed, supplying batteries or bulbs for the three or four usherettes, Burnett had sometimes to supervise the ejection of difficult patrons, usually drunks who'd got entangled in the horror movies unwinding inside their booze-blitzed heads. Big Snowy, of course, would be on hand to see to the physical side of the ejections as he would later when the show was over and he and Matt Lucas would scour the auditorium to winkle out the odd dosser who, now'n again, would try to hide himself in order to extend his stay into a warm night's kip. It was also routine to check out the toilets in case somebody was sitting stone dead on one of the pans, his breath having been taken away by the fumes from the disinfectant cubes as they sizzled violently in orange pools of piss. Burnett's sister came for him each evening in her car, a wee Morris Minor, and drove him back to their home in Burnside. Not once had I ever seen her set foot in her brother's pictorial pesthole.

On the yellow door in the corner somebody – probably Cullen – had daubed 'Apehouse this way!' in choppy green letters. I pushed it open and began the tough climb up the dusty flights of stairs. The Planet's op-box was so primitive Edison would've condemned it: two vintage Ross projectors and a slide-lantern took up most of its available room. These antique kinema relics were juiced by electrical junk so out of date that it moistened the eyes of the greybeard who very infrequently dropped by to perform routine servicing. Adjoining the box was a claustrophobic spoolroom so cramped for space it was possible to get a high from the film cement.

Matt Lucas smiled at me as I came into the box. He was crouched by the take-up reel of number two machine, tucking in a film tail. 'Hullo, Tommy – it's yourself. Still snowing ootside?'

'No as heavy as in here,' I said and stepped across to the monitor to tone down the sound of a raging blizzard. 'How'd the diving trip go, then?' I asked.

He pulled a face. 'Flippin hopeless. A gang of tearaways tanked me wae snowballs in Bedford Street, must've been twenty of them, at least. Went doon on ma bahookie, so I did. Soaked right through.'

'You were daft tae dae it in the first place.'

'Ach, it's always another dollar towards the wife's anniversary pressy.'

'S'that all the bugger gave you – five bob?' I shook my head. 'Don't suppose he went the distance, did he?'

'Mr Burnett, you mean?' He shook his head. 'Slipped off into the Granite Bar, to phone his sister, he said.'

'Is he back on the bendy juice again?'

'Looks like it.'

Something in the corner, near the record player, caught my eye. I grinned: there, sprawled in the battered armchair in glorious bevvycolour, was the magnificent sight of Paddy Cullen, second-class operator and first-class drunk. He looked well gone, down there with his winklepickers dancing on the hobs of Hell. It was long odds against his surfacing before the Anthem was rattling through the sprockets. I replaced the *Evening Times* which'd half-slid from his sweaty face. 'Hellish, is it no, what you find in the papers these days?'

Lucas closed the lower spoolbox door then crossed to the monitor to fade further the grunts that passed for Hollywood Eskimo. He returned to the resting projector and swung up its arc-chamber door. As he set about replacing the burnt-out carbons he glanced through a porthole at the screen. 'Wish I'd a harpoon,' he said. 'I'd know where to stick it.'

'How aboot a snawba doon his neck?'

Lucas gave his head a disgusted-looking shake. He was a frayed wee man with a severe squint and a shimmer of panic about'm that suggested he'd make a fertile breeding ground for stomach ulcers. 'A stick of gelly widnae shift'm.' Lucas hurried round to the running projector to adjust its carbons. 'I've had to run the show myself tonight. No playing the game. Know what he done on the first run?'

'Crashed the carbons, maybe? Missed a change-over?'

'C'mon Tommy, that's par for the course. I'll tell you what he did – stuck parts three and four of the wrang film on, that's what. One minute it's your posse chasing the baddy, the next, it's a polar bear biting the bum off an Eskimo. That's no it finished. When Maisie Templar phones'm up to tell'm (I was stoking the furnace at the time) what does the brainless bampot go'n do? You've guessed it – sticks five and six of the Eskimo film on. Blooming mess!'

Me, I found the whole thing hilarious. 'Think about it Matt – the possibilities. A whole new seam: *The Sheriff of Kayak Creek*, starring Husky Mush and Aurora Borealis! Or, how aboot, *The Snawba Fight at the O.K. Coracle?*'

'I'd prefer a winos' ward starring him,' Lucas said, then immediately fed his own addiction by popping a Mint Imperial into his gob, which he then began to rattle zestfully around his wallies. A chain-sooker, that's what he was. I settled into the creaking basketchair by the radiator and reached for my pack of cigs. Lucas adjusted the mirror on the running machine, a practice more habitual than effective for the Eskimos were fighting a losing battle with Burnett's flawed screen, most of them floundering from sight into its dusty crevices; the scar left by that long-ago flung dagger marked out one of the Arctic's finest for an early death when it appeared like a flash of black lightning, zig-zagging across his brow in close-up. Cullen continued to give his impression of a Harley-Davidson Special doing the ton on a gravel beach.

'Time he got a grip on himself,' Lucas grumbled. 'Think's sobriety's an illness. Okay, we all like a wee snifter now'n again but he's always got to go over the score.'

I nodded. 'A hollow leg oor Paddy has.' I glanced at Lucas. 'Away across and have a quicky yoursel, wee man – I'll mind the shop.'

'Thanks, Tommy, you're a champ. After the change-over then.' He glanced through the window of the top spoolbox. 'Only a couple of minutes left.'

With the change-over completed Lucas stuck on his coat'n bunnet and headed for the Dog. I trimmed the carbons, squeezing as much light as was possible from the flogged-out rear mirror, then I went through to the spoolroom with the loaded reel from the static projector. As I rewound it I accepted that the chance of a couple of jugs in the company of Paddy Cullen was no longer a runner. Just as well, maybe, for I'd need to keep some loot by for tomorrow. Skint on a Saturday – what could be worse than that? I'd nearly painted myself into a corner by hinting to Rhona that she might be onto something special this xmas. A flank musquash for chrissake! Some hopes. Aye, it was all right for they Eskies –

94

fur-coats came chapping on their doors at midnight. A tough life just the same, for when you got auld and your teeth started to fall out (around twenty-five on average) the Midnight Sun mob papped you out on the tundra for bear-bait, no messing. I slotted the rewound reel into the film cabinet and withdrew the next one in sequence. While I was doing this I got to puzzling over the Zebra-bunneted merchant who'd been doing his nosey about me. Hard to figure who he might've been. In addition there was the London *Times* in my stairhead closet. 'Don't forget the snowballs,' Jeremiah put in. I grinned. 'No Balls in the Dark' – a good title for a number on the Eunuch's Hit-Parade.

When I got back into the op-box with another reel of Arctic hokum a surprise jolted me; a real, live non-celluloid chick was standing at the running projector, gaping at it with such an awed expression you would've thought it was an example of newly-minted technology instead of a crap bundle of light and sprockets. She'd the face of an angel – one of the fallen variety. I figured her to be in the 22/25 bracket though sans underpinning she might overflow 25. Her pancake fakeup had been trowled on so thickly it made Dusty Springfield's lavishness in the same area look positively nunnish. You could almost feel the draught from her sooty eyelashes, a startling contrast to her bottle blonde hair which, stiff with lacquer, looked as if its beehive style had been lowered onto her head by crane and welded into place. A blue nylon coat overall was half-buttoned over her red woollen nearly-dress and she wore sandals of the same colour. Her lips which I've deliberately left until last (just as women do when they're chucking on their warpaint) were fascinatingly repellent, corpse-white, of course, in deference to the anti-natural look which the face-graffiti gurus were telling daft wee lassies was absolutely *de rigueur* this season. De-whut? Never you mind about that, hen, just splodge it on. D'you maybe want a shot of my grease-gun?

As the door thumped shut behind me her glance darted in my direction. Because of the layers of cosmetic gunk it was hard to figure what initial impact I was having on her but I took the fluttering eyelids to be a favourable sign. 'Hullo,' she said, and her voice had a nice warm core to it, 'I was just having a look.'

'Be my guest.' I presented my face in profile. 'They tell me this is my best side.'

She smiled. 'No I meant . . .' She hesitated. 'I've never been in a projection booth before.'

'Projection booth, eh?' I loaded the reel into its spoolbox then hurried around to the running machine and tightened the gap between the carbons – night suddenly becoming day would baffle the few patrons who might still be down there. I tried without success to sharpen the focus on an Eskimo who was gnawing at something – a seal's asshole, maybe.

'It's smaller'n I expected,' she said, an observation which MacDougall had been on the point of responding to when I cut in with: 'Aye, it's as tight as a herring's face,' which was one of Da Clay's daft expressions, one that always made me chuckle – God knows why. It seemed to have the same effect on the dolly-bird for her smile blossomed into a silky sort of laugh, a sound to treasure as the monitor continued to spit out gelid chunks of Eskimoese.

I returned to the static machine and began to lace the film leader through the machine's sprockets. She watched as I made the necessary loops. Jeezuz – that dress of hers! 'I just thought I'd come up for a wee peep,' she explained. 'Couldn't believe it when I found the place running itself.'

Squinting into the gate I ran some film through the projector. As I swung the lens down into position I nodded in the direction of the snoring Cullen. 'You'll have met twinkletoes?'

She shook her head. 'Been warned about'm, that's all.'

'Warned?'

'That he's more arms than an octopus – one to be watched.'

Cullen groaned then sank with a gurgle onto the mired bed of his dreams. Octopus? More like a big Fenian haddy caught on a tartan hook.

'He's in some state.'

I nodded. 'Works hard at it.'

'Shouldn't you waken'm?'

'Got a stick of dynamite on you?'

She took a tortoiseshell fag case from her overall pocket and flicked it open. 'Is it all right to?'

I produced my lighter and presented its flame to her with Hollywood knackiness. Her long pale hands and manicured nails suggested that housework wasn't the lady's strong suit. 'Where've they been hiding you?' I asked, ensuring that the confab didn't rise above Tinsel Town tattle: B movie dialogue for B movie situations – saves the hassle.

Her words came out on a tickertape of smoke. 'Peggy's sick, you see, and she asked me to stand in for her, just tonight. What with this talk of a bonus when the place shuts she . . .'

'Peggy's your old lady – right?'

'Sister.' She smiled. Her teeth made a real shiny mouthful and managed to hold their own for whiteness against her pallid lips. I retrimmed the carbons and footered again with the focus. 'What's up wae Peggy, then?'

'Her chest's gone again.'

This invited an obvious flip response but I resisted it. Dropping the sound a notch or so as an MGM blizzard began to have its way with a huddle of igloos, I asked her what she was called.

'Rebecca – Rebecca McQuade.'

I went over to the carbon box and took out a couple of fresh rods, motioning as I did so towards the basket chair. 'Park yourself for a bit, Rebecca.'

'Becky.'

'Okay, Becky. Take some weight off.'

She shook'r head. 'I'd better get back.'

'Finish your fag first.'

An expression I presumed was one of gratitude tried to struggle through her face-pack. 'Ta. Don't think I'm cut out for this sort of work. My dogs are barking.' She lowered herself into the crackling chair then, slipping off one of her sandals, began to massage her foot. To do this she'd to cock her leg some and, given the pelmet of a dress she was almost wearing I was granted a generous view of her suspendered stocking top. My old ticker all but got its diastoles and systoles in a fankle and MacDougall began to get ideas above his station. Hellish what gonads can do to a man, have'm jumping through hoops, oinking lustfully, smacking his flippers, performing in the spotlight of his libido for the glittering prize, that erotic titbit women from time to time choose to toss our way.

She lowered her leg but not MacDougall's temperature. 'You must be Matt Lucas,' she said.

'If I must, then I must.'

'I imagined you'd be . . . well, older.'

'S'that so?'

Cullen groaned again as maybe a bottle of Scotch fell from a ledge of his mind.

'Hadn't you better give'm a shake?' she asked. 'What would Mr – Whitshisname?'

'Burnett. Oswald J. Burnett.'

'Right. What'd he say if he found him up here in that state?'

I shrugged. 'Not a lot for he'd probably have snuffed it.

Burnett's got a dodgy clock. Hasn't made it up them apples and pears in the last ten years.'

She eyed the comatose Cullen. 'Can't stand drunks.'

'And drunks can't stand.' I nodded. 'Aye, it's a hard auld life, eh?'

A lone Eskimo was floating off to his death aboard a chunk of ice roughly the size of Millport when he'd been lured onto it, but which had soon shrunk to the dimensions of a doormat. The brave lad, becoming aware of his plight, muttered something northpolish like, 'Fuck this for a game of sodgers!' I adjusted the mirror again and realigned the carbons. Through the observation slit in the projector's belly a tiny but fierce sun could be viewed, could be manipulated.

'Where you from, Becky?'

'Govanhill.'

'What does your man dae?'

'Lorry driver.'

'Long distance?'

She nodded then in one stroke changed the game's direction. 'The longer the bloody better.'

The doomed Eskimo was going under with unlikely stoicism, the world's door closing on him with an icy slam. A loose joint skittered through the machine's sprockets but made it without splicing. 'Any kids?' I queried.

'Who knows? Haven't been to Dagenham to find out.'

'Is that where he is the noo – Dagenham?'

She plucked at the hem that was her dress. 'Must be – his belly pills were away this morning.'

With that obscene rapidity Hollywood imposes upon ethnic minorities the relatives of the doomed Eskimo were already shrugging off his loss: many tasks to be completed – tundras to be ploughed, seal pups to be slaughtered, boots to be gnawed.

'How come you escaped?'

I looked across at her, 'Eh?'

'Never got married.'

'Who says so?'

'Me. You live with your sister in Crown Street.'

Amusing all this confusing. A tripartite monster was breaking from its ironic egg, was clawing its way into the realm of possibility: Clay-Cullen-Lucas – Clayculluca!

'Peggy's really been filling you in eh?'

An elegant shoulder shrug was her response. And what a shoulder to be shrugged at by. I imagined it to be of a peachy hue, much like the rest of her voluptuous body, this shade being the one that gets the greediest brushlicks on the pornographer's palette. She'd me hanging out to dry, this chick with the long, restless legs in their tautly suspendered nylons. With one twitch of her classy clav she'd got me more lit-up than Osram's test-bed. Not that I needed much enticement for I'd been on sexual iron-rations for far too long. As a result of this nooky-deprival I'd got me an affliction, a Midas-like syndrome only in this case the sense of sight and not touch was the transforming agent: everything my glance alights on takes on an erotic sheen. Objects like car headlamps, trees, violins, are effortlessly shaped by my spunkified vision into the contours of the ideal Woman, she who haunts boys' dorms and monks' cells. Talking about monks, why's there so much hoo-ha about St Anthony's battle with concupiscence? The guy endured nothing more than a randy itch, a mere storm in a scrotum, compared to the sexual siroccos which buffet me both by day'n by night, aye, more especially at night when lying alone in my austere cot I watch ceiling stains assume Siren shapes, see them become wet-lipped succubi with a coffee warmth to their nude hips, pale amber-haired houri beckon and tease, flaunting their taut, yet deliciously trembling rose-tipped – enough! that's just my ceiling, by the way; as for my wallpaper, I'm expecting the vice squad to raid it any day now.

Yawning sensually, so that beyond her opalescent lips the ruby arch of her mouth could be glimpsed, she stretched back in the basket chair which crackled with the sexual static her body was giving off. The hem of the demi-dress rode up the shine of her slightly parted legs. As if I was a brainless rustic who'd somehow or other managed with his simple pole to hook in a legendary fish, MacDougall, fearful that in my clumsiness I'd lose it, was delivering a series of near-panicky instructions: 'Careful now . . . don't jerk your rod . . . like that . . . play it gently . . . watch, you're going to lose it . . . for heaven's sake . . . give me the thing . . . Jeremiah was trying to get his tanners worth in as well, but when you're on the point of landing the big one who'd give ear to a bumptious bailiff prattling about rules and regulations, or what penalties I might expect for this flagrant sexual poaching? Probably it'd all end in a soggy anti-climax and I'd fish out an old boot or something. The Woman, archetype of all women probably wasn't there. Her ugly name, Becky, hinted as much. What I had in tow here was more likely to be just a blonde scrubber, one well deserving those cheap epithets: like dolly-bird or teenage junk phrases such as a 'right little raver', 'awesome chick' and so on. Nevertheless, there I stood (MacDougall likewise) vibrating with lust. And what was this juvenile rigmarole coming from my mouth? Could I really be saying something as corny as, 'Did Peggy no mention I've a helluva weakness for blondes?' Aye, the grottiest of patter right enough but when the mysteries of the legs feminine are being inch by inch revealed to you, anything goes.

'Have you?' she asked huskily (goddammit, there's no other adverb – her voice was definitely husky!)

'Incurable.'

With a whickery sigh of abandonment, the chair — No, let's make it: with a feeling of tingly tumescence the projectionist (boy was he projecting!) fiddled with the mirror control knob. Decking her fag stub, with the sole of her sandal she reduced it to an amber smear on the floor. 'I'd better get back,' she said; that damned huskiness was still there.

The projectionist moved in an oddly lateral kind of shuffle towards her, reminding you vaguely of poor old Quasimodo, whose hump, whose unfortunate protuberance he no longer found riseable — I mean, risible. 'What's the hurry?' I asked her. 'Big Snowy'll catch anybody trying to escape.'

Her hand was already on the doorknob, 'Nice to've met you, Matt.'

'Listen,' I said with carnal urgency, 'how about a wee drink later, eh? Just the two of us.'

She played on me her very candid stare, at the heart of which I could see two nude and very active figures floating away on a chunk of blue ice. Seeing her this close, it was apparent that if she used a lighter make-up trowel and shed those eye-flappers, then she could give Kim Novak a run for her money, and that's my highest accolade.

'A wee drink?' she repeated, her speech lightly peppered with sarcasm. 'And what pavement had you in mind? Or are you thinking of packing the Eskimos off early to bed?'

'Carry-out; half bottle of whisky; a few cans. Okay?'

'What'd your sister say?'

'Forget her.' I took a firm grip on her arm and a slackening one on my morals. 'Listen, there's this mate of mines, got a pad in this very street. He's working doon South just now, so I promised to keep an eye on things. You know what they're like around here — screw their granny's coffin for its brass. Well, what d'you say?'

She hesitated. 'It'd only be for a wee while?'

Vigorous nodding on my part. 'Aye, as long or as short as you like.'

Astoundingly, her lacquered helmet was nodding, was giving me the come-on. Nod, nod. 'On one condition,' she added.

'What's that?'

'Make it vodka instead of whisky.'

She moved quickly away passing through the doorway and going off down the stairs on her sexy red sandals. 'Becky,' I called down after her, 'meet me in Marco's chippy, Cally Road. Wait inside for me — it'll be warmer . . .'

Ever the thoughtful lover!

She continued her descent without reply.

'A loada shite!' Paddy Cullen muttered. I wasn't sure if this was a lag thought jailbreaking his mind or a comment on my immoral advances. It'd already dawned on me that Becky must've come up here expecting to find Paddy. Some broads can't resist the challenge of trying to cook a bang from a wet squib. Maybe she'd seen Lucas heading for the Dog and got to thinking: 'Aha, yon auld garter-twanger's up there on his ownsome. Maybe I should — ' Naw, that couldn't be; she'd mistaken me for Lucas hadn't she? What if — any why not? — she'd spied me loping past in that sexy lithe way of mine's? Who could blame her for murmuring, 'Gawd, who's that hunk, and where's he happening?' Yeah, a moviehouse Messalina with the instant hots for yours truly. I smirked at the inert Cullen. It's your own fault, boyo, shoulda kept your powder dry.

I glanced through a porthole at the screen then dashed round to the running projector. The carbon tips had drifted so far apart it looked like the movie was having a cardiac arrest. Working the feed knobs I pumped light onto the cyanotic screen. In the film itself things had been tobogganing along from one healthy patch of carnage to the next. Loads of whip-cracking, and berg-cracking, but a lot less wisecracking since a missionary dude had turned up to scatter his priestly frost around. The Eskimo chieftan was getting all hot under his furry kaftan because this alien, a right knobless ninny, had turned down his offer to spend a long night in the loghouse with his wife. Now I could've seen the guy's point if what was on offer was your traditional bag of blubber sequinned with fishscales, and smelling like a breeze from Buckie, but he was turning down a tanned Californian chick with blinding teeth and a smile that would've melted an igloo in about fifteen seconds, a solar sister who, until now, had probably never encountered anything colder than the rocks in her daiquiris. But, here was the pious goofyballs saying in effect, 'It's bad luck but I can't fuck . . .'

Once Lucas returned I'd see about a carry-out. Paddy'd need one as well. Trouble was I hadn't much bread on me right now. I still had the seven sheets for the Sherman's pram: Phyllis hadn't asked for it and I'd neglected to remind her. Tomorrow, being Saturday, there'd be lots of things to be bought, like loaves, milk, coffee and flank musquash coats. It was Cullen's habit to stash his loot in the inside pocket of his jacket. I went in after it and fished out a bulky roll of folders. From it I took a couple of quid and stuffed it in to Paddy's top pocket – this was for running expenses until he got back to me for the rest. It was an old arrangement between us, a way of safeguarding his dosh from his sister who was in the habit of going on midnight safaris through his pockets. Next, I did something that hadn't been prearranged between us – a real oddball action: quickly, I opened the chain-catch of the small crucifix Paddy always wore around his neck. He gave a wild snort as I pocketed the thing but he soon subsided into his drunken stupor.

Down there on the screen a polar bear, with one swipe of its massive paw, clouted the heart from the missionary's chest.

11

Cullen and I floundered along the snowy pavement that lapped
brightly against the grafitti-scarred hulk of an evacuated
tenement. Sometimes he staggered forward in a kind of jerky trot
and the snow registered his stuttering gait. A skilled observer
following an hour or so later would've been able to figure out
which of the two men was the most bevvied, though the fact that
this turned out to be a weighty man in winklepicker shoes
might've thrown him some. Big damp useless snowflakes kept
seeding cataracts in my eyes and clogging my earholes. The deep
boom of Cullen's voice haunted nailed-up closes. He hit a patch of
ice and almost decked it. I grabbed his arm. 'Steady, Paddy.' He
backed against a snow-wrought railing. 'It could've happened to
anybody, Tam. Anybody. I told Purdon that. Don't worry aboot
it. You thought you were in the cludgie, right, against the
weighing machine, right? I told Purdon that tae.' He clapped my
shoulder and tried for a palsy-walsy wink which didn't quite
come off. 'Tam. Purdon's for having your card. "Fucksake," I says
to'm, "barred just for being Moby Dick ower the jukebox!" Mind
you, you shouldnae've made yon crack aboot Sinatra. Purdon's
hellish fond of Sinatra, so he is.' He lurched from the railing and
with its snowy imprint on his back he staggered forward a couple

of steps. His head must've been birling for he raised his hand to it then groaned: 'For ony favour tell the pilot to land this fuck'n thing.'

We went slipping and sliding down a snow-clogged lane. The tale of the dishonoured jukebox continued. Cullen had obviously scuppered it by barfing into its mechanism though now he was attributing this to me. As if I'd up chuck on Frankie boy when there were croakers like Roy Orbison or Val Doonican to be aimed at. Paddy's voice struck fuzzy echoes from the glazed brickwork of the lane wall. By the gaping doorway of a deserted workshop, an icy puddle fiercely clutched a collection of random junk; pramwheels, a headless doll, a cracked sink, a lavvy pan, and a paint-spattered boilersuit which lay spreadeagled like a slain man.

From the lane we came into a place where new apartments were being erected. In the snowy weavings of the wind as it played amongst the mounds of sheeted materials and whirled smokily between the raw concrete pillars of the rising structure, it looked like the future was shaping to be about as bleak as the slummy past. As we neared his close in Crown Street, Paddy suddenly stuck on his brakes and clutched my arm. 'We've still time for a couple in The Mod.' A skullcap of snow had gathered on his head and I got a foreglimpse of what Cullen might've looked like in senility, though the odds were heavily against him drawing the pension. He was for dragging me across the road to the Moderation Bar.

'We'll chap the door. We're quoted, Tam.'

A bizarre tug-of-war started with me trying to urge him forward while he sought to pressure me to the pavement edge. The mythical snowtracker would have seen on this spot a confusion of footprints then, on the edge of the tango of willpowers, two sets of footprints resuming their forward direction though those made by the winklepicker wearer showed a smudge of reluctance. From Cullen's closemouth, which now echoed to his loud and friendly cries: 'Ya bass, Tam – you should've woke me fuck'n earlier . . .' a lone set of footprints set forth and with only a little meandering, went on without pause to Marco's fish'n chip shop in Cally Road. No matter how skilled the snowtracker had been he would never in a month of Sundays have jaloused that these tracks had been made by the sexual scamperings of a Gorbals mouse which had taken advantage of the cat's absence to come sallying from the skirting board for some nookery-pookery.

12

Becky McQuade wasn't where I'd arranged to meet her. The queue had installed itself as planned (those standing near its tail were appropriately snow-dappled), and Marco himself, with a vigorous play of his hairy arms, was scooping a gold and crackling catch from the smoky pan and with bouncy thumpings of his wire net was lodging it in the serving compartment. Amongst the sauce and pickle jars a white plastic wireless played Acker Bilk's 'Stranger on the Shore'. Outside, the set-designer, by the juxtaposing of the shop's neon sign with snowflakes, had achieved the pleasing effect of confetti cascading down the steamy window.

Exit a scruffy old man with a carry-out bag jammed beneath one arm. His downmouthed expression suggests that he has suffered a recent set-back, a disappointment of some kind. He pauses to finger-comb his snow-caked hair and as he does so the years drop from him so that soon he's become a man in his mid-to-late twenties. He turns up the collar of his army jacket then suddenly an umbrella blooms in the snow's coilings; from beneath this brolly a voice asks him:

'How did you get here so soon?'

She wore a plum-coloured maxi-coat with a twinned row of

black buttons running in military style down its front. On her piled-up hair there was a light headsquare of a translucent lilac stuff in which silvery threads glittered. A massive black handbag was hooked over her shoulder. I ducked under the brolly's awning on which snow fell with a light ticking sound then, taking her by the elbow, I guided her from view of anyone who might be watching us from the chip shop. Since I was taller than she was it was obvious that if we intended to chat on the hoof then I'd have to tote the umbrella, which suited me just fine since it offered both concealment and an immediate sense of intimacy.

Watching my step I, nevertheless, put my foot in it.

'But if you were seeing yon drunk eejit home,' she asked no sooner had I done explaining, 'then who was up in the projection booth?'

Now there was a thing – I'd forgotten who I wasn't!'

I managed to flannel around this gaffe by telling her that Archie Killoch, the Planet's unofficial nights-off man, had agreed to run the last reel so's I could give the drunken Paddy a butty up the road. This seemed to satisfy her.

'I think I saw'm,' she said, nodding. 'A wee man with a squint?'

'Aye, that's him.'

Another lie. If there really was such an entity as the human soul then mines would be packing its astral bags and getting ready to ram the clenched gates of my body. What self-respecting spectre could endure being trapped inside this stewpot of mendacity.

Up the wilderness pavement of the Scabby we came, a couple of ghosts from a Russian novel; me, laden with beer, vodka, and guilt, my companion – the bringer of light to a darkened Planet – plodding along at my side and thinking thoughts I'd never be party to, never hear vocalised. This amazed me, the two of us walking so intimately beneath that whispering umbrella, complete strangers who'd met only a hundred or so words ago, yet, already, here we were heading for an assignation as brazen as any hooker with'r client. Who whispered that'n my sinner ear? Jeremiah, of course, that dwarf on moral stilts. Are we Scots never to be free of such Knoxian nattering? Him and his grousemate, Calvin, a right pair of theological clots who've combined to form an embolus that soon shuts off the heart from its lifebeat. What's needed is a modern day Walt Whitman to muck out this byre of a country, someone with fire in his belly like Willie Blake whose sturdy besom would've sent these pious turds flying.

We went under Scobie Bridge with its dismal sound of dripping water and the depressing sound of pigeons moaning softly in the dark of the rusty girders. Becky's fashion-boots made a brief erotic chatter on the shit-starred pavement then they were hushed again by the snow as we emerged from beneath the bridge. At my closemouth I collapsed the brolly and returned it to her. She shook snow-water from it then, keeping her head slightly lowered, said, 'I'm only stopping for a wee while, remember . . .'

'Aye, sure . . .' I was nodding but she saw that my attention was elsewhere.

'S'there something up?'

I shook my head. No, there was nowt wrong. Something had in fact righted itself; the lamp-standard outside my close was once again tossing down its dim hoop of light. Into this dull but gratifying spotlight there slunk a gaunt Alsatian dog. It glanced in my direction, pausing for a moment as it did so, then passed once more into the outer darkness.

13

I opened my eyes. Morning, peering through the Judas, tipped me the wink: another stay of execution. Comforting, but one shouldn't get too complacent. I reached out to the bedside table for my cancer kit. The traveller's clock, a luminous liar, claimed that it was nine-twenty a.m. Having been denied travel of any kind – its métier, after all – the thing'd taken to messing around with duration, going fast or slow, as the whim took it. Occasionally, it stopped for an entire hour before treacherously restarting. I hadn't helped this ticker's accuracy any by chucking it at Ramensky, a greedy wee bugger of a mouse who could crack any container, no matter how robustly sealed it was, just so long as there was something edible within to make the effort worthwhile.

In the half-light the room looked like a cave into which the heaving ocean had puked. Blearily, my gaze took a tour of the night's flotsam: clothes, mostly my own, hung over Rhona's armchair where I'd flung them; some change had dropped from a pocket to spangle the carpet; on the table there was a muddle of beercans, glasses, and records sleeves. Outside, the wind barged around like a bad-tempered angel and hailstones tut-tutted on the window panes.

Restlessly moving her legs, Mrs Rebecca McQuade, yesterday's stranger, muttered something as she turned her face to the wall. MacDougall, who was up early this morning, suggested that I might tug back the sheets a little so that he could have a peep at her delectable derrière. I squashed out the dog-end then shoved the ashtray'n stuff back onto the bedside table . . . As I relocated my head in the pillow socket Jeremiah came on the air with the prediction that the harlot I'd bedded would bring the house down about my ears – an unimpressive forecast considering that the demolishers were scarcely more'n a block away. Spitefully, he began to hassle me about the penalties for adultery. Conning writs, subpoenas, and citations, from time to time he read aloud shadowy passages which he deemed relevant to my coming downfall. Last night delight, this morning penance – it was the usual Presbyterian penalty, the fine that had to be paid to the uttermost farthing.

Nietzsche, the Leipzig Lip, had been hot on matters of conscience. That one-liner of his, how'd it go again? Aye: 'If one trains one's conscience it will kiss us as it bites . . .' It was hard to figure why the iconoclast supreme could've taken on board yon eternal recurrence crap – the moronic notion which maintains that everything keeps repeating itself without deviation or change. Put simply, the theory asserts that yesterday hasn't vanished forever but, like the merry-go-round horse, has merely passed from sight and is doomed to return exactly as it was before with the same rider, the same music, the same everything. This hellish idea is often cited as an explantion for the universal déjà vu experience the 'I've been here before' intrusion, time giving a little stutter.

There're yesterdays I'd shoot without hesitation should they poke their heads above history's trench, that one, for instance, when my old man – he'd lain on this very spot – had risen, then begun to stuff his clothes into a battered suitcase. Because its locks had been broken he'd cut a daud from Ma's clothes-rope and tied it around the case. He'd hoisted the case onto his shoulder and left us, looking like an old salt on his way to rejoin his ship. Much later I was to learn that he'd voyaged no further than the district of Langside where he'd tied up at the vacant berth of a Mrs Clare Cavendish, a name gobbled whole by Ma Clay's memorable: 'Yon scheming, double-dyed black widow . . .' which, if anything, taught me that spite can jag as good a phrase from a fiddle as anything that can be wrought by the dour elbowing of virtue. Years afterwards, when slyly questioned by me, Ma Clay proved to be ignorant of the spiderish connections to her description. She maintained that by her remark she'd been referring to her rival's terror of grey hairs and of her constant need to do 'bottle' with them. Nor, it seemed, was she aware of the black widow spider's tendency to off its mates after its bobbin had been screwed. Aye, from out of the mouths of babes and sucklings – not forgetting wee aggrieved Gorbals womenfolk – can come some right foe-withering stuff. With a venom no footling spider would've secreted she'd invoked woe and damnation on the heads of Da Clay and the Black Widow, a contract which the gods in their usual sloppy manner had grotesquely overfulfilled.

Adulterer! Jeremiah spitefully repeated in my ear. He'd a new noun to play with: adulter . . . adult – erer . . . adult error . . . Turning my head I looked out again at the cluttered set onto which, shaking the snow from our clothes, we'd made our dual entrance. At first we'd played our parts so woodenly, fumbling our lines, gesturing awkwardly, but as the fire took hold and the booze began to flow there'd entered a fluency, an assuredness (aye, cock-suredness, says MacDougall).

Thomas, Thomas, try to remember who you're supposed to be. You're Matt Lucas, a film projectionist – remember? Okay? This isn't your home. You're a stranger here, too. Reinforce this. Don't march directly to the correct cupboard when looking for glasses. Look around like you're a bit lost. Make mistakes. Demonstrate your lack of familiarity. Now, let's take it from, 'D'you like some lemonade in your vodka?'

'I'd prefer a touch of lime if you have it.'

'Nope. Don't think so. Let's see what he's got. How about this?' From the cabinet's clutter of bottles – most of them empty – I winkled a small tomato juice. 'A Bloody Mary to go wae the bloody weather, eh?'

She eyed the bottle I was flourishing. 'Looks a bit stourie.'

'Everything's stourie in this dump.'

She nodded. 'I'll risk it.'

Kneeling by Clay's record-player, a Pye 'Black Box', her fingers went prowling through the glossy sleeves of my stuff. 'He has hellish taste in music, your pal. What's he called again?'

'Clay,' I said then wished I hadn't.

'What's his first name – Cassius?'

'Tommy!' I decided another pseudonym would've been too much to handle. A wee bit needled, I asked: 'What's wrang wae his records?'

'Can't stand Country'n Western.' Her fingers roved to another compartment. 'This is more my bag,' she said: 'Sinatra, Como, Buddy Holly, Englebert . . .'

'I bet you've never even heard of Woody Guthrie, or, for that matter – Jimmie Rodgers.'

'I've heard of Roy Rogers. Ta.' She took the Bloody Mary from a frowning Matt Lucas. 'I take it you're into his kind of stuff.' She shook her head. 'Bellyaching on horseback, that's what my Dad used to call it.'

114

Who was this dumb chick kneeling there with her hemline around her throat, drinking Clay's booze, and dumping on his discs? Who'd invited her? That randy wee bass, Lucas, that's who. No wonder he's cockeyed. Chrissake, she's for playing the Singing Specs!

'Those are hers,' she said, indicating the Tin Pan Alley trash she'd spread on the carpet. No way was I going to play Royfuckn Orbison!

'Hers?'

'Aye, his wife's – Mrs Clay.'

'Who said he was married?'

She shrugged. 'Must be kinky, then. Or maybe that skirt over there was left by one of your strays? And yon talcum powder's hardly – '

'They busted up,' Lucas said.

'Where's he now, then? This one,' she added, handing me not Roy Orbison but that maker of euphonious farts, Mantovani. As I stuck the thing on the turntable I recalled the Donnybrook its purchase had provoked, a row that'd ended with Clay, the cowboy, threatening to mosey from the bunkhouse for keeps if his spouse so much as put a finger near the disc while in his presence.

'He's down in The Smoke,' Lucas said, closing the lid gently on Clay's beloved 'Black Box'. I glowered at her. 'Whadja mean – "wind up?"'

'It looks old-fashioned enough,' she simpered as she settled with her Bloody Mary in Mrs Clay's armchair. Looking around herself, she added: 'See yon old-fashioned kitchen they've got in the People's Palace – this puts you in mind of it, only the one there's a lot more tidy. Where'd all those beercans come from? You an alky or something? Place needs a good gutting. Talk about a coup.'

One should keep it in mind, Mr Lucas, that these remarks are not being directed at you personally, but to a Mr Thomas Clay whose general domestic sloppiness is well known. The voddy drinker's dismissal, however, of his 'Black Box' is not justifiable, it being a very efficient and superb example of mid-fifties accoustical engineering.

'Nothing like a touch of auld Mantovani,' said Lucas, becoming mesmerised by her frisking limbs. He took his drink, a stiff one, then went round the table and parked himself in Clay's fireside throne. A right classy pair of gams, she had. Sexist stuff, that. Aye, you'd better believe it! Wonder if a half-bottle will do the trick. Have to. Where's she off to now? Won't sit'n her ass for five minutes. Better slap some more Ivan into'r. Don't tell me she's going to make some scabby remarks about Clay's books.

'What's this Clay bloke work at?' she asked as she ran a well-manicured nail along the books on a crowded shelf. The fire, gnawing with green teeth on a chunk of Granny Finnegan's dresser, suddenly spat a flaming splinter onto the hearth rug. I quickly flicked it to safety; one must be careful not to burn one's fingers.

'He's a banana-packer,' I said.

I knew she was going to laugh – and she did. 'A banana-packer!' (Chortle, chortle . . .) Probably, like me, she'd assumed the labels grew on the bloody things. 'His books're even worse than his records,' said Rebecca McQuade, Professor of Literary Studies, dismissing in one brisk sentence some of the finest minds this and the other side of the Pond. At least there was some consolation for as she announced her dire verdict she put away, as a sort of visual exclamation mark, a fair measure of her drink.

'Is that not lovely?' She must mean the voddy, for surely she couldn't be referring to Mantovani. She pounced now on a fat paperback, one I'd quarantined from the rest of my books. It'd come off the 'Harold Robbins' assembly line and been passed on to me by Toff Thompson who read the *Glasgow Herald* as a cover for his slovenly approach to literature and enjoyed the slightly dubious rep of being a pub intellectual. Becky flipped through the rape-infested pages. 'Harold Robbins, he's smashing, eh?'

'He gave ink its great breakthrough,' said Matt Lucas, the sex-mad toad. He took her empty glass from her, muttering as he did so something Hollywoodish like, 'Can I freshen that up?'

'I just loved *The Carpetbaggers*,' she said as she took her now replenished glass for a walk around the kitchen, a wee tour of inspection. Clay wasn't too happy about the way she poked and pried, but Lucas, who saw her as the means whereby bolts of erotic lightning could be made to play over his naked body, smiled indulgently. 'Are there any snapshots of them?' she now asked.

'Eh?'

'The Clays – snapshots?'

'Naw – don't think so.'

Her prowling was definitely making Clay jumpy. All she'd to do was open the second-top drawer of the dresser and there she'd find a photograph of Mr and Mrs Clay on their wedding day, the pair of them fresh from Martha Street Registry Office, standing, looking slightly stunned, by the Cenotaph in George Square. He'd often wondered why Cullen, his best man, had chosen that particular background. Maybe fallen bachelors and fallen soldiers were one and the same in his book. Becky began to mouth a spate of daft questions about the Clays: what they looked like; what she wore; why they'd busted up – stuff like that. Lucas, swallowing lager from a punctured can, responded as best he could to such nosiness, but he saw clearly that he was in danger of being upstaged; if he didn't start to assert himself soon then the vodka gurgling all the way down her throat would be on a wasted trip.

'Tell you one thing,' she said, moving to the sink where she played with the tap, looking amused by its quaintness, 'they're as different as chalk'n cheese.'

'How d'you figure that?'

'Stacks of ways. Not just from his records and daft books. Other things like – '

Something gratifying had happened in the world of vacuous violins. 'It's stuck,' Becky needlessly said. I nodded. If I'd been a stylus playing Mantofanny that's exactly what I would've done. I rose and crossing to the record player wiped the syrup from the turntable and stuck on some gritty Earl Bostic. A mending of glasses now took place. 'You trying to get me squiffy?' she asked with a titter. This was more like the thing. Aye, this was the way to Nookyville!

'Are you close pals then, Matt? You'n the banana-packer?'

'Like blood brothers. For a shandy?'

'Okay. More lemonade than beer but.'

I went over to the drinks cabinet to do the needful. This bugger, Clay, kept intruding, making his presence felt.

'D'you work Becky?'

She reached out for the shandy. 'Mmm, nice,' she said, sampling it. She lowered the glass. 'I'm a trouser machinist. Work for a Jew up in Pollokshaws. Bloody sweatshop. Wages wouldn't buy poverty. The boss wears a black tie on pay day, so he does.'

She came over to resettle herself in Rhona's chair. Despite the brevity of her dress she'd somehow contrived to hitch it up even further. As far as concealment went she would've been better with the bloody thing off. She knew she had me on the boil all right which was why her legs continued to frisk all over the shop.

'I suppose this dump's for coming doon shortly?' She looked around my cracked cave and nodded. 'About time, eh?' She took some more vodka. 'See that Govanhill, going to the dogs as well so it is. Pakis moving into it in droves. Brown faces everywhere you turn.'

The Pakistani, the Indian, and the cook from Canton, are the Eskimos of our society. Cold-shouldered, frozen out, they live their lives in that wilderness our prejudice has exiled them to, the frigid reservations we've afforded them in grudging payment of our colonial debts. Is it any wonder that they make us feel uneasy, those spicy shadows trotting at our heels, and who beg nothing save the alm of mutual recognition, something we're loath to bring ourselves to offer lest it demeans us, such a fate being anathema to a race of cultural pygmies.

Reluctantly, at her request, I forsook the flipside of Bostic's biscuit in favour of Englebert Humperdink's *Pretty Ribbons*, which, if not proof of the white man's hypocrisy is indicative of the depths he'll sink to in order to enjoy a session of vigorous carnality.

And so to bed.

Not until we'd finished the vodka, of course. Then, in that cluttered overheated little room which had been officially deemed unfit for human habitation, we danced boozily together, me not minding her need to bawl the entire maudlin lyric of 'Am I That Easy to Forget' in my earhole. Thereafter there followed a little Simon and Garfumbling on my armchair where, come midnight, the sexual guards quitted her no-go-areas and my hands were free to frolic like frisky salamanders in the brief flame of her dress. By then there was what old Walt Whitman calls 'libidinous prongs' forking up through me, that carnal revving of the senses as the moral brakes ease off.

It was not the classiest of couplings; this has to be admitted. It might've been a bit more elegant than the sealion screwing I'd seen in yon Eskimo movie, but it was gross nevertheless. When it comes down to it, the sex-act's gross to start with, especially so if your ticket to ride takes you no further than the bleak station of Lust. It's a bit nutty, too, screwing: all that panting and peching so's you can get a temporary projection of yourself into a temporary surrender of herself. Of course, that's just post-coital cynicism. At the time, when I was up to my ears in it, entangled in all that slippery, sensuous insanity – the coiling limbs, the entwining tongues, the gush and the give overlaid by a coarse fuckalogue, the sexual commentary of that lewd maniac who lives in the skull's boiling attic, and who at one point was hoarsely assuring the sniggering dark that a set of perfectly average breasts were a 'pair of hot honeys', a claim to which she responded with language that would've made a brickie blush, inciting me to perform acts that some men are doing time for, then you're in no state to philosophise. No, you just want to get the job done, to plough your furrow, sink your shaft, willingly offer yourself to become a cosmic jerk, a dupe of planetary regeneration.

Becky was clean-shaven where it's at – the first beaverless woman I'd done sack time with. 'A door like this doesn't need a rug,' she'd randily whispered in my ear, then, as her seducing fingers closed around an ecstatic MacDougall, she'd giggled: 'But what's a door without a knob?' I don't know if she made that up on the spot. I doubt it, but I'd no chance to share her amusement for, after getting her tongue further down my throat than my own one was, my depilated demon went into overdrive and laid on me such a sexual scorch it's a wonder my scrotum remains unblistered. She seemed to be like five women coming at me from as many angles, so much so that there scarcely seemed a moment when any of my orifices was free from her erotic intrusions. But, since abstinence makes the hips go faster, I was your randy reamer all right. That tuned-up chassis of mine was a busy blur as we went barrelling round sexual hairpin bends, doing the ton in built-up areas, outstripping the world and all its tame velocities. Aye, quite a performance, one to bring a glow to the cindery memories when you're sitting all soft-dicked and useless in Time's waiting-room. 'Did I ever tll you about the night me'n a lassie called Becky McQu – '

'Aye, a thoosand times, faither. Noo, zip up your flies and don't be disgusting!'

But, if I turned in a personal best in that memorable sackrace, Becky herself was no slouch. That woman knew more tricks than an extended Whist Drive. A tireless performer, even after MacDougall was limply declaring himself to be knackered, drained, done-for, why her electric digits, not to mention her electric tongue, would soon tickle a dream into'm, and in no time he'd be standing all aquiver at her rugless door. Renewed and ready for action.

Afterwards, we lay in silence watching the rubescent dramas that were being projected onto the walls by the firelight. Maybe because she'd read too much of Harold Robbins stuff or had seen too many movies she seemed to presume it was incumbent upon clandestine lovers to tell their life-stories. It was a boozy little biog, peopled by the usual stereotypes: a drunken father, an ill-used mother, and a husband who, in her own words 'should be hanging from a hook in a butcher's window'.

I dozed off and dreamed that I was an insect, a strange insect with the time marked on its back (quarter past eight, as a matter of fact). Donald Strang, ex-pawnbroker and latter-day soul saver, came along, and with a cold pair of tweezers lifted me and dropped me into his collector jar which was filled with broken butterflies and crushed beetles.

'Don't say you weren't warned, Thomas,' he said.

14

There we were, Rebecca McQuade and me, quite the domestic duo, sitting at the cluttered table, scoffing bacon sannies while, outside, the hailstones were softening to snow again.

'You didn't tell me this place was haunted,' Becky said.

'Haunted?'

'Ghosts'n that.'

'Garbage.'

'You think so? Did a policeman ever live here?'

'Polis? In the Scabby, you mean? Aye, sure. Peter Manuel used to drop by every Sunday to play'm at chess.' I laughed. 'The Pope'd last longer in the Govan End at Ibrox.' About to scatter some milk powder into my char, I thought the better of it. 'Listen, if a pig screwed up badly on his beat, let's say he raided a Brownie Pack and got a tankin, something like that, they'd say to'm, 'Right Constable, what's it to be – your P45 or the Scabby? You'd better believe he'd be grabbing for his cards, pronto.'

'Well, there was one here last night, that's all I'm saying. Aye, laugh if you like. I woke up and there he was.'

'Polishing his truncheon?'

'Plain as day.'

'At night?'

'You know what I mean.'

'Say what he wanted, did he?'

'You, by the look of it.'

'Me?'

'Definitely.'

With the ball of her thumb she wiped bacon grease from the corner of her mouth. 'He sat there by the bed. Ages it seemed like. Then he was gone.'

'In a puff of Mace smoke?'

'Eh?'

Jeremiah, often dons the chequered cap and lurks at dream crossroads awaiting old irresponsible me to come bucketing down a hairy gradient on a bike with shot brakes and buckled wheels. Could it be that he'd – Naw, that was crap. Shag Jeremiah. For the time being I intended to savour my status as a house guest, a sexual tourist like Becky here.

'D'you do it a lot, then?'

'What?'

'Dream aboot the fuzz.'

She lowered her cup, placing it delicately in its saucer. 'So, I was dreaming was I?'

Except for a pair of shiny blue briefs she was naked under Rhona's old housecoat with its torn pocket and its grubby braid. My judgement no longer foxed by booze, I saw that she was certainly no Kim Novak, but neither was she a look-alike for Marlene Dietrich, hunched over a fag at dawn. Her hair, that sculpted creation in which not a single strand had been out of place looked now like a burgled haystack. She flourished a hand. 'This looks more like one – a dream, I mean.' She took up the cup once more. 'I keep expecting to wake up beside old Sweaty Drawers.'

'He's in Dagenham, remember?'

She nodded. 'He'd better be, for both our sakes.'

'Sorry there's no cow juice,' I apologised. 'Daisy's never been the same since she got her horn crumpled.'

She shrugged. 'It's okay. Proves it, I suppose, that it isn't a dream – powdered milk – '

' – and the fags running oot.'

'There's some in my handbag, but they're tipped.'

As I stretched towards her bag she made a sudden, snatchy grab for it herself. Secrets, eh? Funny folk, women. This particular specimen had invited me, no, had encouraged me to explore her most intimate nooks and crannies, had given me the lowdown on her sexual topography on a scale that probably her gear jockey of a husband had never been granted. Yet, here she was, coming the coy nun-caught-naked routine. We lighted up and appraised each other through the smoky curlicues. On the mantelpiece the tranny, its delivery at demi-volume, was playing Bobby Gentry's 'Ode to Billy Joe'.

'It must be hellish quiet here,' she said. 'Spooky even.'

'We back to ghosts again?'

What she was experiencing was an absence of sounds in general, not my own peculiar distinction of noises no longer heard: the screeching of pulley-wheels as rainyday washings rose to beflag the ceiling; the thump of doors closing; footsteps going or arriving on the stairs; prams thumping closewards burdened with weans or steamie bundles; the sound of human voices; kids crying; kids laughing; coughs; whistles; and from a long way off a rag'n' boneman's bugle sounding the last post for the old way of things. No more the tiny uproars that thrum through the living tenement, the absence of which made me feel like a spider dwelling at the heart of a busted guitar in which dying sounds faintly resonated.

'Where'd she go, Mrs Clay, I mean?'

She'd returned to her favourite subject. Like playful seal pups her breasts kept peeping forth; the urge to stroke their sleekness was becoming mandatory.

'Dundee,' I said, taking my cue from a tartan ditty the Alexander Bros had begun to kick around the tranny like a set of duff bagpipes.

'Seems funny, just up and offing like that, leaving her stuff.'

'They'll be back soon,' I told'r. 'They're going to have another duffy at it.'

'A what?'

'Duffy. Y'know – another try.'

'Come back to this hole!' She shook her head, looked dubious. 'She must need her head seeing to. How come they weren't rehoused? Everybody else's flown the coop.'

'No everybody. Apart from them, the Clays, there're a couple of kneecreakers.'

'Knee – what?'

'Kneecreakers – pensioners.'

'The Clays've had offers, then?'

I nodded.

'But they turned them down?'

'Have you seen what was on offer?'

She shook her head. 'The Black Hole of Calcutta would've been preferable to this dump.'

'You been up the 'Milk recently?'

'Must still be some good bits. It's not that long ago since they were balloting for a house up there.'

'Aye, afore they fun oot the Planners'd built the moat *inside* the castle. Damper than Neptune's willie, I'm tellin ye. Weans are being born there wae webbed feet.'

'If they keep turning down offers they'll get turfed out.'

I flicked some ash from my fag. A subtle alteration in the chat's bias was called for. 'See yon Moss Heights – they're twice as bad for dampness.' I stubbed out my fag-end. 'It's time they got round to building Mudscrapers, y'know, doonwards.'

'I don't see the advantage of that.'

'D'you no? Think aboot it. For starters, no windaes to wash; no sunshine tae bleach your furniture; no wind, no rain, and no sparras to drill your eardrums at five in the morning; no traffic noises, and – '

'Down there with the rats and the mice, and all those creepy-crawlies?' She shuddered. 'No thanks.'

'Mice'n cockroaches up here. What's the difference? And I've just thought, we'd be out of the road of the noisy supersonics. Aye: nae sonic booms in the tenement-tombs!'

'Horrible.'

'No way. We could have mega subschemes like . . . let's see, aye, Beetlemilk, Grubchapel, Fossilpark, Wormhill.' My levity had done the trick and it was easy now to steer the confab to safer subjects like the weather, the price of coal, the Beatles. Coincidentally, as we were discussing the Fab Four, 'Hey, Jude' came on the tranny.

'I'll need to be making tracks soon,' I told her.

'Tracks is right,' she said with a nod to the window where snowflakes had begun to birl with a renewed vigour. 'Cosy here. What's the point of going out in that stuff?'

'I've got to see somebody about a job.'

'You have one.'

'The Fleapit shuts soon, remember.' Deftly I slipped into the persona of Matt Lucas, chief projectionist of the Planet Cinema, but it no longer fitted snugly, being a bit puckered and rough to the touch.

She shook her blonde head. 'That dump'll fall down before its knocked down. Just a hangout for hobos, somewhere for them to sit'n sup their rubbish. And the stink! They must wet themselves where they're sitting.' She pushed her cup'n saucer away from her and stood up. The housecoat swung open to reveal her sexy blue panties and, of course, her peerless paps. 'Bonus or no bonus, you'll not catch me going back there . . .'

Which was very good news for Thomas Clay, esq.

An embarrassing moment now ensued which the host handled with superb aplomb. The lady visitor desired 'to go a place', and, to judge from her pained expression, the sooner the better. Skirting explanations that while the stairhead facility remained, surprisingly, functionable, it was unwise to use it unless caught in the terminal throes of Montezuma's Revenge, he drew her attention to the presence, close at hand, of a wally receptacle which he was led to believe Mrs Clay resorted to when the weather was inclement or the hour too late to make a visit to the outside lavatory a prudent venture. He, Matthew Lucas would make the chilly descent thither, thereby affording his guest a discreet period of privacy.

'No bloody wonder that Clay woman high-tailed it,' said a scunnered-looking Becky McQuade as she trailed across to search under the bed for the Edgar Allan. I unhooked the 'air-raid' flashlamp from its nail ben the lobby then followed its paltry glow down the stairs to the haunted cludgie. When you think about it, Hollywood has tended to tip-toe around the fact that from time to time we humans have to discharge waste matter. It seemed it was all right to show in some detail the lady making love, but to see'r making water – no way! I hope they keep it like that; the thought of Kim Novak being watched by millions as she – No, I won't even inkify the thought.

Cautiously I prodded open the cludgie door. It swung wide with a raw squeal. What did I expect to find in here? A phantom cop twirling his truncheon? Mrs Muirhead knitting her shroud?

The gauzy image of an adolescent having it off with flying hand over some half-naked starlet in *Picturegoer?* Although I'd stuck on a tee-shirt and a sweater, goosepimples stood out over my entire body like braille. The wan spotlight flitted from pan to bleach bottle, then to the bumpaper holder. Something struck against my foot and I bent to pick it up. It was an empty ciggy carton. Well, well, Passing Clouds – the very brand you'd expect a spook to puff. I dig mysteries, a touch of the uncanny: a caller leaves his card in the shape of a London newspaper crossword clue; before this discovery snowballs are pitched at me by an unknown person, or persons, a stranger dressed in a leather jerkin and striped cap has been making enquiries about me. Should I include the erratic behaviour of the street lamp? I think not. The empty fag carton must be included though. MacDougall directed a fierce jet of piss into the pan. When he was done an innocuous thought trundled across my mind then suddenly exploded. Paddy's loot! Christalmighty, I'd left it stashed in my jacket pocket. I fled the closet and sprinted up the stairs.

Becky was monkeying around with the bottles in the drinks cabinet. 'Saved!' she exclaimed as she held up a Martini bottle which contained about an inch of the highly-overrated stuff. If that was enough to 'save'r' then she certainly had a problem. 'Think I'm going diabetic,' she announced as she added some lemonade to her glass. The housecoat kept floating open but for the moment eroticism had to play second fiddle. My hand dived into my jacket pocket. Panic over – the roll of notes was still there.

In no hurry to be off, Becky was quite content to slouch around, Martini in one hand, fag in the other. On the tranny Dylan was making it with 'Subterranean Homesick Blues'.

'If I get this job, I'm off to London,' I told her.

'Lucky old you.'

A wee bit sulky looking, she crossed to plant her cheeks on the bed then she bent to the floor to lift her suspender belt. I poured what water remained in the kettle into the basin and gave my face'n body a quick slunge. Drying myself with an exaggerated vigour, I turned to face'r. She was just sitting there, stretching the suspender belt between the forefingers of either hand. I wondered what I'd be like getting up in an igloo on a Saturday morning. The wife away for the *Record* and the rolls, myself, lighting the first husky-shit fag of the day while listening to the wind's hard drumming on my ice-bubble, sadly aware that the legs, I mean, the walrussing would probably be called off due to adverse weather.

Becky was watching me. She'd posed herself like one of those judies who'd sprawled across the front covers of the Hank Jansen paperbacks we used to knock from Clatty Kate's shop in Rutherglen Road. 'Matt,' she murmured, and her voice was indeed as they used to say in those penny pornos 'silked with invite', 'surely you don't have to go right away?' The housecoat slipped from her bare shoulders. 'I mean, what's an hour or so on a rotten morning like this?'

Lucas flung aside the towel and moved towards her.

'I suppose,' he said as his hand reached for his belt-buckle, 'an hour widnae be here nor there . . .'

15

Joe Fiducci's shop was all but empty.

I sat slumped in the chair by the window while Joe, himself, fussed around me. His lather brush chuckled in the mug then its bristles fizzed warmly on my stubbly chin. In the battered wireless a guitar plonked hopelessly.

'Irish racing today,' Joe said.

The old man waited for a response. Joe never risked so much as a tanner on a horse, but he was your trad barber – nothing like the cuddies for a racy conversation. Weather substitute: going to be another fine horse by the look of it. Might get a little filly later but.

'You having a bet?'

'Haven't studied form, Joe.'

The familiar creaking sounds of Joe's sandals as he moved around the chair. The ticklish flurry of the lather brush on my flesh. It's indecent to talk about things that really matter. Time, for instance, why can't we discuss the concept of duration or hazard some notions on the nature of eternity? You just can't somehow. Upsetting. Imagine me remarking off-the-cuff to Joe, 'Say, man how d'you dig this acid of being we're all frazzling in . . .' No way was it possible. Too embarrassing. Joe's wife is rumoured to be dying from a cancer which is located in a most unusual site for that disease. Me, I'm just dying to ask'm about it, but won't. Depressing. Funny stuff is Time. It gets into your hair eventually, can't be scraped off the face. When you thought about it, Sweeney Todd with a cut-throat razor welcoming you into your last chair would better personify urban death than yon undernourished gink with the scythe. The grim reaper. Aye, grim wasn't the word for it. Business was bad. I squinted along the empty chairs to my right. Old Pat Mooney, the usual watery drip at his nose, was sweeping up the morning's clippings. You're never alone with a strand right enough.

'Things're quiet this morning, Joe.'

He delathered the cut-throat on the soggy pad of newsprint he'd perched on my towel-wrapped shoulder. Bladed light lit up his morose features. An Italian shoulder-shrug as he said, resignedly: 'People go – they take their hair with them.' Snow on his roof, ash in his smile. 'Not be too long till I'm saying arrividerci Gorbals myself.'

'When're you quitting?'

'Soon now.' He sighed as the blade made creamy upstrokes. 'They make the clean sweep, eh?'

Aye, a clean sweep all right – like Mooney there, brushing himself onto a shovel:

SITUATION WANTED

Owing to circumstances beyond his control, senile snipper requires sit. Trembly-handed, a tippler, over-fond of punting, but wonderful with children.

HAVE SCISSORS – WILL TRAVEL.

Joe was moving into his son's fancy uptown shop. Hard to imagine him in a hair boutique. He'd be there to collect the money and exchange weather opinions, to blow the dust from lotion bottles and try to avoid the meshed glances of that useless twin in the mirror.

Before we parted – in the close as it so happened – Becky'd gone up on the toes of her fashion boots and laid a little cheeper on my lips. 'Good luck with the job,' she said. 'Be seeing you.' And she exited, stepping behind a curtain of snow. Gone. Such emotional neatness, so admirably adult.

'Why don't you retire, Joe?'

'Who? You talking to me?' An uneasy laugh unravelled some more of the frayed stitching of his mouth. 'Whadda I do, retiring?'

'That's the point – do nothing. Just lean on the fence for a change.'

Soap flew up to spatter the mirror. 'Not work and sometimes not eat, eh? Maybe not have a house too soon. I just wear out at the elbows leaning on this fence of yours.'

'Sure, see Naples before you . . .'

'Food on the table, that's all I want to see.' He smacked his fist on the radio, clarifying a Morse-signal. 'Lean on the fence. That's a good one . . . Lean on the fence.'

Mooney was still skulking around looking for hairs (maybe he got paid by the hundredweight). A bald barber made a poor advert for his profession. I looked into the mirror as Joe towelled away the soap traces. A fine healthy glow. This was one of the last remaining shops in the Gorbals where it was possible to get an old-fashioned shave. The cut-throat razor had the edge on those electric jaw-mowers; the one gifted to me by Rhona was at present gathering dust in the Three-Balled-Blessing. My suit has storage place in there, too. Sometimes when I pass the premises I could swear I hear it plaintively singing: 'I know that my redeemer liveth . . .' Only just, believe me. Bending forward I plucked a comb from a brush on the shelf and tugged it through my hair. The old locks were getting to be on the longish side. Rhona scolded me about it on every visit. Her mother had gone so far as to say it was a 'dampt disgrace'. What kind of father was I going to make, running around like a hippie eejit?

'But your Jesus had long hair, had he no?'

'We'll have none of your wicked blasphemy!'

I stuck the comb back in the brush. The mirror I was looking into was fast running out of faces. Mooney sat on the end of the wall bench near the gasfire. He was hunched over the sports section of his newspaper, studying form. Cigarette smoke dribbled up his finished face. Hands slack with defeat, scissor-grooved thumb a-tremble. He was digging out his three-cross-doubles and a treble, warmed by the prosect of it coming up, an unlikely outcome. I went over and sat on the bench. As I lighted a smoke, Joe crossed to the corner where his stropping belt hung. Soon the razor was cloff-cloffing on the worn strap. In the radio, a finely drawn-out thread of sax music abruptly snapped.

'When you take a house?' Joe asked me. 'Soon they throw you out, eh.' He held the stropping belt between thumb and forefinger: a man at the end of his leather. A lop-sided glass shelf on the wall next to the card of Durex Loveskins moved, perhaps a millimetre per day, towards the moment when it would cascade its stourie lotion bottles onto the floor. The gasfire flames wavered and sputtered as the door was nudged open and allowed a gust of wind to swirl into the shop. The head of Caesar, a thin, snow-stippled Alsatian dog appeared. Its melancholy gaze raked the empty chairs then withdrew. A sad business. Once the faithful companion of Tammy Cook, a Scobie Street punter, it had, ever since Tammy's passing, been mourning around, checking out its master's old haunts. Joe said that something should be done about the dog. Mooney was of the opinion that it should be put down. Funny how callous some folk can be; an animal gets into a wee health scrape like, say a broken tooth or a loose claw and right away the howl goes up: 'Give it the bullet!' 'Away wae it!' I asked Mooney how he'd feel about being put down because he'd a pluke at the end of his neb. Without apparent affront he replied: 'Aye, suit me fine that would. They can stick a gun against my heid anytime they like – jist as long as it's no sore.'

Joe folded the cut-throat's gleam into its handle then he came across and stood with his back to the chair directly in front of me. He studied me for quite a time before he asked, 'How long I know you, eh?' Holding his hand palm downwards, close to his bulging midriff, he answered his own question. 'From this high, that's how long.' He stepped to one side and indicated the chair he'd been leaning on. It was an unassuming piece of furniture, solidly built, but completely lacking in stylistic folderols. For donkey's years the chair had served as the weans' seat. 'Do you remember,' Joe asked, 'when you sit on a flap of wood here, eh?'

I nodded. 'You'd a spite against my heid, Joe: it never seemed to hing the right road for you. Know what us kids used to call you: "Tugger the Bugger".'

He grinned but his hand remained on the chair, fingers stroking its polished back. 'Still,' I conceded, 'you were never as rough as that boy of yours, Luigi – the way he scalped a queue you would've thought he'd lost somebody close to'm at the Battle of Wounded Knee.'

He laughed outright, a short burst of amusement, then reverted to a serious mien. His hand clapped the chair back, 'D'you know who made this for me?'

'Jesus of Nazareth?'

He ignored my quip. 'I'll tell you who, your Grandpapa.'

I think he expected me to rise and go across to touch the relic, maybe even to make some comment like: Granda Gibson – well, I'll be damned!' Instead I blew a thin jet of smoke into the air. I was surprised, amazed even, but I just sat where I was and said nothing.

'Before you were born, he made it,' Joe went on, as if this info added to its wonder. He knuckled the top of the chair. 'Craftsmanship – built to last!'

'That's oot the windae these days, Joe,' I told'm. 'Make haste to lay waste's the modern code.'

Joe fondly regarded the old chair. 'This was built to last. Your Grandpapa was that kind of man. Patience in his hands.' He nodded and gave vent to a deep sigh. 'You're right, you don't see much of that nowadays. Nobody take time anymore. Nobody care.'

I realised that the old man was obliquely censuring me. The chair stood on the tesselated floor like a ponderous chess-piece. Here, Joe was in effect saying, is patience, the prime attribute of John Gibson, cabinetmaker, my grandfather. Against it, all I could field were a few transient pawns, a cluster of short-ranged ambitions.

I finished the fag then getting to my feet tumbled a couple of florins into Joe's overall pocket. 'I'm sure gonna miss you when you're gone, Joe,' I told'm, and I meant it.

16

Crunching across the street, heading for Shug Wylie's Bum Boutique, I saw the man, himself, struggling at the lavatory's entrance with two vaguely human things. These entities were mostly rags and seething grey hair, and the one I presumed to be male suddenly sprouted a humanoid hand which curled its yellow fingers about the snowy railings and was not for letting go, while its companion, with equal tenacity, clung to its coat. They were whining, no, more like keening, these tattered things as the mannish heap fought against their being pried loose, torn from their place of refuge to be cast onto the street's bright torrent.

'Let go ya bugger!' Shug kept shouting as he clubbed with the side of his fist at the thing's talons. 'Let go, I said!' Shug, the officially-appointed Keeper of the Keechs, was wearing the approved uniform for such a position: brown dungarees, cap, black wellies, and an expression of outraged authority on his face which was appropriate to a man who took his job and his bog seriously.

Shug went on pounding at the male thing's talons. 'Let go!' And being such a scrap of a thing it had eventually to submit, to release its grip. Both it and its tattered attachment drifted away, mewing like outraged seagulls they were, but soon their cries grew fainter until the ragged pair disappeared around a corner at the far end of Scobie Street.

Later, as we sat in the cramped quarters of his neuk, both of us with a mugful of Shug's unique char – so strong it was almost unspillable – the attendant, still panting a little from his exertions, reminded me of the dire consequences those 'auld germbags' could've wreaked upon the humble convenience. 'I'm tellin ye, Tam, if meths drinkers so much as think aboot pissing – the game's a bogy. No a stink in the world like it. Lasts forever, so it does. You see,' he went on, 'they dossers are no allowed to kip in the brick kilns anymore – no since they found one of them deid – hard as a tile they say he was.' He nodded. 'That's how the place's hoaching wae them – like bloody cockroaches looking for a bit heat.'

'You never can tell,' I warned him, 'it might be you've just changed world history.'

'What're ye on aboot?'

'Well,' I said, 'what if that was Joseph'n Mary looking for a place tae kip? It could be you've snookered the Second Coming!'

'The Second Humming's more like it.' Shug laughed and bent to flick off a bar of the electric fire.

'Good brew this, Shug,' I said. 'Put a shine on your shit, this stuff.' I chewed on a mouthful. 'Ran out of milk this morning. Bread was hard as well. Wife's only been in dock five weeks and already things are coming apart.'

Said Shug: 'If they keep shutting doon the models what can they expect. Soup queues and hymns urnae the answer.'

'It's that auld effer, Wattie, up the stairs. Taps me stupid: a wee bitta this, a wee bitta that.'

'Bloody miserable, right enough.'

Aye, 'miserable'. Trees don't know they're miserable; only man knows that. So had said Monsieur Pascal, that wee Frog croaking so ardently down a well of doubt. I remember, back on the railway, my driver, Wee Tully, plucking a Penguin paperback from my overalls pocket and greasy-fingering through its pages. 'What shit's this you're reading noo, Tam. "Pen-sees" What the fuck're pen-sees when they're at hame?' I corrected'm. 'Oh, Pong-sees, is that what they're called? Beg your pudding.' Later when we got the go-ahead and were hammering up the loop line past the chemical works Tully'd waved me across at his side of the cab. He'd pointed to a man who was shovelling bone-white powder into a wheelbarrow. 'There, yar, Tam,' he yelled over the steel-clashing bedlam of the engine. 'That's how your gonni wind up. Pongsees or no fuckin pongsees!'

Maybe he'd been right at that: too many books, too few answers. Donald Strang the pious pawnbroker had been bang on the mark yesterday. His remark about my need to avoid hill-climbing could've been a dig, a sly allusion to the towering edifice of my ego, a reminder that – pride does indeed come before a fall. Shug, catching up with my gab, said with a grin: 'Aye, it's great what having to wash their own shirts can dae for some folk.'

I shrugged. 'Maybe there's something to be said for gettin things in a shambles.'

'S'that so?'

'Think aboot it.' As Shug wheezily bent to kill another fire-bar, I asked'm, 'What's the key to a well-run home? Routine, right? And routine breeds habit. Okay? Habit, what does it breed? I'll tell you – sleep, that's what. The more you do something, the less you do it. Sounds screwy but it's a fact.'

'So, there's some sort of salvation in a pile of dirty dishes?'

'There's friction, and that's important – things no goin smoothly.'

'Right, if you go oot there into your favourite box and trip ower a big stale shite, you'll be back to shake my hand, eh?'

I laughed. 'I'd stick it in your teapot.' I fired a fag; it crackled and blue smoke rose twistily into the air. 'Y'see, Shug, the mair friction, the less chance there is of you goin skimming doon the ego-chute like some bloody imbecile. You get stuck up there. And that's when you start asking yourself questions.'

'Are you stuck, then?'

'You kiddin? Right now I'm coming doon so fast you'd think my arse was French-chalked.'

Shug took a slow sip of char. He shook his head. 'You're a right funny bugger, Tam. You'n your daft ideas. Here's me wondering where my next breath's comin fae, and there's you trying to make things hard for yourself.'

I held up the fag. 'S'this botherin you?'

'Naw, naw, it's you that bothers me. You'n your batty notions. You'll be tellin me next your wife'll be the better of a hard delivery.'

'I never said anything aboot pain being constructive, Shug. All I'm saying is that we should welcome the odd poke in the eye from life, anything that'll jab us from oor comas.'

'Try selling that yin tae Talky Sloan, this morning.'

'What's wae him, then?'

Shug, surprised looking, put down his mug; 'You've no heard?'

'Don't tell me he's lost his voice?'

'He's lost mair'n that, Tam. He copped an arseful of bus in Croon Street last night.'

'You tellin me he's deid?'

Shug nodded. 'They'll be picking bits of'm oot the radiator yet.'

Yon inane remark so often prompted by news of sudden death flew from my mouth.

'Aye,' said Shug, 'saw'm myself in the Dog. Chirpy as a sparra he was.' Shug flicked off the remaining fire-bar and we watched it die through the family of reds. A picture skimmed across my mind, that of a wee skeleton lying on the beery counter, myself saying, 'Awfy unlucky, a thing like that . . .' The quirky notion came to me that if I hadn't knocked the wee effigy from Eddie's car then dumped it in the stout, Talky might've been alive right now. Not impossible. The incident could've given'm the wind up and made'm steam into the bevvy. As a result he could've left the Dog later than usual. Who's to know, he might've been brooding over the demon in his drink as he began his last walk across Crown Street.

'Salter'll take it bad, eh?'

I nodded. Poor auld Salter. It'd be like having his head jammed in a wet coalbag. Many a time I'd watched Talky doing yon thumbo-jumbo stuff on the blind and deaf-mute's hand: discussing the runners, tapping out the favourites. Talky, the lantern of his life. Another way they had of communication was via the Jaw-hold method, when Talky would offer up his mandible to Salter's clamping mitt while he spoke, reading the vibes, so to speak. Bar the old man's sister, Talky was the only punter on hand who could release him from that dark closet of the senses that imprisoned him. Not that this ability gave Talky any pub-prestige. 'Look at'm,' Danny Dimes said to me one day, nodding towards a corner where Talky was doing his palm-patter with Salter. 'Even the deef urnae oot-o-range of that bletherin wee bastard!'

A story there for any writer worth his salt. It was too bad that the blind in literature were doubly disadvantaged; readers tend to assume they're symbolic: 'I presume your blind chappy represents the spiritual myopia of contemporary society?' 'Well, naw, as a matter of fact he jist couldnae see!'

'Mind you,' said Shug, 'He could talk the hind legs off a donkey, go rattling on like a stane in a boiling kettle. D'you mind

140

yon time he – ' Shug's jaw sagged. 'Jeezus wept!' he cried. He got rapidly to his feet then slumped back down again. Staring into the neuk through its sparkling pane was Death himself. He wore a long brown duffel coat, the hood of which was drawn tightly about his skeletal face with its graveyard grin. He opened the door and shouted: 'C'mon oot – your time's up!' Death had on patched wellies and a pair of industrial gloves which bore bright spatters of buttercup paint. He shook the hood loose from his head, dropping it back onto his shoulders, then shoved the Halloween skeleton mask up from his face, lodging it on the crown of his bald and scurvy skull. The real face was no improvement on the mask. In fact, it looked as if the Midday Scot had been using it for buffer practice. Apart from the severe structural damage it was also studded with inflamed boils and pustules as well as greyish hair-tufts.

Shug, recovered now from his original shock, was back on his feet. 'C'mon, you,' he snapped as he confronted Death, bravely squaring up to'm although he scarcely reached to the bony one's shoulder. 'Bugger off! You're no getting in here.'

Death grinned at me. His teeth reminded you of a vandalised graveyard, mossy molars pitching every which way but loose. 'Shat yersel there, big man, eh?' He tapped his lips with two leprous looking fingers. 'Any smokes?' I dug out my pack. Death snatched away a fag, a couple, in fact. As he bent forward to take a light from me a stench so rotten it would've given maggots the boke polluted my nostrils – the lighter flame turned green. Shug, getting more pugnacious by the minute, began to shove at the tall, skinny intruder. 'Out of it. C'mon – on your way.' I hoped things weren't going to get physical. I mean, being spotted slinging Death from a shithoose! Man, that'd be tough to live down, especially when the Salty Dog wags got to hear of it. 'Look, Boss,' he pleaded, 'I'm no askin tae sit doon or anything. Just a wee

141

wash, that's all I'm after. Surely you'll no grudge a man a wee wash?'

'The flame-thrower's out of order,' said Shug with a nifty turn of wit. 'Out you go!'

And would you believe it, Death turned out to be a right crapper. He gave a cheery wave. 'Ta for the smokes, bree,' he shouted. 'I'll be back for ye in ninety years, if I'm no too busy.'

Shug, ever more emboldened, gave Death a hefty shove from the doorway. 'Bugger off, I said.' And without so much as a departing retort, some face-saving insult, the duffel-coated rickle of banes slunk off. Having sorted Death out, Shug returned to the neuk. 'Aye, you can laugh, Tam,' he said eyeing me reproachfully while he laboured for breath, 'but I'm just sick'n tired of it, so I am. Bloody hobos and half-wits crawlin doon here. And the stink of them – turn your stomach.' He sat down, looking even more irritated by my continuing cackles. 'C'mon, lay that egg and be done wae'it.' But I just couldn't get the clamps on my hilarity which had passed over into near-hysteria, when from a not very great height Death pissed on us. Down the stairs it came, a livid arc of urine that thrashed on the stone floor outside the neuk, japping the window-pane as it did so.

'Ya durty swine!'

Shug was up and running. The neuk door crashed back on its hinges as he flung it wide and charged up the stairs in pursuit. What a gas – Death being chased by a lavvy cleaner! A sight to behold, the sudden emergence of this grotesque pair, looking, no doubt like they'd bounded straight from the caverns of Hell. It was to be hoped that there weren't any kneecreakers with wonky tickers on the go up there. It was real acid-head stuff – the Scabby on a trip.

Shug returned, red-faced and panting, to his keechdom a couple of minutes later. Death had given'm the slip. 'Legged it up one of they closes,' he gasped. 'Lost the bugger . . .' I poured some char and let'm bellyache for a bit although I found it hard to keep a straight face and a laugh bobbed dangerously at the base of my throat.

While Shug, still grumbling to himself, mopped up outside the neuk door I had a wee shufty at my mail. To save the postie's legs I'd an arrangement with'm for my mail to be dropped off in Shug's Bum Boutique. This accommodation, of course, allowed me to boast the unique Glasgow postal district – WC1. There were only two items of mail for me this morning; a chrissy card and a business envelope with a LONDON postmark! The auld chest-walloper kicked off its klaxon and my nerves began to riot. Was this then THE MOMENT, the clap of thunder before luck's lightning cleft my former self from top to toenails, heralding the new man?

No, it's bad luck to anticipate events. Play it cool. Don't let on you're affected by it. Put the letter to one side, that's the way. Yes, open this nice big xmas card your thoughtful and thoroughly delightful sister-in-law has thought fit to send. The card was from the Shermans right enough. You could tell by the faint tang of venom coming from it. Aye, Her Ladyship's fair hand had penned this. Look at those twanging loops, the slightly crushed consonants, signs, I believe, of suppressed eroticism. MacDougall, slumbering peaceably on my thigh twitched. He seemed to think I was referring to Phyllis Sherman's actual hand for sleepily, he says, 'Let's have it gloved in black translucent silk so that when it gently falls upon my inner thigh . . .'

Fucksake . . . what gives? 'Don't come the innocent with me,' MacDougall warns. 'I've got your number all right. This morning you had Becky McQuade on the bed, then, just for the heck of it, had second helpings on the table amongst the breakfast debris, your randy head rapping on a sauce bottle, your bum wag-

wagging between her spread thighs as you took your timing from the Zombies' ancient biscuit: 'She's Not There', which, of course, she wasn't. How could she be there when you weren't even present yourself? Yeah, you were real gone, man, reported missing, a randy AWOL on a mind-fuck with Mrs Phyllis Sherman. Yeah, giving it to her strong on one of the back pews of the Bleaker Memorial, while she yelled: 'Gun me Patton! Gun me . . . !'

What utter garbage! MacDougall needs seeing to, he really does. The christmas card itself has this coach laden with lardbuckets waving with festive bonhomie to an assortment of bedraggled peasantry, most of whom were up to their bucolic butts in roadside mud but still able to return the waves and smile their delight at God's little manger pressy. Lots of robins too, the whole design neatly rounded off by the Sherman's monickers appearing in copperplate writing, so much more with it than the bookie-pen scrawl I served on such fripperies.

Is that everything, then? Why no, here's another letter I've just noticed. From the Smoke too. Shall I open it now? Oh, very well. Casually rending the envelope and frenziedly pluckin forth its contents, I smoothed out the single page letter with sweaty fingers. Ah, yes, just as I expected: it was a wistful reminder from a record club (a warp on your waxings!) with an enquiry regarding some Dylan discs I'd ordered while the balance of my mind had been disturbed. Their non-return seemed to indicate that I'd decided to keep the aforementioned discs. Would I, therefore, honour my part of the agreement by forwarding the now grossly-overdue remittance? Thanking you in anticipation and taking this opportunity to wish you the compliments of the season.

'It ain't me you're looking for babe! It ain't me you're looking for.'

144

Anyone glancing into Shug's neuk would've seen a stricken looking man (how manfully stiffened was his upper lip!) casually scribbling upon an envelope. 'Building gone away: addressee demolished. Return to sender.' Placing the aborted correspondence into an inner pocket for future mailing and still bravely masking his chagrin, he gives Shug's electric fire a hard kick with the toe of his shoe, then taking up a newspaper limps painfully out to his favourite stall, number four.

Ensconced on one of Shug's wally thrones I raked through the *Daily Express*. Of a nauseous world the inky vomit. Nothing in it about the death of a dosser in a city maternity hospital. They were still giving it big splashes for the spacemen. Lots of speculation about the DSM (Dark Side of the Moon). The consensus of scientific opinion is that it'll be very dark, very quiet, and very far.

I don't dig this space travel guff, the New Frontier hyperbole. It's a pity we hadn't developed a Time Machine technology. Even a very primitive one capable only of a couple of frog leaps into the past, a century or so would do. An interview could be set up with an old Sioux chieftain. He could be questioned about his attitude towards the expansion of the New Frontier. Did he not agree that the Conestoga Wagon was a worthy symbol of the civilising process? How exciting it must be for him, a semi-moronic savage who looked, by the way, with all those stupid feathers like a turkey with high blood-pressure. Yes, onward. Ever onward rolled the wagon trains, from sea to shining sea they came, dropping buffalo and Redskins, not to mention names like Little Big Horn and Wounded Knee. Out of the Conestogas fell the seedcrop of tomorrow's greatness, frontier towns, schools, churches, jails, forts, hooch, brothels, syphilis, dysentery . . .

I suspect that old Sioux chieftain, fetched out of time on the hook of devilish white technology wouldn't say a word. For answer he'd merely point to the hectares of dust and scrubland the Washington Chiefs had given them with a grandiose flurry of speeches and lies set down by a buzzard's feather tricked out in gold. The Red Man had long come to distrust the white noises that came from these fork-tongued fraudsters, especially the long words like Democracy, Freedom, Dignity. The one most to be feared in that hissing pot of lies was a peaceable-looking viper called Civilisation. From out of Eden they say it came, just as from the east rolled the unstoppable Conestogas.

(Strike up Stars and Stripes here please.) Yes, you riders of Apollo, you well know what immense odds are stacked against you for the camp-fires of your foulest foe, Ignorance, blaze on the star prairies of that still to be won Frontier we call space!

(Careful, Thomas, you'll bust a snackpipe with all that straining!)

Ah, here we are. Poor wee Talky, the most important event in his life, namely his death, has through the machinations of the capitalist press been shunted onto a news branchline. His demise merits no more than a single sentence, an inky toeprint on the beach of history:

'A man knocked down and fatally injured in Crown Street, Gorbals, Glasgow last night has been identified as Charles Sloan (62) of Eglinton Street, Glasgow C5.'

17

The Salty Dog Saloon was heaving. Harry trotted to'n fro, ducking the lusty calls for pints as if they were thrown knives. Milly continued to carry all before her, while Stirrat stuck up the stout with his usual gruff charm. Auld Fergie, who had the Gaelic and a paunch that piled on the counter, hummed a Teuchterish dirge from the corner of his mouth. An outburst of laughter suggested the presence of Freddy Green ben the Lounge. The Dog fondly enclosed us all, revelling in our masculine growl; it encircled us with varnished wood-panelling and cast benign winks from its gantry. At the till, Sad Sam Murney edged nearer and ever nearer to that glorious moment when he'd chance his first smile. The bog leaked a steady stream of punters and a darts match narrowed to single figures: the Salty Dog Saloon at lunchtime on a Saturday, but, alas, now drawing its last beery breaths. Soon nothing but dust and fallen ceiling plaster, gantry stripped of its bottles, a wreath of holes where the dartboard had hung, and a thin rat singing: 'I'm just wild about Harry' – Harry, himself, signing on at the buroo: 'Sorry, there's no demand for hump-backed barmen at the moment . . .'

'D'you hear aboot Talky?' I asked Paddy Cullen.

He nodded. 'Aye, had an argument wae a 37.'

'What time'd it happen?'

Paddy shrugged then made a beckoning gesture with his hands. 'Hope tae fuck you've got the readies?'

I nodded, then taking the wad from my pocket passed it to him: this was one thing we never joked about. Quickly, he stashed it away. 'Thank Christ,' he muttered.

'What's that?' Paddy bent his head closer to mine. 'A carry-oot? When?'

I tried to sketch in a few details of the night before but, as usual, it proved pointless: for Paddy, yesterday by now was just another crate of empties. I nailed a few time slats into the rickety fence that kept him from blundering off the planet but omitted to mention Becky McQuade or the fact that for the sordid needs of my libido I'd made off with a background and several biographical details not my own.

He squinted at the drained glass. 'Must be a hole in this shagging thing.'

I took the hint and got a round in.

When I began to tell Paddy the laugh about Death dropping into Shug Wylie's bog he seemed to only be half-listening. His whisky was over in one go and again he bad-eyed the glass as if it'd short-measured'm. The beef about his sister came up again. 'See her, it's like being tied to wan of they wee yappy terriers, "Yak, yak, yak", night'n day. Nae kiddin, I'd be better off'n a dosshouse. Every morning it's war-bulletins – ham'n egg and pincer attacks.' Drolly, he imitated his sister: ' "Are you for another buttered hand-grenade, Patrick? Or maybe a wee daud of shrapnel on your toast?" ' I laughed, you just had to, but he didn't join in. 'I'll be hung for her wan of these days, so I will.'

A shrew she might be but, nevertheless, Nora Cullen was the main prop that kept the roof from caving in on her alcoholic brother: remove her and those dark workings through which he fumbled from day to day looking for god knows what (do any of us?) would collapse.

'Where's that wee shit, Killoch?' Paddy wanted to know as he glowered around him at the massed boozers as if they were part of a conspiracy to conceal the only man who could save'm from having to perform the matinee run at the Planet. He glanced speculatively at me but I moved quickly to nip hope in the bud. 'Sorry, Paddy, no can do. Got something on this afternoon.'

After about half'n hour with no sign of Killoch, Paddy was forced to knuckle under. He trudged from the warmth and jollity of the Dog with all the enthusiasm of a man thrusting his plums into a fast-closing vice.

I took my pint for a wander into Commie Corner. And there they were, the same old mammoths with their redundant tusks still patiently waiting for the political polar caps to melt and to flood Europe with the warmth of socialist brotherhood, to fissure and finally sweep away the bergs of capitalism on which their titanic dreams had so often foundered. All the regular Moscow tuskers were there except, of course, Talky Sloan, whose absence in fact seemed to've given them a renewed zest, more vocal elbow room maybe.

Gunner Langford held the floor. In his hodge-podge of military clobber he looked like a drop-out from some rag-tag army. A vintage greatcoat swamped his meagre frame and on his glengarry a badge gleamed. His feet were thrust into a pair of well-bulled army boots. Langford was making a verbal meal out of some guy, a stranger who'd probably wandered down from the publess plains of Castlemilk. A right crabbit bastard was Langford. Once, he'd excluded me from a debate because I couldn't tell'm where the US Seventh Fleet (or was it the Sixth?) was foregathered. 'The planet's supreme bastion of seapower and you haven't a clue where it is!' he'd raved. 'Out! Go on – bugger off!'

The Castlemilk guy was now frazzling on the business-end of Langford's dialectical blowtorch. 'Nothing of the kind!' snapped the pub's supreme bastion of warlore. 'Where'd you read such shite – in the bloody *Hotspur?*' He leanded towards his victim who, with eyes rolling, was giving a good impression of a pug who's just realised he's climbed into a losing ring. 'For your information, Mister, the Battle of Kasserine Pass began on Christmas Day, forty-two. And it wasn't Rommel who got the ball rolling. How could it've been when he was tanking across Libya to get to Tunisia? I'll tell you who it was – Arnim, that's who – Arnim of the German V Panzers.'

Stevie Urquhart sidled up to me. I shrugged his greasy paw from my shoulder. Urquhart, whose napper'd suddenly erupted through a bountiful pelt of coppery hair (how bloody vain he'd been about those locks!) to leave'm nothing but a pair of rust sideboards and a perpetual 'Why me?' expression, said, 'That mate of yours is for the high-jump this time, eh? I hear the Committee's talking *sine die*. Can count himself lucky he's no on a charge.'

Again I shook off his clinging hand and backed away a pace. 'What're ye on aboot?'

His lips, forced by the sudden dismissal of his dome crop to assume the role of his prime physical asset – some blind tart once told him that he had Paul Newman's smile – wriggled like a pair of ardent worms having a screw as he tried for that megastar's wry grin but looked more like Cheetah having a shit: 'Surely you've heard?'

'Heard what?'

'Aboot Paddy? Y'know, pissing all over the Club's jukebox.'

I shook my head. 'Sick ower it you mean.'

His nude head was waggling. 'Naw, naw, Tam, he definitely

pissed on the thing.' In the passing he hooked in an impromptu witness, Sammy Willis. 'Sam, tell Tam what his china did up the Club.'

Sammy, a witty wee punter, stepped back a bit to mime the wagging of an invisible willie. 'Gave Ol' Blue Eyes his first number wan,' he chortled. 'A sight tae see, they tell me, Paddy staunin there wae something like a French loaf in his haun, men fainting and wimmin climbing ower tables for a better look. Best cabaret turn ever. Wish I'd been there.'

Sammy went on his way while Urquhart's lips cooked up a greasy smirk. 'What'd I tell ye?' He nodded. 'Aye, your pal might be hung like a stallion' – his hand rose to tap his bleak skull – 'but there's nothing but donkey-droppings up here.' That creepy mitt of his kept tethering itself to me; it was like talking to an animated cobweb. 'He says he thought he was in the lavvy and mistook the jukebox for the weighing machine. Some excuse, eh? Committee'll jump all over him. His feet'll no touch – telling ye.'

I shrugged my shoulders. Aye, it seemed the Social Club was going to lose one of its outstanding members. 'By the way Tam,' Urquhart was now saying, 'get your tank on Flying Fox in the three-thirty the day. A skoosh case.' He rejoined Lapsely and McPake, his drinking pals, and soon had both glimmerbrains in stitches at the things his versatile lips could come out with. I'd meant to get the SP on Urquhart's tip but it didn't really matter since any nag he recommended was bound to be a surefire binger. Well, at least he'd shortened the field. I borrowed the *Express* Racing Section from Mooney who, having apparently found the chasing of hairs to be a thirst-making business, had dropped in for a wetner. A barney had broken out between two men, both of them demolishers, who'd been christened 'Hammer'n Tongs' by Freddy Green. Always needling, ever ready to knock lumps out of each other, neither, as far as I knew, had so much as struck a blow in earnest yet. 'Right,' said the one called Hammer, 'ootside and we'll settle it!'

'What's keeping you, then?' Tongs asked. He'd already pushed the door wide to admit a snowy blast. Both men stormed out and the door swung shut at their backs. It was proof of how routine their phoney jousting had become that nobody stirred a leg to go out with them to spectate. 'They'll be chipping snawbaws at each other,' some wag shouted and there were laughs all round.

A rapid eye-rake down the three-thirty field produced a twitch for a nag called Caesar's Revenge. It dawned on me why: Caesar was the late Tammy Cook's Alsatian dog, the very one that'd taken time out to drop by Joe Fiducci's shop to give me the nod. Caesar's Revenge was an 8-1 prospect while the plodder Urquhart had hexed was evens fav. From my Hardship Pocket, a wee zipped aperture sewn into the lining of my combat jacket for no purpose I could think of, except maybe for a suicide pill or the last bullet, I dug out the pram money, seven pounds in all. About to take two notes from it I changed my mind. Mooney nodded when I asked'm if he was hitting the bookies later. I gave'm the bread. 'Caesar's Revenge in the three-thirty, Pat. On the nose.' He looked at the fiver, looked at me, shook his head, then tucked the five spot away. Next, jamming his mouth close to my lughole, shouting against the pub's uproar, he wanted to know if the horse was a 'good thing'. 'Naw,' I shouted back, 'I was just getting fuck'n jiggered humpin that heavy fiver around!'

Suddenly, the pub's spiralling decibel ratio dived to a low-voiced buzzing in which the name 'Salter' was busily repeated. And there was the man himself, a thin streak of misery in a snow-speckled bunnet, brown overcoat and black shoes, the handle of his white stick cleeked over his arm. Today he was being escorted into the Dog, not by his sister, Bunty, as was the custom, but by Danny Dimes, his next-door neighbour. As Dimes, a wee bit self-consciously, led Salter to his favoured corner — it was already being rapidly vacated for him. Somebody at the doms table, Billy Bannerman, I think it was, shouted, 'Hey, Danny, has Bunty told'm?'

Dimes stopped, too quickly as it happened, and Salter, lurching from his grasp, collided with a table and sent a beermug crashing to the floor. Salter, lost at the heart of silent darkness, would know nothing about this mishap, for him only the valved droning of his blood as it made its perilous circuits, and the touch of hands as they guided him to his seat.

Dimes lifted a jagged slice of glass. 'Told'm what?'

'About Talky?'

'What aboot'm?'

Colin Cowie, standing near Dimes, chipped in. 'Talky got hamburgered wae a bus in Croon Street.'

'Christ,' said Dimes, 'I hidnae heard. Is he deid, then?'

Cowie who was infamous for his mordant humour, nodded, 'They think maybe his tongue'll pull through if they can catch it long enough to get it nailed doon.' This provoked a burst of laughter, but some of the punters in the kneecreaker division were shaking their heads at the disrespect of it.

'Where's Bunty, then?' Jock Gebbie asked Dimes.

'Her leg's in plaster.'

'The auld fella knows, does he?'

'Aye, he was there when it happened.'

'When Talky got killed?'

'Naw, when Bunty fell on her arse and broke her ankle.'

Salter, seated, his cap removed, now placed his hands palm upwards on the table, the usual signal to Talky to indicate that he was ready to converse.

'Hey, Danny,' Bert Shaw shouted, 'can you dae that deaf'n dumb patter?'

Cowie snorted. 'You kiddin – that bass couldnae spell egg.'

Danny bridled at this. 'Look, I was asked tae bring'm. So I've brung'm. That's it.' He dropped the daud of glass into the pan Stirrat had brought to the scene then, turning, he muscled his way to the counter and ordered a drink. Salter's usual tipple, a bottle of strong ale, was already on its way to him. Those punters sitting near to him had a sort of skulking look about them, as if shamed by their inability to rap out something meaningful on that proferred palm. How was yon palm-patter done? Maybe along the lines of the grid system lags used to rap to each other through adjoining walls. Salter sat in our midst, an affront to all of us. There he was, hunkered down in his soundless pit, awaiting Talky, the lantern of his life. For some reason back into my mind swam the image of yon shark I'd seen on the telly last evening, the brute's teeth biting a chunk from the diver's airline, then its victim tumbling away into the suffocating muds of the abyss, beyond all hope of recall. The plight of Salter was similar; he too was flailing around in the oppressive night of his sealed senses. Though he sat very still and looked completely calm who knew what internal convulsions were wracking the man.

'Somebody should tell'm,' Gebbie said. 'Cannae have him just sittin there.'

'Should be ta'en hame, so he should,' said another.

'Hey McLaurin,' shouted Gebbie, 'Your auld man was cornbeef, was he no?'

McLaurin, at the doms table, frowned. 'Aye, ya daft bugger, but he wisnae blin and dumb intae the bargain.'

'Here,' said Tipsy Tomlinson who claimed to've been drunk since VJ night – and looked it, 'I'll get'n touch wae'm. Watch this.' And we did, every man jack of us (big Milly included) as in almost total silence Tipsy staggered to Salter's corner. He stood there for a time, one hand on the table propping him up while with the other one he searched himself, going from pocket to pocket but bringing out zilch. What was he looking for? A pen? Some money? His specs? Nobody asked. The pocket-patrol was just one of Tipsy's 'things', one of his pub oddities. A shrink would've probably suggested that by his public body-search Tipsy was externalising his anxious desire for cohesive selfhood, that his self-frisking was symbolic of his desperate attempt to 'get it together'. Which is about what you'd expect from those theorising assholes. Me? I figure it's Tipsy's way of playing for time while he waits like the rest of us for the surprise of his next action. And a surprise it proved to be. Giving up his search he now raised his right hand with a wiggly motion, like a fakir putting on the fluence. Next, he bent over the table and made passing movements over Salter's open palm, then his own palms rose with his gaze to the rafters but soon sank again as in a low sottish voice he crooned: 'Talky, are you there? Talky, can you hear me?' He rapped his knuckles three times on the table then again sought spiritual aid from the rafters as with both hands held aloft he intoned: 'Talky if you're here – send us a sign!'

It came almost immediately and, surprisingly enough, via auld Dan Murchie who, sitting to the right of Salter's table suddenly raised his gouty left leg then sounded one of the longest, the loudest, and the most ambitious renditions of bowel music ever to be produced by the anal sphincter. The Fart of the Century, it was a stentorian stinker with the collective energy of a dozen Krakatoas simultaneously blowing their tops. It was a fart with 'professional' written all over it and beside which the raspers the gifted Paddy Cullen could summons from his snack-pipes were revealed for what they really were – the prissy pimpings of a gifted amateur. To hear a fart being transformed into jazz, raw bowel gas becoming an art form was enough to bring tears to the eye. Well, at least it did to those sitting in the immediate vicinity of Murchie. As the last triumphant notes of 'the impromptu' faded away the pub erupted into wild, uncontrollable laughter and for a long time bedlam reigned. Dan Murchie remained seated on his 'instrument' while grinning punters crowded around him to shake his hand and offer him drinks. Meanwhile, a million light years beyond laughter, Salter sat awaiting the touch of a human hand. The sight of him prompted me to split. It was appalling that he'd never ever get in on the joke.

The door flapped open and in came Archie Killoch. He looked like a snowman who was trying out walking for the first time. There was certainly something bedevilling his gait – one foot seemed keen on getting to the bog while the other one was more intent on heading for the counter. 'Archie,' I said, tugging at his snowy sleeve, 'Paddy was looking for ye.' He replied in fluent Martian then stumbled to the bar where Freddy Green was heard to exclaim, 'Clear the decks, lads – I think it's one of ours!'

Behind me, Gunner Langford was saying, 'and another thing Mister – No sit doon, I'm no finished – another thing, it was what was left of the 26th Armoured Brigade. That's right. Rommel sent in a tank column led by a captured Valentine – took everybody on, that did . . .'

I went out into the snow. Hammer'n Tongs were shaking hands. The snow had plastered them so that they looked like a pair of amiable spooks. One of them, Tongs, I think it was, gave me a stupid wink as I crunched past. I tried to dismiss the image of Old Salter, sitting there with his outheld hand, dumbly pleading for the alm of meaningful touch. And Talky, himself – what of him? He'd be laid by in a drawer in the mortuary, his tongue at long last idle and unmoving in his frozen mouth. Such thoughts did I entertain as I made my way through the snow to my date with destiny – my fateful meeting with the Banana Baron.

18

'The wages aren't much cop,' Uncle Billy admitted as we sat by a blazing fire in his drab little igloo, 'but at least it's better'n your dole money, and it's regular.'

Steam rose from my soaked jeans, and already my hair was beginning to dry. In a corner, a muted TV set huffily flicked through its programme of unwatched sporting events: two heavyweight boxers were to be seen swapping ponderous punches, fathoms deep beneath a sea of sadistic faces; then, two Asiatics, armed with tiny bats, began to twitch a ping-pong ball from one to the other, an activity made all the more meaningless by the imposed silence.

The living-room was one of those narrow closets into which for generations working-class people've been stuffed. A closed fist of a room: scuffed carpets and faded wallpaper. Near the TV set was a bookcase, its contents in chaos like an idiot's mind. By the window an empty birdcage and on the far wall a mirror reflected sharp angles of furniture and caught a glimpse of William of Orange, mounted on a white charger as he triumphantly crossed Boyne water, a tatty print which was complemented by a photograph of Glasgow Rangers FC.

It turned out that Billy boy was really hooked on bananas.

With an enthusiasm I found laughable he informed me that the nana world was up for grabs. If I got stuck in, really rolled my sleeves up, why there was every possibility of me rising to the dizzy heights of Cutter, or even Weigher. From there it was but a short step to go on and claim the Brown Coat. The B.C. is the Oscar of the nana-packing world; to don this garment proved you'd become Staff, a position which entitled you to the stupendous windfall of a free, aye, FREE hand of bananas every week. From then on it was promotion all the way, unless, of course, you were unlucky enough to get nipped on the arse by a scorpion or copped it in the neck from a bad-tempered Black Widow spider. The gab now veered to the interesting creepy-crawlies to be encountered in a banana warehouse, a subject which naturally brought us around to discussing Ma Carlyle.

'How's Lettie's back these days?' Billy enquired.

About as dilapidated as her front, I was tempted to say, but instead registered a shoulder-shrug.

'Aye,' Billy sighed, 'she's put in a sore time of it with that back of hers – ever since she was a young lassie, it seems!'

That my mother'n wrath had ever been a 'young lassie' just wasn't on: I knew for a fact that she'd arisen fully-plated from Loch Ness between the Wars. To my dismay, the Banana Baron, mumbling something about 'auld snapshots', rose and crossed to the bookcase.

The album which he placed across my lap exuded a crypt-like odour, a cold resting place for its stiffened humans. Leaning over me, Billy's banana-blunted forefinger guided me through the Carlyle/Dalrymple menagerie, a tedious procession of aunts, uncles, nephews and nieces. A pale moth of a girl in the chrysalis of a wedding gown emerged, to my disbelief, to be Letitia Dalrymple on her wedding day, and the rumpled gamp suspended from her arm proved, in fact, to be Archie Carlyle, himself, her brand-new husband and the elder brother of Billy here. Letitia Dalrymple Carlyle always managed to imply that she'd married beneath herself. Right enough, how wee Archie persuaded her to share the same cloud of confetti was a real brow-wrinkler; the short time I'd known him he'd been about as dynamic as a grease-spot but maybe – who knows? – when he'd been a young buck he'd something going for'm. A locksmith to trade he'd been, but I figure he'd never succeeded in cracking the cage of contempt his wife'd thrust'm into as punishment – despite the boon of her windfall – for not really making it in the business world.

By chance during this all but comatose crawl through the album's pages I came across a snapshot of Rhona. She must've been around eight or nine at the time it'd been taken. She wore a billowing white dress and was to be seen tossing breadcrusts to down-swooping seagulls on Rothesay Harbour. How innocent she looked with the sunlight pouring cleanly upon her and no shadow of the hawk, Clay, yet fallen on her virginal world. 'Cast your bread upon the waters and after many a day it'll get soggy and sink . . .'

'That's me to the left of the banner.'

Billy was pointing to a besashed and bumptious-looking punter who, along with others in Orange Lodge regalia, marched resolutely through a Catholic-inspired rain. 'A grand Walk that was,' reminisced Billy. 'Terrible weather, but we turned out in strength just the same.' His finger jabbed the photograph. 'See that fella there, his boy was all set to sign for Rangers when he got killed in a docks accident. Aye, John Purdie he was called.' I was tempted to ask'm if a heavy Catholic had fallen on Purdie junior, but held my wheesht: the boring journey from Victoriana to religious mania had served its purpose: surreptitiously, I undid the top button of my casual shirt.

'Will you try a wee sherry?' Billy asked as he returned the album to the bookcase. 'It's a wee tate somebody left last Ne'erday.' The 'sherry' turned out to be a close relative of the 'Jungle Juice' Glesca winos traditionally dement themselves with, something I'd expected from the pains he was taking to hide the bottle's label. 'I'll have a wee dribble myself, just to keep you company like,' he said as he splashed a rim-hanger into his glass.

We sat there for a time in drowsy silence by the fire, looking, I thought, like one of those telly commercials: 'Billy's Brew'll make you Spew!' On the sideboard a clock started awake and began to froth chimes. It was a handsome piece which had probably been presented to Billy after he'd cut his millionth banana. 'Is that the time already?' Billy exclaimed with an urgency that suggested he was about to catch a jet plane to Venezuela, or was on the point of receiving a visit from the Lord Provost himself. After scattering a few more chimelets the clock dozed off again. Uncle Billy subsided with it, a clockroach safely under its stone. A quick image flashed across my mind, that of Granda Gibson's hand flicking back the silvery lid of his skull-shaped tobacco bowl and his fingers tearing at the orangey shag within. It looked a painful process, but the skull – it'd been nicknamed 'Cripps' – had gone on grinning until the day it took a tumble and scattered its amber brains on the hearth. Why that image? Who knows? Billy, the banana beetle, turned his antennae to the ghostly TV set, fed on its flickerings for a few moments then, gushing little sighs, reabsorbed himself in prehistoric man's telly – the fire with its languid blades of flame.

'Are you still scribbling away then, Tommy?'

He asked this as if he was enquiring about some disease which might not yet've run its course. My shrug seemed to signal that a cure'd been effected. 'Ach, aye,' he said, 'writing books is fine for them that's nothing more to do with their time.' With a surprising expertise for one who claimed to be a teetotaller he flipped over the last of his drink then placed the drained glass on the ledge of the tiled fireplace. 'Anyway,' he announced, indicating the wally dug on the mantlepiece – a cretinous-looking beast with a sawn-off face – 'your books'll soon be as auld-fashioned as one of these things. D'you not think so yourself? This time, next century, they'll be playing bingo in your libraries. Mark my words.'

Aye, nuclear bingo: clickety-click the planet is sick.

I undid another shirt button.

'You've not'd much luck with the book I'm hearing.'

That had to be the understatement of the year. The novel, written by me during my self-allocated sabbatical, had been rejected four times thus far. I've no doubt that behind my back the family were having a good snigger. Rhona of course had been the loyal exception though I admit that her piteous expressions when the thing limped home battered and bloodied by franking stamps, were harder to bear than her sister's outright sarcasm: 'Has your boomerang got back yet, Patton?' she'd enquire, while her husband Jack would give the knife in my back an extra twist by asking if I'd managed to sell any of my daubs? Which meant that he presumed I'd jacked in the railways to pursue a painting career. Maybe I should have. The manuscript had begun to show the bruises from its days, weeks, and months buried in the 'slush piles' of various publishing firms. After it'd been returned for the third time it had scorch marks on several of its pages, as if someone had been trying to thrust the thing into the furnace. Last time out it returned stained by beetroot juice and ketchup which suggested the reader had considered eating it then chickened. So far on this its latest journey southwards, it'd produced an acknowledgement of receipt then thereafter entered into the agonising silent phase which apparently the current Apollo spaceship will encounter when, going behind the moon, it will temporarily sever contact with its Control in Houston.

Actual criticism of the novel by its rejectors was very thin on the ground, although the consensus of opinion seemed to indicate that its main weakness lay in its apparent 'lack of plot'. You can bet your granny's boots and braces it lacks plot. Plots are for graveyards. I'd rather drag my eyeballs along barbed wire than read a plotty novel. You can almost see the authors of such contrived claptrap winding up their childish prose toys, before sending them whirring across their fatuous pages in search of 'adventures'. See how perkily they strut and stride; observe the zany intermingling patterns they make with their inky bootees; listen, and you'll hear their valorous hearts grinding within their heroic breasts.

What I'd written was a simple tale about a guy called Webster, based loosely on Da Clay though I'm bound to admit that his rumbustious character failed to make the journey intact between penpoint and paper. It deals with the last few years of his life when a tragedy befell him that transformed his existence – he fathered a monster, a hydrocephalic babe who was destined to die before her second birthday. His partner, the Black Widow of real life, Mrs Cavendish (in the novel she's Amy Struthers) cuts and runs, but Webster, knowing full well that his daughter's life will be both harrowing and brief, nevertheless chooses to dedicate himself to her care. He gives up boozing and gambling, finds work in order to pay for her medical fees. Brian, his legitimate son, by whom a part of the novel is narrated, expresses his puzzlement and his hurt over his father's apparent disinterest in him. How could it be that the shallow Webster had after all profounder depths to him, depths he was only willing to plumb for Brian's blighted half-sister? Why was it that all his father had to offer him was 'the bleak sight of his retreating back . . . ?'

Billy had asked a question.

'Sorry, you were saying?'

'Your book – what was it about, then?'

I noted the posthumous phrasing of his enquiry. 'A lavvy attendant,' I said.

There was a whirr of surprise in his grey, pleated throat, 'A lavvy attendant?'

'There're still some around.'

'Aye, but it's not very often that you read about them, y'know, in books.'

'It's a whodunnit,' I blandly told'm. 'A sort of Sweeney Todd thing. Clients, usually rich wans, sit down on bog number two then vanish through a trapdoor.'

Maybe it was the wine but Billy's eyes had taken on a glassy look. He fiddled some baccy into his pipe bowl. 'Unusual, right enough. And have you a publisher for it?'

I shrugged. 'Things are a wee bit bogged doon at the moment.'

With his pipe going to his satisfaction, smoke squirting from the corner of his mouth, his lips making rapid putt-putting noises, Billy became at ease again. 'Aye, Tommy,' he assured me, 'it's a tough auld life right enough. If you don't give, you don't get.' His glance returned to the wally dug – it was proving to be a useful prop. 'What stands still gathers dust, there's a fact. My auld faither (God rest'm) used to say: "He who hesitates gets bossed". Always remembered that.'

I loosened the third and final button.

In comparison to this crap, the blizzard raging outside had become immensely seductive. Uncle Billy continued to lumber through the script Ma Carlyle had obviously written and produced for this occasion. 'I know you'll agree that it's the young ones we've got to think about. There's your Rhona wae a bairn on the road, I mean, rich or poor, we all start out in a single-end, if you get my meaning; it's what comes after that counts, eh?' I raised my hand to my shirt collar; his eyes followed the movement then visibly widened as they beheld the unbelievable. He looked quite overcome, apoplectic as they used to say in Victorian novels. Hastily, the telly hid away its swimming-pool nymphs, replacing them with an ad for bleach that seemed potent enough to liquify granite. 'Tommy,' Billy said in a strangling voice, 'what in the name's that you've round your neck?' By the sound of his voice you would've thought he'd swallowed a couple of gallons of the super bleach.

Hamming puzzlement, I casually flipped out the crucifix, 'This, you mean?'

He cringed from the sight of it with all the comic revulsion of a Hollywood Satanist. 'And . . . and what would you be doing with the like of that on ye?'

'It's a crucifix.'

'Aye, fine well I know that.' His struggle to find words would've made even the sloppiest of directors frown. Hope flared anew in his troubled eyes. 'It's one of they hippie ornaments, is that it?'

I tucked the crucifix back inside my shirt. 'It's real enough.'

'C'mon Tommy, what are you playing at? Take off that Vatican brooch. Imagine a good Proddy like yourself – you're having me on. It's a joke, right?'

Solemnly, I shook my head.

From the strangling roots of Uncle Billy's bigotry there arose a great orange lily of wisdom. 'Tommy, you can't cure popery with penicillin. It spreads, son. Aye, they bead-rattlers make sure of that.'

Suppressing a grin at the thought of Billy here sneaking past chapels wearing a smog-mask, I got to my feet. 'I'll have to split.'

Looking like a guy who's just won a Firhill season ticket, the

Banana Baron, glowering darkly from his scorched fireside throne, gave tongue to a timely warning: 'You can't turn your coat without showing the seams, Tommy.'

Aye, nor could you walk through a blizzard and not get your jacket soaked. I stuck it on, tholing the arctic hug of the thing as one might endure the ghostly embrace of a departed loved one. Up'n heaven, Ma Clay popped her head from a daffodil-yellow window and chirped: 'First the sneezies, next the wheezies, then the De'il does as he pleases!' The window tittered shut. Meanwhile Mrs Clay's anti-bellum offspring was zipping himself into an obsolete warsuit, having sold himself, as usual, for short-time gains – a mercenary of the passing moment.

'I'll have to chat to Father Cullen about it,' I promised.

Billy rose from the armchair. 'Who's this Father Cullen, then?'

'I'm attending his pre-convert classes.'

The image of Paddy Cullen got up in a reversed collar and hassock – no, not hassock, that's a cushion, I think – cassock, that's what I'm after. Aye, Cullen in a cassock and zonked out in the Confessional, having stuck away a flagon or so of communion wine, the thought of this put a severe tax on my laugh-restrainers.

'I hear you're an atheist, anyway?' Billy said huffily.

I shrugged. 'You shouldnae believe everything you hear on the Carlyle tom-toms.'

Eastern mysticism, that's what I'd chucked, being taken to the spiritual cleaners by saintly curry-bashers and Tibetan spivs. The yogi-bogi men as well, with their asanas that drove western man bananas – circus tricks and claptrap, it amounted to nothing more. Koans and cons, and meditation is the first symptom of narcissism. Take a gander at those psychic fat cats who preach poverty and practice wealth. Lazy bastards, every last one of them. Be sure that when shit wants shifting they'll be on hand to flog you the bucket'n spades. Sacred India my ass! I tell you, there're more ramps, cons and stings going down in your average ashram than there are at the Fiddler's Ball.

I turned up my jacket collar. 'Be seeing you,' I mumbled.

He really did look put out. 'I don't suppose Rhona knows about this?'

I shook my head.

'Aye, well, you'd best be keeping it that way. It'd be bad for her, bad for the . . . the . . .'

'Baby?'

He nodded. 'That goes without saying. A bad deal all round. I hope you're ower this daftness afore she's by.'

He showed me out, anxious now, it seemed, to be shot of me. I stepped out onto the dismal landing. Snow sluiced through a broken pane on the half-landing and above us a gas-mantle flung a shivery light upon the name-infested walls. 'I'll see Mr Mellish on Monday,' Billy said and I was pleased by his downbeat tone. 'He'll maybe drop you a line for the interview. Oh, and Tommy,' he added with sledgehammer subtlety, 'I'd keep my shirt buttoned if I was you — Mr Mellish is a heid-bummer'n the Masons!'

Mr Mellish, your bigotry's hellish!

I made my way down slanting, snow-leprous streets to my bus-stop. A wayside church billposter reminded me that JESUS SAVES! I fell in line with that all right. Surely the distribution of bananas was a minor item in his Dad's agenda. As it happened, Donald Strang sent me a telegram. It was delivered by a spiritual hobo, one of those pamphlet machines which, operated by a tiny battery of faith, give service for years. The tract was as green and as moist as a lettuce leaf with tiny caterpillars of wisdom wriggling whitely all over it. Strang, in his inimitable style, presented the rumour that the universe was more or less jiggered. Very soon now, perhaps on a run-of-the-mill Saturday like this one, the cosmic ringmaster would heave a disappointed sigh then give the word for the Big Top to be struck; the sustaining pillar of creation would be removed and the spangled canvas of the heavens would flop into chaos. For is it not said in the Book of Zephaniah that 'the great day of the Lord is near'? And what a day was being laid on, an Armageddon spectacular. Nothing was to be spared: 'Clouds of thick darkness'; 'Trouble and distress' by the bushel; they were really digging deep into the human misery-bag for this one. The frogs, locusts, and pestilential what-nots the ancient Egyptians got plagued with for coming-the-turtle over exit visas for their Hebrew tribes was but a series of mild irritants compared to the woe and desolation already in the mail to us. Our planet, need it be said, is in a very bad way. The real mystery is how human hope came to flower in its strangling clays, how myths of continuance beyond the final heartbeat came to germinate in a rind of corpses a half a mile thick. There's nothing to be depended upon, nowt at all. From the first yell life has us on the ropes and there's no trick, no dirty tactic that pugilist won't resort to, from kidney-punching to ear-biting, to stretch you out at his feet. Only one fact is certain in this uneven contest – the fight's fixed: the Ref has your card marked, even before you've laced on your gloves. When you dive – as dive you must – all you can do is to try'n make it convincing, to go down with some style.

As for yon longbeard, Zephaniah, he, like Steve Urquhart, couldn't have predicted an outbreak of shit in an exploding latrine. Proof of this was blazing across the screen of a TV set in a store window: Caesar's Revenge, my selection, had obliged at the sparkling odds of 10-1!

Roll on Damnation.

19

It turned out that Zephaniah, professional whinger (grouses by arrangement) had gotten it completely wrong, he'd been wildly OVER-optimistic!

As I returned to the Scabby – my body by bus; my mind on the back of a winged Irish colt – I savoured the treat still to come, when old Mooney would make with the bread, and my mitt would close around fifty-odd scoobies. Meanwhile, over and over, I ran that reel which depicted Dan McGarvie, turf accountant, dishing out the dosh, a grudging hand-thump to each departing fiver.

But Joe Fiducci soon brought me down to earth, aye, he clipped Pegasus's wings all right.

'Gone?' I echoed. 'What d'you mean – gone?'

Joe, who was trimming the hair of an albino kid (odd to see those white locks tumble from such a young head), wagged his own grizzled thatch. 'He go to the bookie; he come back; he think maybe he have the flu; he put on his coat then – arrividerci!'

The child's mother sat polishing the lenses of her son's specs with a hankie. She wore a shabby fur-coat, a flank musquash, maybe. Leaning forward, she whispered an instruction to Joe. He nodded. 'Okay, I do that . . .' The boy, sitting on the wooden flap that'd been laid across the arms of Granda Gibson's chair, closed his pinkish eyes as if it was hard for'm to watch his hair snowing onto his shoulders then dropping to the chequered floor where the grey clippings of old men lay.

Clippings of another kind were being swept up by Barrel Broon, McGarvie's obese boardmaker. Barrel brushed betting copies – loser's stuff – ahead of him like a wedge of soiled snow. From the blower in the corner a gritty voice mouthed football results. The Pools Panel had sat today. Balding soccer stars of yesteryear had foregathered at the Hotel Olympus to examine the entrails of a freshly-shot spectator. Nice number, sitting there in a cosy room, a brandy handy, and maybe one of Cuba's costliest reeking in your word-hole. Very tasty. It was a much better deal than the punters who'd shivered it out in this dump had got. There'd been nothing make-believe about their task for they played the reality game: get it right first time pal, or you're broom fodder!

McGarvie, looking like an albino himself with his pale hair lying on his narrow skull, stared at me through the steel-mesh screen of his skinny payout window. McGarvie didn't dig me, an aversion which was the result of my old man (nom-de-plume 'Shiny Shoes') clinching the padlock on McGarvie's brother Jake's turf parlour with a fantastically-priced Yankee bet. Although the shop's 'limits rule' was triggered it'd still been a hefty chunk of loot Da Clay had strolled off with. Jake had decked it with a heart-attack shortly afterwards and had lit out for wherever bookies head for when time's no-limit wager finally comes up.

Aye, punishment for the wins of the father shall be visited upon succeeding generations right enough.

When I put it to McGarvie that Old Mooney might've been lucky at the Irish meeting, he got cagey. 'Aye, he could've won a poke of tanners. So what?' His shoulders twitched in response to my next question: 'A ten-to-wan-shot? Aye, maybe.' Seeing no profit in me he was already turning away. I tried again, but this time the verbal response was sourer: 'Fuckall to do with you what he won!' He rid himself of the fag-end that'd crept to within millimetres of his mouth, crushing it to a black dot in an ashtray. Period. End of conversation.

I'd two choices, no, three; (i) I could lie in wait for the albino kid's maw and blag her fur-coat; (ii) make a tour of the Oatlands pubs where Mooney did his Saturday night boozing; (iii) return to my abode, have some nosh, a change of footwear, then maybe saw-the-log for a bit before my visit to Rhona. I opted for the latter and stopped by at my local dairy for some breakfast tack. It was to be hoped – bloody well expected! – that Mooney would drop by the Dog this evening with my winnings. The possibility nagged at me that he hadn't laid the bet, but had stuck my fiver in his sky-rocket. Maybe he did have the flu. It could be that he'd had a slice of the action himself. I trudged homewards through the snow and the more I thought about Mooney drinking around with my crackle in his pooches the deeper were the footprints I left behind me.

Like a ghost from the past (do any of them come from the future? There's a thought!) Granny Ferguson disguised as a pile of woollen cardigans, stood guard at our closemouth. Apart from the fact that she'd had the wacky notion to apply lipstick to her mouth rims – missing by a good half inch or so – she wore a sartorial novelty in the shape of a mink-furred Cossack hat. This headgear had been skewered by a massive hatpin which from its angle of entry gave the impression it had been rammed clean through her skull. Not that this was anything to get alarmed about – there wasn't much in there to damage.

As I approached the warpainted crone she was uttering her battlecry of old: 'I'll have the polis on ye so I will. Aye, don't you worry aboot that. They're coming . . . they're coming. I've got your names.' And so she had, well most of them: Rudge, Lyons, Green, McMahon, Milligan, yours truly, of course, the rotten apple of her eye. Naturally it was to be me who fulfilled her prophecy of the outcome of our street fitba — I broke her window, knocked out a complete pane.

There'd be no snow, no freezing winds whipping across the landscape she was peering out at; more than likely her old mind was locked into a summer day, back in the forties maybe, when life, raw and vital, had rampaged in the Scabby; disease too, of course, and plenty of deaths but always in attendance was that overwhelming sense of gallus being, especially so in childhood when there hadn't been the time to get all the things you wanted to do done. Probably those raggedy-arsed kids, the bane of her life, jiggling a tennis ball out there on the chalk-scrawled street, were more real to her at this moment than was the spectral creature who now stepped on out of the winter-to-come and placed his icy hand upon her.

'Is there something up, Mrs Ferguson?'

The summer blinked out in her mind. 'It's you, is it?' She shook off my hand. 'Ready to muck up the close wae they Parish boots of yours. Aye, gie me your muck, that's what tae dae!'

In fact, the close hadn't seen either cloth or mop since Rhona had gone into hospital. It was littered with trash blown in from the backcourt and demolition stour clung thickly to the walls. I tried to coax the old woman into her apartment but she was having none of it. 'C'mon, Mrs Ferguson, you'll catch your death oot here. Tell you what, you go in by and I'll bring you doon a nice bowl of broth. Okay?'

No, it wasn't 'okay'. As far as she was concerned nothing about me would ever be okay. I belonged in a wrecker's yard for I was an expert at breaking things; plant pots, window-panes, and hearts

171

too maybe, nothing fragile was safe in my presence. To accept food from my hands was to invite death by poisoning. 'You'll roast in Hell for what you've done!' she suddenly screeched. 'Aye, and a lot sooner than you think.'

It spooked me a bit, the old dame's forecast, as it tailed me up the trample-delved stairs. She was still shouting as I reached my own landing.

In my living-room I tip-toed around, dousing decibels wherever I could so's not to rouse Wattie Mullens from his wine stupor and have him legging down to see what was for grabs. Cannily, I took a pot from the press under the sink and emptied the gunk which its label claimed to be 'Scotch Broth' into it. While I waited for the stuff to divide, multiply or whatever it did, I got the fire going with a splash or two of paraffin on the hot cinders.

With the bowl of broth steaming in my hand I tried one last series of knocks on Granny Ferguson's door, but she was not for opening it. The dotty witch, it seemed would have no truck with the Borgia Meals-on-Wheels Service. Instead she seemed content to gab to her household spooks; I could even hear her laughing at some posthumous crack. Mission abandoned. I was about to head up the stairs when Cyclops arrived. The one-eyed moggy looked wabbit from trekking snowed-up pavements. 'You've knocked it off, son,' I said and lowered the bowl to the close's gritty floor. The furry ingrate sniffed at what was on offer then took off with a huffy miaow. 'You'll lick where that lay tomorrow,' I scolded, using an expression Ma Clay used to dish out at the table when I'd taken it up my humph not to dine on her hamely fare. Dead parky it felt on those stairs. On my way up them I took swig after swig from the bowl and had emptied it by the time I gained my own landing. 'All quiet on the festering front!' as Da Clay put it, which was just the way I liked it.

I sank into my armchair with some fresh cuts of bread and another bowl of so-called broth. When I'd finished my scoff I turned the socks I'd left to dry over on the fender then settled back for some shut-eye. I'd this weird wee dream; I saw myself on the stairs, going down to the haunted cludgie. Pushing its door wide I was confronted by a full suit of armour arranged in a sitting position on the pan. I began to footer with its visor and eventually it sprang open. It seemed to be empty, the suit, but couldn't have been for something inside was on fire. Smoke began to pour from the casque and soon the suit got so heated it began to glow brazier red. It would've all been very symbolic, a meaty diagnostical bone for any Freudian fart to've had a good gnaw on: Herr Clay, I haf to inform you that your psyche is for der Kibosh!' if I hadn't wakened to find that my socks were on the point of incinerating themselves. I stuck them on, enjoying their scorching contact.

I stared across at the dumb TV in the corner. It was having a nightmare called Vietnam; kids being napalmed; eggshell villages being stomped upon by GI Joe's converging mortar rounds. Before the mind could assimilate what the Pentagon's real intentions for that woebegone land were, we were whisked away to view some xmassy schmaltz in Trafalgar Square. And just to ensure that no memory vestige of human carnage remained, we went off now on a zoo trip. A beaver flicked along a snowy tree limb then there followed some funny footage of a penguin skidding drunkenly around on some tundra: it looked a lot like wee Archie Killoch's efforts to remain upright in the Dog this afternoon.

I updated my journal, a broad sweep of the day's events thus far, headlines which I'd amplify tomorrow with a bit more time. On flipping through the pages of one of my 'Red Nerves' jotters I came across a quote from Talky Sloan himself:

'Freedom for the working class means that although you're not going to get a bit of Granny's dumpling, you're completely at liberty to go without it . . .'

Nice one, auld timer!

20

When I went into the Maternity's Day Room Val Doonican was on the box. A charming Irishman, he was by profession a kind of singing sedative which no doubt accounted for the state of collective narcosis being evidenced by his viewers. Wagging to'n fro in a rocking chair, he plucked soporific chords from his guitar, and the public yawn, touring the mouths available to it in the room – six of them now that I'd showed up – was fielded to me by a tallow-pale woman who sat close by Rhona. My jawbones crackled lightly as the yawn tautened them. All over Scotland punters would be fighting off waves of fatigue as they elbowed themselves across their living-room rugs to get at the TV channel selectors before it was too late and they were sucked into that psychic black hole, that snore-pocket from which they'd emerge to be confronted by the direst prospect on this or any other planet – the Scottish Sabbath.

Rhona alas remained all too wakeful to the shortcomings in her life. Once again I got sandbagged for my scruffy appearance. 'Think you'd been flung off the back of an army truck . . .' Inevitably my long hair got short shrift. When had my shoes last seen a brush? And why had I brought chocolates? A whole quarter pound too – my my, it'd be miniatures of Lucozade next. Disdainfully she'd pushed away the choc-box.

'But they're brandy liqueurs – your favourite.'

'Is that where the smell of booze is coming from then?'

'Only had the one, Rhona.'

'I thought I asked you to change my magazine.'

'Did you?'

'All you get in this rag's Liz Taylor and how to detect cancer.'

'Sure, how I gotta knowma carcinoma.'

'Shut up!'

Next came the ever-recurring wrangle about the Futility Furnishings payment book. 'Beautility,' she snapped. 'Why've you always got to give things such childish nicknames?'

'Such as?'

'Well, Fat Wallet for – '

'The Nat Smollett Estate. I like that, it's apt and it's – '

'Stupid. Time you grew up.'

Aye, once again I'd forgotten to bring the never-never book. I was hiding something. She knew me all too well. Could pick up a lie before it tripped over my lips. What was I up to? Might as well tell her. She'd find out in the end. I better not be lying about contacting the Gas Board to have the meter emptied. Did I want one of those Salty Dog low-lifers to do the job for me? I protested that she'd no right to call my fellow-drinkers 'low-lifers'. She nodded, 'Maybe I am being hard on them. Your real low-lifer would be someone content to sit and sup tea in a public lavatory.' I'd told her the anecdote about Death having called at the Bum Boutique and it had gone down a treat – quicker even than the Titanic.

All in all this visit was proving to be as about as relaxing as had been my ascent in yon creaking coffin they call a lift. 'Okay, folks, this floor for grouses, groans, and girns. Don't forget to visit our sob-spot for a right good greet. Next floor, complaints, censures, beefs and bellyaches . . . Stand clear of the gates, please. Sonny, keep your dabs off this here emergency button.'

The bell rang and I rose to my feet as if I was scared they'd change their mind and declare an extension to our visit. Rhona had been in the middle of something really interesting and was now shrewdly observing that 'houses won't get off their bricks and walk to you – you've got to go and – ' Damn, that bell, just when I'd been starting to get into things. Around me the good Scottish husbands had risen to their feet too, and were to be seen planting sedate Scottish (who's looking?) kisses on their respective spouses' cheeks. My attempt to join the pecking order had been restrained by an upheld hand. 'Don't,' she hissed, 'your breath would melt iron!'

21

On the trail of Mooney while his spoor remained fresh, I checked out the Salty Dog's lounge where he was known to knock back a noggin or two before getting down to some serious boozing along in Oatlands. The joke about the lounge – it'd been nicknamed 'The Kennel' – was that it'd once been a thieves' kitchen until the thieves complained to the Sanitary Dept about the conditions in which they were expected to plot crimes. Many famous personalities had passed out in The Kennel, Benny Lynch surprisingly enough not being one of them, although every galoot who stuck a few bottles on a shelf and called himself a Gorbals Publican usually claimed that the pawky wee pugilist had been one of their own: 'Och aye, many a time your man gave us his crack, standing in the selfsame spot you're filling now, sir . . .' A punter wandering back from the forties would scarcely recognise the place, what with the fancy lighting (bulbs with shades noo, be jeez!) and, on the floor, waxcloth your feet just sank into; the walls looked much the same – like they'd been sprayed with liquid horseshit; the 'oak' beams would've been a novelty mind you, as would the service-hatch extension – it had formerly been a mere slit in the wall, hardly wider than Dan McGarvie's pay-out window. The coal fire'd been replaced by a pair of smoky paraffin heaters which excited so much coughing among the customers the place sounded like a TB ward. The coal fire, by the way, was at the centre of one of the Dog's renowned tales, for it'd been the very one into which Gimpy Lawson's gammy leg was tossed by Dykes Deacon, a Toonheid hardman. As the leg burned Deacon is said to've growled after the panicking Gimpy who was hopping for his life to the door: 'That's jist for starters, ya bastard – I'll be back for the rest of ye later!'

I drew a blank in the Kennel: Mooney wasn't there, nor had he been seen earlier. Hatchet Hannah and Chibber Freeland were present though, and making it known by their singing of a raucous ditty which Freddy Green was doing his best to shush since the song drew its inspiration from Harry Moffat's spinal protuberance:

> Where did Harry get his hump?
> Where did Harry get his hump?
> Was it oan the Govan Ferry
> Fae a Dublin dromedary?
> Aye, that's where Harry
> Got his hump.

From a murky corner, cave-dark, where fags flared then faded and furtive eyes blinked on and off, the stupendously ugly kisser of Jake Mannion darted forth to put the bite on me. His tactics rarely varied and hard listening was called for or you'd miss the pitch. First the handshake, accompanied by a Masonic rigmarole of knuckle tweaking and palm sliding; this followed by an overt try at reducing your mitt to pulped bone, this pressure intended to convey the hearty honesty of the man. Next the patter: 'Tammy Clay – son of Shiny Shoes, the man who broke the bank of Jake McGarvie, lend us a quid.'

179

I gave'm the 'I'm skint' sign which is mainly done with a slow lift of the shoulders and a rueful expression. The handgrip increased but I managed to wrest my mitt free. He diverted his annoyance by plucking the bunnet from Keith Kinsale's bald napper and chucking it across the lounge. It cuffed auld Ned Sheldrake's empty tumbler from the table and sent it crashing to the floor. Ned, who until then had been peaceably lost in the smoky dream of his pipe flared up like a mini-volcano, scattering ashes and sparks as he shouted across. 'Ya silly fucker, ye.' Mannion gave'm the finger then began to use Kinsale's head for a bongo drum, slapping his hands on it, and none too lightly at that. Kinsale, who was obviously stoned out of his gourd, merely smirked at the maltreatment and simpered, 'See, there y'are. Telt ye it wid turn tae rain . . .'

I went through to the bar. It was plunging and pitching like a runaway roller-coaster. Wall-to-wall bedlam. Paddy Cullen was there, sat at the doms table and looking cracking in his deepsea diver's suit, with a bottle of stout cooling in the snow-filled helmet at his feet. 'Hey, Tam,' he shouted, 'draw up a body and sit doon.' He gave me a wave and seemed surprised when the three of us waved back. No sign of Mooney. In the lavvy there was this punter leaning his back against the tiles while water dripped from an overhead cistern onto his turnip. He peered at me through slitted eyes. 'Lo, son. Helluva night, eh? Nae sign of that bloody bus yet?'

Back in the bar's uproar I put the message out for Mooney's home address. Leave it to the Sooside Mafioso: before I'd time to sink a pint, back came the FOUR places he was definitely staying at. A harder one this time: what was his favourite Saturday-night watering hole? In no time at all I'd the choice of half a dozen boozers. Well, thinking and drinking never really mix do they?

The Oatlands drinking fraternity proved to be a suspicious lot.

Barmen who watched too much *Eliott Ness* had me down for undercover fuzz or maybe a glimmerbrain who packed a blade and a grudge. The punters mostly tuned out right away, or gave me bum steers. Eventually though I got lucky. 'Aye, what's yours?' a barman challenged. I trotted out my question. His eyes fleered, then with his elbow he nudged one of his mates, a beefy guy with a mane of white hair which was so intricately piled on his head that it seemed a stray thought might cause it to avalanche. 'Sammy, d'you know a baldy barber name of Mooney?' Sammy put a hand on his hip, camping it up something rotten and in sugary tones, eyelids flapping, he cooed in a voice that would've made Liberace sound like Lee Marvin, 'No, but I know a hairy stoker called Wullie!'

The drinkers at the bar played pass the snigger. I bought a pint and lit a fag. Some Saturday night this was shaping out to be. Where was Mooney? In a boozer with a Vat 69 or in a sickbed with a Fahrenheit 103°? What if the old bugger was selfish enough to croak on me? It'd be hopeless trying to wrest my loot from his mourning relations. No, it was better that he was hale'n hearty, even if he was gilding his tonsils at my expense. In one of my worry-centres a teleprinter with a direct line to Jeremiah began to clack. The tickertape spewing from the doom machine bore a sombre forecast concerning my future – the consensus being that I was running out of it at an alarming rate.

Something was nudging me. I glanced down. A wee greybeard was there. 'Hey, big fella, you looking for Pat Mooney, works as a barber down the Scabby?' I nodded. 'Well, he disnae drink in here any mair so he disnae.' I nodded again. The midget showed me his empty tumbler; I had another one filled for'm. He nodded his thanks then named the pub where I'd find Mooney. 'Aye, just across the bridge yonder – cannae miss it. Saw'm in there aboot hauf'n'oor ago.'

He could've been fannying me along but I decided to buy it. With my collar jerked up and my hands stuffed into my jacket pockets, so's I'd still have'm should they snap off at the wrists I went out past Shawfield Stadium. No duggies in there tonight, the action being over at White City. I hoped Mooney hadn't gone there. A mugs game, the dogs. The fact that the skinny bastards started from traps was warning enough. I trudged across the bridge into Bridgeton. Enemy territory this. The old stamping grounds of the Norman Conks, the Fleet, and the San Toy; Eastend gangs who used to come across the Clyde in pre-Sillito days to mix it with the Beehives and other Southern tribes. Nowadays this was Tongs territory. A faint tremor travelled my bones. The Eastend on a Saturday night was no place for a pacific Soosider like myself.

Mooney wasn't in the pub; what's more, nobody'd ever heard of'm. It was your basic boozer, cheery enough staff, but the regulars kept giving me that cold eye reserved for strangers. As I swallowed lager I figured it would be too late to get back to The Scabby for a last pint with Cullen. That doomladen hour when they 'bung the barrels and the landlord snarls' was fast approaching. I could, of course, hit an illicit tipple in the Mod Bar. I grinned when I recalled Gus Hagen's reason for calling his joint The Moderation Bar. 'It's so you can say when your doc asks if you're a heavy drinker, "No me, doctor – I drink in Moderation".' Cullen would probably be there by now. Now that I thought about it, what'd that crazy bass been doing in the diving gear? I frowned. Here I was, solo-supping in a cruddy Eastside pub. I'd scarcely parked my arse on the Big Wheel of Fun before they begun nailing it down for the night. Off with the lights. Saturday's kaput – a box of spent matches. My own fault, of course; always place your own bets. The golden rule.

I was maybe four gulps from the bottom of my glass when into the pub limped none other than Horace 'Dicky' Harte. The 'dicky heart' pun's right enough mind you, for the wee man's clock's about as reliable as the kind you get in Paddy's Market for a halfcrown and change back. The nickname, though, stems from a more obvious foible – Horace whistles. Horace whistles a lot; all the time in fact when he's not rabbitting he's making with the cheep-cheeps. Aye, quite the wee canary is Horace, though tonight in that long snow-dappled coat with its grey fur collar he looks more jackdawish. He was also wearing a classy scare-piece, a choice bit of wiggery; you would never've guessed that just before leaving the house he dunked his turnip in a bucketful of tar.

Approaching the counter, Horace dunted snowflakes from his coatsleeves. The coat itself was exactly as I'd imagined the clerk's looked like in yon Gogol story before he decided to trash it and have a new one made. So pleased was I to see Horace that I shrank behind a pillar, hoping that even with his streaked 'granny' specs he wouldn't spot me in the gantry mirror. I studied him as he began to remove his gloves then, changing his mind, quickly rolled them to his wrists again – but not quickly enough: something purplish and nasty was spawning on the backs of his hands. It had to be admitted, though, he looked a lot healthier than when I last saw'm – he was good for another fortnight at least. Heavier too he was, well past the seven stones mark. And his hepatitis looked to've cleared up a treat.

Horace Dicky Harte was a medical phenomenon. His flayed body had played host to more bugs than a modelhouse tick. When last we met he claimed to be suffering from an exotic disease called – what was it again? – aye, 'Adiposis Dolorosa', something like that. Anyway, the malady was supposed to be a condition that made fat people feel melancholy. When I'd pointed out to Horace that he wasn't exactly shipping much lard around, he nodded, 'That's just the point – skinny folks like me have nothing to fight it with!'

No sooner had Horace clambered up onto a stool than his obsessive chirruping began. 'Whistle, and I'll come tae ye, my lad . . .' A barman approached. 'A vodka with some orange, please, a half-pint of your heavy; and a packet of potato crisps, plain.' It was as if from the trashy workings of a tranny, already mouldering on a rubbish dump, the mellifluous voice of Richard Burton had unaccountably blossomed forth. But believe it or not the speaker was none other than Horace. Not only was he big in the canary world, he also packed a gold-lined voicebox. Horace had been born of decent working-class parents. Glaswegians both, the salt of the earth, the Hartes were folks who didn't shrink from bending the stiffening lead of so-called 'received English' to their needs. But look what they'd got for their efforts, those socialist paragons – laddy-bloody-lah, Horace, that's what. He did it for badness of course, just to jive up his parents with his BBC enunciation. It was a rave though, listening to'm picking over his vocabulary – a mere saucerful of words – with such fastidious concern. No wonder the barman, having served'm, was edging away from the wee man and his well-modulated patter about how after catching a cab to Shawfield he'd found the stadium 'not to be functioning'.

'Look what the wind has blown in,' Horace suddenly exclaimed, not so blind after all, as he located me in the gantry mirror and by a familiar puckering of his boil-scarred snout indicated that the find narked him very much indeed, thank you. It served the little creep right, poking around in mirrors at his age. As yet reluctant to brave the third dimension we chatted barbershop-fashion, yon oddly artificial duologue in which you and your clipper watch the lips of the phantom pair in the mirror, eavesdropping, so to speak, on their flannel about the cuddies, boxing, and fitba. How bloody boring it was, I assured Horace, to bump into'm again, and should he feel like having a fatal stroke or a cardiac arrest, why go right ahead, no offence taken; the facial fuzz was a great idea which he might well care to extend to the rest of his gong, thereby screening us from its simian offence. Naturally, this was all conveyed by tonal inflexion while my two-dimensional mouth got on with the cowardly conventions of life. It should be noted though that my approach was languid, bored even; 'Lo, Horace, didnae know you there wae the whiskers. How goes it?' That kind of stuff.

His gloved hand stroked his chin. 'Did yours curl up and die, then?' he asked, referring sarkily to bygone days when I'd let my chin do its own thing; not, in Rhona's judgement, a great success. Phyllis opined that it made me look like a horse with its feeding bag on which, in her opinion, was a considerable improvement. Since Horace and I both utterly detested one another our chit-chat soon fizzled out and once more he took up his whistling.

I first met Horace when I hung about the Chameleon Bar, an upcity pub which was one of the first into C & W music. That was around the time when singing cowboys drifted in from the electronic prairies, rhinestoned dudes all riding the gravy train which had been set in motion by the Carter family. I'd been a regular punter at the Chameleon just when the old haunting tone of American folk music was giving way to the voice of protest (as if Woodie Guthrie's life hadn't been one long, agonised howl at the world!) Singers like Dylan and Baez had joined the pantheon of photographs which covered the pub's walls, but I continued to dig the old stalwarts like Jimmie Rodgers, Woodie Guthrie, Leadbelly, Betty Lomax and, of course, Hank Williams and George Jones. From them you got stuff that resonated with hard-times America, a tonal bleakness that spoke of a world of wet freightyards, hobo woodsmoke, and night trains coming down.

185

We used to have some good rap sessions in the old Chameleon, me'n Ciggy McQueen, Benny Spencer, Frank Lipton and Caz Carruthers. Horace had hung around our company like a sort of pestilent mascot, a bug to tread on when life got boring. It has to be admitted that I'd stamped on'm more often than anyone else had.

Maybe to shut off his mouth-music and to allay my curiosity, I asked Horace what'd become of the old gang. Did they still jar in the Chameleon? He slipped down from his stool and reluctantly, I did likewise and came around the pillar to meet him. Since halitosis was a marked feature of his three-dimensional entity I breathed shallower than a guppy and stuck away my lager so rapidly my Adam's apple must've been a blur. In that incredible plummy voice of his, his vodka'n orange clutched in a hand that was now stripped of its glove to reveal the opening spoors of a dermatological newcomer, he explained that the old folk-train's lum had been belching dreamsmoke and had eventually been derailed by a succession of drug busts. All had not been lost, however, since the selfsame choo-choo was now to be found stationed in a rowdy bar up the Possil. Yes, most of the old crowd were to be found there, although Mountain Maxwell, the hum-dinger-twelve-stringer, had 'changed instruments', a coy way of saying that he'd snuffed it – a harp for a guitar. The big man'd been taken out by a massive stroke. Who? Ciggy McQueen? Yes, he was still hanging around. Benny Spencer and Lipton too. Caz Carruthers, though had gone Stateside and the last heard of him was that he was doing his DJ for a radio station in Seattle or somesuch place. Horace now went on to explain that he himself only looked in occasionally; since his last op he'd had to cut back on the booze. Hastily, I smacked my glass on the counter. 'Have to split man, too bad we didn't bump into each other earlier. What?'

'Why don't you come to the shindig?'

'Shindig?'

He nodded and the dead crow on his noggin all but shook loose. 'The lads always have a bit of a do after the pub shuts. Ciggy'll be there, Lipton too I imagine.'

'Where's it at?'

'Up Possilpark. Be a great night.'

'You going then?'

When he nodded I didn't think to ask myself why anyone'd invite typhoid to a party. Horace was a reminder to all that life is a risky biz – having him in close proximity to you was as chancy as playing tig in a leper colony. For the first time on that screwed-up Saturday I began to get positive vibes. Maybe a few live embers could be coaxed from the ashes after all. I began to get really hepped up about seeing Ciggy McQueen, Lipton, et al. It'd most probably involve a carry-out though. I put this to Horace and he nodded. 'We'll go halfers for the booze, all right?'

'You're on,' I said, and on impulse shook his Martian mitt where the purplish lumplings seemed definitely to be multiplying.

22

Heading westwards in the company of a whistling dwarf, my stomach dancing from the stink of him, my disquiet mounting at the taxi-meter's hyper-activity, I found that the compiler of this monochrome evening had prepared an elegant coincidence, arranging for it to flower at Glasgow Cross. Our cab, which seemed to've a turtle instead of a tiger in its tank, had just settled for a quick snooze at a set of traffic lights when an ambulance giving it the crisis bit – flashing lights and yowling siren – came breenging from the Saltmarket, shot across the mouths of London Road and the Gallowgate, and went wailing up the High Street. Immediately behind the ambulance there came a hearse, complete with snuff box, and going at a fair lick for that normally sedate vehicle. Our driver grinned from his smoky compartment. 'Business must be slack, eh?' I was smiling at that one when I saw, following the hearse, a black Volkswagen Beetle. Although its roof was thick with snow its number plates had been cleared, and it was because of this I was able to confirm that it was none other than Eddie Carlyle's car. Eddie and his mother'd been attending the Jesus Jamboree at the Tent Halls. Right now they were heading in the wrong direction for home but being kind and thoughtful Christians they were no doubt giving someone a lift.

I'm not too superstitious, but I could've definitely done without that bizarre nocturnal convoy. The same goes only double I suppose for the victim in the ambulance, or the bod in the box, assuming that there was one. It was really far-out. Why should a hearse be going like the clappers through the streets of Glasgow at this time of night? Definitely one for the 'ideas notebook'; 'While they tried to assure him that he was okay, that he was going to make it, Clay, squinting through the ambulance's rear window, saw that they were about to be overtaken by a hearse . . .'

Well, we're in that fix from day one – all of us, right? Nowt to be done about it. Could've done without the heavy reminders but. Prompted by the sight of the ambulance Horace laid off his Ronnie Ronalding to announce the forthcoming event of his revolutionary hip-joint operation. I wasn't sure if by 'revolution-ary' he meant that he was going to be fitted with a revolving hip; or that the surgeons intended to circle him on rollerskates while they were wielding their scalpels; or that he was to become the beneficiary of some medical neo-wizardry. Who cared? Hearses and hip-joints were hardly a turn-on for the generation of an upbeat party mood.

'I'll be one of the first in Scotland to get it,' Horace boasted.

Hip-hip-hoo-fuck'n-ray!

Let's say it as is – it wasn't so much having witnessed the meatwagon and the corpse-crate charging through Glasgow Cross that was bugging me as Argyle Street crackled blackly under our tyres. No, it was that bloody Beetle that was getting to me, the way it'd ran so darkly across my path (can a snow-smothered car do anything 'darkly'? Aye, if it's intent I'm getting at) with its moral backspray which'd all but doused the wee fire of optimism I'd been blowing, flame by flame, to life.

'What're you playing at, boy?' a voice suddenly asked inside my whoozy head. It was Jeremiah, of course, crudely impersonating

'Bunsen' Turner, my old chemistry teacher, a man with frosty mandibles that squeaked when he was moved to verbal rage – about once every three minutes. This'd been the very man who'd told me after I'd ballsed up some cosmically significant piece of test-tubery that I'd never amount to more than a 'pig's fart in a cracked bottle', a vulgarity that'd been received with much chortling from those bright sparks who'd somehow or other managed to hatch crystals from a solution of copper sulphate. What was I supposed to be doing? Jeremiah wanted to know. I mentally shrugged. I was just going to see a few pals, y'know, to shake hands with yesterday. Where was the harm in that? I knew in my heart of hearts that it was a futile pursuit, about as pointless as cheating at Solitaire. It's an odd thing how the gift of recall so quickly degenerates into nostalgia. The neurologists know all about what's going on inside that thought termitarium we call the brain; any day now they'll announce the chemical's identity, you know, the one that can remind you that your mother once wore a hat which so strongly resembled a snail that it slowed down her thought processes. The act of remembering is nothing to get mystical about. After all, it's merely the reactivation of neurological patterns laid down in the cortex and –

'Chuck that!' snaps the voice in my head. 'Don't try to snow us with that quasi-medical mush. Let's face some home truths, Clay; you're a moral skunk, a feculent fuckup of a man. This diseased midget by your side, this homunculus, is by comparison as pure as the – '

'For chrissake, Horace,' I grumbled as I stared out at the driven snow, where is this fuck'n place?'

For some time now we'd been zipping here'n there amongst pearly Possil streets with a blizzard of debt raging in the fare's meter and a driver who was pursuing a topography that'd been mapped by his own mercenary mind and which bore no correspondence with the urban reality. (I was sure that this was the second time I'd seen the Blind Asylum go by). We were definitely retracing our tyremarks, had in fact been doing so since Horace's original guess as to the whereabouts of the shindig had backfired.

'We must've overran it,' he whined. 'I know the street is after a red furniture shop and a surgery.' When I uttered an oath he complained that everything looked the same in the snow. Different, he meant. How could things look the same? 'Try the next one, driver,' he instructed in that fruity voice of his. 'I think I'm starting to get my bearings.' So long as his meter kept hoovering up a bob a minute, the driver didn't object to skittering from one location to another, in fact, he seemed more than willing to explore every backstreet, sidestreet, and frontstreet Possilpark had to offer. I should've known better, allowing myself to be driven off to an address as vague as the one supplied by Horace as we clambered into the cab, for after naming a street, he'd added: 'At least I think it's called that, but I'll know as soon as we get there.'

This Hubris business the old Greeks went on about, this was me getting a double dose of the stuff. I could almost hear them, yon Olympus mob, sitting around in their nightshirts and scoffing grapes. 'See this Clay fella, no playin the game so he's no. Wife in hospital and him nookying around like he's single or something. No giving a monkey's. Time we put a spoke in his wheel . . .'

Aye, they'd done that all right – and how; trapped inside a money-mincer on a Saturday night with an amnesiac dwarf!

The longer I sat there the more I got to feel like a participant in one of those arty-farty movies they show up the Cosmo. Le Taxi they'd've called this one with maybe Jean Gabin as the cab driver, myself played by Alain Delon (well, why not – it's my movie!), and with José Ferrer recreating his Lautrec role as Horace. The film,

191

as is the wont of yon avant-garde guff, would've been a boring mile or so of speckled celluloid which depicted nothing more than a repeated shot of a taxi being pelted by luminous snowballs as it entered then reversed from the same street. While this is going on Gabin grins evilly at his clients through the rear mirror; Horace Lautrec, whistling furiously, goggles through the patch he's rubbed clear in the steamy window; Delon, meanwhile, is seen metamorphosing into a fares meter, a nasty metallic business of which the first indications are the ghosts of rapidly multiplying numbers flickering across his eyeballs. Slowly, but not all that slowly, the meter was turning to solid gold; there was about half a week's wages in there now. And it wasn't as if we could cut our losses by getting out, paying off Onassis, then hoofing it to wherever the ding-dong was. Wandering around Saracen Cross with a pokeful of beercans was about as safe as Haffey's goalmouth, Wembley '61. There were gangs hereabouts that made the Hell's Angels look like mobile monks.

The carry-out bag in Horace's lap rustled as he leaned forward. 'Down here, I think, driver.' We went lurching down a street that looked as if the Luftwaffe had only just left it after a highly successful bombing raid. On a gapsite between two crumbling tenements a bonfire was blazing and lethal-looking kids galloped around it. These mini-Goths were skelping each other with snowballs, while others, seemingly finding this pastime to be too tame were heaving bricks and knuckles of iron at each other. Already, snowballs were cracking against the cab's windows as it hirpled over the snow-covered debris which gave the street its sinister lumpy appearance. On its back near the bonfire lay the shell of a Hillman Minx; snow melted from its underparts as a small brat, the perfect sociological model of your multi-deprived urbanite, was being compelled by his hooligan genes to give the Minx's exhaust pipe laldy with a length of steel

tubing. Graffiti, the psoriasis of the slums, besmirched every wall
– threats and more threats, the territorial claims of gangland. We
lurched past jiggered shops, their windows boarded up, though
some of the planking had been swiped, probably by the bonfire
merchants. Since the only tenement windows that could be seen
were bedroom ones, they were mostly unlit, giving these demi-
buildings a deserted appearance. At the bottom of the street but –
it must've been the swanky end! – a few brave xmas trees glowed
here'n there. Every now'n again a curtain was tweaked aside as
tenementers checked out what was no doubt the rare phenomenon of a cab in their midst.

Obeying Horace's instructions, the taxi driver brought the cab
to a halt. In the close opposite us a nervy gas-mantle jittered light
along the flayed walls. Snowballs continued to thud against the
taxi. I glanced through the rear window; the apaches had
multiplied which made me nervous. What if they'd tired of
burning wood and were on the lookout for a more novel
combustible? The same thought must've paid a call on our cab
driver for while I took it that he was raking around for a sack large
enough to hold our fare, he, in fact, brought out a truncheon,
a heavy-looking fuzz-issue noggin-tapper. This he placed by his
side. Interesting.

'I'll just check it out,' said Horace as he opened the door and
was on the point of taking his leave.

I grabbed at his arm. 'Check what?'

He blinked at me indignantly then pointed to a lit window,
one-up-left. 'That's it. Best to make sure there's been no change
of venue. Take us ages to get another cab.'

I nodded; it made sense. Horace stepped from the cab then
began to fumble with the carry-out bag. From it he withdrew a
paper-wrapped half-bottle. 'Your whisky,' he said as he passed it
into me. I took it and stuck it away. The driver was taking a beady

interest in the proceedings. I jived my thumb on my index finger. 'The moolah, Horace. We agreed to split the fare, right?'

At that moment the little sod was caught in the vortex of some well-aimed snowballs – one of the missiles almost hooked the specs from his face, while another one nearly had it away with his wig. 'I'll fully reimburse you when you come up.' More direct hits flared on his back as he scurried to the closemouth. He paused there, then turning, one arm raised to ward off the salvo of incoming snowballs, he shouted: 'I'll give you the okay from the window. Keep watching . . .' Swatting snow from his coat, he legged it up the close and had soon vanished into its murky flickerings.

While I kept tabs on the window, awaiting the summons to Joyville, the driver abruptly demanded his fare. I'd no choice but to hand over the best part of next week's housekeeping money. I think the bugger was even expecting a tip – a rap around the earhole would've been more like it. The fleecing moment had unhooked my attention from the window and as my gaze returned to it I was just in time to see its curtain twitch back into place. It must've been Horace giving me the come-up wave. Not that it mattered, for the driver – an impulsive chap – had decided to get shot of me. After an increase in the bombardment (some of the thrown objects were definitely not snowballs), he snapped: 'Right, pal, that's it – eff-off!' Some gratitude; I'd given him enough for a downpayment on two flank musquash fur-coats and, yet, here he was – 'D'you hear me, china?' His lifting of the fuzz-stick was, I thought, a bit over-dramatic. Mind you, I could've done with that skull-lumper when, seconds later, after hitting the pavement at speed, I nevertheless got everything those multi-deprived morons could bring to hand, snowballs, stank lids, boulders, you name it. Cursing them on the hoof, I fled up the close.

As I jouked around the close's elbow and prepared to launch myself up the first flight of stairs, I scarcely gave the driver a thought, though it was on the cards that his cab would be reduced to a metallic smear and he'd end up having his balls barbecued – one can but pray. I glanced at the nameplate on the door to my left: J. Frost. Very apt that was for there was a draught, cold enough to freeze the plums from an Eskimo, raking down the stairs from the smashed window on the half-landing.

But all was not bleakness and blight: a youthful slum-ite on a creative jag had sprayed a spider's web on the wall, its silver threads cast in just the right position to catch the glances of upwards plodders. A niftily executed job this web was, complete with the Reverend Humphrey Weaver, himself, who squatted at the heart of the matter in his spider disguise, dreaming sermons. No doubt chuffed by this artistic effort Possil's Picasso'd gone on to depict the intricacies of the female pudendum and its interaction with the male reamer, a conjunction not consummated and which gave rise to the risible notion that the randy sprayer'd been interrupted by a parental clout on the lug just as he was getting to the tickly bit: coitus interruptus! The stairhead bog had an occupant who, judging from his pained grunts and groans, was pressing hard to relieve himself of a jaggy brick. I hoped for his sake that he'd a gasmask in there with'm. Holding my breath until I was by the cludgie door I went up the second flight of stairs. The murals here were the work of lesser artists, humdrum hooligans who'd been unable to raise their game above gangland conceits.

The landing, lit by a poisonous-looking gas-mantle, would've been just the job for a Beckett play: main prop – a bucketful of ashes, tea leaves, vegetable peelings (played, perhaps by Nicol Williamson) stands on the gritty concrete, midstage; the landing has three doors, two of which – the left-hand and the central one, create the impression that they've been copiously vomited upon, then clear-varnished; the remaining door, on the right-hand side is painted a violent ox-blood colour, and has a terrazzo doorstep – a symbol of tenement affluence in the early fifties. This door is half-open and from within the flat can be heard the strains of C & W music, in this instance, Johnny Cash singing 'Orange Blossom Special'. Clay approaches the door and stands hesitantly before it. He looks dishevelled, his jacket splotched with the damp imprints of effectively-aimed snowballs. He pushes his longish hair from his brow then draws the paper-wrapped half-bottle from his pocket. He knocks on the door . . .

I liked the music, but not the vibes, coming from the flat. The nameplate said Pike, a not over-friendly handle but, come to think of it, I'd once known this guy on the railway, name of Broozer, who'd turned out to be a fairy. Nobody seemed to hear my knocks so I knuckled the door a bit harder. Johnny Cash had started on 'The Long Black Veil' which was a shade on the morbid side for my taste but at least it was quieter. Still no reaction to my knockings. No Ciggy McQueen, no Benny Spencer rushing out to greet me, to exclaim with hearty shoulder slaps: 'Tam Clay – you poxy midden! How goes it? Long time, no see . . .'

I heard the stairhead bog being flushed then the sounds of its bolt getting waggled free. From the sighs and groans of him, I figured that no fit guy full of the joys of life was about to breeze into view. And I was proved right: the ruins of what must've been a strapping man in his prime limped onto the landing. His duds were all over the place, the elasticated waistband of his drawers curled over his unbelted trousers, his fly-zip was down, and his stained grey cardigan was buttoned out of sequence. From his chest, as if it housed antiquated machinery, came sinister crepitations, a sort of death-rattle rehearsal. Dead, but lacking the sense to lie down. How wrong can you get? The greybeard proved to be a spunky old sod. He came closer and I got a whiff of him, a real nose-wrinkler, strong on piss, gumrot, and unwashed oxters. 'Is that the bells already?' he wheezed and reached out a mucky claw to touch the half-bottle. 'Don't even mind of Christmas going by.' I drew the bottle away from his covetous attempts to take hold of it. 'Whaur's your lump of coal?' he now enquired. Just in time he caught his putrid pants as they were about to plunge anklewards. He hauled them up with his right hand while with his other one he waved me into the flat. The lobby was in darkness except for a wedge of light thrown by a half-open door. On a seedy carpet a grey cat drifted like a patch of moving fog. 'She walks the night in a long dark veil . . .' Johnny Cash was singing behind a closed door. From the room within I could also hear the sounds of voices and laughter.

The greybeard signalled for me to follow him to the half-opened door of a room which housed either a TV set or a radio going full blast, 'C'mon intae ma nest and see if you can fix me a better picture.' I followed him into a crypt of a place, so cold it would've made a corpse shudder. And the stink! A real skunkbox it was. The room's wallpaper was being devoured by a roving fungus and a chunk of ceiling plaster near the curtained window had collapsed to expose the lathes. It wouldn't have surprised me one bit had a rat stuck its head through that hole and waved a white flag at us. On a bulky dressing-table, dimly duplicating themselves in a cracked and dusty mirror, were piles of paperback Westerns and boxing mags. The telly was on a low bedside table surrounded by enough pillboxes and medicine bottles to cure the sick of Bombay. The stark iron bed on which several heavy coats served as additional blankets looked as if it'd been party to a lot of dying. The old man shucked his slippers then with an assortment of creaking noises – either the bed or his skeleton was coming apart – he got under the coats and covers. I nodded towards the gasfire in the corner, a toothless-looking specimen due to several of its chalks being missing. 'You'd be better wae that on, auld yin.'

He shook his head. 'They'll no let me, son.' His puny shoulders trembled. 'Cauld enough tae kill a husky so it is — and they'll no let me.' He waved an almost transparent hand towards the flickering TV set, 'C'mon, then, do your stuff!'

I began to jiggle with the wire hoop aerial that stood on top of the telly. The set was so ancient it was miracle enough that it was generating wobbly images of a sort of electronic limboland in which faces, clouds, and smoke writhed in spasm after spasm across its stourie screen. An old tatty yesterday, all blotched skies and speckled motion, jittered into view. Writhing clumps of shadow divided then divided again into the darting tadpoles that become people. A king, or one of those feather-brained ambassadors who crowed and preened themselves on the dungheap of a pre-war Europe, was to be seen at a racetrack surrounded by sycophants. A jockey, so tiny he looked like a silk-clad puppet, had his elfin hand pumped by the visiting dignitary. The camera lied, blatantly burlesquing motion, giving such a froth of speed to each event that it was small wonder that Europe itself was dashed to pieces the very same year. I shifted the aerial. A beard sprang from nowhere onto the VIP's face and he developed a sudden limp. An obese doll with medals as large as lollipops on its chest shot from a model train. Traffic spluttered around. A carpet unrolled its tongue. The ambassador strutted through the murk to disarm a smiling traitor with a handshake, then both of them popped into a cavernous car. Black flowerings of people on the wet streets . . .

'That's a loada shite,' said the greybeard.

I thumbed a button. Ice-skating; not a bad picture. 'That'll dae me,' said the auld yin with a lecherous grin. 'I like seein their wee knickers.'

He raised two nicotine-fouled fingers to his lips and mimed a smoking motion. 'Give's a gasper, son.' I held out my pack and the fly old bugger grabbed three ciggies from it. 'Seeing's I missed Christmas, eh?' He winked then made with a grin that starkly exposed his beige gums. 'And while you're aboot it,' he added, 'a couple of strikers, as well.' From the box he clawed about six or seven matches and stuffed them into his cardigan pocket. Keen to get away from the stink of the place, I moved towards the door. 'Mind, noo,' he said and looked as happy as a pig in shit, 'if you've the mind to first fit me, you know where I bide.' He did something really loopy now: raising his finger to tap his temple he then pointed with it to the wall through which music faintly leaked. His meaning was evident – clearly he considered the shindiggers next door to be prime candidates for Rubberland. I left him drooling over the gyrations of a thick-thighed ice-maiden.

In the lobby the grey cat, having decided to gatecrash the party, lined itself up alongside me as I paused for a moment to make myself presentable. I hand-skiffed a smudge of whitewash from the sleeve of my jacket, finger-combed my damp hair, then with the half-bottle held palm-upwards in a manner I hoped would look indicative of friendship and generosity, I opened the door and with a slightly overdone bacchanal swagger, breezed into the party.

23

There was a party in that room all right; the only trouble was that it looked like a lynching party. It consisted of four men in shirt sleeves who were playing at cards in such an up-pouring of smoke you would've thought that their table was on fire. A dog was present, too – living proof that the wild wolf was anything but extinct in Scotland. On initial impact the room looked like an ongoing collison between a brewer's truck and a secondhand furniture van. Beercans and bottles were everywhere – on the drinks cabinet, around the Dansette record player, amongst the xmas cards that lined the mantelpiece, on the dresser, where for the second time that day I saw King Billy mounted on his Boyne beast, not a picture this time, but a small porcelain statuette. More beercans crowded the table, they stood amidst the choked ashtrays, cig packs, and the tinfoil containers carry-out snacks had been eaten from. Then there were the glasses, some empty, some half-full, not forgetting the money – more bread than I'd seen this side of a bank vault.

I don't have the maths for it, but take my word, Time's lethal trot can be slowed, maybe even stopped. For that's what happened when I stepped into that room – Time was syphoned from it, motion too. Like a waxwork tableau depicting variations on a theme of evil, the gambling quartet sat transfixed around the table. One of them, an immense man wearing a dark blue shirt bestrewn with stars, had been frozen mid-deal, this arrested moment allowing me, almost at leisure, to see how small and dainty the cardpack was made to look in his shovel-like hands. Beside him, with a neb on'm like a shoehorn, a man sat motionless in the act of counting a wad of dough; another card player had been petrified as he'd reached for his lighter; the remaining guy had his forefinger raised in a hectoring manner which suggested he'd been making some point with considerable intent before my interruption of it. As for myself, although adrenalin washed through my system, pounding glands and yelling RUN! I just stood there as fartless as those Pompeian punters had been when Vesuvius greeted them by doffing his hat. The grey moggie, of course, had skedaddled via the door and could be heard pelting to safety along the lobby carpet. To the accompaniment of a low rumbling noise from the cur's throat, it was left to the giant with the shirt-of-many-planets to break the spell by rising (it seemed he'd never stop getting up) to his feet and lumbering towards me. This was the signal for everything to unfreeze again, my asshole especially, as the dog dashed to within knee-cropping distance. But this was only a half-started motion, Time being played at the wrong speed, the very opposite, in fact to the auld guy's telly. For now events crawled frame by slow frame into existence. 'It aint me, babe, it aint me you're lookin for, babe . . .' Cash was growling in a wound-down voice that seemed to be coming from his boots. An instruction crawled from Starshirt's mouth and the Alsatian dog's intention of snacking on one of my kneecaps was stymied. It stopped, backed away a pace, and although it was still horripilating with malice it sheathed its thwarted fangs. Another instruction sent the animal loping past me to take up guard duty by the door. The dog's master, his flabby pecs lobbing the stars

201

around, tramped in my direction. He stood around six-four although if he claimed seven foot I wasn't about to dispute it. So fiercely cropped was his hair that it dappled his skull like iron filings – you could've sharpened a ploughshare on a dome like that. All in all, his gudgeon-like mouth, and a sort of black energy flickering around his eyes, had the effect of making a bronto-saurus look cuddly by comparison. He stopped within about a foot of me, then, slowly tilting his enormous torso, he brought his face close to mine, rocking me with his tartan breath. He asked two very basic questions: 'Who the fuck're you?' and, 'How d'you get in here?'

It's difficult to explain to a giant that you've been duped by a dwarf. The best thing is to stick to the basic facts, the most basic of these being that while in search of a party you'd been stupid enough to wander into the wrong pad. Apologies were, naturally, called for and these I spouted in abundance with what, I hoped, was just the right mixture of humour, self-denigration, and contrition. A bad mistake to make. Jings, aye. The auld man'd let me in. He'd been doon at the lavvy, you see. Asked me in to fix his telly. No way would I've come in otherwise. No siree. Definitely not. I must've got the wrong close number. Easily done, what with the kiddiewinks having some innocent fun by battering me with snowballs and stanklids. Sorry, sorry, aye, really sorry, big man. Aye, and when I laid my hands on that wee bastard, Horace, he'd be a whole lot sorrier. He'd obviously set me up – gone through the close's backdoor and got off his mark. The mystery cab tour had been his way of rooking me. Now I thought about it, didn't the wee shitpot actually live up in the Possil? He'd decided, it seemed, to make me pay for those past insults, had been nursing a long-held grudge. And now this, his pièce de resistance, getting me lumbered with what looked like a quartet of Possil's choicest psychopaths.

I could be wrong, though. It was possible that Horace'd been devoured boots to wig by Blightfang, here, the moment he'd planted his size threes on the lobby carpet. For all I knew, he could be hanging like a skinned weasel in the scullery from a meathook. The old nutter in the bedroom might at this very moment be spooning, as a treat, Le Cerveaux de Horace onto the moggie's food-dish. No such luck! Horace was off and running, legging it through a snowy maze of backcourts and sidestreets with the bulk of my carry-out clutched to'm, chirrupping homewards to the security of the boulder beneath which he lived out his plague-ridden existence.

The Sky-at-Night was laughing. Was this a hopeful sign? Probably not – Peter Manuel had laughed a lot, hadn't he? Half-turning to the trio at the table he said: 'Hey boys, get a load of this: see this punter, here, you know what? – he's lost a gay'n hearty! What's your name, son? Tommy, eh?' He turned to the gamblers again. 'C'mon, where's your manners? I said, Tommy here's mislaid a party.' From the trio there arose in unison a mock 'Awwwwh.' The starry giant nodded. 'That's more like it. It's only a wee hale'n hearty but, Frankie, see if maybe it's fell doon the back of that table.' Frankie, an evil-looking sod with a scaly brow and a dot moustache actually went to the bother of physically checking before he dourly shook his head. 'Nothin here, Malky.' The big man shrugged. 'Maybe it's in wan of they pockets, Bilko'.

Bilko, wearing a white shirt and a black waistcoat began to pat his various pockets. He was a burly man with black hair sprouting extravagantly from everywhere but his head; it coated his throat'n chest, his arms, and the back of his hands, making him look like a bald panda. But the eyes behind the chunky glasses were as soulless as those of the shark I'd seen only yesterday – it seemed centuries ago – on the TV set back home. Bilko tapped one of the waistcoat's upper pockets. 'Eff all,' he said, then, suddenly, he whipped from the remaining pocket a small, square pack which he brandished aloft. 'Whadye know – eff-ell this time!'

They all fell about laughing. The stars on Malky's shirt heaved in chaos while the three men at the table collectively cracked up. I figured it might stand me in their favour if I weighed in with a few titters of my own. When the cackling had ran its course the man with the shoehorn sneezer – his pinky had resumed patrol of his flattened left nostril – was addressed by Malky. 'Anything doing up the auld trumpet, Cadge? Naw? I thought maybe we'd knocked it off there.' Malky turned to me. 'You're out of luck, son – nae party here.'

I was nearly daft enough to thank'm for trying. 'I'd best split then,' I said. 'Sorry bout the mix-up.'

He nodded while the others drank their drinks, smoked their fags, watched. I took a couple of backward steps. A throaty growl from the dog made me pause.

'Be seeing you,' Malky said.

'Ta ta,' Cadge said with a smirk.

'D-d'you think you could call your dog off?' I asked.

'Call it Off?' He shook his head. 'Naw, naw, I think it's got used to Shane'.

A cue for more laughs.

'Cadge,' Malky said, 'away'n see if faither's okay.' Cadge rose and passed us both. The dog gave a sharp bark but was quickly silenced by its master. The door squealed open as Cadge headed for the auld yin's room. Johnny Cash was droning about a lifer who kept staring at his prison's walls and of how he hoped one day to be up and over it. I was in a similar fix myself, although my problem concerned not wall-hopping but wolf-vaulting. The solution lay literally close to hand – the whisky bottle. All that was needed was a quick hip-swivel, arm up fast, bottle down even faster, and – splatt – Shane's brains everywhere. But my hips remained unswivelled. If wrestling with a wolf wasn't on then neither was Pike-grappling. He pointed to one of the battered armchairs that flanked the fireplace. 'Park yersel.' When I showed reluctance his request switched to command: 'Sit on your best features – there!'

I sat.

Cadge returned and once Shane had resumed his Cerberus role he grunted that the old man was okay then resumed his seat at the table. Pike dumped himself in the armchair opposite mine. I made a point of not glancing too often at the table for there was a hellish amount of bread on it, maybe too much to be legal. It was to be hoped that I hadn't interrupted them as they were divvying up the proceeds from a blag – if so, then I could expect to be divvied up myself. No, more likely all that table lettuce was made up from the clippings from gamblers who'd got busted and had left. Surely all the empty booze bottles and cans couldn't be down to just this foursome; they'd be paralytic by now. Pike was lighting a cheroot. When he got the thing going he resumed staring at me. I began to realise how Fay Wray must've felt when King Kong was running his inflamed peepers over her. He turned to the table. 'I'll drop oot for a bit,' he said to Bilko who was restlessly boxing a card deck. 'Give youse a chance.' His gaze swivelled back to my face and the cheroot tip flared as he took a drag.

'What's your line of toil, son?'

A nice friendly question the brontosaurus was asking. Good. We're going to have a wee pally blether about this'n that while his chums, up to their elbows in loot, slugged their booze and made gamblers' wisecracks. Maybe, before we got too settled I could take Shane for a pee-pee – there was a good-going bonfire out there I could sling the bastard into. Pike grinned when I told'm my occupation. Aye, that's right, a humble nana-packer. (The more I tried on this particular hairshirt the better I'd be able to endure it should the worst come to the worst and I was forced to take the bloody job.) The cards trio were making animal noises. Cadge, in particular was doing a witty impression of an orangutan, a a real belly-heaver, it was. Weren't we all having a real wacky time!

'A kinna funny bastard'n job that,' Pike said.

Right on the nail that was. Aye, a funny bastard'n job, right enough. Who could take bananas seriously? To prove this Bilko told a cracking joke about a nun and a green banana. You just had to laugh – even Shane was showing his teeth. If only Big Malky would chuck that staring act of his. Mentally, I smote my brow with the heel of my hand. How thick could I get? Instead of seeing my half-bottle as a potential weapon I should've been considering its use as a passport. Through the machinations of evil Captain Horace I'd been marooned on a hostile island with four savages – well, maybe 'savages' was pitching it a bit strong, although the description was apt for the dingo by the door. What had been expected of me, what they'd been waiting for, was a demonstration of friendliness. In their primitive minds whisky was an equivalent to baubles'n beads – liquid wampum, it was – they awaited its distribution. And, indeed, they would have some – have it all as a matter of fact. Then I'd be free to go on my way.

Tentatively, I held out the bottle to Malky, their chieftain. 'This magic flask, warmed by many summers; makeum warriors' hearts heapum brave . . .' I didn't come that gumph, of course, but said something more to the point: 'D'you fancy a drink?' He plucked the half-bottle from my grasp and hefted it in his meaty palm. 'Is it the good stuff you have here, Tommy? The auld usquebaugh?' I wasn't sure what kind of whisky it was for that wee bastard Horace had got the carry-out while I'd gone cab-hunting. I nodded just the same though I expected it'd be cheap rotgut of some mongrel distillery, certainly not the pedigree malt Pike seemed to've set his tastebuds on. With a friendly swing to his jowls he got to his feet and began to rip off the paper wrapping. 'See your vodka,' he said, 'no worth a fuck, ne'er it is. Ruskie hair-tonic that's – ' He stopped mid-sentence. The wrapper had fallen from the bottle which now glittered nakedly in his grasp. 'Aw, for fucksake,' Pike growled.

There it was, winking darkly in the light from the table-lamp – Horace's last laugh: a half-bottle of Dossers' Drambuie, Scud, Electric Soup, Mortified Wine, Bum's Beaujolais, Jungle Juice, Embalming Fluid, Paupers' Plonk – call it what you like, but it was the lowest of the low, the dregs under the dregs, the lousiest insult ever perpetrated against the humble grape. Pike's immediate reaction was disturbingly mild. Sure, he slammed the half-bottle down on the table with ferocity enough to make the glasses as well as his muckers jump, but apart from muttering, 'What a diddy!' he'd done nothing, as yet, about what must've seemed a wilful piece of piss-taking on my part. At the very least you would've expected'm to have given Shane the opportunity to have a random chomp at my anatomy. In fact, he was acting like the executioner who says solicitously to his victim as he mounts the scaffold to be deconked, 'Have a care on them steps, Sir, the blood tends to make'em slippery.' Cuffing beercans from the Dansette record player's lid, he lifted it and flipped the disc. 'Mamma, you've been on my mind,' Big John began to growl. Pike stood for a few moments, a morose look on his face, as he stared at the whirling record then, with a surprising gentleness, lowered the player's lid. He waddled across to the table now to watch a card hand being played out.

Cadge lifted the half-bottle and eyed its label. 'Makes you fart cartoons this stuff,' he said to nobody in particular.

'Bastard!' Frankie'd been full-housed by Bilko and obviously, wasn't too happy about it.

Pike rubbed a hand over his shorn skull, making a sinister rasping noise. From the table he seized up a can of lager, punctured it, then offed its contents in a oncr. He crushed the empty container before lobbing it at the already overflowing coal-scuttle. He looked grim, unforgiving, like a judge retired to his chambers to consider his sentence. The gamblers took a break from cards. They yawned, they stretched, lit up fags and freshened drinks. I could've committed genocide for a cig or a slug of lager, but being under literal house-arrest I reckoned such luxuries would be denied me.

'Listen,' Cadge said, 'much d'you reckon he's worth?'

'Who?'

'Your hippie, here.'

'Fuckall.'

'C'mon now,' Cadge was grinning, 'that jaicket must've set'm back a half-dollar at least. Early Korean by the look of it.' He waved a hand in my direction. 'Let's bet on it.'

'Bet on it? I widnae fuck'n wet'n it.'

'No the jaicket – him, the Banana Boy.'

'What's he oan aboot?'

Bilko shrugged and riffled the card pack. But Pike was listening. The table creaked as he leaned on it.

Cadge explained, 'We lay bets on how much dough we think he's got on'm. Whoever guesses right, or nearest to, lifts the lolly.'

'Much?'

'Fiver?'

'Tenner,' said Bilko.

'Awright for you – you've been raking it in.'

'Chook-chook-chook-chook . . .'

208

'Okay, a tenner it is.'

'Where's a pen?'

'Up my arse!'

'Handy for your brains, then.'

Pike sat down. The bet seemed to interest him. My opinion wasn't sought. 'Tenner each in the pot, then,' Pike said, setting himself up as Rulesmaster. 'A spot-on guess lifts double the kitty; nearest guess takes the pot as it stands, but, if there're two winners . . .'

'How'd that come aboot?' Cadge asked.

'What?'

'Two winners?'

Pike shook his head, 'What've you got atween they ears, fuck'n custard? Look, if the wino's got a fiver on'm and you guess four'n half sheets and I'm in for five quid ten, then you've – '

'Oh, aye, I get ye noo.'

It was high time I wasn't there. Tactics: make a breenge for the door, pulling off jacket as I did so: throw jacket over the cur's head; apply heavy footwork to its ribcage; open door; off through the lobby at the speed of Spanish diarrhoea.

Cautiously, I began to inch down my jacket's zipper.

'There'll be two guesses apiece,' Pike declared, further refining the rules.

'Two guesses?' Cadge queried. 'How come?'

'Let's get on wae the bloody thing,' Frankie was getting impatient. Stiletto-thin he was, his flesh taut to the bone. Of the four men seated around the table he looked the one most likely to come up with some sadistic way of giving me a hard time. My zipper was almost halfway open by now.

Pike tapped the pen on a scrap of paper. 'Who's first then?'

There was one consolation, they weren't drawing lots to see who'd get first kick at my cheenies – not yet, anyhow.

'Two quid, two'n a tanner, and two quid five'n a tanner,' said Bilko.

'You've got to be really skint tae bevvy the scud,' Cadge reasoned. 'I'll go for a quid'n tuppence, and one quid, three bob.'

Pike wrote it down.

Frankie fingered his wee tash. 'Two pounds, twelve'n a tanner, and two quid thirteen.'

Pike repeated this then scribbled in onto the paper. 'Right, that leaves me.' He considered for a moment then, his mind made up, said, 'I'm for seven'n a tanner, and eight bob, dead.' Having written down his choices, Pike lifted the paper. 'I'll read out the guesses, so there'll be no grumpin later.' He did this, then tipping the contents of an ashtray into an empty tinfoil holder, he shoved the ashtray nearer the edge of the table. With a twist of his head he signalled for me to join them. 'Right, winemopper,' he said, 'get your arse ower here.' This was my chance to make a run for it, but the thought of the wolf's teeth ripping chunks off my flesh made me lose the bottle. Tamely, I rose and crossed to the table. Pike indicated the ashtray. 'Right, stick your tank in there.' Noting my frown, he grinned, then encouragingly added, 'Don't worry, we'll maybe let you have it back again.'

Cadge snickered. 'Be a honker if the bastard's no got a light.'

I was tempted to tell them all to get stuffed but thought the better of it. 'Dignity's an expensive shroud,' Ma Clay used to say, a homily that always baffled me, but I think that I was finally getting her drift. 'When it's springtime in Alaska,' Big Johnny was singing, 'It's forty below . . .' I reached into my jeans pockets. The fearsome four craned forward as I began to dump my loot in the ashtray: first a wrinkled pound note; then a creased ten bob note; followed by some silver and some coppers – total amount £2. 7s. 7½d.

'I'm fuckt, already,' Cadge groaned. 'You tae, Malky.'

Pike said nothing.

I rummaged through my jacket pockets but there was no more bread. 'That's me,' I said.

'Hippie bastard!' Frankie scowled as he lost out to Bilko who was already punching the air in jubilation. Pike shrugged, then his chair crackled as he leaned back on it. I'd've preferred the big man to've won; it might've put him in a better frame of mind. The lack of reprisal for the whisky-into-wine business still bothered me. Frankie, naturally, would've preferred Frankie to've won. A sore loser he was, for as Bilko reached across to scoop in the pot he placed a restraining hand on his arm. 'Hold it. How'd we know he's coughed up the lot?'

Bilko half smiled. 'Come off it Frankie.'

Frankie appealed to Pike. 'I say he should turn oot his pockets so's we know it's above board.'

'Fuckall difference to me,' Cadge said as he began another nostril finger patrol.

Pike nodded his massive head. 'Aye, Frankie's got a point.' He scowled at me. 'Hing oot your linings jugheid.'

I began to shell out the contents of my pockets, placing them one by one on the table: a comb, a biro, a hankie, a ciggie-lighter that needed a flint, fags, matches, a catarrh inhaler, an unopened packet of Spangles, a shirt button, house keys, a small screw-driver, a pocket knife, and, from the inner pocket of my jacket, a paperback on the life of Pirandello. I indicated that I was through but Frankie remained unconvinced. He came around the table then seizing my jacket by its lapels yanked it open. His hand jabbed into the emptiness of my inner pocket then he spotted my 'last ditch' or 'poison-pill' hole. 'What's in there?' he asked.

I shook my head. 'Nothing.'

He prodded at it. 'You're a liar. There's something in − ' He yanked down the diagonal zip then delved his fingers into the tiny

211

aperture. They came out bearing something that pried gasps from the others and had my asshole semaphoring maydays; dangling from its chain, light winking from its gold-plated surfaces, was Paddy Cullen's crucifix. With what looked like a genuine shudder of revulsion Frankie rid himself of the thing, tossing it down amongst the banknotes, cans, bottles and tinfoil crap. 'What d'you know,' Frankie said, 'we've got oorselves a Tarrier!'

If looks could kill I would've been dead already. It didn't take yon wee Dutch dandy riding his white charger on the dresser to endorse what I already knew, their brutal glares were enough for that, as were their arm tattoos – these bears were militant Prods, no-surrender merchants hooked into history by a shared party line the number of which was 1690. Pike, hands folded on the table, began his address to the jury: 'To think I nearly let the dug chew aff his cherries, as well.' He shook his head. 'Could've pizined itself.' The others laughed. Bilko gathered in his winnings, separating the notes according to value into different piles. Frankie howked amongst the beercans in the corner, tossing empties aside until he came upon a full one. He sauntered back to his place at the table. Cadge's search of his nostrils continued.

Shaking his head as he stared down at the crucifix, Pike went on: 'You can see noo how he's such a tit – heid's full of green cheese.' I was about to interrupt him, but thought the better of it. No point in claiming my Proddy origins; Proddies didn't wear 'Vatican Brooches'. Useless to suggest that I was an exception: I wouldn't have believed a word of it, myself.

'Tell you something,' Pike said to me, 'You're only the second Fenian to've stepped intae this hoose'n twenty years. A young bead-rattler it was, made the same mistake as yersel.' He nodded. 'Aye, we posted'm back tae Dublin, a wee bit at a time, so we did.' Although his fellow Proddies grinned their eyes remained hostile. Pike lifted the half-bottle of wine. 'Too bad,' he said, 'you canni take this tae Hell wae ye. It'll be fuckn perishin doon there, what wae Popes, Bishops, and Parish priests warmin their fat arses at the Fire.' He winked at the smirking Cadge. 'Away ben and fetch faither's pisspot. If he's used it so much the better.'

Cadge needed no prompting. In a matter of seconds he was on his feet and scurrying to the door. The cur which'd been whining restlessly loosed a loud bark but a command from Pike made it slink to one side so that Cadge could pass. My mind had been made up for me: as soon as Cadge returned I would have to go for broke. The dog'd be a bit distracted by the door opening and I – The escape plan, scarcely conceived, had the skids put under it, for suddenly Cadge, preceded by a suffocating cloud of acrid smoke, came breenging in like an imp from Hell, bawling at the top of his voice: 'Malky! Malky! It's your faither – he's set his fuck'n room on fire!'

Much smoke and much confusion. Chairs toppling, the dog going bananas as the men rushed the door. Shouts, curses, coughing now from the lobby. With the smoke all but levering my lungs into my throat I snatched up my belongings from the table not, amazingly enough, forgetting Paddy's crucifix. I crammed the stuff into my pocket then got down on the floor and elbowed my way to the door. When I got there I took a deep breath of the dwindling fresh air remaining at this low level, got to my feet and sprang into the mêlée of bodies, thick smoke and heat in the lobby. Catching just a glimpse of the inferno that raged in the bedroom I cannoned into somebody – Cadge, I think – stomped on Shane's balls and as it yowled hideously I stomped even harder on an accordian, though, on later reflection I suppose it must've been the moggie, then I went barrelling towards the open door. Brushing aside Bilko who was bent double and coughing his guts up I burst through onto the landing.

With my lungs well'n truly kippered, tears pouring down my face I immediately took a flying header over the refuse bucket, almost giving my right arm a new hinge as I decked it. I was on my feet in an instant, and went hammering down the stairs, three at a time, pelted the length of the close, then with snow fizzing around my busy feet I blistered along the pavement, charging, I hoped, in the general direction of Saracen Cross and a taxi.

Almost halfway around a tenement corner I pulled myself up sharply then back-tracked. Trying my best to suppress my cough and at the same time struggling to get a few molecules of oxygen down into my vulcanised lungs I dodged into a darkened closemouth. My old ticker was racing fit to bust as I made my way to the close's rear exit, but escape via this route was barred by a massive puddle. Still trying to convince my lungs that breathing was possible just so long as they unknotted themselves, I coughed my way to the entrance once more.

Their voices could be heard now, and the soft pounding of their feet. If any of the approaching group had spotted me, then my tea was out. It was either a Possil hunting party returning from a foray, or a tribe from a neighbouring territory on the look out for local scalps. Some luck at last! They didn't come my way but headed straight on. I peered after them from my dark refuge. About a dozen or so braves, bunched together, they ran in easy loping strides. All of them were probably tooled-up. Only when they were well on their way did my lungs start to pick up on old habits like processing air. I granted them the encouragement of a few deep grinding coughs and from all over the place, dogs began to bark in sympathy. I moved off rapidly. I'd had quite enough of four-legged fiends for one night.

On a main thoroughfare, near a fish'n chip shop, drawn by the sound of female screams, I saw a crowd gathering around something on the slushy pavement. Holding my gowping arm, and still coughing like a pit pony, I crossed to peer over the shoulders of the onlookers. A bloodstained youth lay calmly on his back, totally unconcerned by the shrill keening of the girl who knelt by him and of the attempts of a railwayman to render first-aid. 'Give'm room for chrissake,' a man ordered, and the circle of rubbernecks relaxed for a moment or so but soon grew tight again.

From somewhere in our midst the shocked voice of a woman rang out: 'Aye, a gang of boys did it. Stabbed'm and ran doon yon street there . . .' Then, another voice: 'Here's the ambulance now. Naw, it's no – it's a fire brigade.' 'Stand back!' a man shouted. 'Give'm air!' and on the fringe of the crowd, a wee Glesca punter with a pinched cigarette and the mark of the dosshouse on'm, was saying with a shaking head, 'He's had aw the air he'll be needing, that fella . . .'

24

How's it possible that I could be having a chinwag with a gabby cabby about the unlikelihood of Glasgow Rangers FC taking the League flag this season when, only a short while before, I'd been party to the torching of a pensioner's pad? Okay, I'd given him the matches in all innocence but that didn't let me off the hook. For instance, why hadn't I when I was legging it down the stairs from Pike's place hammered on several doors to raise the alarm? Hadn't I also ignored, at a later stage of my flight, a telephone kiosk which just might've been operable enough to summon the fire brigade? Worse, hadn't I taken time out to do some rubbernecking, maybe even secretly relishing the sight of somebody more down on their luck than I was? I've no doubt that my excessive attachment to this bundle of bones of which I at present hold the sole tenancy turned my head in a direction contrary to my civic duty. May I also at this juncture ask for a petty crime to be taken into consideration. I regret (no, I do not regret) that such was my haste in removing myself from that scene of personal and quite unwarranted humiliation that I, inadvertently (no, quite deliberately), scooped from the table some banknotes that were not my own – a few only, certainly not sufficient to compensate me for the harassment I suffered at the hands of that vile quartet. I can see now, in fact, what a fool I was not to leave that table with my pockets brimming over with bluebacks. 'Be ever alert,' M. Sartre says, 'for the Destiny Leap may open like a chasm at your feet at a moment not of your own choosing,' or, as a less well-known philosopher, Vic Rudge, put it, 'There are nae fuck'n pockets in a shroud, Tam, grab all you can when you can!'

'Aye, you're right there, pal,' says the cabby, 'we'll never see the likes of Jim Baxter again, no in oor lifetime.'

'Cough-cough-cough,' I said. 'Cough-cough-cough-cough.'

'Do yourself a favour, mate,' says the driver after I'd heaved myself from his cab, 'don't start War'n Peace, and don't be buying any long-playing records – sounds like there's only wan mair shirt for you. Ta-ra . . .'

He gave me a cheery wave then departed.

Although that God's reject of a Saturday had pounded my brain to runny porridge, a few neurons still managed to bleep faint warning signals the moment I set foot in my close. Footprints, fat, freshly made ones that went on up the stairs. Whose? They didn't belong to auld Wattie Mullins, his prints being of the long and narrow sort and, anyway, no way would Mullins be out at this time of night (or morning, was it?). Warily I mounted the stairs. I was chittering and my arm was louping some, especially when a coughing spasm seized on the old bronchial tract, the bone-deep pain would shoot agonies into my crippled wing. The higher I climbed, the fainter the footsteps became. They'd all but vanished by the time my rasping lungs and sodden feet had delivered me the way an ocean dumps its dead on my own half-landing. I stood there, my fairly plain self having become one huge convoluted ear. Listening.

From the haunted lavvy there came the sounds of heavy

breathing: the phantom was in its lair at last. Although our meeting was by now long overdue, I decided that bright morning was the best time for uncanny intros. After all, I'd my broken lungs and singed arm to consider – not forgetting the old ticker, mind you, you only get one per kit; it needs special attention. I was about to tip-toe past the closet's closed door when the spook's breathing upped some on tempo and this was accompanied by a quickening series of moans which gradually flowered into that most banal of sounds – the human sneeze! Several human sneezes. Somehow a spook with flu seems a less scary entity: I relaxed. Besides, I figured I knew who the maker of these nasal explosions was. I took out my lighter and flicked it several times without result. No flints! I'd forgotten. So, it was a lighted match that, after kneeing the door open, I shoved into the closet's darkness. A squadron of fresh sneezes rocketed forth and just about snuffed the match flame.

'Bless you, Paddy!'

He was sitting on the pan, dressed in the diver's suit and the helmet was on the floor between his feet with a can of beer and one of stout stuffed into it. One of his hands held an unstoppered, half-bottle of Scotch; the other rose to shield his eyes from the match's glare.

'S'that you, Tam?'

'Who does it look like?'

'Al Jolson.'

'Eh?'

He touched his face. 'You been up a lum or something?' He struggled to rise. 'Anyway thank god you're here.' He wagged the whisky bottle. 'Hadnae been for this I'd've been fartin icecubes.'

The reason Paddy had taken to gallivanting around the Gorbals in a diving suit was perfectly rational, nothing bizarre about it, at all. Quite simply, during a quiet night at the Planet, Paddy'd sloped off to the Dog for a couple of crafty ones. As insurance for his return Matt Lucas'd insisted on taking possession of his overcoat and his house keys, a banal ploy since Paddy would've walked in his bare scud to the North Pole if he'd been convinced that a bottle of whisky'd been buried beneath it. Anyway, as he passed the Rectifier Room on his way down the stairs he spotted the diving suit lying across wee Matt's workbench and he stuck it on for a bit of a laugh with the Salty Doggers. After a few goldies and a half gallon of stout Paddy'd reckoned that any attempt to resurface too quickly could be fraught with danger, so he stayed put until closing time then got a lift in Mickey Dalton's taxi to the Moderation Bar. It was only after John Barleycorn had'm well in his thrall that Cullen remembered about the housekeys being still in his coat-pocket at the now locked-up Planet cinema. Since chapping up his sister while drunk and in charge of a diving suit seemed a trifle dodgy, he'd decided to crash in good old Tam Clay's pad. And, here he was.

'Tam?'

'Aye, Paddy?'

'They were some sausages were they no?'

'Same wae the lager, ready for it I was.'

'Tam.'

'What?'

'You cannae beat a bit scoff, sure ye cannae?'

I was in bed, lying on my back, and nursing my sore arm. Paddy had an oddball aversion to beds and did most of his kipping in chairs – at the moment he was stretched out between a couple of armchairs with some blankets thrown over him. In a moment of alcoholic revelation I'd once heard Paddy refer to beds as, 'They fuck'n grave-trainers.' His dislike of beds, though, isn't a lifelong one; it began, as I recall, around the beginning of the sixties when a whole scad of popstars were snuffing it through ingesting their own puke while stoned out of their tiny nutshells. 'Remember Kopax Brazil,' Paddy'd warn, then, to your inevitable response he'd groan, 'of course you havnae heard of the fucker – he ate the same supper twice, didn't he?' 'Remember Kopax Brazil' became one of our coded phrases which, in this case, meant that Old Morto didn't give squat for talent, either when it was in bed or in bud.

Firelight flickered on the walls, just as it had the night before when Becky McQuade told me of how at her wedding McQuade had punched his brother Pat's eye clean out of its socket. Pat, according to Becky, was McQuade's favourite brother. What might happen to those folk he didn't dig was something I preferred not to dwell on. The living-room smelled of our recent cook-up: we'd sorted away flat sausages, tottie scones, and eggs, some black pudding, and thick slices of heavily-buttered bread, the lot washed down, in my own case with lager while Paddy saw off the can of stout and some of his whisky. Wolfing breakfast in the smaw hours; life was becoming more'n'more ballsed up.

'Know what I was thinking, Tam?'

'Naw.'

'That there'll soon be fuckaw left. In a couple of months just empty space.'

'Aye, it makes you think.'

'Nae Salty Dog, nae Planet, the shops away as well. Bugger all left. Christ, even the Jerries couldnae manage that.'

On he droned while his shadow on the wall from time to time raised its shadow bottle to its shadow lips. His theme throughout was transience, the swift and continuing loss of familiar landmarks. I grunted the odd reply, but mostly I was thinking, not so much about how tenements, iron bridges and marble banks soon enough become fog in the air; no, I was considering the things in life that aggrandise themselves and become a burden too heavy for our glass frames – sickness, disappointments, the ache of years life freights us with. What was it all for?

'What'd you get up to the night?' Cullen was asking.

'Nothing much. I was taken for a hurl by a poison dwarf, made a prisoner in a giant's castle, nearly eaten by a wolf, then I torched a pensioner's bedroom.'

Paddy chuckled. 'Ask a daft question.'

With my good arm I punched some shape into my pillow. 'Paddy.'

'Uh-huh?'

'How come you go to chapel?'

'Coz it's there, I suppose.'

'D'you believe in this heaven'n hell stuff, then?'

'Aye, definitely. If it wisnae true there widnae be sausages.'

'That's helluva deep that, Paddy.'

'You Proddies are dead ignorant, so youse are.'

'Good night, Paddy.'

'Night Tam.'

25

We sat in a small restaurant with red chequered cloths on the tables and with tiny impressionistic paintings – stamps from the foreign countries of the mind – decorating every inch of the ceiling. The proprietor's name, which had been inveigled into the plate-glass, appeared as a straggling little vine of conceit beneath the brawny efflorescence of the establishment's name, 'La Veglia', solar forgeries of which scattered themselves with chlorophyllous abandon amongst the animated diners. For instance, on the pale brow of my companion, Mrs Rebecca McQuade, a verdant 'I' could be seen to flare then dim again like an unresolved ego problem. Dressed entirely in white, for she'd newly come from attending her husband's funeral, she lighted an elegantly stemmed clay pipe which had tiny pink rosettes embossed on its cheeks and gracefully sipped dainty wisps of smoke from it. Merrily, we were discussing her husband's fortuitous demise – trekking through the Arctic on some glimmerbrained expedition to bring the haggis to the Eskimos he'd been struck dead by a school bus driven by Joe Stalin on a day as fair as any you might expect to enjoy in heaven. On the table between Rebecca and myself stood a tall bottle of blonde wine which – the fantasy of sots – no matter how often we replenished our glasses from it, remained undiminished. Very pleasant it was, this amiable tête-à-tête; not even the presence of Eddie Carlyle, who with lugubrious servility was trying to pass himself off as a waiter – his continual hrrumphing was a dead giveaway as I suppose, were the green rubber boots he'd chosen to don – could dilute our enjoyment.

After a time Talky Sloan appeared with something concealed beneath his coat. The hidden object turned out to be a human skull which he placed on the table beside me. Having done this he launched into a verbose account of the delay he'd suffered at the customs all because he'd lacked a certain document which had only been legitimised that very morning. To Talky's claim that the document was still in the birth channel, that the existence of it had not yet attained reality, the customs officer had slyly asked: 'If it don't exist how come we're discussing it?' It was an altogether tedious tale which was mercifully abrogated by a blacksmith who in his leather apron, spiked with tools, came clanking in. He was brandishing a pair of lengthy tongs in the jaws of which there was clamped a glowing horseshoe. Acrid smoke filled the restaurant when Vulcan, with great deliberation, as if he was performing a bizarre coronation ceremony, lodged the fiery 'crown' around the skull's brow. Immediately, the blower in the corner coughed into life and a grating voice said, 'They're under orders!' I leapt to my feet but Strang, dressed as a dentist, and wearing in addition a blood-spattered clerical collar, shouted, 'I can't stop it!' as again and again, he tried to staunch the life-taking torrent from my mouth. He shook his head and stepped back a pace. 'It's no use – you're gushing like a tap!' He held up a fur-coat and its crimson lining oozed to the floor. Whimpering, I tried to lift it. Rhona, with a child in her arms, appeared. She was dressed for a funeral. 'Hurry,' she urged. 'They've found out!' We ran together down a segmented bone corridor where workmen with blowlamps were trying to fuse broken sections of the breached wall. Lights writhed in ceiling sockets and giant scarab beetles ran muttering about our feet. Although all of these creatures were winged not one of them chose to take flight. Rhona fell: still clutching the baby she went skimming along the floor then, with a voluptuous smile, vanished into a wall cavity. I charged through the doorway and found Paddy Cullen in harlequin dress seated on a lavatory pan. He was eating slimy objects – maggots maybe – from a diver's helmet. He invited me to share his pullulating meal. 'Make a good arm poultice,' he suggested.

I shouldered my way through a flimsy wall into the Planet's Rectifier Room. Da Clay was there. He took up a glass billiard cue then proceeded to poke it through the Rectifier's grid. This provoked an electric growl from Freddy, the luminous ape who was imprisoned at the heart of the machine. From a spigot at the base of the howling apparatus Da Clay now let flow a torrent of molten metal into a clay cup which he then passed to me. I drank from the cup and immediately ulcers flowered on my tongue and palate, and all the soft machinery of my throat seemed to be eroding. Naked, except for his shiny shoes Da Clay performed a robotic-looking waltz with Phyllis Sherman, who wore only a pair of blue silk panties and stiletto-heeled shoes. I tried to shout a warning to my father but my voice had been burned out. Alone now, for his partner had become a she-wolf that sat upon its grey haunches and gave vent to long desolating howls, Da Clay danced around the Rectifier, ululating like a shaman. The head of a child, a monstrous head began to solidify in the machine's shrieking mists. 'Behold!' my old man cried, 'the head of the Gorgon!'

In panic, I seized the head from the Rectifier, then shoving it beneath my Lifebuoy's jersey – the same way I as a kid used to conceal my bible from sabbath scorners like Hatchet Hannah or

Vic Rudge, I ran from the chamber. A pack of wolves began to pursue me. Through grey street after grey street I ran. My boots struck sparks from the cobbles but the wolves were gaining on me. I sprang up a fragile staircase that was made from dust'n moonbeams and it collapsed with a silvery sigh in my wake. My arm was suddenly seized by the rending fangs of some creature. I struggled through a skylight onto the roof of an immensely tall building. Still wrestling with the thing that'd laid its tenacious teeth on me I let the head fall from beneath my jersey. It went bounding down the moss-scabbed slates and lodged itself in the guttering. I stared down at it: mutilated by its fall, grey and ferocious looking in the moonlight, the face of Pike glared up at me. I felt the power being sucked from my hand (my other one had been reduced to a fingerless mash of bone'n gristle) and my grip slackened. Slowly at first then rapidly gaining momentum, I went slithering down the incline . . .

26

Just as Socrates died from the feet upwards, so Paddy Cullen came from sleep in the same direction. I stopped writing to watch. First, a quivering in the toes, a dabbling with them in the flux of day, then retreat; but soon, renewed animation as the toes now fan out through sock holes, like sea anenomes' feelers, to nibble at the light; wavelets of energy pulse upwards through the legs before lapping into the pelvic area and on higher into the trunk; the arms and hands reluctantly follow. But for a long time yet the head resists the Cullenizing process. At last, the eyes spring like deck hatch covers and the unsheathed gaze blearily takes a fix on the ceiling's worn chart. Positional readings are taken – the SS Cullen is underway.

'Good morning, Paddy (cough-cough).'

'I'll take your word for it.'

He sat up and began to scratch himself. Jeezus, he looked like he'd aged by a decade during the night. He began to search around himself, a sort of threshing movement that became more frantic the longer it went on. His hands delved beneath the blankets. 'Gotcha!' He fished out a rancid-looking upper-denture plate. He clicked it into place like a machine part and instantly looked two days younger. 'Thought auld Shanksy had'm again,' he growled. His feet swung onto the floor. 'S'that char you're drinkin?'

I nodded towards the blackened teapot that sat on a fire-bracket with a cheek to the flames. 'Bit stewed.'

'Aye, like masel.'

He seized hold of the teapot and jawed some tea into a mug and heaped in about four sugars. Next, he got down on his hunkers and groaned around for a bit until he'd found his whisky bottle. He held it up to check its contents; about a man-sized slug remained. This he poured into his tea then, no doubt respectful of his moiled headgear, quietly paddled a teaspoon in the turbid stuff. He downed several gulps of the char which I figured must be as flavoursome as a cheap paintstripper.

'Time's it?' he asked.

'Dunno,' I said. 'Your feet must've knackered the clock. Stick on the tranny.'

'No be able to hear it wae you barking like a seal.' He got up, dragging the blankets on the floor, crossed to the mantelpiece and tuned in to 'Slipped Discs', a prog. in which the jock took requests from his listeners regarding which record they would like to hear publicly demolished – this was done by sound-effects which were meant to convey the impression of an almighty sledgehammer pounding a record to vinyl dust before our very ears. The world of Disney Exist kept stealthily extending its borders. What with pools panel experts inventing imaginary soccer results and Scottish disc-jockeys with transatlantic twangs to their verbal gibberish pretending to be demolishing – ach, why go on? Scunnersome, that was the very word for it – scunnersome. Cullen dragged the blankets back to Rhona's armchair and dumped his fat butt into it. He wriggled his yellow toes in the direction of the fire. 'What you up to?' he enquired.

'Mm?'

'Who you writing tae?'

'Myself, I suppose.'

'Yersel?'

'Aye, it's a kinda diary.'

He frowned. 'You write things doon that've happened to you – s'that it?'

I nodded.

'Like "Today I scratched my bum – yesterday, I didnae bother"?'

'The very thing.'

'Complete waste of bloody time!' He glanced over at me as I tenderly stroked my throbbing arm. 'Is the auld wing still playing you up?' He shook his head. 'Many a time I've decked it efter havin a bucket – but never through trippin ower the damned thing. Anyway, if that bark of yours keeps up you'll have kicked the bucket afore the arm draps aff.'

'Ta, Paddy.'

'Don't mention it.'

Paddy began to hum along with a so-called 'doomed disc' they were lining up for pretended pulverisation. Good, it was 'Stranger On The Shore' that was under the Hammer. Unlucky song, my ass. How could there be such a thing? If it was possible then there'd have to be 'lucky songs' as well.

'D'you hear aboot Burnett?' Cullen asked.

'What aboot'm?'

'Got mugged.'

'You're kidding me.'

'Naw, seems this dosser-type jumped'm as he was getting into his sister's car. Ran off wae his hat. Y'know, yon furry thing that looked like a well-shagged squirrel.'

I nodded. 'Did he lose anything else?'

'Holy Mother of God!' Cullen suddenly exclaimed. You

would've thought that a spider had bobbed up in his tea. Rapidly, he crossed himself.

'What's up?'

'This.'

He held aloft his crucifix.

'So?'

'I lost it but – '

'Now it's found, Hallelujah!'

He shook his head. 'Naw, naw, it wisnae there, I'm tellin ye. I lost it. Woke up yesterday morning and it was away.'

'Middle age, they call that.'

'Definitely missing, it was.'

With something approaching religious awe registering on his booze-zapped face, he studied the crucifix. It was like a scene from one of those Pat O'Brien priest movies – the reprobate finds god again – poor script, putrid lighting, and duff acting. 'I thought the chain must've snapped and chrissake . . .' He turned the revered object over'n over between his fingers. 'It definitely wasn't there. I noticed it'd gone when I was shaving.' This was doubtful; shaving was for Paddy a most dangerous task; while he was doing it he'd eyes for but one thing – safe passage for his tremulous cut-throat blade as it passed over his carotid artery.

I closed the journal I'd been writing in and went across to increase the tranny's volume a little. Paddy continued to sit there with the same saft look of piety on'm and a wee mobile nugget of light dartin across his pagan features. I guess at that moment all the catechisms and beatitudes, the novenas and suchlike stuff that Catholic weans've tattooed onto their brain lobes when they can't do much about it had come up with a Jesuit jackpot. To say he was transfigured would've been going over the score, but 'religiously exalted' wouldn't have been too far from the mark. The obvious solution, that the sod who'd knocked the crucifix in the first place had simply restored it, seemed light years away from dawning on'm.

With a couple of electric snorts the tranny cleared its tubes of music then came on with a news bulletin. The usual Sunday morning crap: strife between nations; some daft fart lost on Ben Nevis; a youth stabbed to death in Possilpark (which was hardly news to me!); a compensatory item about the brisk sales xmas trees were producing this year; then – I shushed Paddy as maybe he was about to reveal the Secret of Fatima – Old Pike was dead. He'd perished in the fire. Pike, himself, was in hospital suffering from burns and smoke inhalation. Also detained were three other men who'd not yet been named; all of them were suffering from the effects of smoke. Pike, it seemed, had made valiant efforts to save his father. There was also some guff about Shane, the family pet, having raised the alarm. Although Pike's flat had been gutted, the fire brigade'd managed to prevent the inferno from spreading to neighbouring homes.

'D'you know them, or something?' Cullen asked.

I shook my head. 'Any more char in that pot?' Cullen nodded, then lifting the pot from the fire bracket, approached with it.

'One slice or two?' he asked.

27

Having borrowed a coat that I'd last jagged around in during the fifties – the days of wine'n throwsies, with the stains to prove it – Cullen had gone off to mass. Such a figure had he cut with his pouched fish-on-a-slab eyes, brambly chin, and the tail of the gaberdine shortie-mac halfway up his ass, that passersby would've promptly taken'm for a drythroat on his way to a shebeen, or maybe even a gangster enroute to some underworld crime bazaar to do a little gun shopping. A more discerning observer, a neighbour, say, might've detected the change in the man and remarked off the back of her hand to a companion: 'Yon Paddy Cullen's fairly picked himself up since he got back from the swineherding!' There was no doubting that the miracle of the cross had had an impact on the man: ever since its occurrence he'd gone around with this saft look of piety on his clock that to a pagan like myself soon got to be a bit wearing. I'd no doubt whatsoever that Paddy's state of grace wouldn't outlast twelve-thirty p.m. when the Labour Club opened its doors and Auld Nick gave'm a crony's wink from the fiery pit of a whisky glass.

After attending to the cliché of the man on his tod – the delft-chocked sink – I began to round up the scattered empties which, without so much as a 'gardyloo', I chucked from the window into the backcourt. In complicity with me, the thick snow cushioned the impact of their fall then set about covering them. It was just as well, for I didn't want Wattie Mullens to become aware of my tenemental delinquency. During the last summer that'd ever visited Scobie Street – now there's a sad wee thought – I'd had to pull Wattie up for lobbing packets of shit from his window because his cludgie was knackered, and Rattray, the Factor, had stalled over calling in a plumber. Caused a fly-plague Wattie's 'wee presents' did – the bloody place became the tour centre for Bugland: 'Doing a Scobie' became the in-phrase in the Bluebottle Flyaway Brochures. Flight after flight of the droning buggers arrived and not just the blue yins but green and orange as well, and an exotic purple-backed mob who, being a bit on the clannish side exclusively sunned themselves on the midden roofs. Wattie'd asked me if he could use my squat-box until Rattray relented and hired a Yellowglove to make the necessary repairs but I knocked him back; he could take his pestilential ass across to Shug Wylie's place. As far as I knew he was still doing that. It could well be, though, that he's started crapping in his own nest again, but there're some things in life I don't want to know, far less think, about.

During the clean-up I came across a full can of lager, a wee reward for facing up to the hoovering singlehanded. I didn't really get beasted in to my household chores for I'm a staunch believer in the theory of Pellmellicity which holds that, come what may, all things eventually find their rightful places in the gravitational fields. A lacksadaisical piece of charring, I suppose it might be called; a man dividing his attention between a machine that wheezed at his feet like a dropsical pug and a paperback which contained the aphorisms of the Leipzig Lip, would, I suppose, be sight enough to crimp the brow of any zealous dust-distributor.

Unaware that the 'pug' had suffered some sort of inner convulsion, had shocked its system into reverse and was vomiting the contents of its mouldy guts – sweet-wrappers, milktops, fishbones, wool, paper scraps etc. – I reread a particularly piercing comment by Herr Nasty: 'In order to look for beginnings one must become a crab. The historian looks backwards; at last he also believes backwards.' At that very moment I glanced down and saw the sick thing at my feet regurgitating domestic history, its wretch-reflex howking so far back into its gut that it'd managed to barf out a daffodil petal. Surely, the bag had been emptied since Spring? With a crochet pin it'd also gobbled I raked amidst yesterday's leavings. Norman Mailer used up gallons of ink to infer that the fate of anyone can be deduced by an examination of their shit. He was more than vague as to the mechanics of the business but he remained convinced at the end of his convoluted essay that while the yogi-bogy brigade hummed and hawed about the 'itness' of existence, more honest progress could be made if we addressed ourselves to the all-pervading stench of Time, in other words, to the essential shittiness of the mind-sanitised cosmos. The crochet pin flicked something from the rubbish. It was a folded pound note, the very one – I was convinced of it – that'd gone missing one rainy Friday and all but wrecked my marriage. Rhona had been too free with her innuendos that the quid in question had more than probably been sucked into the maw of my back pocket. Now, here it was – vindication, proof, the restoration of honour. It'd probably cost me the newly-found note and more to get the sucking thing fixed. Meanwhile, I went over to the broom cupboard and took out the brush'n shovel. 'I chant the word pre-electric!'

Having raised some dust and some sweat I soon called it quits and sank into my armchair with a fag and Nietzsche's nattering. The vibes, though, had gotten loused up and I could no longer connect. I ended up wishing I'd put a match to the book and read the cigarette. I went over to the 'Black Box' and stuck on the *Dustbowl Ballads*. From the piles of books, sheets of paper, maps and stuff, I dug out my notebook and jotted down, 'A man is vacuum-cleaning his carpet. Machine goes into reverse. Amongst the debris he finds fragments of a suicide note in his wife's handwriting . . .' I shoved the notebook aside and took up my current journal. Re-reading the 'Pike incident', I clearly saw that despite my avowed self-promise to set down what befell me as objectively as possible, sparing neither my dignity nor pride, I'd come nowhere near such a lofty ideal. It was so easy, this self-suckering. By the erasure of a verb here, the promotion of an adjective there, through subtle or unsubtle inference, not to mention an irritating prose jauntiness, in essence, the very beat and rhythm of chickenheartedness, I'd managed to camouflage the funk I'd been in throughout the Pike business.

Would Narcissus have landed himself with Anorexia Nervosa if he'd been encouraged to keep a journal? Probably not. Journal jotheads are to be numbered with shit-wavers, those I-guys who, having produced a stool, cannot bring themselves to commit it to the democracy of the sewer without bidding it a fond and lingering farewell; ditto, the snotamours, those self-weaning bugle blowers who have the nauseating habit of examining the outcome of the nasal explosions – what can they hope to find in their germy hankies – a pearl? or maybe even a ruby? Other members to be associated with the Brotherhood of Journal Keepers are the solo-lovers, that pervy gang of monosexual mirrorgasmic, self-respecting wankers of which Horace Dicky Hart is definitely a member. Me? I'm a journal-junkie, a history-shooter forever craving an ink-fix. I know what I have, all right – Pepys's Syndrome, that's what.

I tried to smoke another fag but my soot-streaked lungs kicked up such a fuss I'd to abandon the idea. I popped the lager can and took a gulp from it. Yeuch, I wouldn't be going back for the rest; it tasted the way I figured the Clyde would taste this dead-end time of the year – brackish with an undertow of drowned dossers. Right now even Woodie Guthrie's strident voiced socialism had a man-perishing sound to it. No guesses as to why – Old Pike's ghost had come to haunt me. Okay, let's face the facts as I knew'm: I'd been involved in his death but there was, as yet, no proof that I'd been the direct cause of it. The blaze could've started through the TV set blowing up or as the result of an electrical fault. Now, it's a fact of life that you can't help but affect, even alter or reshape the fate of those around you. Ghosts, after all are 'holes in the happenings', and therefore remain potent in their absence. Even if you've taken to hermitting it down a fifty foot concrete oubliette, you can't help but get entangled in the fact of living. But the changes you wreak simply through being, needn't be for the worse. Let's say that you stop a guy'n the street to ask directions. This casual, unplanned intrusion into his life could be enough to save'm from meeting up with a certain fateful truck which all his life, from when it was ore in the ground right up to the fully manufactured product, had been on its way to eviscerate him. I didn't get the chance to analyse this further.

The knock on the door was unfamiliar to me. It certainly didn't suggest the beggarly presence of old Wattie out there, for his knock is more an accoustic apology for breathing. Nor was it the sombre knuckling of Eddie Carlyle which invites comparison to the sound of nails being knocked into a coffin lid. I switched off the record player and went out to open the door.

Becky McQuade stood there. 'Oh Matt,' she wailed, 'am I glad to see you!'

28

I, Thomas Patrick Cullen Matthew Lucas Clay had to think nimbly in order to keep apace of this drama which had erupted on my doorstep then rapidly spilled into the living-room. Acting – no, more like reacting, to the part thrust upon me, the tripartite role of the Clayculluca, I paced to and fro on the threadbare carpet, while Becky, having flung herself into Rhona's armchair, had straightway plunged into a tear-sprinkled tale, the sob-plot of which aptly enough centred on a burst water pipe.

Around midnight, Friday last, a waterpipe had fractured in the McQuades' apartment and had soon flooded through the ceiling of their downstairs neighbour . . . On receiving no reply to her knocking the neighbour'd contacted Becky's mother-in-law who lived close at hand. The 'auld besom' – Becky's definition – kept a spare set of keys to allow in tradesmen, etc., when the McQuades were absent. An emergency plumber was called and he'd soon repaired the leak. As a result, of course, an awkward question had emerged: where was Becky? Her mother-in-law had presumed she'd stayed overnight at her sister Peggy's place along in Oatlands but, come morning, this presumption had been scotched by the arrival on some errand or other of Peggy's husband. So, an unsuspecting Becky'd arrived home around noon, Saturday, to find herself facing the music. Where had she been all night?

So hostile, so laced with innuendo had the old woman's questioning been that gradually it began to take the shape of an interrogation. The upshot was that Becky'd lost her rag and ordered the 'auld besom' from her flat. And that was how things stood now – her mother-in-law fizzing with resentment and scarcely able to contain herself as she waited to spill the beans on Becky as soon as McQuade returned.

I paused alongside Becky and said to her in a growly sort of voice: 'Greeting'll no help matters. Get a grip of yourself.'

I resumed my toing and froing.

Jeremiah considered it was the opportune moment to announce the arrival of this my first home-to-roost chicken. There would be many more to follow he prophesied. I'd nobody to blame but myself for this calamity. Hadn't it been me who'd scattered the seed in my very own yard? I wasn't about to deny it. Yet, I admit to being surprised, shocked even, to see Becky McQuade coming through my doorway, closely pursued, no doubt, by an invisible horde of Pandora's unboxed and unbridled nasties.

In Scotland, domestic crisis is generally faced up to with the proverbial 'Nice wee cuppa tea' or a smoke. I chose the nicotine route, to my regret. The very first puff provoked a lung riot that folded me and all but shut me down for good. It was in a voice that sounded to start with like Donald Duck on helium but which gradually normalised, that I said to Becky: 'Don't know what you're getting so worked up about. Just tell'm you spent the night in a pal's hoose. Chrissake, surely you've got pals?'

She adjusted her ridiculously small hankie and dabbed with it at her mascara-smudged eyes. 'You don't know'm,' she warbled. 'He'll dig'n dig till he gets at the truth.' Speaking of which, said

Jeremiah, why don't you come clean to her about who you really are?

He had to be kidding. How'd it look if upon hearing that her husband might soon be on his way to bootalise me I instantly sprung a new identity?

Don't you mean brutalise? asked J.

No, I don't smartass. I'm talking boots here, size ten tacketties with steel toecaps cratering my corpus crusty.

Surely you're aware that by your continuing deception you've placed an entirely innocent man in jeopardy? I'd no intention of letting wee Lucas take the bust for my lust. Pity, though, I'd be depriving the newspaper industry of a fine alliterative headline:

DEEPSEA DIVER DENTED IN DEVON STREET!

Still dabbing at her streamy eyes with her linen 'snowflake', Becky seemed to be regaining control of herself. The thing I found just a wee bit odd was how a woman, weighed down with apprehension at the imminent arrival of her husband who, according to her, would not be slow in dishing out the GBH, could've found the concentration and the emotional stamina to mount that magnificent blonde edifice on her head? It looked like the work of a topiarist though, doubtless, it'd been created by her own bare hands, a blowgun, a gallon of hair-lacquer, a few hundred hairpins, clasps, and side-combs. With its French-combed flying buttresses, curlicues, intricately-coiled donjons and barbicans, it, apart from being a hairstyle, might also qualify as a listed building.

'D'you want a cup of coffee?' I asked her.

She shook her head. Although she was still doing a bit of facial mopping up, the weeping jag was effectively over. 'We'll have to think of something,' she said. I sat down in my armchair and stared into the fire, the interweaving flames of which were reminiscent of Becky's hairdo, hoping to spring a few notions from this antique device. The best, or worst, it could come up with was a mutual suicide pact which given that McQuade was snowed-up in his lorry somewhere down the A74 was a mite premature. Slowly, I began to cobble an idea together. It left a lot to be desired but then so does this planet of ours and its maker had a whole seven days at his disposal.

'Listen Becky,' I said, 'let's run this one up the flagpole and see if it's worth saluting.' I winced. Only the Yanks can come that movie-talk, make it sound natural. 'There's this auld woman lives on'r tod, first door you come to doon in the close. Let me finish. Granny Ferguson she's called. A bit dolly dimple, she is. Queues for'r pension at three in the morning, talks to'r shadow, y'know the kind of thing. Now Friday night last, after you left the Planet, did you no happen across the auld sowl, plowtering about in the snow she was. Didnae know whether she was going or coming. Being the kindly person you are, you didnae want'r to catch pneumonia. A wee boy told you where the auld woman lived and you took'r hame. You made'r a cuppa tea – no, Ovaltine; she always has Ovaltine last thing. While she drank it you went to look for a neighbour but there didnae seem to be any so you went back to Granny's flat. She begged you not to leave her. Cried her eyes out, she did. What else could you do but spend the night with'r. In the morning a relative dropped by to take'r off your hands. Well, what d'you think?'

She took one of her filter tips from her tortoiseshell case and lit it with sharp, jerky movements. Smoke twisted from her pale lips like ectoplasm. Hadn't a ghost of a chance my story by the look of it. I was right. 'D'you really expect'm to swallow that rigmarole?' An impatient toss of her head during which the haircastle didn't even sway but remained rock solid. 'This is John McQuade we're talking about – the worst bugger this side of Hell.

And even if he did buy it – this old bat you're on about, she'll deny everything.'

I shook my head. 'Her skylight's bust, I told you.'

She shook her head. 'You don't know'm – a right jealous ratbag.'

'So he'd come to Granny Ferguson's tae check your story oot?' She nodded, but dubiously. 'Good,' I said. 'So, I'll give you the lowdown of her living-room, where the furniture's placed, what kind of pictures she has on the walls, ornaments and stuff to be found on the mantelpiece and around the place, wallpaper, that kind of thing. Oh, and while we're aboot it – when you came across Granny she was wearing a mink-furred Cossack hat. Got it? Aye, it might sound daft but – '

'It all sounds daft if you ask me'.

I rose and crossed to the table.

'You somewhere to go?'

'How?'

'Your eyes are never off that clock.'

I told her about taking young Jason to the Art Galleries. I'd goofed, strayed from the genealogy of Lucas into that of Clay's but she didn't comment on it or react in any way. 'I'll have to be getting back, anyway,' she said. 'That auld swine'll have her spies posted.' She exhaled some smoke, seemed a bit more relaxed. 'How'd the interview go,' she asked.

'Interview?'

She nodded. 'Aye for the job you were after.'

'Oh, aye that,' I nodded. 'Think I did okay. They'll drop me a line.'

'You'll be off to London then, if you get it?'

'That's right – the Big Smoke.'

'What're you looking for?'

'In London?'

240

'No, here.'

'Pen, it was there this morning. You got one?'

She shook her head.

I resumed my table search, sifting amongst books, mags, newspapers, typewritten sheets, maps (lots of them, I love maps), record covers, and so on.

All I came up with was a pencil stub with a shoogly lead but on reaching for the sharpener I knocked over a paperback novel of Bellow, the one in which Charlie Citrine figures, and from it there rolled a red-inked pen. Ta, Humby. The search for a pen had uncovered testimonies of infidelity: a clasp bearing several strands of hair which if plaited might yet hang a man; a wineglass from which a seductress had sipped; dabs by the dozen, including a significant find – an almost entire palm-print with lines of life, fate and head clearly distinguishable, and a ketchup smut kindling an ironic stigmata at the heart of it – the accusing hand of Rhona.

I began to sketch onto a largish sheet of paper the plan of Granny Ferguson's kitchen. As line by scarlet line the details grew and conjoined, so too did a frown, line by line, begin to pleat Becky's brow. It was obvious that she didn't dig this approach to our problem, this effort to extricate us from the sexual swamp into which we'd blundered. Banal, I guess she thought it was, maybe even footling. Her expression was now one of deep sulkiness.

'Silkiness?' MacDougall pricked awake. 'Did you say "Silkiness".' Ignorant, as always, of what was taking place at the pragmatic level where the real levers of power are, he launched into his masturbatory mumbo-jumbo, an incantatory invocation to the rousing thunder, the Lazarus-raising forces of 'what if'. Aye, what if she's starkers beneath that coat of many buttons. Eve-suited. Uncupped breasts, beloved of babes and babbling men. Find the right combination to those buttons and all shall be revealed.

Beneath my active pen the mystery of the Red Room unfolded; to each item, be it furniture or a mantelpiece trinket, a numeral is assigned which is placed within a bubble then tethered to its object by an ink-thread. The bubbles, unclouded by my life-breath float free, a poor bet for longevity in this sharp-cornered world. Granny F., herself has been granted the numeral (1) who, on referring to the descriptive list we learn is a widow in her eighty-fifth year; not quite five feet in height; weighs little more than a sackful of ping-pong balls; she has a wall-eye, her left one, and a carbuncular-like growth on her right cheek; chin moles sprout silvery strands of hair, as tough as fifteen-amp fusewire. And so on.

The plan's major drawback, apart from the fact that it is a contingency one and therefore as unpredictable as the flightpath of a bullet in a tin lighthouse, was that it was pitched a tad too near the action. I would've felt more relaxed it it'd lead Becky's homicidal mate to somewhere on the other side of the city or, better still, the planet. Contingency plans have much in common with those pioneer aeroplanes that flapped like gross parodies of birds from their drawing boards then, after only a few timorous hops into the air were recaptured by that stern warden, Gravity, and smashed by him to matchwood for having had such aerial presumptuousness.

29

Young Jason had so far spent over ten minutes staring in at the diorama in Kelvingrove Art Gallery and Museum, long enough for most modern kids who, weaned on television, tend only to snack on reality. But this quaint box of tricks, a cousin of the magic lantern and the flannelgraph, had the boy hooked. So, there I stood, a prisoner of low wattage sunrises, watching the seasons come and go, seeing the stoat, the mountain hare, and the ptarmigan changing alternately from their summer garb to their winter one, then back again. It made me uneasy this gawping at the torrent of days as they disappeared down Time's plughole. This silent doombox, this cube of light, was a die rolled from a craps game in Hell. It served as a reminder that Time, Auld Nick's hitman, was up'n hustling.

'No, I want to see it again!'

I hauled the kid to another inset window which, on cue, extinguished its light.

'What're those, Uncle?'

'Snow White's Jewellery.'

The fluorescent rocks brooched the darkness with blues, greens, reds, pinks, and amethysts – the cold fires of minerals. Memory began to round up Disney's dwarfs and, to light their way home from the gem quarry, strewed their path with rubies, diamonds, opals, zircons, emeralds, and topazes, but, quick as adulthood, the magic grotto vanished in a blaze of vulgar light. Since chunks of lifeless quartz held no appeal for the boy he began immediately to strain in the direction of the diorama. I led'm firmly away.

'Why didn't the rabbit move?'

'It was a hare.'

'Was it dead?'

'No. Bored stiff maybe.'

We wandered into the Wildlife Section, a misnomer if ever there was one. I'd never seen such a bunch of tamed-out stiffs. The tiger, for instance, was a ripe old bag of stripes. And call that a lion? I've seen a fiercer looking carpet slipper. At least Homo sapiens was living up to the section's 'wild' tag. The place teemed with'm, tiny manlings, their feral screams, laughter, and chatter-ings issued from all corners of the manmade jungle. One of them – a Castlemilk Cro-Magnon, possibly – was trying to shinny up one of the legs of an immense stuffed giraffe which dominated the main floor space. No wonder the Animals' Prayer begins 'Heaven protect us from Homo erectus'. But since Heaven has a hard enough time protesting its own existence, protection has been delegated to a bunch of artguards who've about as much jungle cool as Barton MacLane after a bad day at the ivory mill. My own manling, from whom I scarcely removed a vigilant eye, was proving to be no tamer than his peers. He'd insisted upon bringing along his model Spitfire with which he'd already strafed the battle fleets in the Model Boats Section, and right now was on lethal safari somewhere over Africa. 'Di-di-di-di-di-di', each bellicose foray left spittle patches on the glass frontages of the exhibits, but disturbed not in the least those dusty beasts that stared out eternity in their post-taxidermal paradise.

Staring in at a sea-lion, nailed forever to its slab of fake ice, my mind suddenly hiccupped and had me stepping back into yon frozen moment in Pike's lair: 'A Tableau Depicting Variations On A Theme of Evil'. What was the quartet doing right now? Coughing up blackness, probably. I could visualise Pike, in mummy swathings, lying on his back and staring up at my image nailed like a wanted poster to a wall of his mind. And, inside his broiled head revenge, in all sorts of sadistic manifestations, flaring then dimming.

'Di-di-di-di-di-di', that was the koala bear getting his. You're next, wallaby! A liveried attendant fixed a severe Sabbath eye on me and I suggested to Attila the Gun that it was time for his fighter to touch base for refuelling. The same attendant frowned when I coughed all over a wild boar which had got loose from its case. The animal didn't seem to be up or down about it but the attendant tagged after me for a time, probably just in case I got within bronchial range of a Rodin or took my vandalistic hackings amongst the precious pots of the Sung and Ming periods. Passing the giraffe again (the manling had been lured down from its leg with a banana or something), I recalled an anecdote I'd read about Captain Cook's ship. It was claimed that while Cook's vessel was anchored in a certain bay that, despite its immensity compared with the local craft thereabouts, it had remained unnoticed by the natives because (a doubtful proposition) it lay outwith their perceptual frame of reference. Remembering this, I strove to direct Jason's attention to the huge Long Neck.

'Look up there, son. What d'you see?'

'Can I get a lolly, Uncle?'

The boy's lack of response, the facile ease with which his attention had been drawn to the immediacy of a kid noisily sucking an ice-lolly tended to validate the Cook theory.

'Please, can I have a lolly?'

'Later, first, tell me what you see up there.'

'I want it now.'

'Don't you see anything?'

'Please, can I have one?'

'If you tell me what you see up there.'

'It's a giraffe, mister,' the lolly-guzzler informed me.

Jason, bribed with some Jelly Babies until we came across an ice-lolly shop, was now giving an elephant the once-over. He shook his head, dissatisfied. 'Why won't it move? Has it stuck?'

I parked myself on a bench and wished I could light a fag, but it just wasn't worth the bronchial uproar even a couple of puffs might spring. Thinking about coughing of course immediately unloosed a bout and I went through my repertoire from mucousy minor to rib-cracking major which didn't help my sore wing any, the pain of which came on all the meaner from having been ignored. 'Arm With Sore Man!' – an abstract picture of misery. Likewise Jason, as he glumly surveyed the petrified jungle, searching for something – be it a limping natterjack toad, anything at all so long as it was blessed with mobility. Surely, it wasn't beyond the Museum's technical ability to implant a device that would simulate breathing in some of its larger exhibits? Why, yonks ago, at the Glasgow Green Carnival, I remember seeing Sleeping Beauty lying in her kip, her wee bellows going like billy-o as she awaited a cheeper – a hundred years in the promise – from her slowcoach Prince. That she'd been hooked up to a crude motor-driven air pump was obvious but still the sight of her wee bosom heaving then subsiding was worth twice the entrance fee in the opinion, that is, of Thomas Clay, who at that time was suffering the woe and the joy of early adolescence – pimples and prurience.

I stared across at the boy and felt in some daft way that I'd let'm down. Kids nowadays were a right thrillproof bunch. The

Armoury Section had, unexpectedly, proved to be a real mood-clunker.

'Where're the men?'

'What men, son?'

'You said there'd be men-in-armour. But they're empty, aren't they?'

I'd nodded. 'Aye, you're right – they're empty. But look, that's what battle horses wore.'

'They're not real horses.'

'No, but – '

'Then, how d'you know the armour's real?'

'Oh, I'm sure it's the real McCoy.'

'They'll fall quite soon.'

'Fall? Why should they?'

'Because I say so.'

'Di-di-di-di-di-di-', his Spitfire, banking steeply, hosed me with bullets. Take that you fork-tongued fraud for coming the con! Jason had a hang-up about the imminent collapse of things. Maybe this was down to him having an old man who daily bucked gravity on the highwire of finance. (Don't upset Daddy – the pound's fallen again . . .)

For the boy, buildings seemed especially vulnerable. Might they not fall? What held up the sky? Was it the tin-tack stars? Although I'd enjoyed the poetic sheen to this query I'd withheld my praise. It wouldn't do to have him growing up a misfit with a lyrical limp, would it? Certainly not. You're quite right, Phyllis, one monster per family is one too many. Jason had wanted to know what thunder was, and wee Florrie Monks almost got her jotters for telling him that it was just God rearranging his furniture. I remember Da Clay's scatological comment when one evening thunder had come clattering over the tenement rooftops. 'Aye, aye,' he'd said, thumbs hooked into his galluses, 'it sounds as

247

if St Peter's been suppin the beans again!' A right kerfuffle that'd caused in the Clay household as Ma got stuck into the blasphemer for such irreverence in front of the boys.

For a piece of porcelain, solemnly viewed, Jason had but one comment: 'Who dropped it?' A statue of Buddha, smirking no doubt over how gullible people were, was curtly dismissed. 'He must've rubber legs!' We trudged around this cultural tomb witnessing the trivialised fall of things, the neatly ticketed debris of dismantled centuries. And throughout the boy had remained impassive, unimpressed. Why didn't things move? Why did they just stand there? And soon my imagination had also been sapped of its mobility, so that it too moved from object to object in a kind of torpor, irked by the boy's refusal to be astonished.

When I hang out in Bluesville I tend to get philosophical. Okay, maybe I'm not up to comparing Hegel's 'intricate being' with Kierkegaard's 'double-mindedness', but this much I've got figured – when god chased us from Eden after Adam's rib-tickler got suckered by the serpent, he could have been yelling only one thing: not yon gross malarkey about us bumptious bipeds having from then on in to earn our bread by the sweat of our brows. No, what god'd really been bawling would've been along the lines of 'Out damned hypocrites! Out!' Aye, hypocrisy is numero uno in Satan's vice league. Take that guy sitting next to you on the bus, he looks a real honest Joe . . . But maybe only an hour ago he'd been forcing his odious notion of sex on his baby daughter? And who's to tell if yon woman with the bunch of flowers, so modest looking, isn't on her way back home to inflict more bestial cruelty on her crippled mother? It happens all the time, in every city, and no doubt in every hamlet and village as well. Open any newspaper, glance across any telly-screen, and you'll find that the moral grotesqueries outnumber the funnies ten to one.

Take myself – any self will do; they're all equally bogus – I'm up to my neck in hypocrisy. In fact, if there was such an institution as the Museum of Morality, I'd occupy a prime spot in it – a glass case all to myself, complete with identity tab, Urban Hypocrite: A striking example of a Twentieth-Century Urban Hypocrite. Note especially its thick skin which possesses a chameleon-like ability to blend with its background. Mark too its easily detachable features, exchangeable teeth, and reversible eyeballs, plus its readily adaptable limbs. Another significant feature is – '

I was up off the bench and running. I caught up with Jason seconds before his Spitfire could rake the sunrise derrière of a magnificently-robed negress who'd happened amongst us that Sabbath afternoon with the Garden of Eden perched on her plum blue hair. And what a powerful sermon that exotic hat with its cutesy little serpent was preaching to us drablings:

My friends, Jesus was cool. He wore psychadelic sandals and wouldn't have been seen breathin in no khaki kaftan. Don't let's forget what he say about Solomon. He say even when that gaudy ol'rooster was spazzed up'n his tux, why he still wasn't no match for them switched-on lilies of the field. So grab yoself a rainbow for a hanger and drape it bright in Joseph threads. Ain't no grey in Heaven folks. And, if it happens there is – then I ain't going . . . Hallelujah!

And on she sailed, her ebony face as calm as the best night sky you ever remember seeing.

Jason and me paused to view an insult to the Japanese empire. Four stooges, purporting to be typical members of a Japanese family but who were patently a quartet of Martians who'd given Ray Bradbury the slip – his lyrical clawmarks were plainly visible – stood together in a sort of glass wardrobe. The father in his robe looked a bit like Nöel Coward with conjunctivitis. If these dummies were supposed to be typical Japs, what would they be palming off on the public a couple of centuries hence as your 'typical Scots'? Wee tartan bendy gnomes, maybe, with their eyeballs glued to their assholes to guard against any new poets who might be on their way to disturb the kailyard calm.

Aye, twad fair mak ye grieve Christopher, wad it no?

Intending to take Jason to the Eygptian Room I found a 'Keep Out' notice posted at its entrance. From behind a canvas screen there issued soft rapping sounds, made perhaps by a mummy knuckling the inner lid of its sarcophagus. 'Lemme out! Lemme out!' But, gently, Old Salter was pressed back into his fold in oblivion. 'There, there, you've just had a bad awakening, that's all. Noo, coorie doon – have another billion winks . . .'

Three men sit in separate rooms eating their breakfasts. There is a likeness in the deft manner with which they handle their eating tools and, perhaps, a correspondence in the tone of their chit-chats with their respective wives. Later, one of these men will casually place the shelled brain of Talky Sloan on the weighing pan; another of the trio will rake through the ashes of a Mr Pike then lay out his semi-cooked organs for inspection and analysis; the remaining man will from the gash in the chest of a murdered youth pluck a hypothetical weapon and other men will go forth in search of its lethal reality.

Behind the canvas screen the tempo and volume of the rapping sounds had increased. Maybe, after all, they were cobbling a few random dynasties together or patching up a pyramid. But we'd never find out – Ancient Egypt was shut today 'for restoration purposes'.

Since we were in the galleries I decided, in a roundabout way, to satisfy the boy's notion to see a man-in-armour by taking him upstairs to view Rembrandt's masterpiece on that very subject. On our way there I'd to explain to Jason that it was unlikely we'd come across any ice-cream vendors in the galleries, no, not even in the Italian one.

Jason, unimpressed by mere masterpieces, had settled for the living tableau of the floor beneath us, relishing the opportunity to look down on people for a change, to escape the bondage of diminutive size. Leaning my elbows on the rails I watched for a time, idly observing the antics of those mice who'd been lured from the grey skirting board of pragmatism to nibble at the cultural cheeses on offer. To'n fro they scurried. The children's activity was especially frenetic; in fact, from this height they looked as if they were performing some kind of courting ritual. Randy wee buggers, they probably thought that 'carbon dating' was something new on the nookie front. Later, while wandering a corridor, I was to see a young girl fingering a man's penis. The man in question was made of bronze, and, judging by the lustre of his prong, was well used to such frontal assaults. The groperette and her giggling pals made off amidst hoots of laughter.

In pacing those galleries, pausing, going on again, you find many portraits of civic gangsters who've stuck up the bank of Fame and got clean away with a reputation. Most of these mountebanks and lady-do-nothings you wouldn't supply with a hard chair never mind wallspace, yet here they are, protected by alarm circuitry and artguards, safely lodged at the plush heart of the social pyramid, booked in for eternity, or at least until Ivan the Tourist comes snapping with his IBM flash camera. As I patrolled these slick, echoing chambers, young Jason toddled on ahead of me as if for him the paintings were changing patterns in a rainbow at the end of which he'd find the legendary crock of gold. Sorry, son, there'll be nowt there, except, maybe, God and the Devil playing at fitba with da Vinci's skull.

Rembrandt's 'Man In Armour' was placed in a sort of cultural spotlight, and roped off from the public, which numbered about half a dozen folk when Jason and I approached to join their reverential gawp. Today I discovered that Rembrandt's gallus use of light was failing to illuminate yon wee patch of inner dread and darkness which is sometimes referred to as 'the soul'. The artist's perceptions, those insightful arrows, rattled faintly on the great bell-jar of tedium that enveloped me. When before had I ever paused to consider what the actual man might look like once he'd crawled from the enhancing hug of his grandiose armour: a pale, wormish runt maybe. It was probably down to a constellation of events – Old Pike's death; the nagging ache in my arm; sexual self-loathing, the aftermath of adultery, I don't know which, but my cultural asdic was definitely on the blink. A lassie in a burgundy-coloured maxi coat with buttons as big as hand-grenades, and who had a ski-cap thing pitching like a yacht in the dark blue storm of her hair, rescued us all from our inarticulate-ness when, having sped her flexible and knowledgeable glance across the masterpiece remarked to her boyfriend, 'He's a dead ringer for Kirk Douglas, sure he is?' I stopped off at Dali's 'Christ' but found it to be more vapid than ever. I yawningly loitered to examine a Degas bather washing the varnish of classicism from her body, then I continued past those multicoloured boils that'd flared up in the face of European puritanism. I spent a much longer time though staring at 'The Adulteress Brought Before Christ'.

I took Jason down the stairs and, at his request, we revisited the Evolution Room. A sandpit contained the blackened remains of a child, if you believed the affixed notice. To me, it looked more like a burnt-out campfire. Maybe old Pike'd looked like that when the firemen finally got to'm. Huh, so it was still there – the old Clydesdale horse. Daylight sluiced through its bone cage, spotlighting places it'd no right to be. The 'auld hairy engine' as Wattie Mullens would say, deserved better treatment than this, being shamelessly exposed to the very core of its former power for the feasting glances of idle visitors, those carrion eaters of history, who left it with fluid belches and the stink of death on their chops. Da Clay, who'd brought me on a rare visit here, had assured me that the skeletal Clydesdale had once been Benny Rooney's coalhorse. 'Aye, he steyed ower long in the boozer wan day and that's how he found it when he came oot,' he'd grinned. 'They could fairly go their chuck yon Florence Street weans.'

The Weaponry Room next. Wandering amongst carbines, rifles, elegant pistolets, and all the other despoilers of the flesh, their grave-filling capacities lovingly detailed, a skunk memory flushed in the passing raised a sudden stink in my mind. Simon Rattray (note the conjunction of rodent and stinger in the very name) had been our factor in the Scabby. A weasel of a man he'd been, with a skull that looked like it'd been flattened by a shovel, the same stroke having rammed his head so deeply between his shoulders that he'd appeared as neckless as he'd been ruthless. His evil bones should've been preserved and hung back there in the Skull Chamber as a salutory warning of the degenerative possibilities which haunt our race: Rattray, the Leeching Man.

Rattray had been the Agent for a Miss Euphemia Pursemore of Cowes, IOW. How's that for a debt-making duo – Pursemore and Rattray! The story goes that a certain John Divers – the Scabby's political shaman – aware that Rattray was becoming too lazy to even turn a blind eye to the squalor being forced on his tenants through lack of repairs and downright custodial neglect, obtained by his usual devious means the absentee landlady's address. As a consequence, one bright Cowes morning her ladyship found herself opening a bulky package which turned out to contain a dead rat – a whopper by Scobie Street standards – to the verminous body of which was attached the following limerick, said to've been composed by John Scobie himself:

Dear Miss P.
To give you a whiff of your slum
I could've wiped this with my bum,
But, since you're such a louse,
Here's a Scobie Street mouse,
With roaches and rats still to come!

I looked around myself. Many a gun was pointed at my heart. Older, slower guns now, dischargers of sluggish bullets which had been the fastest means of death in their day. Such progress since. A mere half-ounce of thumb pressure was enough these days to off an entire city. This bugbear of living your life at the heart of an omnipresent arsenal, the feeling that you've a button-implant at the nape of your neck and the itchy thumb of some political misanthrope hovering over it night'n day. Oh Hiroshima, Nagasaki, now we know the world's gone waki . . . No sign of Jason. Expecting to find'm around every corner I worked my way amidst the tools of homicide. These modern kids, what was to be done about them? The way they madcapped around inside their brand new senses, going off the road every five minutes, scaring the hell out of their demented instructors. Five minutes later – still no sign of the boy. Down the bellicose centuries I strode. By the time I'd got to the stab'n hack days of claymore and battleaxe my neural circuitry was locking into an amber condition. Where'd the kid got to? I shouted his name a few times, expecting to hear the clatter of his feet as he came to me. No response. Conditon red declared. This is not a drill. Klaxons began to honk. Red alert . . . red alert . . . this is not a drill . . .

'Have you seen a fair-haired boy in a red anorak carrying a toy plane?' Over'n over this same question put to that stupid armadillo called The Public which was pebbled with inanely staring eyeballs and from which the same stupid counter-query arose: 'Have you lost'm then?' I stopped an artguard. He looked like a smudged V. Van Gogh self-portrait, and was in fact checking out one of his ears as I spoke to'm. He promised to keep an eye open for the lad. 'Make that both eyes!' I snarled, angered by his tepid interest. Maybe a missing troll was down as a bonus in his book. I continued to jitter around, trotting out the same harried question. Just as I was about to succumb to full-blown panic it dawned on me where the little squirt would be. I went there pronto. A bunch of kids were staring in at the diorama. Jason was amongst them. What a relief! I leaned over to tap Jason's shoulder. He turned his blond head as the diorama pulled off its stale trick – summer becoming winter. The boy had been transformed too: eyes, the wrong colour; front teeth missing; face too pinched looking. My hand slid from the shoulder of the red anorak. 'Sorry, son, thought you were somebody else . . .'

Recalling that Jason had shown a spark of interest in the Locomotive Models, I hurried there. A retired colonel type, all tweeds and plummy twang, looked up from the steam engine diagram he'd been studying in the company of a Joe 90 lookalike, his grandson, or nephew, probably. 'A red anorak, you say?' The colonel checked out his moustache for crumbs or something, then shook his head on which a deerstalker hat had been firmly clamped. 'Sorry, can't say that I have. Awfully sorry. Lost the little chap, have you?' There was about as much concern in his voice as there was humour in the chunk of machinery being examined by Joe 90. 'Carrying a Spitfire?' Again the colonel wagged his head. 'Haven't laid eyes on'm. What about you Timmy?'

The boy who looked as if he was about to climb into the piston chamber, now said: 'It wasn't a Spitfire.'

I stared down at'm. 'What was that, sonny?'

Timmy, who'd what at school we'd called 'swotty' eyes,

looked at me with far less interest than he'd devoted to the workings of the steam piston. 'It was a Hawker-Hurricane.'

I grabbed at his shoulder. 'You saw'm?' A different nod. 'Where?'

'With a man.'

My internal klaxons were shrilling now all right. 'What'd he look like?'

'Blond hair, red anorak . . .'

'Not the boy – the man?'

'Same as you, almost: old US combat jacket, tartan scarf, denims, scuffed pair of shoes.'

I sighed, but not with relief. Obviously, the little bugger was responding logically to the questions as framed by me. Had he seen Jason? Yes, he had, but when I'd been with'm, not as it'd first seemed, in the company of another man, a stranger – at least there was that. But they did not go away those images of some stone-faced pervert bundling the weeping Jason into a snow-covered car then driving off.

'Where was this, then Timmy – the Evolution Room, eh?'

'Ornothological Section.'

My scalp prickled. We hadn't gone there, Jason and me. He'd said he didn't want to look at dead birds and we'd bypassed it. 'This man,' I asked, 'it was me, wasn't it?'

'Wasn't it what?'

Plainly, he was getting bored. This was becoming a mess, I could've strangled the little bugger. He was shaking his head and sending longing glances towards the piston exhibit.

'What makes you so sure?'

'His jacket was cleaner than yours. The scarf was Stewart tartan, not MacGregor, shoes were different, and he didn't wear a CND button.'

'Thanks, son,' I said, though why I was thanking him for

doubling my dread I don't know. I hurried off. 'Hope you find the little chap,' the colonel called after me. I waved an acknowledgement but by then Timmy had already succumbed to the far more seductive appeal of the nineteenth-century steam railway technology.

Anyone viewing my antics during the next five minutes or so, say from the upper galleries, could've likened my behaviour to the malfunctioning, not of antique machinery, but more recent technology – a Dalek gone wonky, its circuitry imploding, its mind smoking through metal seams and grilles, its gyrations becoming more and more manic. I claimed every artguard I came across and gabbled out my story. Much nonsense flowed, I wanted all doors locked, loudspeaker announcements, organised search-parties. The boy had been snatched. That's right, by a man dressed much the same as myself – But what was the use? These dust'n debris agents were tuned into yesterday: give them a sniff of a knight's codpiece and they'd deliver the aristo in no time at all. I demanded to see the curator or whoever was in charge. This meant that I was getting desperate, for what would an arts expert know about red-anoraked waifs carrying model aeroplanes? The attendant I happened to be berating for stepping away from me to chin a wee lassie about dropping a sweetie wrapper on the floor suddenly smiled. I turned to follow his pointing finger: toddling towards us in the company of another grossly-underpaid artguard was Jason.

'Uncle Tom,' he cried, 'can I get an ice-lolly now?'

'A chap found'm wandering,' the guard explained after I'd thanked'm and taken a tight grip of my charge's hand. 'Tell you an odd thing, though, this chap who found your youngster, he was . . .'

'. . . dressed much like me?'

He nodded. 'Same everything.'

257

I touched my scarf. 'Except this was Stewart tartan. And correct me if I'm wrong, but I don't think he was wearing one of these – right?' I was pointing to my CND button.

The guard who wasn't to know I'd been chatting to the great, grand-nephew of Sherlock Holmes, himself, looked quite impressed. 'Aye, now that you mention it . . .'

A minute or so later saw Jason and myself back at the diorama.

I got next to nothing out of the boy about my dress-alike. Presumably, since the guard hadn't alluded to it we bore no facial similarity, me'n the kidnapper, which was just as well for that dopplegänger stuff gives me the willies. They say that if you meet up with your double then your tea's about out. Mine, then, must still be in the pot, but for how long? Jason's story had such a matter-of-factness about it that I couldn't help but sense he'd been put up to it, rehearsed; I mean the explanation bore vocal prints that weren't his own. He claimed that he followed my dress-duplicate from the Weaponry Room thinking he was me. When he'd found out that he'd been tagging after a stranger he'd started to cry. The man had taken him to an attendant, and that was all there'd been to it. Nothing to write home about. A mere blip tadpoleing across the screen of normality. Step down the red alert, lock away the launch codebook. Make a brief report in the Incident File: 'Loss of minor communication 1530 hrs. due to sartorial misidentification. Located and rectified. Normalcy restored 1550 hrs. (approx.).'

Just as now'n again startling pains transit through your body, so unexpectedly and so overpoweringly, that you instinctively sense that if they were to remain for only a few seconds more, your dying from them would inevitably follow, so certain life-events, odd occurrences, convoying through your existence, can bear the same lethal threat. The boy waited with uncomplicated optimism for the rebirth of a new season but this tiny episode was serving notice on me that no longer need spring follow winter with the same old sun-plodding docility.

Jason chortled as once again the shabby trio re-emerged in their winter woollies. In a more sombre frame of mind (my arm was really giving me gyp now), I found myself thinking about Old Pike, Talky Sloan, and the stabbed youth, a trio who hadn't made it back from the dark. My parents came to mind, too. It was really heavy, this knowing that for them continuity – well, spasms of return – into this life were chiefly down to me, to my ability to rekindle them in the spirals of my memory. So much for that splendid immortality Ma Clay had so fervently sung for in the Bleaker Memorial Church. Was this what the forever holiday in God's Country amounted to – a will o' the wisp in a forgetful son's head?

For a long time after his burial (an entire month, at least), I'd fully expected to hear my brother Martin's special tune – 'Pedro, the Fisherman' – being whistled by him, its melody jarring a bit because at the same time he was pelting up the tenement stairs, two at a time, to reach our joyous houschold and to receive the exuberant cuddles of Ma, Da, and me. In this fantasy Da Clay always had on his slippers which meant (no promises, mind) that maybe he'd bide a wee while longer. Martin, spanking gravedust from his clothes, would tell a breathless tale of escape, of how Granda Gibson'd come to his aid, showing him how to howk out a tunnel, bracing its roof with dead men's thigh bones. He was often set-upon by Eastend gangs and plagues of red-eyed rats but, eventually, he'd burst through the putrid soil and sucked in great draughts of air. I hooked my arm about my brother and squeezed him with all the love and affection that I could muster.

'Uncle Tom,' he said.

'Mmm?'

'Uncle Tom, you're hurting my shoulder.'

'Sorry, son.' I relaxed my grip on Jason.

'I think I saw the bunny move,' he said.

'Aye, we'd best follow suit. Your Maw and Da'll be daen their nuts.'

A smile creased the lad's lips. In front of'm I'd blatantly committed an anti-Shermanism, a thou-shalt-not. I gave the back of my hand a couple of light, mocking slaps and grinned down at the boy whose lingual purity I'd sullied. 'Sorry. I meant that your mater and your pater might be getting somewhat concerned about our prolonged absence.'

The wee rogue gave me a briber's wink which implied: 'I won't tell about the man if – '

I was sentenced to another three ptarmigan-hare-and-stoat summers and the same in winters before I was sprung from the tyranny of the doombox.

Outside, nature's diorama had got jammed in its winter phase; the snow gushed unstaunchably from the black hole that was the sky. As my hair whitened with the stuff I put on the trembly gait of a greybeard and tottered forward on an invisible walking stick. Jason's whoops of laughter ceased abruptly when in the snowy phantom of a car by the kerbside a funereal window rolled down to reveal in all its glacial majesty the face of the Wicked Witch of the North.

'For any favour, do hurry along,' she commanded. 'We haven't got all day.'

30

'I hope you like yellow nosh,' said Phyllis with arch slang. 'Wan Tun soup this is called.'

I paddled my spoon in the foggy stuff, half expecting to find Wan Tun's sandal. Young Jason, who wasn't sophisticated enough yet to know that food can serve wilier ends than mere nutrition, murmured, 'Yellow nosh,' a couple of times then began some vocal experimentation: 'Yellow nosh . . . Red nosh . . . green nosh . . . purple nosh . . . posh nosh . . . squash nosh . . .' a colourful chant which was given the chop by the sound of his own name, burred with reprimand, as it flew from his mother's lips. The boy now studied his reflection in the bowl of his as-yet undipped spoon. He breathed on it then restored his image again with a quick wipe of his serviette. Again his name, fizzing with the kinetics of censure, came hurtling across the table, but this time tagged by a weary postscript: 'Jack, speak to him. Really his manners . . .' Sherman, whose blankness of expression suggested that he was off on one of his internal audits, maybe evaluating the costs incurred by some financial tornado, hastily rejoined us. He mouthed some vocal guano about his six-year-old son's need to stop behaving like a child of six, and to remember that Santa didn't bring toys to ill-mannered boys.

Jason chewed on this for a time then flicking a cheeky glance in my direction chirpily asked, 'When Baby Claus disnae down his scoff, does Mammy Claus dae her nut in?'

Phyllis's eyebrows nearly shot off her forehead. 'What did you say?'

'I said . . .'

'Don't you dare repeat it. I've told you before about bringing gutter language into this house.'

'But – '

'No buts about it!'

Sherman nailed the lad with a hard stare. 'Right, settle down. This is your last telling. C'mon, set to.'

Jason was dining on hamely fare, his favourite grub – tomato soup, mince'n tatties with baby carrots, followed by a tub of custard trifle. Both parents began now to probe him about what he'd seen at the Museum. 'Nothing moved,' he told them. 'And the armour was empty.'

The boy ate while he talked, both acts performed with such a rapidity that I was reminded of the constraints imposed upon my gustatory galloping when I was a kid. 'C'mon, noo, son,' Ma Clay would scold, 'let your stomach see the daylight.' The boy had in fact dispatched all three of his courses (very minute portions for a growing lad, I thought) while we were still dawdling with Wan Tun. Jason was given permission to leave the table, which he did only after extracting the grace of being allowed to play with his train set for half an hour, after which it was beddy-bye time. The boy, chancing his luck, made a further request. 'Definitely not!' Phyllis snapped. 'Uncle Tom won't be coming through to tell you one of his stories. You've enough rubbish in your head as it is. Now kisses all round and off with you.'

Second course: sliced duck with bamboo shoots. The Shermans were expert with chopsticks, easily carrying succulent portions of my ego to their voracious mouths. It was just a knack really they assured me, and with hooded smirks allowed me to pig it with knife'n fork. The wine, to judge from the superlatives they heaped on it, had originated in prestige grapes that'd been trodden by the feet of angels. Their sophisticated palates fused with the mystery of growth and maturation, while my gross tongue, numb as a stone, let the bon vin slosh over unpraised and unappreciated.

We were dining in what they referred to as 'The Dinette', an alcove off the kitchen area which was roomy enough to accommodate six chairs around a table. About a dozen species of pot plants swarmed across the alcove's wood-panelled walls where ledges and nooks housed an aviary of porcelain birds. A nocturne of owls glared balefully down from what looked like a genuine tree limb bracketted to the wall. I was reminded of a childhood terror – the glass caseful of stuffed birds that'd dominated the hall at Killynowe Farm, in Dumfriesshire. Jackdaws, ravens, hoody craws, magpies and wagtails, all seemed to fix their cruel eyes on me as I scampered past them on my way to bed. But, how bold I was when Mrs Irwin, with a tread that wasn't going to falter for some footling phantom, went on ahead of me, her paraffin lamp with its puttering flame routing the shadows while I crept along in her stout and steadfast shade, brave enough now to even outstare the evil magpie and his gang of graveyard croakers. In the morning Mr Irwin would leave his room with a scad of farts, his heavy tread making the staircase creak like the timbers of a clipper going round the Horn. I always imagined the birds in the glass case being stirred to a black frenzy as he padded past them, rifle shots volleying from his abundant behind.

In the Sherman household there was – just had to be – a much grander place than this humble noshery-nook to celebrate the belly's needs. This banqueting chamber, within which I hadn't even been invited to step, far less chew a chicken bone in, was always referred to as the 'Big Room' by an awed Florrie Monks. Naturally, the Big Room was for Big Occasions and for the Big Folk who attended them: the Dinette, on the other hand, served the day-to-day eating of the Sherman family, and was also deemed suitable for minor visitors such as myself. In the Dinette, the diminutive dominated. Serious conversations were not expected of you here. Over this table chatettes were more the vogue, and maybe the old laughette while you sipped coffee from a tiny black cupette. This evening the topic turned out to be the social value (if any) of museums, art galleries, and such-like history warehouses. To this subject Phyllis contributed the oddball notion that it would make an interesting addition to every home if its occupants were to convert a small boxroom into a sort of family museum. This could contain a grandfather's favourite pipe, an aunt's treasured bible, the very telegram that brought dreaded news from the War Front, and so on. When I reminded her that in some households the grandfather, the maiden aunt, and the bereaved family might still be living on top of each other in the boxroom, she said huffily that even a corner would serve the purpose. To introduce a whimsical note I suggested that my own 'Family Shrine' might very well display my Mickey Mouse gasmask, ration book, Da Clay's last pair of shoes, Granda Gibson's spare set of wallies, his yellow long johns, complete with escape hatch, the wee white tin that'd contained my first set of loveskins, and the poignant card on which the War Office had tersely informed me that because of my scarred lung it was judged that I wouldn't be sufficiently robust to endure the sheer manly hell of the NAAFI queue. My contribution proved to be a blunderette for it promoted what could be called a 'Chinese

Silence', a kind of audible hush on the surface of which words float like so much trash. This persisted long after the last beansprout or almond had been cleared away with the debris from the fortune cookies.

'You for another?'

I nodded and gave Sherman my glass. The first dram had done little to strip the lead from my mood. We'd transferred from the Dinette through to the lounge, although, for the moment, Phyllis was not with us, having gone to make a phone-call. Her absence was one of the few things to be enjoyed in this most pretentious of pads. The drinks cabinet said it all. It had this gimmick, so corny it made you want to giggle. When you lowered the serving flap the cabinet chimed out a wobbly version of the Blue Danube.

This crass novelty could be suppressed by thumbing the cork of a bottle which would've been a familiar prop to acid-heads, shaped as it was like a ruby snake streaked with lemon markings, and so weirdly contorted it looked like it'd sloughed a dimension. Sherman biffed the cork with the side of his fist. I'm sure he felt its trite tinklings demeaned him, being too frivolous for a man of his substance. Aye, he'd fairly piled on the substance – two stones of it, at least – since last I'd seen'm, where was it again? Aye, Dad Carlyle's funeral, the day we'd locked the locksmith down. Just over two years ago. A grizzled touch to his still ample locks, I noted. The 'executive look' they called it nowadays which is just one more euphemism seeking to mask the bald facts of human perishibility. His face, the focal point of the disintegrative process, seemed wired to a subcurrent of unease, like a man receiving the first mild buffets from a hurricane that is swarming with ruin for him. The hieroglyphics of anxiety were there for the reading on Sherman's dial. But whatever it was that was kinking his colon had, for the moment at least, been assimilated, tucked out of harm's way, just as the body can accommodate a bullet at the heart of its major functions, the vital business of living tip-toeing around it, but going on just the same.

Sherman was drinking at an almost reckless pace, faster'n I'd ever seen him putting the stuff away. As I tried to figure out why, a dazzling fissure opened in my mind and I saw an Eskimo spinning off to his death on a splintering chunk of ice. Intuition, the mind slipping on those spooky goggles which enable their wearer to see around Time's corners and to pass with ghostly scorn through the jailing walls of Newtonian physics. This paranormal peek was enough to reveal to me that Sherman was in some kind of fix – about to shoot the rapids in a lead canoe. A hitherto solid certainty in his financial world had melted out from under him, this catastrophe due to unforeseen movements in the dollar icecap; he was certainly going to get his feet wet. Was this why he'd quizzed me about various benefits a man in my financial straits was entitled to? It'd almost seemed as if he'd decided to take a crash course in failure, to get the going rates in the grey world of grits and handouts chits.

Sherman unstoppered the bottle and jawed whisky into the pair of glasses, doing so without caution and with bags of panache, three fingers apiece as Peter Cheyney's dipso dick used to put it, completing each pouring with a jaunty elbow lift to produce a last golden jag of the stuff. He took up the syphon and rammed a hard shunt of soda water into each drink. As he moved away from it, the musical cabinet allowed some semi-quavers to escape from its throttled mechanism. Sherman paused to glare back at it and with a series of cowed and fading chimes the thing shut down. Quel homme!

'Damned box,' he said as he handed me my drink. 'Soon as it starts up my liver runs for cover. Enough soda?'

I took a sip and nodded. Sherman, merely by seating himself, all but vanished into the capacious maw of his floral armchair. It looked like one of those man-eating orchids Tarzan used to wrestle with. As he slipped further down its variegated throat Sherman raised his glass in what looked like a farewell toast. 'Slainthe!' he said, and I mouthed the customary echo.

For a time we gabbed about this'n that, the growing popularity of holidaying in Spain, then onto some stuff on the production of single malt whiskies. This got me onto an anecdote about a teuchter who used to drink in the Dog. Magnus McPherson, he was called, and his claim to fame was his assertion that he'd been stillborn, and could prove it. When sufficient scoffers had laid bets against'm Magnus would produce his creased and tattered birth certificate which bore the Registrar's signature, official stamps, and also detailed that he'd been born in the mash room of a far northern distillery. What his mother had been doing in such a place at such a time, Magnus wasn't for saying.

In the wide hearth plastic facsimilies put on they were smouldering logs, and over by the door Faraday lay sprawled in sleep, looking, I thought, like a half ton of cleverly moulded gypsum. In the hall, Phyllis was exercising her whinnying laugh. Behind Sherman to his right, the xmas tree flickered with escape plans but couldn't snap its luminous bonds. Even the shu-bumpkins seemed programmed to a tedious circuiting of their green world in which the barnacled lid of a toy treasure chest, minute by minute, opened to release a torpid pearl of oxygen. It didn't throw me none to hear the master of the house confess that during those rare occasions when he managed to get in some goggle-boxing he mostly dug wildlife films. And why not? It was perfectly natural for a man seated between the jaws of a devouring orchid, while dressed in pullover, collar'n tie, to placidly observe a pair of manitees having it off on the ocean bed. Whatever turns you on, baby! I'm told, but remain sceptical, that there're even glimmerbrains around who'd rather watch whelks shitting than listen to Jimmie Rodgers singing 'T for Texas'. And why shouldn't Sherman, as he was doing now, entertain his guest with some creepy-crawly lore? My antenna was really buzzing with the tales he had to tell about Bugland and its busy denizens. Seems, if you're to believe it, that there're wasps, beetles too, that can con board'n lodgings from ants by selling them a kind of chemical dummy. A 'Pheromone' it's called, or so Professor Sherman told me. 'The wee buggers leg it up to the anthill's door, flash their pheromone badges and bingo – they're in! Makes no difference if the bug's got a tartan head and a star-spangled ass, so long as it's got the right chemical credentials they hand it the key.'

Suspicion tickled my brainlobes. Was he laying this stuff on me just to take his mouth a walk, or could he be insinuating that I was some kind of hive-crasher, that I spent my time pheromoning my way into situations where I could indulge my dronish tendencies. I doubted it. Sherman kept his edge for those gory sharkpools where the feasting on busted companies took place. To him I was little more than a ditch chokeful of dead sticklebacks, a welfare pisshole.

'Tell you something that bounces me,' said Sherman, though he twisted the promised info into the inverted hook of a question, 'those animals that can mimic their surroundings – how the devil do they do it?'

I laid a suggestion on him but he shook his head. 'No, that survival of the fittest stuff doesn't count here. There's a hidden dynamic at work, a force that not only can unpick molecules, strip down atoms, but can rejig genetic blueprints.'

I shook my head, 'It's reaction, not intention.'

'Eyes,' Sherman said.

'Eyes?'

'Cave fish don't have any.'

'So?'

268

'You'll be telling me next that all those blind creatures way back at the beginning got fed up bumping into each other so they decided to have eyes. And how'd they go about it? According to you, no doubt, certain cells became increasingly sensitive to light . . .'

I smiled at the casuistry of the man, at this ventriloquist act he was pulling by popping questions into my mouth then answering them himself. 'But tell me this,' Sherman now asked as a roll of drums rose from the orchestra pit and, quitting the trapeze bar, he performed a triple somersault then, so confidently, stretched out for the spar now starting its swing towards him, 'if those creatures were blind in the first place, how come they knew there was such a thing as light to specialise in?' Gasps from the audience – sustained applause . . . 'Aye'n he does it without a safety net, y'know!!'

Bergson had produced a heap of metaphysical sawdust by sawing at the same log. Not much you could do with the stuff though, except maybe to scatter it on the floor of the Kickstone Tavern (so called after Ben Johnson's witty demolition of Bishop B.'s anti-matter theory) where of a night a merry crowd of materialists would gather to quaff pots of really real ale and swap anecdotes about things noted, and events experienced in the great out-there, the palpable, structured universe. And what guffaws assailed the roofbeams as Mr Simon Squiggs, mine host of the Tavern, scorning the assistance from his burly flagon-filler, was to be seen giving M. Henri Bergson the Flying Farewell, the old heave-ho. And as the pauvre Frenchman biffed the cobbles with a Bishop-denying howl, Squiggs refilled his chair on the rostrum next to the definitely really real ale taps and addressed the claret-mottled assembly: 'Keeps on arskin for sommat called "Ailing Veetall" he does. An when Bertie 'ere tells'm there baint be sucha concoction this or tother side of the bleedin universe, says he, the

269

Froggie, "May nong, mong sewer, zee Ailing Veetall eez zee breath of God Heemself . . ." Cries of shock'n horror from the logico-posits as – '

'What d'you think yourself?' Sherman asked.

Unable to recall what he'd been saying I busied my lips with some Scotch.

'Jason liked it, anyway.' Sherman's forefinger pinged a little asdic-sounding signal of distress on the side of his glass. 'What was he on about – the rabbit and the lights going out?'

Rabbit-light. The two verbal prods were enough to jab me from the attractions of the Kickstone Tavern, back to the drab world of what-is. As I filled Sherman in on Jason's fascination for the diorama, the lounge clocks, with more metallic fuss than a jail closing down for the night, rose to welcome a new hour. It was time I was high-tailing it. Judging by the way Sherman was shunting the Chivas a lift in his car, even as far as Bishopbriggs, no longer seemed a runner. Maybe it was for this very reason that he'd been skelping the booze. Well, I could always get a taxi, that is if they hadn't been forced off the road by the arctic conditions.

'You don't seem too enthusiastic yourself about them.'

'Mmm?'

'Museums,' Sherman said, 'stately homes, refurbished castles, that sort of thing.' I shrugged, and he went on, 'Odd, that is. I would've thought the opposite. I mean, it's obvious that you over-invest in the past.'

'S'that so?'

He nodded. 'More than obvious.'

'No way ye.'

Like a conjuror about to pull some digital wangle (would the empty glass vanish in a puff of amber smoke?) he held up his hands. 'Well, look how long it's taking you to get your backside out of – what's it called again?'

'The Scabby.'

'Scobie Street, that's it.' He tilted his head in the direction of the hall, keying into Phyllis's phone gab, trying to judge if it'd last long enough for him to make another raid on the drinks cabinet. It seemed not for he dumped his glass on the tray that his chair wore on its massive wrist like a toy watch. 'From what I hear,' he told me, 'you'll be hitching a ride on the last demolition truck out of there.'

'What's it to you?'

Despite a flawless dress-rehearsal the conjuror had screwed up: cards, doves, silk ribbons, paper flowers and rabbits, were erupting from his person; the jaws of hidden pockets sagged; endless flags of distress were being hauled from between his faltering lips, 'Well . . . I suppose it hasn't . . . not really . . . family'n that.'

'Family!'

'Yes. Family. Okay, maybe we should see each other more often but . . . well, it's only natural that Phyllis should . . .'

'What?'

'You know, be concerned for her sister's welfare. Surely you can see that?'

I said nothing because there wasn't anything that could be uttered without risk, no phrase that wouldn't be inflammatory. Deep down in the very marrow of his bones, Sherman was shit-scared of me. I was a reminder to him that poverty might only be a toss of the dice away. In the Monopoly world around which he so deftly hopped there might yet come a go-to-jail day with no bail card on hand to spring him.

'I'll have to split,' I said. 'Get my jacket, will you?'

He rose. 'I'll give you a lift to Bishopbriggs, if it's any help.'

'What like's the bus service?'

'Still in the garage, I shouldn't wonder.'

'Could you call a cab, then?'

Phyllis swept into the room with her pacy sense of overdrive which — I submit this only as a theory — is a quirk of the prematurely-born, an impetus those rawnecks seem to maintain throughout their existence, giving us womb-turtles the finger as they blaze along life's highways, their speedo needles to the pin, every town they flick through called 'Goodbye'. Here's another try-on-for-size: couldn't it be that the frenetic, high blood-pressuring hustle of the modern world is down to the technique called 'Birth-induction', a form of womb-robbery which is sweeping our assembly-line hatcheries. You'd think with all the insomnia-plagued and dream-dogged nights yet to come that they'd at least let you have your first nine months in the maternal hammock undisturbed. But no, if it's not a sinisterly gloved hand coming through the litterbox to grope you, or pipes with eyes on their noduled ends rising through the floor to ogle you, then it's the worst of all possible intrusions: you're just turning over onto your other side for some prenatal zeez when BLAM! the womb-door's booted open and in stomps Sister Pulham and her gloved and masked accomplices, vaseline and crowbars at the ready.

As she came round the mountain that was the sleeping Faraday, Phyllis said to her spouse, 'Jason's got his rails in a twist again. See what you can do, will you?' As soon as he'd left Phyllis immediately confiscated the whisky glass from the tray on Sherman's armchair when with that sardonic smirk which adorns the facial putty of Eliott Ness as his boys with their sobering axes bust the liquor barrels, she marched across and claimed mine too: no more blue danubing tonight, folks! She placed both glasses on the hostess trolley then crossed to straighten a cushion on the settee.

I wondered if Phyllis, like me, had picked up her husband's distress signals. I remember once hearing this widow saying of her husband who'd died of a coronary, 'I saw his attack coming when it was still miles away.' I got this picture of a grey-jowled man gamely digging in his windowbox and dreaming of nasturtiums, while his partner, staring over his shoulder, is watching the formation of a blue, heart-shaped cloud on the horizon.

Phyllis now turned to confront me.

A book I'd been reading recently about human body language had claimed that the cross-armed position (CAP), which Phyllis had now adopted, was NT (Non-Threatening). I doubt if its author had done any researching in Glasgow, for up here the jaggy-elbowed stance accompanied by clamped lips and a fierce rocking motion of the head can look decidedly menacing. Oddly enough, she now hit me with a query connected with elbows. 'What's wrong with your arm?'

My stoical shrug seemed to make'r all the crosser. 'Why d'you keep rubbing at it, then?'

'I bumped my elbow, that's all.'

'Falling off a bus?'

'Eh?'

'Or was it a bar stool?'

What was the X-armed bitch on about?

'. . . by the look of that army rag of yours . . .'

What had she said? Missed a bit . . . Dosser, I see. I look like a dosser. I ponged like one too. Stink of booze never off my breath. A walking brewery. The son of Shiny Shoes and with the same whiff of recklessness about me . . . The penny finally dropped. Now I saw the way the shit was shifting. This was me getting a sherrikin – verbal abuse, Glesca style. It was obvious to me now that Sherman had been delegated by the family to sort me out, to let me know that my infantile irresponsibility was no longer to be tolerated. But he'd fallen down on the job – messing around with metaphors just wasn't his bag. Phyllis knew what was what but.

No ego-whittling with a dainty penknife for her; by the look on her face she was about to do the full machete number on me.

'How did you manage to lose Jason?' she asked in a tone more suited to the Nuremburg Trials than to this temple of tackiness. Shit, the wee yin had gone'n cliped on me. Had promised he wouldn't as well.

'Lose'm? C'mon that's a bit strong, is it no? We're only talking a minute or a minute'n half at the most.'

'You don't deny it then? you did lose'm?'

'Well, if you call being out of sight for – '

'What happened?'

I filled her in but scratched the doppelgänger stuff – a gaffe as it turned out.

'What about the man?'

I met her stormy gaze. 'What man?'

'The one who took Jason from under your nose – that man!'

Willie Congreve, auld son, you had it wrong – Hell hath no fury like a woman conned, it should've been.

'Don't know what you're on about.'

She unclasped her arms but her behavioural stance became very worrying: semi-crouched she was, rage blinking on like neon along the slender bones of her face, while the forefinger of her right hand was going its dinger at me, as was her tongue. Stop lying in your teeth: a man took Jason away – the child told me; the man said it was a game of hide'n seek. They watched you running around like – a headless chicken. That, by the way, was the man's expression. Jason didn't make it up – couldn't have. After quite a long time – about ten minutes, Jason says, the kidnapper took'm to an attendant. That's what happened and I want to damn well know why!'

Me, too, lady – believe me! I've a stack of mysteries piling up, from haunted closets to leather-backed snoops, not to mention this latest brow-wrinkler – the Kelvingrove kidnap. 'Listen,' I said, 'a bloke did find'm, that's right enough, as for the rest, well – '

'Dammit, how long was he missing for?'

'I've told you – two min – '

'You're a liar! Ten minutes, Jason says.'

'What's a wee boy know aboot judging time?'

'You damned eejit – that man could've been one of those perverts. Places like that hoach with'm. Come clean – how long did he have'm?'

'Two minutes at the outside. Get a grip on yoursel. That guy'd been a perv, d'you think he'd've taken the boy to an attendant? C'mon, think about it. Another thing, the man didnae lure Jason from me – Jason followed him because he was wearing the same clobber as me. "Hide'n-seek" my eye. There just wasnae the time for it.'

Although I was fairly certain that the boy hadn't come to any physical harm – taken to a wc and interfered with, I mean – I didn't dig this being forced into lying complicity with my dress-alike. Jason, like most imaginative kids, hadn't been content to tell of the incident as was – he'd jived it up some, flung a few more squibs on the fire. Still, all wasn't made explicable by a childish sense of the dramatic – the happening in the museum remained criss-crossed by disturbing shadows. Phyllis moved away from me. She began to prowl around the lounge, adjusting an ornament here, a lace doily there. 'You're too damned careless for words,' she scolded. 'We entrust you with Jason's care and surprise, surprise you made a mess of it. We must need our heads examining, giving you custody of anything – never mind an infant. Putting you in charge of anything has to be about as clever as tap dancing in a minefield. I just knew something was going to happen. Knew it for sure. And, as usual, you didn't let me down.'

My chair creaked as I rose. 'What d'you mean "as usual?" ' I snapped, the old dander getting up. 'When last did I – '

'You're careless. Nothing matters to you but yourself. If anything had happened to that child – '

'Nothing did happen. How many times're you wanting told.'

'No thanks to you.'

'Does the same go for your mother, then?' A fine time I'd chosen to start juggling with nitro-sticks.

'What about Mother – what's she to do with your negligence?'

'I heard tell, a couple of weeks back, she lost Jason in Woolworths.'

'That's different, and you know it. He simply wandered. She didn't stand around daydreaming while he was kidnapped from under her nose.'

'He wasn't kidnapped. How many times do I have to tell you?'

She approached me. There wasn't one single body-sign favourable to my continuing health. A smack in the gub seemed about to unleash itself. 'Find a mirror,' she growled, 'and take a good long look into it. With a bit of luck you'll catch a glimpse of what the rest of us see all too plainly: a tramp, that's what, a tramp mooching from one day to the next, no pride in his appearance, not an ounce of ambition in his head. A fag in one hand, a pint-pot in the other and you're as happy as Larry.' She sighed and slowly shook her head. 'Why our Rhona was stupid enough to – '

'Go on,' I said, feeling really needled, 'stupid enough to – what?'

She took a step nearer me and her words came out in a kind of semi-shriek. 'Good God, man, don't you know how dangerous high blood-pressure can be during pregnancy?' On a much lower register now, in a voice that expressed all the contempt she felt for me, she murmured, 'Why don't you just get out of my sight?'

An astonished-looking Sherman came in with my jacket over his arm. He looked from Phyllis to me then back to his wife again. 'What on earth's going on?'

I took my 'army rag' from him. 'It's all right, Jack. Phyllis here was just giving me my marching orders.'

31

In the first place Jack Sherman shouldn't've been driving. He should've been at home sitting in his upholstered 'orchid' with his slippered feet parked on the slopes of his comatose St Bernard; he should've been conducting his musical cocktail cabinet while coaxing fiendishly innovative trumpetings from his rudewind section; he should've shoved off to his bedroom to savour the eroticism of being rubbed down by his wife with scalding teabags; in fact, he should've been doing anything but just sitting there like a gringo awaiting the garrotte while one of St Mungo's finest came crunching towards him across the deep and crisp and even. From this law guardian's chest there issued crackling bursts of crimespeak, impressive proof that he was in direct contact with his mother ship. Of the legendary pig-poke there was, as yet, no sign. Maybe, at this very moment, his companion was crouching in the front seat of the Panda swigging neat brandy before cooking the crystals – just a wee jag to get them going.

Green means GO – go directly to Jail: do not collect £200.

Sherman was wheezing like a set of knifed bagpipes. He rolled down his window. He said, 'Oh God!' three times. He also farted, which interestingly enough corroborated the claim that even the most hardened criminals frequently get their bowels in a twist during the commission of a felony. Jeezuz, the post-gut stench of Chinese wokery is unforgivable – a real friend loser. The officer stopped alongside Sherman's door, then a startling face appeared in the window aperture. It had a stony sheen to it, implanted with eyes that brimmed with hostility, and its blue jaws jived on a wad of gum. The eyes focused on the driver and Sherman after Sherman rolled away onto the crime-greased spool of Panda-man's mind. The darkly-garbed statue now spoke: 'Excuse me, Sir, are you the owner of this vehicle?'

Let's cut to a happier moment, the start of the journey, maybe, when I found myself agreeing with Phyllis that her husband, having shifted the Chivas some, not forgetting the table wine, should sensibly refrain from driving. No, let's skip that bit too – I can't stomach being seen to be in agreement with that bitch. How about Sherman bumming about his car? Aye, that'll do. A peerless set of wheels, just right for a man who, although no longer a kid, still packed plenty of whizz – or so he liked to think. An MG 1300 saloon, one thousand sovvies to put on the road, a couple of whiskies to put it off again. Right, let's have some autospiel. 'She's got a new transmission system that gives synchromesh on all gears.' Definitely handy stuff to know that. Such info'll go down a bundle in the Dog. 'She's powered by a 1275 cc four cylinder engine, in other words, a detuned Mini Cooper S engine.' Did you hear that? Dead impressive. Just think, here I am, sitting at the heart of a thousand quids' worth of freshly-minted technology. Me, who only the other day had been seen in a junkshop selling my tipper-tapper for two measly blues. What a jalopy. A man could be forgiven for warbling with pride in its ownership. Sherman, in fact, was practically yodelling as he took me on yet another tour of the walnut fascia which I was thrilled to learn had been affectionately based on the dashboard of the old Reilly. 'Oh, really?'

As in wheelsure fashion we were descending the shiny brow of an avenue, and he was explaining to me some technical tosh about the MG's ability to get from standstill to crimespeed in so many seconds (I've never quite grasped the need for such a coveted facility in a family saloon; surely it's a perk only the Brands Hatch boys and bank heist merchants would dig?) a series of vocalised yawns broke from my lips. Sherman immediately drew the car in to the kerbside, braked, killed the engine, nailed the wipers and jabbed at the radio's buttons. As the sound of Donovan's bland voice evaporated – he'd been singing his indigestion number: 'Catch the Wind' – Sherman uncellophaned a cigar which looked like a small cudgel. But, not even after he'd sucked some fire into its snout did he indicate why we'd stopped. I lighted up one of my skinny plebeian weeds, took a cautious puff on it but a bout of coughing started just the same and I'd to ashtray the fag. I sensed that a lecture was coming on, and I was right: out of a Havana cloud came forth his voice, employing that grandiose tone Hollywood accords to God when in biblical epics he starts rabbitting from behind a choric thunderhead. It was a stylish Orson Welles performance in which it was possible to detect his egotistical pleasure in the low, manly rumblings of his voice, a temporary timbre loaned to it, I suspected, by an incipient bronchial condition.

He began with some routine invective about my lifestyle in general, the spur for the entire verbal charade about to unfold itself being down to the fact that I'd yawned in his illustrious presence and, worse still, while he'd been expounding on the merits of His Car, an insult in Jack's book on par with scratching your ass while shaking hands with royalty. 'I mean,' he said, 'where d'you get off looking down your nose at people? The only outstanding thing in your life so far's been your backside hanging out your troosers . . .' My attitude was all wrong. Why, even back at his house I'd sat there with the usual cheap sneer on my pan, as if I'd the key to Fort Knox wedged up my jaxie. Who did I think I was kidding? Certainly not Jack Sherman. No way. He'd my number all right. There were hamsters that'd a better lifestyle than I had. I was a walking zero, a complete zilch with loser written all over me. (Must be helluva wee writing, Jacky boy!) It was criminal the energy I was willing to expend in order to avoid working for a living. That religious malarkey I'd tried to pull at Uncle Billy's yesterday, that was me to a tee. Had I really expected him to swallow such guff? Credit'm with some commonsense. It was high time I grew up. Toilet-training time was over – from now on I'd have to wipe my own bum. 'You get nowt for nowt in this world.' For a start – housing. It was high time I'd dropped the notion that I was too good for the likes of Castlemilk. The truth was that Castlemilk was too good for me. Was I blind, or just being plain stupid in my inability to see that jumping on and off the dole, being on the panel for weeks at a time, meant the loss of crucial housing points? I'd end up in another pesthole like Scobie Street. Was that fair to Rhona? Was it fair to my unborn child? Maybe I thought that since Ma Carlyle had provided storage room for my stuff, that should the worst come to the worst I could plonk myself down rent-free in her spare room. Well, I'm here to tell you – forget it.

He shut up for a few moments, winded, maybe by slamming those non-returning balls over the net. I guess he thought that I'd dummied up because his home truths had humiliated me. Where'd he got hold of the idea that I was trying to get cheap lodgings in my murder-in-laws's pad? I'd rather share a kennel with a rabid Doberman pinscher. I was peeved some to learn that Uncle Billy hadn't after all taken on board my possible conversion to the Catholic faith. I should've guessed he would twig.

Screwball notion, anyhow. A cross and a whole lot of bother. Right now, because of it, I could've been slabbed out in the City Mortuary, alongside Talky Sloan, Old Pike, and the knifed youth. Closest call yet. No doubt convinced that his manly growlings had wiped me out, Sherman now eased up on the slag-pedal, and with what was supposed to pass for an avuncular smile creasing his clock, he said, 'I'm only telling you for your own good, Tommy.'

For my own good, eh! When I think of the confolk who've sapped me with that line! Everytime I hear it I check to make sure I still have my shoes. Take Ma Clay for starters: 'You've got to be cruel to be kind, son,' she'd say as with unwonted vigour she'd scrub the grit from the flesh wounds I all too frequently bore up to her with salty howls from the backcourt. And, days later, when the plaster was filthy and curling up at the edges, came the harrowing exposure of the healed wound – and another verbal rip-off from Ma: 'This'll hurt me more that it hurts you, Tommy . . .' though when the plaster was yanked off it was always me who did the yelping while she smiled and called me a big wean. Medicine, too, was helped over sugared with a lie: 'C'mon, son, though nasty'n soor – the quicker the cure!' I mean if your own kith'n kin were stitching you up something rotten like this, what hope could you have when they trotted you off to those chalky chancers in Scobie Primary School? They knew what was good for you all right, they were experts in that regard. When I was little more than soft-boned bewilderment in short pants they showed me the ropes then promptly proceeded to tie me up in knots. By the second week in that place they'd me eating plasticine and wetting myself. For my own good I was made to stand in draughty corridors and was on sneezing terms with many a dusty classroom corner. With pinches and nudges they'd soon fitted me into my allotted niche in that bellowing asylum for unopened minds. And, as if this enforced 'goodness' wasn't burden enough, they'd a second penal tier waiting. And boy did its warders know what 'goodness' was!

Cigar smoke, the blue convolutions of it on the windscreen. Sherman sighed. At his fingertips, a grandsworth of prime auto; a sheepskin jacket on his back; hand-stitched shoes on his feet; in his mouth a hand-rolled cigar; and yet the man was sighing. Thoughtful of him but to kipper me with the aromatic reek of the thing – gave me an insight, no, wrong sense, an insniff into what I was missing in life, trappings which could still be mine if I settled down to being an industrious clockroach. Sorry, I can't see it being worth the hassle. For Sherman the Havanas, for me – the bananas. Just the luck of the draw, that's all.

'Well?' he glanced across at me. 'Cat got your tongue, has it?'

A grey cone of ash detached itself from the cigar and with tiny red stars winking at the disintegrating heart of it made a soft landing in the ashtray. He indulged in a further sigh, a deeper, more melancholy sounding one. But it was all an act; Mammon's robots aren't wired for empathy, there's no possibility of such greed-channelled androids being able to formulate even a primitive conception of what a poor man's misery might feel like. Sherman's sighs were as phoney as a whore's climax.

'What's to be done with you?' he asked.

Maybe, him being the solar asshole of the family (his very fart it's said can brighten an entire room) Sherman assumed he'd the licence to put such impertinent questions to people. He also had the wheels of course, the means of getting me to some hangdog bus-stop in the Briggs, a district where human life of a kind is lived though I've yet to see the proof. In other words when there's only one parachute on the plane it doesn't pay to bad-lip the pilot.

Sherman, the robot, now did an astonishing thing – he reached up and unbolted his face, plucking from it the vital component that kept it together, namely, his rimless glasses. With haste, as if he knew he was vulnerable, he whisked a white hankie across the lenses. A sight to see, that naked coupon of his. It was like seeing a tyrannical headmaster in his drawers: who could take orders from him or ever again be in awe of such a purblind pod of flesh? Sherman, allowing the hankie to flop into his lap, rapidly seized hold of the specs by their legs and waggled them onto his face. He prodded at the gold bridge until the lenses were comfortable astride his gaze. Amazing how two ultra-thin wafers of glass restored his authoritative air, returned his combative edge. His face was fully functional once more. Just as Adolf H. had been his moustache so Jack Sherman was his specs. His self-image. Were they to get broken or become lost he would be correspondingly diminished. I don't doubt that Phyllis wakening to find his undressed face asleep on the pillow beside hers would suffer a sense of foreboding. Unnerving it would be for a futurist like herself to see that her weighty hopes and plans were dependent on such a paltry and fragile prop as a pair of rimless eyeglasses.

He gathered his hankie from his lap and carefully refolding it returned it to some body compartment. 'Know what I think did for you, Tommy, yon yoga stuff you used to be into. Remember? Squatting on the floor, hoo-hahing at your belly-button.' His smirk deepened as no doubt he saw by certain of my physiological reactions that he was into pay-dirt; probably my jaw tightened, and my hands became fists, a change in my breathing pattern, maybe even a flush appearing on my face. 'You were quite the closet Buddha, eh – the Guru of the Gorbals. I can just see you, sitting there'n your Y-fronts amongst the candles and the joss-sticks making vowel sounds. Or was it bowel-sounds?' He laughed. 'Same difference.' After several attempts at puffing cigar smoke into my face, he managed to ripen a promising cough of mine into a chain-reaction of bronchial barking that left me peching, teary, and extremely irritated. His jibes went on. 'Did you ever see it, Tom – the mystical Third Eye?' He reached out to the ignition key but delayed turning it. 'Maybe you found you'd been sitting on it all along.' He gunned the engine then, as he released the handbrake, he gave me the benefit of some unsought advice: 'Yeah, searching for Samhadi in your simmet's a total waste of time, running away from life by sitting on your backside. It's tantamount to – '

I don't know how the rest of that lecture might've gone, nor shall I ever know for at that moment the panto manager – what an impatient guy he was – waved on the villains.

'Get ready to hiss, kids.'

And they came rolling on in their flashing sleigh drawn by a panda – the giant ogres, Blowdeep and Blowgreen. Their square heads were jammed into chequered hats and their festive nightsticks freely swung. Clayman chortled with glee when he saw how put-out was the evil Goldgrabber. 'Tee-hee,' he said, 'now he's for it! Now he'll get a bumful of holly . . . !'

A most interesting rap this between porker and parker. Having established that the driver was indeed the owner of the vehicle in question, the curlytail next wanted to know why Sherman was parked at the foot of a hill on such a night. Had he broken down? Was he waiting for someone? Or, had he just stopped to admire the scenery? Without being asked to Sherman produced his driving licence and passed it through the window to the officer – the fatal slip, surely, the dead giveaway! The document disappeared from view, was presumably examined, then returned to its quivering owner. I'll never know if the fuzz got an early xmas present that night, a promise-to-pay tucked by to meet such a contingency, the driver's ace in the hole. All I do know is that the pig's highly sensitive snout which at that moment should've been reporting to his brain that it was in the immediate vicinity of a whisky distillery and a Chinese latrine, was, in fact, being withdrawn into the cold night air. I'd advise you to make your journey a short one, Sir — the roads are getting tricky.'

And, with that prosaic piece of advice Blowdeep, five, maybe ten pounds heavier than he'd been on his arrival, went crunching back to his magic sleigh which tinkled, flashed and merrily rang with the sounds of a festive crime wave.

32

About a minute or so after our encounter with the curlytail Sherman was for dumping me in Anchorage, Alaska, or some such Arctic equivalent. It was a scraggy piece of tundra on the Southern outskirts of Fat Wallet, a moiled wasteland modelled on a post-battle Paschendale or Ypres. Excavation equipment, diggers, scoops, and what-have-you lay abandoned by the frigid roadside; a pair of cement-mixers, like fat canonry, presented their snow-packed muzzles to a trio of hag rowans who were conspiring at a crossroads. It was on this very spot that Sherman slewed the car to a halt.

'Out!' he ordered.

Out? Out there? He had to be joking. Like a rookie skydropper who'd gone chicken, I clamped myself to my seat. Out there was strictly for huskies. A wind, armed to the teeth with snow and hypothermia agreed with me as it came smoking along a poorly-lit road that just might be the long way to Tibet. Sherman repeated his insane command. He even began to jostle me. Very uncool. 'You heard'm,' he gabbled. 'Get off the road, he said.' He was trying to reach past me to get at my door handle, but sore wing or not I managed to fend him off. I grasped what his problem was. How much running time'd his bribe bought? How long before those oinks declared open-season on'm again. A genuine worry. But what was an endorsement compared to yours truly being howked like a glazed garden gnome from a melting snowdrift come April next? No contest. The heartless bastard was still trying to dunt me from my seat, every sideways shunt of his forcing a gasp of pain from me. I couldn't tough this out much longer. From Sherman's lips poured fiction about there being a plenitude of hotels, inns, and welcoming peasants all waiting for me around the bend. Could I see it? Aye, with a pair of navy bins I could've zoomed right into a couthy wee tavern where a fire big enough to roast a Jack Sherman blazed in the hearth and a triple measure of the inverted gold awaited my coming. As it was, I'd merely my god-given peepers to rely on and the only sign of human habitation they were reporting was a scattering of construction huts and some vague shadowy things in the snow-covered fields – probably a caribou herd on the move to its winter-feeding grounds.

Sherman slammed into me again and pain ricocheted along my bones, augmenting itself like a fabulous pinball run, racking up the agonies to a score well beyond human toleration. Angrily, I swung round at'm. 'C'mon for fucksake, Jack. What's got into you? I don't even know where I am.'

He told me but it meant nothing. According to him all I'd to do was to keep to the road for ten minutes and I'd be – stiffer'n Casanova's pecker that's what! Sherman began to froth more fiction about how close to civilisation I really was, then seeing that this was leaving no grooves on me, he mounted an even more ferocious assault. A Mafia hitman would've flinched at such callousness. As his shoulder ramming increased he showed his teeth, made savage snarling noises and fisted heavily at my fingers which clung now to the door-handle and prevented him from getting to it to force my ejection. His face, I noted, was becoming glossy with melting veneer.

I jerked my head. 'Back there . . . maybe a mile . . . a hotel . . . Ow, ya bass, that's bloody sore! Take me to it . . . and I'll phone for a cab . . . Right?'

No dice. 'Back there' was where Blowgreen and Blowdeep lurked. Sherman was for another route home. This entailed his turning off right here'n now! The obscene little struggle literally took an even more vicious twist when he seized my crippled wing in his pincer-like grasp and began powerfully to squeeze on it. I let out such a roar it would've alerted the Marquis de Sade, himself, to the code of human decency he was violating. One just didn't do this to people. It just wasn't fuck'n on! My blanched fingers dropped from the door handle. The pincers relaxed, became a hand again, the fingers of which lightly patted my louping arm before falling away, a kind of tactile apology.

As he got the door open harsh blades of snow slashed at the left side of my face and plastered white my shoulder'n arm on the same side. The car's headlamp beams lit a road from which all tyremarks had long been erased. I rubbed at my throbbing arm. 'You're sure there's a hotel?' His head about nodded itself from its rocker. To hear'm you would've believed that only a few minutes away, a quarter of a mile or so along the cottonwool road – you'd know you were close to it when you'd spotted Bambi gambolling with his woodland pals in a buttercupped meadow – was to be found a traveller's haven simply hoaching with hotels, motels and even cartels, not to mention bed'n breakers by the dozen with loads of 'Shangrilas', 'Dunroamins' and 'Restawearies', with white-haired and floral-peenied grannies lined along their well-scrubbed doorsteps waving 'Vacancies' placards to the spoiled-for-choice tourists. In case I needed further persuasion the pincers returned to my sore arm. Not pressuring it, you understand, just there as a wee reminder of how even the best relationships can so swiftly degenerate into brutishness.

Fully aware of the facts of death, I stepped from the car into a snowdrift. The wind couldn't credit its luck: it ran up to cuff'n slap at me to see if I was real, then, finding that I was genuine enough, though obviously a glimmerbrain, it capered gleefully around, running together its luminous palms. Sherman's body was tilted in my direction as he reached to try'n claw the door shut.

'You're a topper, Jack!' I shouted in at'm, 'a real fuck'n top – ' Scared, maybe, that a remorse of conscience might rob it of its big witless playmate, the wind aided Sherman by snapping the door shut. You twat! a voice (it sounded like Vic Rudge's) shouted in my head. You should've grabbed them off the bass! Grabbed what? His fuck'n specs, man. What a diddy. D'you think he really sees you giving him that vicky. Save your fuck'n breath as well, he can't hear you. He's offski. And so he was: fishtailing snow, the MG was soon nothing but dwindling tail-lights, its acceleration honouring its manufacturers promise by getting its speedo to sixty before I'd shouted myself into a coughing fit and, in trying to execute a double vicky, had aggravated my sore elbow so much the pain suggested it'd popped its socket.

Right enough, if I'd only thought to snatch his specs. What a stroke! It would've fixed him good, had him out of the cosy nest of his car floundering after me, begging, aye, just think of that, begging me to – Stop wanking your wishbone, the scunnered voice said, too fuck'n late. Maybe not. I could lay a hex on'm. My days dabbling in shamanism and parawhatsits had given me a few wrinkles in the art of striking one's enemies from a distance. Tuning into the thousand hexoherts range I suggested that a busted axle should befall the MG, anything at all that'd see it getting written-off in spectacular fashion, just so long as the end result was Sherman with his backbone snapped five times over but remaining conscious throughout his ordeal, ultra-sensitive to each'n every pang that visited his flesh – and so mote it be until the uttermost breath had quitted his cracked and blackened lips.

Here, said Jeremiah, that's a bit chancey – laying curses on your fellow man, especially at a crossroads. Don't you know the earth hereabouts is Satan's portion? Why else are suicides buried at such junctions? Be warned, curses tend to redound on their invokers at such unhallowed spots.

Redound, eh? My, he'd dug down to the bottom of the auld word bag for that yin. The act of redounding. Pissing against the wind, he means. Wouldn't it be a pity to put at risk all the good fortune I've been recently enjoying, all the fun I've been having scuba-diving in Shit Lake? All right, I'll lift the hex. Cobble his spine together again and replace those injuries with a bruise to the thumb and simple decapitation.

Safeguarded now in spirit I'd be able to pay heed to the needs of the old corpus crusty. Heat was its primo need, of course. 'You'll no' gang faur oan a cauld firebox . . .' as the cindery wee gem of railway lore has it. Sherman's sheepskin jacket (what garment could be apter for such a lycanthropic owner?) and a flask of whisky, would've made me more confident about reaching the hotel which Sherman assured me awaited just around the next bend in the south-bearing road. Are you listening, landlord? I want to change my order: scrub the Scotch and sub it with a triple dark rum – the banana-flavoured kind – and a couple of green teardrops of ginger. Thanks. Pardon? My ETA? I reckon around ten minutes from now, give or take a grizzly bear or a famished wolf-pack. If I don't show by then you'd best come a mushing with some huskies. How will you know me? C'mon, despite the coincidence of a double-dresser back'n the

Art Gallery there just can't be two of us tramping this white trash with tartan scarves wound about our bonces looking like a couple of spooks trudging home after yet another Wembley débâcle.

It would surprise me none to hear that John Mills, the film actor, had suffered more jawdroop than a jilted pelican during the making of *Scott of the Antarctic*. Those hours spent in the make-up trailer when his gorge rose before the sun did as they tweezered onto his flesh snowblight'n the seven scurves; the long day's battle through phoney blizzards, cussing technicians, and worse-tempered huskies – it's during such grisly episodes in an actress/actor's life, when the studio set begins to look like an illuminated scaffold that the players get a glimpse of the stark reality awaiting them down the road – not the coveted Oscar, that tasteless chunk of metal, but Rubberland, itself, with its simple necessities: a cot, a chair, and a basket-weaving set.

At least at the end of a wearying day in his Spanish Antarctica John Mills could look forward to a shower and a decent meal, unlike poor Scott who, out there in the real, unscripted world, hadn't only been unable to eat in the canteen – he'd been unable to find the bloody thing! What of yours truly, then – was my life about to dribble out in farce as well? Would I be brought back in the jaws of a snowplough, my rigid legs stuck up'n the air in a pathetic last vicky at the world? (In this scenario, which'll be ditched just as soon as the promised hotel hoves into view, the script committee insist on the, to my mind, hackneyed notion of having the snowploughman whistling a few snatches from 'Stranger on the Shore'.) For the moment, though, I'd just have to continue plodding on between the poles of endurance and hope. I've been doing this nearly all my life, usually sans snow, so what's the big deal?

Recalling Scott's entries in his last tragic diaries I began, just to keep the dreaded cranreuch at bay, to mentally jot down some notes for my own journal, if I ever got to within pen reach of it again.

Sunday 22nd Dec. 196-

(I've long been an admirer of the decorous habit certain Russian authors employ in taking a hammer to Time's sickle and flattening the soft lead of the given centuries decade into a flat wee rod of conjecture.)

'For a long time I've been floundering along. My feet sink into the dazzling quicksnow. At any moment I may be taken; a flash of white, a single gulp, then gone, much like the shark victim's last moments. For too long I have lived with this delusion of being a man, and one moreover who had no peers in the art of survival. Too late I've discovered myself to be a mere insect trekking across the wilderness of a teaplate. I turn, and yet endlessly turn, harried constantly by Fate's stubby finger (nicotine stained, by the way) which prods maliciously at me. Sometimes it even flips me onto my back to gloat at my impotently writhing limbs. What frustration when, just as I think I'm making progress his mucky nail flicks me back all the way to the very rim of my journey.'

Shortly before I reached that place of heavenly rest, promised to me by the horned and hooved Sherman, a muster of icy sentinels frisked me to the skin, turning out my last pockets of warmth, beggaring me to my last therm before allowing me to proceed, but only after I'd given them the password.

'Bastard!' I howled. For, having gone round the bend I found nothing but a roofless biggin – the former home of a turnip howker – hedged about with a ha-ha, its interior thickly wadded with snow. Nothing else to be seen by way of human habitation, neither hotel, motel, nor pub – not even a wee pie-stall. The glimmering road went on ahead of me, occasional dim sparks of light, as lustreless as a March xmas tree, a scarcely worthwhile amperage grudgingly shed by some tight-fisted local council lighted the way to yon grim wee hamlet, the name of which never appears on signposts, the one most feared by mountaineers, hillwalkers and Arctic explorers alike – 'Lethal Exposure'.

As I stood there, coughing and shivering, another of Jeremiah's promised chickens came home to roost. 'The Eskimo's Exit', that's what'd been given me. No doubt such a drastic solution to the 'Clay Problem' had been arrived at during a round-table conference of the Family. Those present who'd displayed qualms about offing me would've been quickly slapped down by the Godmother, Letitia Carlyle. I could almost hear her harsh death sentence as she put out a contract on me. 'Best he be put down. Best for us all – especially our Rhona. Some mongrels can't be trained. They spend their lives leaving messes behind them, messes other people have to clean up. But, no more of it – he's got to go! And having thus spoken she'd no doubt arisen and hurried herself off to her velvet-lined coffin for the sun was already high in the heavens and the rays from it drove her quite batty.

The task of my disposal had obviously fallen upon the Family Champ, Jack Sherman. This would account for the way he'd given the booze big belters and provide the reason for his insistence – despite protests from both Phyllis and myself – to drive me as far as the Briggs. After his brush with the curlytail, instead of panicking, he'd kept his cool. You've got to hand it to these money-men, always a step ahead they are, real sharpies the way they can turn a potential disaster into an astounding gain.

A homicide in which the weather, itself, is the murder weapon – it literally took the breath away. And, an important point, the murder was still in progress, my gradual elimination was underway. Right now I was about two parts human to one part cadaver – my feet'n hands were already grave-fodder – and the corpsification of my arms and legs was imminent.

'The body of a man, later named as Thomas Clay (28), of 37

Scobie Street, Glasgow C5 was found in open country several miles south of the Nat Smollet Estate. The deceased is believed to have been ran over by a snowplough, but the police declined to comment on what part of the victim's anatomy was affected when the cruel coulter passed.

As a celebration of my own daftness, this cockeyed heroism in fraught circumstance which is a marked characteristic of your glimmerbrain, my stiffening mirth-muscles managed to crank out a pale facsimile of the John Mill's 'Tuff Brit Grin', the original of which is now in the Imperial War Museum. Encouraged, my ice-locked tongue and throat muscles tried for a chuckle but could produce only a threadbare chirruping sound such as you'd expect to hear from a newly-widowed grasshopper. Still, my show of defiant optimism, allied as it was to a windshift which despite its kidney-glazing potential, kept giving me big shoves in the right direction was, for the first time, granting signs that I was making real progress and not merely marking time on the same snowdrift like a helpless cartoon figure trapped in a scenery whirlaround of repeater trees, born-again boulders, and mimetic mountains.

Hey, s'that no a light ower yonner?

Shhh!

Can you no see it, or what?

Block your wordhole. Course I see it.

Well, then?

Don't want to scare it off, that's all. Sorta creepin up'n it. You crowd them mirages, give'm your scent, so much as step on one little knuckle of ice – and they are gone, man.

I was starting to feel good and that was real bad. Polarnauts take up whole chunks of their snowographies warning against euphoric moods. Mountaineers too. When outfoxed by the overhang and no way of getting back, you start into whistling, cracking jokes, and waving your knife around, your fellow ropees have every reason to reach for their worry-beads. Deepsea divers refer paradoxically to such untimely mood upswings as '*Rapture of the Deep*', though right now my main fear was from rupture of the spleen caused by a drop through the ice of this frozen River Styx I was walking. Tagging along at my heels beneath the carapace I keep getting imaginary glimpses of a huge fish, a pike maybe, which just couldn't wait to get its teeth-bristling jaws wrapped around yours truly. But do I worry? Not a bit of it. If I had lips for it I'd give a little whistle. So what if my elbow was gowping and some rough-handed cove was ramming bales of hot steel wool into my gasbags; I still felt so goddamned good about things, so upbeat and ticketyboo. Shake your heads and mumble doomy forecasts into your frozen beards, you tundra vets – I've gone beyond your reach into gladness. Yup, I was that far out of it!

I recall reading a diver's account of his experience with the '*Rapture of the Deep*' or as he called it, 'giggling with the gudgeons'. Having got a kink in his airline or an eel up his asshole, some such techno-letdown, he'd seen through his facemask his entire family, stretching back for many generations, sitting around a table on the seabed having what he chooses to call 'a sort of Mad Haddock's Tea Party'. It looked like a real lavish spread and his kinsfolk kept waving to'm, urging him to come and join them. He'd been sorely tempted to do just that when suddenly there'd been revealed to'm amidst the multi-hued, dappling interplay of numinous fishes, the very Meaning of Existence itself. So penetratingly simple had been this Meaning that he'd resisted the alluring come-ons of his family at its seabed celebrations and had fought his way to the surface. Once he'd returned to his own element and they'd got'm into a decompression chamber, amongst the first words spoken by him were the very ones that'd emblazoned themselves across his mind while he'd been 'giggling with the gudgeons'.

Gentlemen, he'd solemnly intoned, I am privileged to be the custodian of the Meaning of Existence. Please record the following for posterity:

A FISH MAY RIDE A BICYCLE BUT NOT WHILE WEARING TROUSERS!

Thank you.

Hey, man, those lights, they're getting brighter.

Dummy up. I see'm okay. Play it cool – ignore'm.

But I took another peep at'm just the same. From the mere straw of light I'd been clutching at, the luminous band stretched along the horizon had broadened so that it'd begun to look like a mahogany plank, one strong enough to bear the hope that its very presence signalled the proximity of a townlet or even a village. The wind had dropped by now and the snowfall had lightened to oddly separate cascadings of flakes, like the last sweepings from the now all but empty snowbunkers. Another peep. Aye, the lights endured, pricking to brightness with every slow nearing step. A dog could be heard barking and a raven with one of Noah's waistcoat buttons caught in its beak fluttered past . . . Okay, quit the exaggeration, I think we've got the picture. But just to reinforce the fact that civilisation was close at hand there began to materialise before me an astounding apparition.

Sunday 22nd Dec. 196- (An unexpected PS)

'A miracle! Out here, in this folkforsaken place – a telephone kiosk! And, what's more, not a single pane of it was missing, broken, nor even cracked. It was swathed in a tissue of fine snow through which, here'n there, festive patches of ruby paint gleamed. It looked for all the world like a gigantic xmas present stood up on its end. But as is often the case with glamorously wrapped pressies after they've finally been opened – disappointment: the kiosk was completely gutted, empty, denuded of apparatus, a ghost in the telecommunication's network. Nevertheless, it offered proof that humans had once been here and this was emphasised still more by the presence in the kiosk of a pink sports paper and on the damp mucky floor, looking like a flattened slug – a used loveskin.'

I stood wheezing and coughing in the snow-shrouded kiosk, feeding its darkness with flaring, short-lived matches. The sports paper was too sodden to catch fire, my lungs too twitchy to suffer smoke. A helluva thing is existence: a wee splutter of light, that's all there is to it. You learn to eat; where to shit; what your given name is. You're made to take a job and to live by the rigours of its working conditions; then, one day, usually when you don't expect it – they drop a coalmine on your head. Finito.

Maybe those frozen dadpoles down there on the manky floor had gotten lucky did they but know it. An idea for a short story occurred to me, so at least my fictional gland was still secreting: this guy is walking across the Sahara when he hears a phone ringing. Being a Scot he detests this waste of time and energy. Going well off his route he traces the ringing to a British telephone kiosk which stands on its ownsome in a wadi. He enters its broiling interior and lifts the receiver. A Brooklyn voice grinds into his ear: 'Kaminsky Account: two sawbucks Saloosi, thoid; if bread, dump all, Mighty Fine, de fourth . . .'

My phoneless kiosk, although offering me a modicum of shelter wasn't a place to hang about in. About as chummy as an Iron Maiden, only this version for its fatal hug would use icicles instead of nails. I wound my sodden scarf about my head again, jerked up my collar, then dropped somebody's stone hands into my pockets. It looked, after all, as if the kiosk had been a sucker card in a forked deal, a come-on to the clean-out. But I was proved wrong: the Man started to skim me some potent pieces of pasteboard. I picked up on a pair of lamp-posts, a prile of streets, followed by four-of-a-kind in cottages. Soon enough I'd the makings of, if not a town, then a hamlet at least. This could only be the miniopolis of Crabton. Its streets always have this peculiarly empty look about them. Like now, for instance, when the sole pedestrian to be seen was a snow-drenched transient.

I was drawn to a place of sanctuary. On an otherwise snowbliterated board the words 'Sister of Mercy' reached out to me. Had they been cleared expressly for me by the hand of St Christopher himself? A kindly-looking nun responded to my urgent knockings. In those time-honoured clichés, hallowed down the centuries, the traveller puts his case, with some necessary updating, of course; a taxi would be preferred to an ass, and a telephone to summons one better than hanging about in a gutter shouting. Following an altogether alien tradition, the good sister told me to clear off then gave me a snoutful of door timbers. A merry xmas to all you holy cockroaches. I don't envy your lives one bit. I think your God gave you a bum deal walling you up'n that penitentiary for the pious, that sepulchre which whited with snow 'appears beautiful outward but is within full of dead broads' bones'. Almost word-perfect. The Reverend Weaver would snip a couple of knots from my sin-thread and Ma Clay would be well pleased, too.

I was lured by a bright light down an avenue which looked like a place where birch and poplar trees came to die. Humans, given that there were some hereabouts, were sticking close to their tepee hearths tonight. Any moment now I expected Ray Bradbury's chilling robocar to come on powdery white wheels around some corner, to fix me with its probe while from its personless interior a voice would begin to ask very intimate questions. The upshot? I'd be charged with being a stranger – a very serious offence around these parts.

Mundanely enough, the seductive light illuminated a low squat building which had dithered between becoming a pillbox or a

Martello tower and done neither. According to its noticeboard which by half-turning its shoulder had managed to preserve some of its identity, it declared itself to be a 'Home for the Chronically – ' something or other. The Deaf and Chronically Ignorant was my guess to judge by the way those roasting themselves at fires inside ignored my heavy fistings upon their snow-festooned door.

Hurrah! I was picked up by a baker on his way to perform a nightshift in an industrial laundry. (I know, I know. Let it pass – I was in a very bad way!) Its driver talked all the way to the Briggs about budgies. He bred the little buggers. He'd lost ten of them due to the bad weather. When we got to the Briggs he gave me a couple of bridies that looked like retreads. The wispy blue feathers preserved under the crust-glaze was a novel touch. Anyway, I gobbled them down and wished my saviour many happy budgerigars when they came and the best of luck to Stretchy, his prize cock.

I hailed a cab but its driver gave me the slip. The driver of the next one I signalled to gave me the finger. The third driver had almost to be ambushed, and even after I'd cornered him he wouldn't turn a wheel until he'd seen the colour of my money. Eventually what was left of me arrived in what remained of the Gorbals. By then it was too late to wet my whistle, since Glasgow, that most holy of cities, although it'd liberalised its Sabbath boozing hours a little, still tended to take her pavements in around ten p.m. But even if there'd been time to tie a couple on I wasn't up to it. No way was I fit to 'scrum for a rum, or bruise for some booze' as John Scobie puts it in his 'Heavy Drinkin'.

I returned to base, coughed my way up every flight of stairs, lurched wearily into my cane. I lighted the fire and got a mugful of scalding Bovril down me while I sat so close to the roaring fire it would've looked to any stranger watching like an attempt at do-it-yourself cremation. Eventually I thawed out but it was only sheer discipline that persuaded me to write up my journal.

And then, the unexpected; from out of the blue onto the white I penned:

Letter to an Unpublished Child.

Dear notyet,

Today, take my word for it, you're already heavier than a deluxe volume of *War and Peace*, and displaying such a sinuous complexity of purpose as to rival that opus. There, I knew you'd be pleased. Better still, your tests reveal your remarkable inventive vigour, not to mention your verve'n vivacity (Daddy has sent these v's flying like seabirds to brighten up his craggy prose). It would seem that the passing of your Homo sapiens exam is now a mere formality. Mammy and I are so proud of how you buckled down to your prelimbs. What a thrill the other day when Mammy let me touch a secret spot and I was able to feel the vibrations from that genetic typewriter you pound away at night'n day. An expert on you heroic little terranauts was able by means of a trumpetlike instrument to hear the most promising echoes from your 'wee blood beater' as he so drolly called it.

Things this side of the womb are so-so. Yeah, I'll straightshoot with you, they could be a whole wedge better. But don't you go bothering your bald wee bonce about anything: Daddy'll have a nifty wee nest all fixed up for your arrival. February's such a waste of a month: 'Snaw'n slush'n the lavvies'll no flush', as Mr Scobie puts it, so your advent will be all the more welcomed.

Since you've the inside gen you'll know that Mammy is doing fine although now'n again she gets to feeling a bit clunk. Not to worry, things'll work out, you'll see. So, just you away for a wee paddle in your dusky brook and let me do the worryin.

    Keep up the good work,
                    Love, Daddy xxxxx.

33

Intimations of departure; presentiments of conclusion.

I'm squatting in bog four of Shug Wylie's scrupulously scrubbed crapper, *The Scottish Daily Distress* is spread across my chilled thighs. Most of the paper's prime space has been devoted to the Apollo 8 mission, the purpose of which is to lassoo the moon. A starry-eyed NASA boffin predicts that the USA'll have men on the moon by this time next year, a feat which will be of no interest whatsoever to John Michael Hallison (19) of Burmola Street, Possilpark, whom I'd last seen imprinted on a slushy pavement, Saturday night, last. Stabbed through the heart, he'd been, 'a single, fatal thrust' according to the report. A time-traveller now, the youth had already departed this planet, gone dwindling away on the retrogressive velocities of death, heading for burn-out. To judge from his picture – a smudged teenager on a blurred bike – he'd already shed twelve or so years; by tomorrow he might well be depicted toothless and tucked up'n his pram.

There was mention also of the Pike conflagration. Nothing much, just a wee cindery patch at the foot of a column to inform the readership that Papa Pike was no more, and that the condition of his son Mr Malcolm Puke (stet that misprint!) was giving cause for concern due to severe burns and the effect of smoke inhalation. Three other men who had been visiting the flat at the time of the fire's outbreak were released after treatment.

And what of Horace the Hun? Was he reading this selfsame report while praying with every fibre of his stunted, pox-ridden body that the blaze'd been caused by the spontaneous combustion of a visiting hippie whom the forensic folks hoped to identify just as soon as his dust'd settled. The report concluded with the statement that the Pike's flat'd been completely gutted. My main worry was how complete was complete? A concern which'd acquired sturdy roots and a whole set of poisonous leaves had implanted itself in my mind, so much so that all my other worries – there seemed to be droves of them – wilted in its sinister shade. Pike, and his trio of Proddy goons might've obtained my name'n address. If so then it was down to yon pessimistic pair, Pirandello and Dylan. How come? Simple. Instead of remailing the record company's payments reminder on the Dylan discs, I'd used it as a bookmark for the Pirandello paperback. This book I'd dumped on the table when I'd been forced to jettison the contents of my pockets for their wager. In the hasty retrieval of my personal stuff (and a moderate uplift of some banknotes of varying denominations), I must've overlooked the paperback. Of course, if 'completely gutted' meant just that, then I'd nothing to worry about. But if the Pirandello biography had been salvaged, together with its telltale letter, then a hard rain was gonna fall on yours truly.

Any morning now I'd waken to find I'd become a gigantic clockroach. This morning I'd sure felt like one as I lay there on my back swallowing the disgusting globs of mucous that kept gathering in my mouth. And such bitterness. Had I really been the intended victim of a Family murder plot? It hardly seemed likely. Sherman had been given the choice of an unblemished driving licence and the possibility of my death from exposure. Naturally, since he'd convinced himself that his reputation mattered more than my continuing nuisance value, he'd plumped for his own self-esteem. It wasn't an act of attempted homicide, more one of human carelessness. Similarly, I'd shown carelessness when I'd allowed old Pike to delve into my matchbox even after I'd heard from his own lips that he wasn't allowed to have a lighted fire in his room. Had I stopped to ask myself why this was, I might've twigged.

Although the beaver down by the brook had collected many small twiglets of gossip, I'd small interest in them. I felt completely scunnered. For a start the weather down south had taken a turn for the better. Consequently, the A74 had begun to unclog itself and in bed'n breakers, Greasy Spoons, etc., gear jockeys were being shaken from their enforced hibernation. John McQuade would be amongst them. It's amazing how I've managed – without a flake of evidence, be it noted – to elevate McQuade to gianthood – six-six at the last mention. Also worthy of note, is the barbarian's beard I've clamped on his clock, not to mention having mentally clad'm in a woodfeller's jacket, capacious enough to meet the muscular spread of Paul Bunyan. I've also equipped him with a lethal pair of boots that pack enough steel to armour a Sherman tank. Goliath McQuade – mine own creation! Maybe I've been exaggerating, frightening myself. Could be he's nothing but a wee wetmouth with granny specs and shitty bumper boots, aye'n with the heart of a cockroach. No, I don't think so somehow. Hadn't Becky warned me that he was a 'canaptious big swine' who'd punch you as soon as look at you. Best not to forget either that she'd lulled me to sleep with a tingling tale of how, during one of the many routine scraps at their wedding he'd punched his favourite brother's eye clean out of its socket. No way does this mean that I was about to drop wee

Matt in it. I'd never do that, not intentionally, no, not even if by tomorrow McQuade's grown to seven feet and rising. Let's face it but, when it comes to the pinch (punch) what could I do? I mean I've gotten kinda used to looking at things with two eyes, and – no I'm not saying that. If fists start flying I would be in there giving as bad as I got. But let's live in the world as is – okay? I can't be expected to protect Lucas every minute of the day. No way was it possible for me to bodyguard'm without a break. I'd a whole stack of problems of my own to sort out. 'Ach, tae hell wae it,' as Tiger Wilmott used to say, 'getting yersel born's the hard bit, Tam – the rest is aw doonhill . . .' Tiger, a china of mines, died in the Vicky Infirmary from what he called 'a floating kidney that discovered it couldnae . . .' A helluva guy, Tiger, and a smashing goalie.

Thus far Monday's lived up to its bitch-of-the-week tag. First, had come a real downer: Joe Fiducci was chucking in the towel this very week. He'd intended to hang on for a few weeks more but his son Luigi'd persuaded him that nostalgia was a luxury he couldn't afford. 'He's right,' the old man nodded as he gave me what might be my penultimate shave from him, 'yesterday's never fattened a pig . . .' I hadn't heard that one before; it must be one of those proverbs that get maimed in translation. I don't suppose our own one 'Mony mickles mak a muckle' comes out too well in the Tuscan vernacular.

Old Mooney wasn't in the least upset to hear that he'd soon be out of a job. For this there was a very sound reason – the old bugger wasn't there to hear it. That he'd done a bunk with my winnings was more or less confirmed by his absence. The chances now of getting at least some of my bread back were melting quicker than the A74 slush. Joe gave me Mooney's address in Oatlands. It'd do no harm to check it out, just in case the greybeard had really come down with a dose of flu or something.

More gloom awaited me in the Bum Boutique: the plug'd been

306

pulled on Shug. Earlier, a senior crappy-chappie had dropped by to tell'm that his facility had been declared redundant and would be terminated at the year's end. However, Shug's dedication to hygenic defecation had not gone unnoticed for he'd been allocated a new location – an uptown crapper, a prospect that didn't cheer'm any.

'Just a load of poofs and poncers up there,' he grumbled. 'No a decent shit amongst them.'

In Shug's dookit a buff-coloured envelope awaited my arrival. Opening it, I found myself to be in communication with the Glasgow Housing Dept. Curtly, for they are as economical with their words as they are with their smiles, I was instructed to attend their Castlemilk office this coming Friday regarding the allocation of a flat in the said district. Some years ago this might've been bracing news but today it had all the allure of a cable which read:

'PACK CASES STOP COME AT ONCE STOP HAVE WANGLED US A BERTH ON TITANIC . . .'

'Bad news?' Shug'd asked me.

I nodded. 'I've got ma call-up papers for Legoland.'

'Ach, I don't know,' Shug said. 'You could dae a lot worse than Castlemilk. They used tae be climbing ower each other's shooders tae get a hoose up there.'

I took a bite of Shug's char. 'Naw, if I'm goin anywhere it'll be Myrtle Park. High flats, maybe, but it's only a corner kick fae Hampden Park.'

'Have you enough points for the like o'there?'

'Should think so. Wean on the road, being made homeless – that's enough to be goin on wae.'

'But you're no workin.'

'Soon will be but.'

'Doing what?'

'Banana straightener.'

Shug grinned and gave one of his elegant wee sniffs. 'Never mind,' he said, 'there's wan blessing so there is.'

'What's that?'

He nodded towards the diving suit which I was returning to the Planet on behalf of Cullen. 'When you're up the Milk and get a notion for a pint – at least you'll have the clobber for it!'

34

And so it transpired that with an unravelling psyche I sloshed the slush across to the doomed Planet with a fake diving suit slung over my shoulder, its helmet carried in yon gallus underarm way those Yankee astronauts tote their star-lids. I also carried with me an unholy alliance of viruses which was sweeping to victory on all fronts. My louping elbow was fast reaching that mark on the painometer where shrieking and gnashing of teeth can no longer be stifled. A right flock of ravens, I agree. But, not to worry, I've been down before, like that time, for instance, when I copped a dose of the Spanish Blues. I'd been smitten by a book, the work of yon doyen of the dolorous, Miguel de Unamuno. The initial swigs from his cosmic cocktail with its base of heavy pessimism produced a sense of existential vertigo you might expect to get from hopping around backwards on a hinged pogo-stick with a coal scuttle jammed on your head. But, all things pass, as Emily Dodds, cinema cleaner, might've said as I trailed some sidewalk reality across the muck-whorls her symbolist mop was making on the vestibule's terrazzo floor. 'Up yours too, dipstick,' I said in reaction to her scowls and headshakes, and might've got grosser still if she hadn't been stone deaf.

A tip I got from a manic depressive concerning the common

blues was 'never to try to make it say its name'. In other words don't analyse its whys and wherefroms. Can't do a thing about it anyhow. It's just mental bad weather passing over, its mean rain coming down on more heads than your own one. At the heart of the conventional blues as articulated, say, by an old negro hunkered over his harmonica on the stoop of his lean-to shack, is resignation. Yeah, his baby had indeed done gon'n left'm, and he can take it for sure she definitely aint a-coming back. No, siree. Sing it, man!

> Now, I promised my lovely lady
> I'd dress'r in pearls and silk,
> But now she's wearing charity
> And we're trapped in Castlemilk.
> We got the blues,
> Yeah, we got those damned and deserted
> Damp walls blues . . .

Too right, they have. But for all its hangdog charm, the common blues is losers' music, failure resonating from a busted guitar. It's an extreme expression of a sort of parochial pessimism, a much diluted extract from the draughts of deep angst as poured by Unamuno, Sartre, Camus et al. These spectators of the void were dealing with the same terror which seized Pascal's heart when staring up at the starry abyss he felt the full weight of his snuffability. I suppose what gloomy Miguel had been drawing my reluctant attention to was the fact that the universe at large doesn't give a toss for us earthlings – worse still, it doesn't even know that it doesn't give a toss!

But soon, much sooner than I'd expected, my downbeat mood was lifted some as I climbed the stairs to the lounge by the visions of Maureen O'Hara, Barbara Stanwyck, Doris Day and Esther

Williams, all of them still up there in their gilt frames, and, as always, dispersing the gloom with the ivory lanterns of their smiles, beaming down on me from the tinselly ramparts of the Hollywood Dream. I saluted each of them with an admiring glance and didn't forget to waggle my ears at Clark Gable whose good looks, alas, had succumbed to a green rash which tended to make'm look like a pissed-off Martian. Alan Ladd, though, is still in tip-top condition – sharp as a Bowie knife. I paid my respects to'm by pausing for a moment before his picture. Ladd is the patron saint of punters, the wee man with the big heart, the guy who stoically takes it on the chin for as long as is bearable before he quietly reaches for his gunbelt. Ladd is family, sired on me by celluloid when I was at an impressionable age, that fractured time when the old man was barnstorming in and out of my life like a boozy comedian, stopping by a while to crack some jokes, break a few promises, before he tap-danced offstage again. In his absence, I'd taken my troubles to Mr Ladd. Even if he was busy, maybe serving two years before the mast, or chute-dropping on a Jerry bridgehead, he'd always take time out in one of my dreams to say where it was at. I came to rely on him, that's what made this picture a kind of icon for me, why I'd asked Old Burnett to let me have it when the Planet ran its last reel.

Something interesting seemed to be taking place inside Burnett's office. Exchanging the role of bypasser for that of eavesdropper I paused to listen. First, the doomy sounds of Madge Dawkins, Burnett's secretary, sobbing. Unusual, this aint. Madge cries so often and so copiously that a guttering system strapped to her long, tremulous chin would've saved her a fortune in nose tissues. In a latter-day Canute role, Burnett was trying to baulk the salty tide with a series of tepid-sounding there-theres and phrases like, 'Don't take on so', and 'No need to upset yourself like this . . .' While it seemed that he was succeeding in screwing off her tap Burnett's sympathetic patter was frequently pervaded by unaccountable cloth-rending noises. Had I stumbled upon the unthinkable – the defloration of Madge Dawkins, professional virgin? The rip-ripping sounds were driving MacDougall to an incredible pitch of randy conjecture. If I was to barge in would I find the air thick with flying lingerie and Burnett and Dawkins in – no, it was a combination too bizarre to envisage. Let's grab an eyeful anyhow, said MacDougall, all but bursting with prurience. For sure, there was a sexual shimmer to their duologue:

Burnett: No, hold it there, my dear. A little more firmly. Yes, that's the way (rip-rip).

Madge: I j-just can't (rest of sentence muffled due to resumed snivelling).

Burnett: Well, what with the loss of your poor mother and (rip-rip) so on, you've had more than enough on your plate. This is certainly tougher'n I expected (rip-rip). There, that's got it. Just drop'm on the floor my dear . . .

Madge: (wailing still) But a mummy picture for Christmas – that's just awful!

Burnett: It'll only be for a couple of nights. (rip-rip). We're closed Christmas Day, don't forget. And another way to look at it (rip-rip), we'll have the Beetles for three nights now. We'll soon have things fixed up – never fear, you'll see. (rip-rip).

Resuming my bypasser role I moved towards the door in the corner. Going up the flights of stone stairs I was diverted from my aches'n pains by my childish sniggerings. It seemed that Madge had screwed up the film bookings and landed the Planet with a mummy-movie instead of the Yellow Sub thing. Hilarious! 'And for our Yuletide attraction we present: 'The Turkey Came Dressed!' Poor old Madge, surely she didn't deserve to have her petticoat ripped off because she'd made a clerical error. On the second top landing I paused to catch my breath.

RECTIFIER ROOM – KEEP OUT.

Every time I read those words stencilled on the workshop door (they are theatrically underlined by a zig-zagging lightning bolt) I recall the Orwellian Room 101 in which Winston Smith and other crimethinkers came face-to-face with their dominant dread, the one in which the loudest scream was but a quiet prelude, an indulgence almost, before the messy business of wrenching the ego from its socket began.

I shoved open its door. No Thought Police awaited me there. But there was a monster of sorts – a snoozing Frankenstein job called Freddy. I like to think of Freddy – don't ask my why – as being sort of luminous ape-in-the-making. To activate him you don't have to wait around for a suitable thunderstorm to plug into. Nope, Freddy starts bopping the moment an ironclad wall switch is thrown. Housed in a steel-meshed cage to which Danger tags had been hung (more thunderbolts, by Jove!), once Freddy gets juiced up, he starts to shake those pulsating chains of his and what I whimsically imagine to be 'thoughts', albeit, primitive ones, arc in crackling salvos from his glass chamber head, a real sizzling discharge for Frankenstein freaks like me, all the amethyst and blue excitements you could hope to see, not forgetting the sound-effects, the beast's electric howlings as it storms the tree of life.

'What is it?' I asked Paddy Cullen one day.

'It's a rectifier called Freddy,' he replied.

'Aye, but what's it for?'

'Well,' said Paddy, 'it's no for cookin mince, that's for sure. Freddy disnae like mince.'

Maybe not – but Cullen sure loved talking it. He'd attended Stowe College during his apprenticeship to pick up, as he put it,

313

'A wee daud of electrical know-how.' But the only thing that'd stuck was Ohms Law, which according to Paddy is, 'Never clap strange electricity – the bugger could bite ye!'

I dumped the diving suit and helmet on the workshop bench which was cluttered with tools and speckled with sawdust and wood-shavings. Caught in the cold jaws of the vice was the hull of a model ship Lucas'd been working on. The wee man was dead knacky with his hands, and currently he was earning some nice bread by making and flogging bedside lampships. Lucas had told me that he'd been saving hard to get something really special for his wife to mark their silver anniversary. I stroked the wood's smooth grain and thought again of McQuade trucking up the A74, every heartbeat a wheel-turn closer. Jeremiah'd been right last Saturday. I should've come clean with Becky instead of allowing Lucas to become my sexual stand-in. Yon crappy expedient I'd laid on'r about Granny Ferguson; somehow I couldn't see her going through with it. More than obvious it'd been that she hadn't thought much of it.

'I hear,' I said as I joined Lucas in the spoolroom, 'that Madge's got'r flickers in a twist again.'

Lucas nodded, 'Aye, ever since her mother died she's been going aboot in a dwam. That bag of hers is like a chemist's midden, so it is.'

According to Lucas, the Mummy's Curse must've got to the film as well; every reel was poxed with flaky joints and torn sprocket tracks. 'You should see the cue marks,' he grumbled as he worked at the rewind bench with cement and scissors. 'Talk aboot flak!' He nodded towards the steam-hazed kettle in the corner. 'That's just off the boil.'

I shook my head. 'No thanks, had some char wae Shug.' I heaved myself onto the spool-safe and drew up my legs. 'Has Paddy no trapped yet?'

Lucas jerked a thumb ceilingwards.

'What's he doing up there?'

'Skiving most likely.' He flipped up the joining-block clamp and examined the repair.

'Is he okay?'

'Hmm?'

'Paddy – he's no got a bevvy on'm? I mean . . . up on they catwalks'.

Lucas began to caw the spool rewinder but only a yard or so of film had skimmed between his thumb and index finger before another loose joint turned up. He sighed and took up the scissors again. 'Done a bunk on me, Saturday night.'

'Paddy did?'

'I'd to go withoot a break.'

'Don't worry,' I joked, 'by the look of that mummy crap you'll have plenty of breaks the night.'

Lucas went on with his beef. 'Another thing, I'd to haul they film cases up here myself this morning. You'd think he'd at least take a shot of making up the programme. Fair's fair. Enough on ma platc as it is.'

'How come?'

'Ach, Mr Burnett's asked me to do some more leafletting. You know, tae cover up Madge's boo-boo.'

'You mean – bugger aboot'n that diving gear again?'

Obviously embarrassed, his head waggled. 'No exactly – it's a mummy this time.'

'A mummy!'

'Aye. He found this auld decorator's sheet, y'know, for the bandages, like.'

So that's what the sounds from Burnett's office'd been – him and Madge making mummy wrappings. Any glimmerbrain could've guessed that!

315

'You've flipped, Matt. Definitely gone round the twist. Okay, there's an excuse for Burnett – he's been out to lunch for years, but . . .'

'Ach, ma face'll be covered so who's to know. Widnae catch me doing it otherwise.' The clamp snapped down on another join. 'Anyway, it's always another dollar towards the wife's pressy.'

'What you gettin her – a pyramid?'

Through in the op-box the phone buzzed.

'That'll be Burnett to say your shroud's ready.'

With anxious mutterings Lucas bustled from the spool-room into the op-box, or as Becky McQuade had called it, the projection booth, a fancy handle for a cupboard that generated fog with a sound-track. I got down from the spool-safe and went out onto the small balcony. Laughably, this enclosed area was referred to as the 'Sun Roof' though my abiding memory of it'll always be of raindubs and gullshit. Today though it was decked out with a fleecy white rug Mary'd been up all night stitching for her son's approaching birthday. I tightened my scarf and jerked up my collar. Parky up here it was. I could've done with a fag but resisted the notion. My chest, as a reward for my self-sacrifice immediately tried to evict both lungs simultaneously. Whether it was my coughing or a coming thaw I don't know but an icicle, the largest of a daggerlike bunch suspended from the guttering, cracked clean across and fell with a quick bright flash. The balcony on a day like this wasn't a place to linger for it seemed only to be shored up by the flimsy fire-escape which plunged in a series of flights down the Planet's gale-scarred southern wall.

Cold though I was I was well compensated for my gooseflesh by a panoramic view of the Lost Barony of Gorbals. What set the red nerves twitching was the utter contempt for the working classes which was evident no matter where the glance fell. Having so cursorily dismantled the community's heart, that sooty reciprocating engine, admittedly, an antique, clapped-out affair, but one, that'd been nevertheless capable of generating amazing funds of human warmth, they'd bundled it off into the asylum of history with all the furtive shame of a family of hypocrites dumping Granny in Crackpot Castle.

Much imbued by the so-called merits of functionalism the planners and architects had taken wardrobes and tombstones to be their thematic design models, and had set to work with that civic slapdashery which erecting homes for the pre-Holocaust working classes tends to invoke. Surely, it was with such a sense of transience that Basil Spence had sat down to fashion yon concrete spike he'd driven into the Gorbals' vitals. Paddy Cullen, on a visit to his Aunt Terry who existed in Spence's desolation of corridors, cramped apartments, lonely womenfolk, and trapped weans, tells of the day he'd been confronted, when the lift doors had opened, by a funeral party: 'Aye,' says Paddy, 'there he was, him wae the pine jaicket on, staunin up, same as the mourners, though whether he was on his feet or his heid, who's tae know?' The lift you see wasn't big enough to take a six-feet'n-over stiff; there was no way that the coffin could be laid out horizontally as is dignified and proper.

I stood there, mentally re-erecting the Gorbals of old, running my hands so to speak through the pile of grey jigsaw pieces which depicted fragments of lost streets, shops, and buildings, interlocking a well-known corner with a familiar lamp-post, plonking a lost cinema (the Paragon of Cumberland Street) into the wrong locus – lla-llb Commercial Road, which was where the Wellington Palace had stood, or as it was more popularly known, the B'S. Wee Tam Briggs, the Salty Dog's Memory Man, can reel off the names of every shop in Rutherglen Road from Queensferry Street to Crown Street, as they were in the fifties. His powers of recall are staggering. One night in the Dog when he was dumbfounding some punters by naming the entire Blantyre Vics Squad from yonks back, the door was suddenly flung open and in storms wee Sadie Briggs, his struggle'n strife, with a steaming hot plate of tatties'n mince in her hand. This she smacks down on the table in front of Briggs, then, hands on hips bawls: 'There, yar, Memory Man, you can have it here – seeing's you've forgotten the fuck'n road hame!' Quite unabashed, Briggs had forked some mince into his gub, then with a nod of approval had said: 'I cannae mind who you are, missus, but, I'm telling ye – yer mince is champion.'

In the 'fastest gun' tradition, Briggs was regularly challenged by punters who'd heard of his amazing powers of recall. He was shit-hot on sporting questions, and, to date, I've yet to see'm being outfoxed. One night this stranger turned up'n the Dog – he was a dapper-looking, clean-shaven guy, so he must've been from Rutherglen. Patiently, he waited his turn to have a go at Briggs, and soon enough it came. 'Right,' says the stranger, 'what's this from: "Quinquereme of Nineveh, from distant Ophir, rowing home to haven from sunny Palestine, with a cargo of – " '

'Here,' says a baffled-looking Briggs, 'is this in fuck'n code or what?'

The stranger was smirking.

'Who the hell's this Quinky-whatsit?' a bystander mumbled.

'Must be wan o' they Arab teams,' another suggested. 'Y'know, sandshoe shufflers.'

When it emerged that the stranger had been wasting The Memory Man's valuable neurons on poetry of all things, he was soon sailing through the isthmus of the saloon door and, no doubt, went chugging through the channels of the mad March Streets ruffled and upset and vowing never again to show face in any of the Gorbals' cultureless watering-holes.

I'd hoped Paddy Cullen would've come down from the attic by

now. I was a bit worried about'm . It was a dodgy place to be, especially with a hangover and I'd never known a Monday when Paddy wasn't half-jaked from the night before. Not that I, sober as a Presbyterian goldfish, and about as fit as a legless spider was into traipsing around those catwalks either. Firstly, it involved having to climb something that looked more like a metaphor for rust than an iron ladder. Despite my nagging wing, I somehow managed to heave myself up the thing: it wouldn't do to supply the Thought Police with the info that I was shit-scared of heights – such phobias are the very ones they wind you up with in Room 101.

The ladder rose to another balcony which concealed the Planet's asshole – in other words, its extractor-fan chamber. From here the fleapit discharged eye-watering farts redolent of ciggy smoke, orange peel, cheap wine, and the stinks of the fleshpacks. Beyond the bulk of the extractor chamber was a flimsy door which bore a clumsily-painted warning in red letters: DANGER – KEEP TO CATWALKS AT ALL TIMES! This was the 'Doorway to Heaven', so-called, of course, because of O'Toole's ceiling paintings of angels, stars and planets.

The attic definitely gave me the willies; it was a place to be avoided. I'd the same aversion for it as, I suppose, uncaught murderers used to have for trapdoors.

The lights, such as they were (dim bulbs sown amongst the rafters and stanchions), revealed the dusty spread of the wooden planked catwalks which radiated in lateral offshoots from the central catwalk, the only one I'd risk walking along because I'd been assured that it rested on a stout steel girder that ran the length of the auditorium. As far as the other catwalks were concerned, they seemed to me to be hanging out there on a wing and a prayer, supported by habit and kippered angels. If stepping onto these catwalks was dodgy then stepping off them was suicidal. One false step and you were away for oil – straight through the ceiling's thin membrane to a long screaming fall that'd explode you like a bag of ripe tomatoes on the hard reef of the stall seats.

Wee Lucas tells a good story about the first time he'd been taken on a conducted tour of the attic by the then chief projectionist, Billy Bain, so that he'd know the location of safety-lamps. Every minute or so Bain stopped to repeat his dire warning: 'Never, never, step off the catwalk, not for any reason. You've got to keep your wits about you up here.' So saying, he'd planted his size tens on a sheet of asbestos and plunged clean through the roof as far as his hips before he'd frantically grabbed at a catwalk to save himself. 'S-see what I mean,' he'd panted, his face ashen, 'that's how easy it is!'

As my eyes adjusted to the attic's dimness their lengthening vision saw that something was seriously amiss. 'Paddy!' I shouted. 'What's wrang wae ye?' Before my phobia could stop me I was on the main catwalk and running. Apart from scaring the shit from a pigeon (a dusty percussion of wings), my shouts were having no effect at all on the boilersuited Cullen who lay prone on a skinny catwalk far out above the stalls, face down, his head on his arms, motionless. The powerful flashlight at his side flung a raw beam of light amongst the rafters and some tools lay scattered around him. Normally, the very thought of chancing my weight on one of these lateral struts would've been enough to turn my bowels to slush, but here I was, on all fours now, my asshole, I admit, semaphoring maydays, crawling along that creaking spar until I was within reaching distance of Cullen.

Don't touch! My brain, panicking over the liberties already taken with its welfare, warned me just in time. Electrocution! Paddy might've touched a bare wire and become part of the circuitry. What to do? The speckled memory of an old safety poster reassembled itself . . . Do not touch victim . . . Switch off current . . . Lever victim from live source with a broom handle . . . Artificial respiration . . . Call an ambulance . . . Fucksake, I hope the ambulance brings a broom handle! Power source? Hadn't the foggiest . . . As I crouched there, not knowing what the hell to do or not to do, Cullen raised his head and with a chipper-looking expression on his face gave me a big grin. It was a face I would dearly've loved to've slammed my fist into, non-stop, for about a fortnight.

'You bastard, Paddy!'

He went on grinning as he saw me and my fury shrivelling to that shameful and abject sight – a man in the grip of his phobia, that withering moment when his prime fear sinks its mandibles into his terror-ducts, and he immediately begins to spurt infantilism. Nailed to that catwalk, fully alive to my plight, like a somnambulist peering through the fine mist of a nightmare to find himself on his own high window ledge, I could feel all that space beneath me, the gravitational drag of the void. I couldn't move yet inside me there heaved this great bore-tide of dread, rushing up my arteries, undoing dams, gulping bridges and spitting out anchors as it went, an unstoppable torrent of funk. All those years of training that'd been invested in me were gone in an instant, swept aside; honour, manliness, bravery, self-respect, all were carried off like twigs and me with'm heading for the cataract, and beyond it the cradle: any second now I'd be puking and mewling.

The catwalk seemed to be twisting and buckling under our combined weight, it was shrivelling to the narrowness of a rope which strand by strand began to undo itself . . . Cullen saved me. He did so by simply ignoring my presence. Reaching into his pocket he took some coins from his pocket, then he pressed an eye to one of the holes let into the ceiling to accommodate a safety lamp. Chuckling, he raised his head then began to feed coins through the orifice; after each deposit he'd squint through the hole to mark the coin's descent into the auditorium. The target for this wacky mischief would probably be the deaf Emily Dodds. I could picture her, maggot-sized from this height – the hoovering of the stalls suspended – her mouth gaping as the pennies from Heaven fell silently around her.

'You're a complete bastard, Paddy,' I told'm again. Unabashed he dug into his pocket for more coins. He paid scant, if any, attention to my humiliating exit when, like a half-crushed insect retreating over bits of itself: a feeler, a cracked thorax plate, the torn jelly of an eye, a split wing, and the thin pitiful leg which quivered with the trauma of separation, I followed my tweaking asshole back to the main catwalk.

35

The name Brannigan had been branded on a hardboard offcut by
– judging from the bolloxed lettering – an illiterate joker with a
blunt poker. This nameplate had in turn been crucified on a door,
the portal of which was at this moment occupied by a gargoyle
with peroxide-singed hair and a faceful of fourteenth-century
pockmarks. Looking deeply suspicious she eyed up'n down the
coughing stranger who'd arrived on her mucky doorstep; it took'r
some time to admit that aye, this was the home of Pat Mooney,
her father.

'Is he in, then?'

'Aye, the jile I hope, or better still – the Clyde! What? Naw I
don't know where he is. Try the barber shop doon in Scob – Oh
ye have, have ye? Well, fuckt if I know where'll be.'

Her voice boomed on the tight landing with its name-
infested walls and cratered plasterwork. Behind me a door
creaked. Glancing over my shoulder I saw an old crone peeping
at us. Mooney's daughter – what a spine-melting glare she had
– bawled: 'What's the matter, you nosey auld bastard? Has your
deefy dried up again? I'll try'n shout a wee bit louder fur
you – '

The woman's head, like that of a startled tortoise, was quickly withdrawn into the cracked shell of her kitchen.

'He's no been back since Saturday, you say?'

'Naw, he's no. And we'll no be hinging oot flags for'm when he does get back.' She wagged her ferocious head, 'Anyway – what's it to you?'

I explained about her father collecting my winnings.

'S'that a fact, noo? Ran aff wae your money did he?' She nodded. 'Nae wunner his belly never brought'm back.' Judging from the stench coming from the kitchen's greasy innards Skunk Maryland was the dish-of-the-day. A voice, possibly that of Brannigan himself, growled something deep and untranslatable from the interior darkness. But she seemed to get the gist of it all right. 'Fuck you'n a draught!' she shouted over her shoulder, then she scratched vigorously at her scalp with the spud peeler she happened to be holding (hundreds dead – many injured!): 'How much, then?'

'Pardon?'

'Much does he owe you?'

When I told her she pointed the peeler at me like a dagger. 'And what were you thinkin of doing aboot it? Get the polis, maybe. Well, I'm no stoppin ye. Away and get'm. Go on. They know the road well enough. I'm past shame wae that auld midden. He'll no set foot in here again. Tell'm that if you find'm.'

When I said that I'd no intention of going to the fuzz she about hit the roof. 'Well, don't think you'll get a haun-oot here. Enough fingers in ma purse as it is. Aye'n I don't care if you let the whole bloody world know about it. D'you hear me?'

'Does he have any other relations?' I asked.

She nodded. 'Aye, there's his brother, Sammy. He's the brains of the family.'

'Where'll I find'm?'

'Where? I'll tell you where – in a padded cell doon'n Carstairs that's where!'

I'll say this for Mooney's daughter – when she shuts a door, boy, does she shut it! As I trudged the Oatlands slush I kept checking my lugholes for signs of bleeding.

36

This bloke Plato – a right flannel merchant, eh?

Says he: What you see's not really there. No, it's only a mock-up of something that's always there, always shall be there though you'll never lay eyes on it because it's visible only in the ideal world (Disney Exist), the location of which is being kept under tight philosophical wraps. He claims, Mr Broadbrow does, that his teacher, an Athenian windbag called Socrates, peddled this baloney to a bunch of layabouts with names like sheep diseases. These drones (and, boy, could they drone!) were supposed to be muckers of Socrates though a fair wheen of them had created an ideal vacuum when the hemlock order arrived.

Now there's small use in saying that Socrates's theory regarding ideal essence refers in the main to geometrical figures – circles, squares, triangles, and so on; once you admit even the tiniest of circles there's no way that you can logically reject the other stuff – stuff, let's say, like yon drip accruing at the tip of the old dosser's neb as he stands out there in the sleet watching me as I junket on eggrolls and coffee. The way I figure it, that transient snotdrop must, according to the bane of Xanthippe's life, have its ideal counterpart, and the same goes for the fart released with such gusto by a workman at a nearby table, the potency of which so affronts his mates that admidst exclamations of disgust they flap newspapers under their noses. 'At least,' says the windbreaker, 'mines don't sneak out in their slippers . . .' Now, let's ask ourselves the prime question: was that forthright emission until the moment of its release stored in a kind of ideal fart-vault? And here's a rasper – do ideal farts, the authentic ones upon which our feeble zephyrs are modelled, smell more genuine?

A snackbar like the Maggot (real name, The Magnet, though its drawing power has long since faded) tends to drive its clientele into philosophical reveries. As they sit at one of its flayed tables in the homely reek of the place they find themselves addressing the Big Questions: where have I come from? why am I here? and if I eat this accident on my plate shall I continue to be here? The Maggot is a place much frequented by gastrophobes and gluttons, folks who have a down on their snackpipes and continually bombard them with 'Suicide Sams', a Maggot special which timebombs the system and detonates an hour or so after the consumer has left the eaterie, otherwise you wouldn't get near a table for stiffs.

Me? Why was I in the Maggot? Well, I'd dropped in to brood really. My Kemsley House astrologer has recommended me to find a seat somewhere and to give myself a right good brooding over. Astrologically speaking I'm in a helluva mess: Saturn, it seems, has broken into my House and shat'n the bread-bin. It was therefore the recommendation of my press spey-wifie that for the time being I should keep my head down and remain very very still. This advice I didn't dig. As a fatalist I reckon if your name's on an incoming shell, then you can bob'n weave like the Road Runner, but come the detonation you'll still find yourself fifty or so yards from your blitzed asshole.

Anyway, the breakfast and brooding biz gave me a chance to get things into perspective. My lost winnings, for instance were a contradiction in terms – if they were lost then they were no longer winnings. Just a fog of words. The so-called actual substance was nowhere to be found in the known universe. They just might exist in Plato's ideal world but, as we know, it doesn't have much of a bus service. It's also pertinent to consider that Mooney, himself, no longer exists: like Talky Sloan, he could've been boarded by a bus while perambulating with an incandescent liver across some lethal street. Other possibilities? He might've got board and lodgings in one of the City's numerous iron hotels where tiled walls and barred windows are uniform features. Then again, might it not be that a conspiracy was afoot to conceal from me the whereabouts of Mooney? Yon virago on the doorstep could've been having me on; no sooner had I coughed off than she'd skipped back to the bedroom to press a cooling tenner to her father's fevered brow.

Then, of course, there had been the Three Wise Guys.

Now they'd definitely been taking the piss. There they were standing at the Richmond Park gates opposite Dalmeny Street, looking like an ancient picket line somebody'd forgotten to call off. Taking a pot shot at Fate I'd gone up to them. There's little point in describing them since that'd mean scratching around for adjectives denoting ripeness, not to mention similies for senility. Best maybe to fall back on Mr Whitman's vivid phrase and to say that they made up a trio of 'grave bafflers', and to skip snide remarks about their skin deterioration. After all, if my skin'd fought two major wars it wouldn't've been in any great shape either. One of the ancients had this medal pinned to the lapel of his worsted overcoat and – No, that's baloney – there was bugger all medal, I'd simply awarded it so's I'd have a prop to hang future dialogue on. But the auld joker did keep touching, with fingers that wouldn't have disgraced a dead pianist, the very spot where the medal would've been pinned, had there been one. Words can sure get into a right clutter sometimes. The grind of grammar. 'Thomas Clay, tell the class what syntax is.' 'Sir, it's the amount deducted by the Inland Revenue from a prostitute's earnings.'

I got off to a bad start with the antique trio when, misinterpreting their lack of speech for silence – actually they were reflecting on a remark made prior to my arrival – I blurted out a callow query re the possible whereabouts of a Mr Francis Mooney, erstwhile employee of Signor Giuseppe Fiducci, locksmith to the riff-raff of Gorbals and environs.

'Time to change the rules,' said one of them.

'Suppose so,' said the man lacking a medal.

'You mean wrote doon?' queried the third member.

'I didnae say that.'

'Change,' emphasised the medal-less one.

'The British Constitution,' the third one now mumbled.

'What aboot it?'

'No wrote doon either, so it's no.'

'How come you're talking aboot it, then? If it's no wrote doon it disnae exist.'

'Canna trust what's written on air.'

'What's NO written, you mean.'

'Mince,' said the one who'd the air of a leader about'm. 'The Ruskie's have one. But it might as well've been tattooed on Joe Stalin's arse for all the good it's done them.'

A nodding of heads endorsed this.

I didn't jump in right away with a repeat of my Mooney question. Just as well, for their chief had one shot in his verbal locker:

'No a whole pain left,' he said. 'Not a single dampt one.'

This opaque remark seemed to have the effect of restoring me to flesh'n blood again, rescuing me in the nick of time from vapouring off like the silvery outgoings of breaths from their mouths and nostrils. Their rheumy eyes roamed over me, as if patches of flesh'n cloth were cohering into something vaguely human. I was taken into their heads and through the occult interlocking processes of oldthink they simultaneously — their smirks told all — arrived at the conclusion that I scarcely outranked in significance the scrap of yellow paper which happened by at that moment bearing the announcement that the Beetles, the Dab Four, could be seen at the Planet Cinema in Scobie Street, this very day, and also tomorrow . . . another blatant lie blowing about the universe.

The one who'd been the prime speaker pondered for some time before he chose to respond to my query. He nodded, then with a vague wave of his walking stick, said: 'The rest.'

'Eh?'

'The Auld Folks' Rest at the Ducksy,' said the one in the worsted overcoat.

'Are we talking about the same Mooney?' I asked. 'He's a barber and — '

'Aye, his daughter's merrit tae Brendan Brannigan. Lives wae them.'

I nodded, 'That's right.'

'Seen'm in the Rest bout an hour ago.'

Not a word of it did I believe. Mooney might've been pushing sixty but no way could I see'm trekking off to a kneecreakers' neuk on a snowy Monday morning.

But why should this trio of geriatrics try to bumsteer me? Where was their gain? Probably none sought — they were just chalking one up for the kneecreakers' division, elbowing me in the eye while the celestial Ref's attention was elsewhere. Mind you, it wasn't impossible that Mooney, unable to face up to the prospect of returning home (and who could blame him for that?) had slunk off to the Rest to get his cold, fleshless behind against its cast-iron stove, planning to remain there until eleven a.m., that uplifting hour when courage could at last be purchased in the shape of alcohol's delicious poisons 'through teardrops of gold or scorching pints, cold'. It wasn't likely that I'd find'm in the Rest but I'd still have to check it out. Mumbling my thanks I crunched into the snowy park and crossed the wee bridge beneath which the Jenny's Burn, a sort of ochre-bronze shade today (it derived its colouring from whichever effluent had been discharged from the poisonous kidney of the nearby chemical plant) snaked away beneath phosphorescent trees to its turbid tryst with the Clyde which took place under the planked bridge at the foot of Cuddy's Brae.

An odd thing occurred as I plodded along under a bright canopy of snowbearing trees; I passed what might be called a 'grumble of greybeards' for they all looked as if they'd been mugged for their pension books. As they conversed in angry-sounding tones one of them who'd been bad-eyeing me something rotten flourished his walking stick and shouted: 'They should've all been drooned at birth – the hale jing bang o' them.' His whiskery gang murmured their agreement, and stamped their poorly-shod feet on the bluish glints of the snow-ruts. All the way to the Rest I was to be the target of similar geriatric sour looks. In fact, I so incensed one auld punter that he let fly a tobacco-stained spittle in my direction but it was so poorly aimed it landed on the skip of another codger's bunnet. I left them snarling at each other while my snow-clotted steps took me round to the pond-side of the low building which housed the Old Folks' Rest as well as the premises of a model boat club. More pensioners in groups of two'n three speckled the snowscape. Such a scene would've had Lowry reaching excitedly for his sketch-pad. Right up his street, these diminutive and disconsolate figures who'd been exiled from their erstwhile heaven by a gang of vandals that'd struck during the night, and had busted every window as well as sprayed every wall, interior and exterior with gangland graffiti, the brutish, dayglo signatures of the braindead.

Paralleling this calamity was the one which had befallen the swans and ducks. Until now the pampered fowl had taken the pond to be their man-given sanctuary, but in the night the pond had frozen over and had forced them from their habitat. The irridescent quackers displayed a comical astonishment at the swim-denying change that'd overtaken their hitherto resilient element. Nevertheless, they seemed to be enjoying the novelty as they cavorted and capered around. The swans though took unkindly to the change that'd been forced on them. Huddling together, they looked shorn of dignity as they flexed their serpentine necks and rattled their orange bills on the hard iceplate.

I asked a few greybeards if they'd seen Mooney on their enforced extra-mural travels but from each of them received either a grunt or glower – sometimes both – anyway, the very shortest of shrifts. Obviously they'd me down for one of the tribe that'd raided Fort Senility in the night, who'd poured through the busted windows to take out their societal beefs on a few scraps of helpless furniture.

Before leaving, one of them, their leader probably, had left behind a personality clue – right there in the centre of a ripped draughtsboard was a massive, whorling clot of subhuman shit.

A sudden cracking sound jerked my gaze towards the gelid pond. No, it wasn't my thrumming elbow going for broke – it was the concussive report of the armoured water being breached by a sledgehammer. The hammer was wielded by a parks employee in citron-yellow thigh waders. Within a few minutes he'd smashed a wide hole in the groaning ice. The freed water churned and heaved, splinters and iceshards surfaced then sank again. The notion that the seething waters were boiling persisted beyond the margins of logic. I took an almost childish enjoyment in the spectacle, being especially delighted at the hissing white fractures that forked far out into the still intact integument, messengers bearing news of the mayhem to come.

The ducks stampeded pell-mell into the black swirling water, but the swans, being the huffy, stuck-up buggers that they are, insisted on separate launchings, sliding into the pond a slow one at a time. At that moment a camera-clicking gnome appeared on the scene and began to shoot off with amazing rapidity what must've been about an entire film roll while the fowl, still excited by the novelty of it all, butted their breasts against the ice hole's jagged rim but gradually learned to accept their limitations. The mini-snapper had accentuated his gnomelike appearance by wearing a pea-green anorak with peaked hood, black needlecord trousers, lumpy looking boots and a vivid white beard that poured in a small snowy cataract onto his well-buttoned chest.

The workman, his ice-wrecking mission completed to his, if not to the moody swans' satisfaction, began to wade ashore. His lemon thigh-waders shed chaotic reflections, so that he moved landwards as if tagged by a flickering spotlight. His sledgehammer across his shoulder, he moved directly towards myself and on reaching the pond's perimeter onto which the oily water fell with sullen slaps, he stretched a hand out. With my good arm I drew him up alongside me, and with a grunt of thanks he stood there letting water stream off his waders while from the bib pocket of his overalls he fished out a squashed fag packet and awkwardly, for he was working one-handed, the other one being fully occupied with holding the sledgehammer, he got the ciggy between his lips. I dug out my matches and struck one for him. It was then that I realised that this commonplace little scene was being recorded for posterity by the eye of the gnome's camera, blinking inquisitively in the direction of myself and the parks worker. Click-click-click-click – how much film could that smilebox hold? Talk about Roy Rogers' sixty shooter! Suddenly, the impromptu session was over. The worker turned away, trailing a silver-blue smoke scarf and the gnome vamoosed in the opposite direction without so much as a squeak of thanks.

'Hey, hang on a tick!'

He heard me all right but went on just the same, lumps of snow flying up from beneath his boots. I decided against giving him chase. What the hell! The gnome in his pea-green jacket vanished behind a screen of birches which, coated with snow, looked like they'd just had a fresh paint job. I imagined the sawn-off David Bailey trotting up to a huge hinged toadstool, lifting its whited cap, then vanishing inside. An oddball event right enough. Metaphysical muggery. What was making me so uptight? A wee touch of the atavistics, eh? Fear of soul-possession as exemplified by the jungle innocents when first confronted by the white man's spirit-snatcher. In the eerie red glow of his cave the goblin would conjure up my likeness, stirring it around in a white enamel dish until the image was cooked then hypo-fixed. The hanging process would follow.

Meanwhile, the disinherited greybeards were drifting off along the various exit paths. The parks workman, whose image, like mine, was a prisoner of the gnome's soulbox, was sweeping tinkling ice-shards from the pond rim into the agitated water while, behind him, a fellow worker was brooming smashed glass from the defiled interior of the Old Folks' Rest.

Sam Breene, the Maggot's proprietor, waved a dismissive hand at the dosser who still stood at the window and stared in at us as we gave our ulcers laldy and mopped up blobs of botulism with wads of grey bread. The husk ignored Breene's shooing gestures and went on watching every bite that went down my throat.

Should I save'm a chocky biscuit? 'Have this Wagon Wheel on me, my good man . . .' It looked like his wagon was running on split axles. Aye, when you thought about it, there's always somebody worse off than yourself. Maybe in that black tenement across the road there was a cancer victim enviously eyeing the dosser and saying to himself: 'Would you look at yon ragbag; he staggers around all day in laughing shoes and third-hand tatters, wide open to the wind'n rain. He probably eats rats and drinks from puddles, yet, there he is, able to walk around, aye'n for years to come. While, I, who took care of myself, wore the right clobber, ate health foods, chucked smoking and packed in the booze – I'm for the bloody off . . .' The irony of it. Rhona was fond of quoting yon saying: 'I cried because I'd no shoes until I met a man with no feet.' I'd been quite taken by it when first I heard it but now I can see it's just a lump of keech wrapped in chrissy paper. Having no feet I laugh coz I'll never have corns or bunions! Another way to look at it.

Mind you, it wouldn't surprise me if despite his move-along gestures to the tattered one, Breene was actually payrolling him. It could well be that he's hired'm to stand out there so that his clientele, a real tatty lot, could, as we lapped up our dogmush, relish still further the piquancy of one-upmanship, something we rarely encountered in our flavourless lives. But how far were any of us from the degradation of that loser who stared in through the steamy window? Maybe only a thousand heartbeats or so: the death of a partner; the loss of a job; the tumble down the stairs of some ambition; awakening one morning to find yourself col-onised by a mood which progressively thickens like a cataract; any one of these calamities could be enough to send you looking for brotherly love on a bombsite, squalling, aye, maybe even murdering, for a mouthful of hair-lacquer, lying down until dawn amidst ratshit and ashes. Breene finally went outside and chased the dosser. He returned with a self-righteous gloss to his cheeks and began to rattle crockery onto a rusty tray.

I was all but through with my brooding when an idea sowed itself in my mind then, as in one of those botanical films they used to bore us with at school, it raced through its growth stages at a velocity well beyond the needs of chlorophyll. The motion quickly acquired a crop of forbidden fruit as from deep within my cerebellum a resonating voice said: 'Drop out, Tom!' A worthy suggestion – to vanish, go, disappear, be seen nevermore. Jack Sherman, being interviewed by the oinks: 'You claim that Mr Clay was dropped from your car at approximately 2100 hours. He'd insisted on walking, said he wanted some fresh air . . .' Would Sherman experience remorse? Not a bit of it. Phyllis would probably skip for joy when she heard the news, as would Ma Carlyle and Eddie. And Rhona? Poor Rhona, she'd miss me for a time. Widow's weeds and a babe-in-arms. She'd probably move in with the Carlyles. Aye, it was definitely time to go.

Out into the fake street with its cottonwool snow. The dosser was lurking in a hastily-assembled plywood close (watch, wet paint!) He was probably thanking his mucky stars that this wasn't happening in the real world, the ideal one, that is. Still, you just had to make do with the script old sweaty Fate tosses at you. Like a rooky actor the dosser mumbled his lines prior to their delivery, chewed them over to extract the max in dramatic flavour.

'Hey, Jimmy, see's the bus-fare tae the Western. It's ma brother – his tea's jist aboot oot.' A tricky enough wee line but he delivers it with spot-on fidelity, accompanying it with deferential expression and just a pinch of arrogance, enough to convincingly carry it off. Unfortunately, the gobful of bacteria he nonchalantly hocks into the wind to enhance the authenticity of his delivery is promptly returned and smears itself across my toecap. This justifies a fine of some sort, and my fingers rooting about in my denim pockets allow halfcrowns and florins to squirm through them until I'm able to present'm with a warm-hearted bob.

'Hope your bree makes it, pal,' I tell'm.

He saluted my generosity by raising two fingers to the peak of his gungy bunnet. 'Ta, sodger, you're aw fuck'n heart, so ye are . . .'

37

In the Dog with Paddy Cullen.

Our table was near – too near – the doms table. Those rowdy spot-mortems mired the first and holiest hour with expletives. Dominoes shouldn't be allowed before noon, or at least they should be played quietly out of respect for those who'd come here to muffle their own private dins. Sad Sam Murney, obviously aware of this, warned the spotty ones to moderate their language. Smirks all around at the players' affected response. 'Give'm a swirl, Cyril,' said Billy Bannerman as he cuffed the sleepers into play, while Buff Thomas in a fruity voice cautioned his partner to, 'Keep your eyes on the game, old chap, or else we'll be acquiring an elderly relative . . .'

Cullen eyed me for a moment, his mouth shaped for words but settled instead for a gulp of stout; moistening the roots of speech – overdoing it, as usual. He clonked his froth-laced tumbler onto the seasoned oak.

'You still in the cream puff, or what?'

I shook my head. No, I wasn't in the huff. Narked maybe, aye, a bit miffed as one is wont to be when it's leaked to the public domain that chunks of your mental territories've been invaded, taken over by phobiac squatters. Anyway, most folk had a phobia

338

of some kind. Granda Gibson, for instance had a terror of canaries – even just one on the loose got'm into a right flutter. His idea of Hell (his room 101) was being trapped forever in a coalmine that throbbed with the wings and piercing shrieks of free-flying canaries. And Ma Clay, she used to – ach, what does it matter. Cullen himself couldn't claim that all was well in his own attic, could he? I mean, lying there on his belly papping coins through a roof-hole at a deaf scrublady. According to Cullen he'd been penny-dropping wee Emily Dodds before I'd entered the attic, and that when he'd heard me coming through the doorway he'd just kept his head down to see how I'd react. Sure, he knew about my fear of heights, but he'd hardly expected me to throw a trauma that'd take me to within a whisker of nurseryland.

Here's another poser while we're on the subject: is there a phobia to cover an active dislike of locusts?

'What?'

'It's a locust the day,' the wee woman repeated.

We were sitting in Doc Munn's surgery waiting-room. You always got the feeling that you'd just missed the tide when you stopped by here. The place was damper than Noah's drawers. In a corner a hearty fire blazed, an extravaganza of high leaping flames which would've been greatly appreciated had it been a real fire and not a poster of one! (A fireguard Tames the Flames!) Risky place to hang about in: Jenny Armstrong, Doc Munn's receptionist, was rumoured to've snuffed it from triple-pneumonia complicated by seaweed. Munn hadn't bothered to replace her, so his dwindling panel had to sort themselves out in order of survival – I mean, arrival.

I looked at the woman. 'A "locust" did you say?'

She nodded, 'Aye, Doctor Munn's got a wee touch of the swindles so they've brought in a locust.'

I grinned. 'You mean "a locum" and "a wee touch of the shingles", don't you?'

She sniffed, 'Aye, that's what I said.'

Archie Flood trailed past the doms table and stood looking at me'n Cullen.

'Talky's funeral,' he said.

'Aye, what aboot it?'

'Linn Crematorium, eleven-fifteen the morra. Peacock's organising a mini-bus. Youse gawn?'

We nodded and he jotted down our names into a notebook. 'By the way, Archie,' Cullen asked, 'will Talky be wearing his new blazer?'

Tim Peacock, the Dog's owner, breezed in toting a briefcase and a manifest air of well-being. His Doberman, a light salting of snow glittering on its back, trotted along at his heels. Peacock had a fine monied swagger to'm, the sterling snap of a man who worked out daily in the gym of commerce, unafraid to go the limits. He looked around his life-support system and seemed well chuffed by the turnout for such a shitty Monday morning. Murney took his briefcase and lifted the counter flap but for the time being Peacock opted to remain this side of things, chatting to his clientele, demonstrating that even though he wasn't one of us – and he intended to keep it that way – he wasn't averse to rubbing shoulders with the riff-raff now'n again, or of telling them the odd joke. The punters in his vicinity (many of them no doubt developing liver-rot on Peacock's behalf) shuffled their feet, laughed uneasily, and fingered their tumblers in a kind of furtive way. They looked relieved when he at last left'm and went through with Murney into the cramped dookit he used as an office to hear a rendering of accounts.

The locum plucked my medical record from an index file and placed it on the desk. A painful cross-section of my life thus far bound between common slabs of hardboard and secured by a worm-coloured elastic band. What became of these records when you snuffed it? Incinerated were they? Or maybe left to moulder in paper cemeteries, a means of support for archival nosey-parkers whose forte in life is arranging people into columns before marching them up to the top of the page then marching them down again. Such intimate info should be popped into the pine box with its occupant, or be passed to the deceased's family. Many an absorbing night to be had with the telly switched off, all gathered around the electric log to study what one's kith'n kin croaked from:

'It says here that Uncle Bertie died from an infart. See what I told you aboot haudin them in!'

'Mammy, I thought Granpop bought it from choking on a fishbone. It says here he snuffed it from G-O-N-O-R-R . . .'

'Give me that at once! Now off to bed with you!'

The locum was probably still in his early thirties but already a 'penalty spot' was opening at the crown of his soft blond hair. Chilly looking bugger. His response to my comradely good morning was a curt hand-signal for me to park myself on the hard chair in front of his desk. Just from looking at'm it was obvious that he was of that pragmatic school which holds that a demonstration of objectivity towards patients was the benchmark of good medicine. Not so, old Doc Munn. A fat, friendly soul, he always made a point of asking you to recount your current dreams. I doubted if this organic mechanic who frowned over the desk at me would be interested in such mundane matters. As he with cold finger flicks worked his way through my file, I seriously considered jacking it in, of marching to Hell out of this dump and rejoining the clockroaches. Aye, despite my genuinely sore arm, my prickly lungs, I might just've done that if the locum, a real sneaky bastard, hadn't dropped his pen to the floor, the object of this being, of course, to induce me to bend and retrieve it for'm, thereby proving that my dicky dorsal was mythical. No fuck'n way, locust! He told me to strip to the waist and after I'd done so he enquired how I'd come by my body bruises. He frowned at my explanation that they were due to a fall then he got stuck into my back with such digital vigour you would've thought that MALINGERER was branded across it in bold lettering. 'Does that hurt? What kind of pain? Sharp or dull? Here, especially . . . Hm . . .' He told me to get dressed again. My stooning elbow was cursorily examined then dismissed. 'Badly bruised, that's all – nothing broken.' He reached for his panel pad. As he scribbled on it I asked after Doc Munn's health which going by the locust's frown he considered to be a gross social gaffe on my part, an impertinence. Imagine! A common member of the W.C. an abject clockroach, enquiring after the health of a physician! Next thing you'll know GPs will be getting accosted in the streets by the lowly pests, bullied into conversations without appointments, having, without benefit of consultancy, to give impromptu opinions on the coming weather, assessments on the durability of Polish working boots, and whatever else comes into the pinheads of their loutish interlocutors. This is what came from allowing crass movies about the pranks of student doctors to be widely circulated, of permitting dangerous books like *Black's Medical Dictionary* to fall into the germy feelers of the clockroach tribe, glimmerbrains, all of them, who without so much as a blink will assure you that, for instance 'the Arch of Aorta' is to be found within walking distance of Athens, and that the Great Saphenous had been a famous Hungarian conjuror.

With a kind of 'this'll-fix-you-chummy' sneer on his chops the doctor ripped my Medical Certificate from the pad and with the backs of his fingers steered it across the desk in my direction. I studied it. Well, well, here's a to-do – he's awarded me the

Cobbler's Line, the one before the last. Seven days from now, it was his judgement, I'd be able to scurry on the factory floor with the best of them: it was his further opinion that this time I'd be able to contribute a really sustained chunk of pillar-to-posting.

Amazing beasties these prophetic locusts!

'Am I talking to myself, or what?' asked Paddy Cullen.

'No, I'm listening – carry on.'

'What was I saying?'

'Eh, about Peacock's new pub.'

'Fucksake, Tam – that's history!'

'Naw, Lucas – you were on about him. Right?'

Cullen nodded. 'A mummy wae specs oan – s'that no the limit, eh?'

'Well, there was yon centurian wae the wrist-watch, mind? What was the movie? *Quo Vadis*, I think . . .'

'And blood as well, for ony favour,' Cullen went on, ignoring my reference to the Roman with the Rolex. 'Any diddy knows that they always drained mummies afore wrapping them. Says Burnett, "Aye, maybe, but it proves one thing, Patrick – you ken bugger aw about show-biz".'

'Maybe he has a point.'

'Eh?'

'Another pint?'

'Aye, on ye go.' He laid a ten bob note on the table. 'Get's a pack of smokes as well, Tam.'

While I waited for Sanny Stirrat to pour the drinks, the door opened and in sauntered this dressed in black punter, like a pint-sized Johnny Cash he was in his black leather, six buttons, kneedrop-level coat, his black cavalry-twill trousers, the leg bottoms of which'd been stuffed into a class pair of boots that would've sounded right and looked just dandy on the plankwalks of Tombstone. And what about the skull-warmer! Black leather again, man. A leather Homburg? Aint such a beast. Well, there sure is now!

Didn't Pap used to say as he was forking up them black-eyed peas never to trust a man who turns out dressed in black after a snowfall? But all you beer-guzzling, welfare chisellers can relax, roll away your furtive looks and ready-to-run tenseness for this sombre looking doggy shaking snowsmuts from its hat is certainly no broo-sniffer from NAB county who'll try to sidewind you into his confidence, the way those varmints do. Forget that croc-skinned briefcase he's toting – there aint no welfare teeth in there shaping to put the tax-payers' bite on you: NAB county no-gooders would never dream of packing such a giveaway as a crockosmile briefcase. Be easier trying to remain inconspicuous with a double-b. shotgun down your pants. Best to put it thisaway – whoever you think this small black coyote is – he aint. There, can't say plainer'n that.

Although the Dog was by no means full its strangers alert system still functioned, a fact evidenced by a dip in the pub's vocal output as the Man in Black entered, a blip of silence ( ) passing through, a mere falter in the gabstream but enough to indicate that the new face had been noted and was being watched. As a matter of fact I'd passed this self-same dude this very morning as I was on my way to Oatlands to have my eardrums reshaped by the formidable Mrs Brannigan. 'Nothing occult in there,' as the whisky-priest said to the spookhunter, ' 'ceptin your ornery talkaday skull – but it lights up sometimes.' This a.m. I'd encountered Lucas twice, the first eyeballing being when he was in his projectionist gear and trying to scissor'n cement some continuity into a tattered horror movie: the second time of sighting was through the Maggot's window when he'd been wearing his Egyptian Big Sleep outfit and looking a right tube with those specs of his clinging to his swaddled conk. He'd nudged aside an old dosser then peered in at us as we wolfed our 'Suicide Sams'. Evidently, we hadn't rated a handbill since I suppose he figured we'd be the wrong side of a stomach pump come curtain time.

The stranger got himself one of those wicked wee Scottish ales that usually frequent the lower shelves and are much admired for their sharpness and strength by us bovine boozers as we mill around the draught-trough for our brewer's fart-in-a-tumbler. With his glass inverted over the bottle, making little chinking sounds, he of the black duds crossed to park himself at the table adjacent to the one at which Paddy with enormous optimism and hand-trembling clumsiness was trying to inveigle a fresh flint into his lighter.

Stirrat, who has a rep for his skill in bringing a pint of the Hammond Innes to a state bordering on platonic perfection was cossetting the stout so much you would've thought that his job in Peacock's new liver-grinder depended on it. Such fastidiousness is due some praise I suppose, if only the bugger would stop pouring my lager with all the grace and charm of a cow pishing in the byre.

Just as old movies get eaten by the sprocket teeth that bring them to light, and their continuity becomes damaged by the repair work, revealing this with a series of visual hiccups; their auditory equivalent ( ), a further pulse of silence, passed amongst us as the door wafted in yet another unknown (was it snowing strangers out there?) Speaking of movies, this hombre was a natch for the 'Black Hats Brigade', what with his blocky shoulders and a face on'm like a Marines' drill sergeant who'd been Purple-Hearted in 'Nam. A guy then who'd been a kick short on kindness ever since. He'd an exceptional jaw structure, this honcho, the kind a punch from Muhammad Ali might've knuckle-wrecked itself on. And didn't his chin pack this deep whorling dimple which wasn't prettifying at all, but was a mean looking twister like the indent left by a healed bullet wound. Dressed in a plaid zipper-jacket over a navy boilersuit, his black hair was mostly covered by this black-knitted teapot-cosy affair, the kind tough wharvesmen do their Hollywood number in to a background of dismal-sounding foghorns and the slow slapping of oily waves along the rusty hulls of sea-tramps. Wardrobe had overdone it with the Zapata moustache, though, a whole wedge too much of the theatrical, it was. And surely the director was regretting by now his insistence on yon George Raft coin-flippance – substituting a bunch of car-keys made no weightier impact.

Zapata (we might as well make use of that sub-nostril joke-fringe until we can get a handle on the brute) gave us all the once-over, the twice-over in fact, then his gaze returned along the human rail of jumpy welfare wanglers before he, himself, became part of it by pushing his big shiny boots into a gap and signalling to Harry Moffat with quirking forefinger. The humped one and the unknown did a bit of rapping but fresh uproar from the doms table plus a loud argy-bargy nearby about which route the old red tramcar had taken rowdied out any chance I had of hearing what the big guy was quizzing Harry about. Harry, his old eyes touring faces locked onto Cullen's. His finger now rose to point: That's your man, there. The stranger nodded then moved – drinkless, I noted – in Paddy's direction.

When I got back to the table with the drinks and Paddy's fags, Zapata, who'd planted himself on my chair was saying to Cullen in an amused but disbelieving tone, 'You're having me on – must be.'

From a small white envelope Cullen tipped yet another flint onto his vibrating palm, then pinching the elusive particle between thumb'n forefinger, he tried to maneouvre it into the lighter's aperture. 'It might be hard to swally but – shit!' The flint skited away, was lost. He nodded towards me, 'Tam here'll tell ye.'

'Have I taken your seat?' Zapata asked but without the apologetic half-budging movement that should've accompanied the question.

'It's awright, this hard yin'll dae me,' I said in deference to the man's muscles, and, of course, his big shiny boots.

There was something about those boots of his . . . ?

The short black stranger, I noted, was doing the *Express* crossword (its big one). He was jabbing solutions into the grid at a phenomenal speed. He must pack some nifty neurons under that leathery Homburg of his.

Yet another flint trickled from the envelope onto Paddy's hand. With a nod towards Zapata, he said, 'Tam, this here's Matt's nephew – Billy Lucas. Uh . . . ?'

I removed flint and lighter from Cullen. He nodded his approval. 'Aye, this pub's started tae get helluva shaky since they started the demolishing.'

Lucas grinned and looked around himself. 'Some place eh? First shop I've ever been in that still has sawdust on the floor.'

Endorsing his theory that the greyer its whiskers the better the joke, Paddy shook his head. 'Naw, naw, that's no sawdust – yon's yesterday's furniture.' The big guy made with the guffaws anyway. Paddy took up his fags, shook one out for me, but had his offer turned down by Lucas. A non-smoking, teetotaller – what was he doing sitting at this table? Aye, and in my chair as well!

'As I was saying, Tam – this is Matt's nephew. I've been trying to break it gently to'm that his Uncle Matt's gone roon the twist.' He helped himself to one of my matches, and lighting up a fag, went on. 'So, maybe you'd like to fill'm in on what wee Matt's up to right now.'

Shiny boots?

And so it was told, the bizarre tale of the urban mummy that wore specs and wellies and was at this very moment promoting its curse in a post-slum necropolis called the Gorbals.

With the flint replaced I took a tanner and tightened the lighter's retaining screw. I flicked the sparker-wheel and a light immediately sprang on inside my head. Coincidence, that arch-plagiarist, seeing that I was over-involved with the pangs of this inner enlightenment, snatched the required dialogue from the lips of Frank Wyper who sat at an entirely different table indulging his habit for levity at the expense of his boozing crony, Ned Dorman: 'Take a look at that folks – I think the sun's starting to keek through. The fog's definitely lifting. Any minute now this tree stump'll start talking . . . !'

Maybe I'd deserved the sarky clapping but. What a dumbkopf! Compared with me, Dorman was a polymath. Who else could this lumber-jacketed, big-footed giant be but McQuade? Hadn't I chosen his very wardrobe? The ghost of the beard recommended by me loaned a bluish sheen to his jaws and chin. Billy Lucas his brimstoned arse! This was Becky's betrothed brute all right. He must've kicked Matt Lucas's name out of her; now he was here to perform a frontal lobotomy on the wee man with his size ten boots. One glance at'm told you what he was – a murder machine, that's what. If this demolisher, this walking sledgehammer, ever caught up with Matt, then the wee man would be wheeled into the mortuary on three different trollies.

John McQuade, alias Billy Lucas, alias Zapata, had smiled and shaken his head incredulously throughout the tale of the walking mummy. A good performance for somebody who surely thought he was being conned. It certainly had all the hallmarks of a sting. Either that or somebody'd stuck on the wrong reel: wasn't Lucas supposed to be swathed in bandages *after* he tangled with

McQuade? Must be a bit of a pisser arriving to fulfil a slaying contract only to find your mark had already been seconded to the army of the living dead? Why this bantering tone? asked a shocked Jeremiah. Surely I wasn't going to leave the unfortunate Mr Lucas to the far from tender mercies of this thug? I've already said I wouldn't. How many times would I have to repeat it – no way was Lucas going to take my lumps. Okay?

'Is it urgent like?' Cullen asked Lucas as he stuck his lighter away with a nod of thanks in my direction.

McQuade shook his head. Murderous eyes. Plausible tongue. No, not bad news or anything like that. His uncle, you see, had been saving hard to buy a wee second-hand car – nothing fancy, but not a banger either. A wee Singer Chamois had turned up at the garage where he worked. In right good nick it was. He thought it'd be worthwhile for his uncle to give it a looksee. That was all.

'He might drop by for a pint,' Cullen said. 'Helluva thirsty craturs mummies are.'

Harry Harrison, hirpling past our table, enroute for the lavvy, paused to stare at Cullen. 'Here,' he asked, 'did I see you in a diver's suit, Saturday night?'

'Colour was it?' Paddy blandly enquired.

'Eh, a kinda shitty colour.'

Cullen shook his head. 'Naw, couldnae've been me – mines is a salmon pink wae polkadots.'

'A good match for your arse then,' Harrison said as he thumped off on his walking stick.

McQuade still playing toss'n catch with his keys, said: 'Cannae hang about too long. I think I'll take a wee scout around.' He fingered his moustache. 'I'll probably get lost. On the road here I'd to ask an auld joker for directions to Scobie Street. He told me it was a gonner. Taken away on the back of a lorry, he said.'

Cullen sighed. 'Ach, there're still a few shovelsfy left yet, so there is.'

'You'd think the place'd been bombed.'

Cullen shook his head. 'Naw, naw, yon's just a staun-in Gorbals you're seeing oot there. The real wan's away getting fixed. Be back any day noo – mark my words.'

The man in black hadn't a clue: crossword completed, he discarded the newspaper then did a surprising thing – from his briefcase he took out a creased-looking paperback of J.W.Dunne's *An Experiment With Time*. Opening the book where the purple tongue of a bus ticket poked out, he smoothed the pages then fell to avidly reading a text which had once thrilled me to my existential core. A time-convict, then as now, I'd been tramping the universal round, doing my porridge, when Mr Dunne had slipped me this pass-key. Unfortunately, it hadn't quite fitted any lock of significance but maybe a little more patient philosophical filing would've done the trick . . . Strange it was though to see it again, that quirky little word machine in which its pilot, a level-headed, aeronautical engineer, had taken off on a night flight, plotting his course from the sober star graphs of science. But it was a flight that was to end in disaster with the far from practical aviator looping the loop before he fell in a mad rush of angels' wings, proclaiming in the inflated manner of some hoary patriarch as he plunged to the unconvinced earth that 'Nothing Dies! Nothing Dies!' Aye, he might've been right about things but not people – they certainly snuffed it: Ma Clay – cancer; Da Clay – cancer; Talky Sloan – evisceration; John Hallison – knifing; Old Pike – suffocation.

McQuade got to his feet. 'I'll have a quick spin aboot, then. But if I don't catch up with'm tell'm to give me a bell at the garage. Okay?'

'I'll come with you if you want,' I volunteered. 'Four eyes're better'n two.'

McQuade nodded. It was hard to figure whether he was pleased or not. 'Sure, if you want to. But finish your pint first.'

Cullen grinned. 'Tam's never had any problems in that department.'

As I gulped my lager I glanced at the stranger at the adjacent table. He looked engrossed in Dunne's time-twister, yet I got the impression that this was a pose, that, in a happy phrase that tumbled from young Jason's lips when he was describing a sneaky eavesdropper, 'He was watching me with his ears.' Such was my familiarity with Dunne's book that I could near enough tell by the thickness of the still-to-be-read portion where he was at – somewhere in the region of the Fallacy of the Phoney Pencil, I guessed.

In order to bring a homely cast to this theory the author chose a humble pencil to represent our dynamic 3-D Universe; while the 2-D one, shorn of the dimension of height, was to be thought of as being a gossamer-thin piece of paper, spectral stationery so fine that it is convenient to say of it that it has no thickness at all. Yet, it is into this very non-thickness that the reader is to imagine himself compressed.

A steamrollered shadow of himself the reader is now asked to visualise the pencil passing through the surface of the ghostly sheet of paper, in other words, the 2-D being pierced by the 3-D universe. What results from this is an analogy of growth as we know it here in our own cosmic backyard. Since the 2-D observer is unable to see the pencil in its entirety, his/her knowledge of it being restricted to a changing cross section of it (the smoke machine should be vigorously cranked here!) then, as the pencil penetrates the paper, first of all there will be seen a particle of graphite which the further the pencil is pushed through will accrue other particles and gradually assume the shape of a small leaden disc around which a larger wooden disc will form.

It's at this point that Mr Dunne pulls on his seven league boots and strides across the puddle-like oceans to search for Disney Exist. 'What if,' says Mr D., 'just as the pencil penetrates the paper, our 3-D universe is penetrated by the 4-D one of Time?' A fascinating question if the whole theory hadn't been completely fraudulent from the outset, the sneaking of an entire dimension through the custom post of logic. 'Man's still the dupe of Time'n Tide – the woman's brolly's in the Clyde.'

I finished my pint and got to my feet. The man in black also bestirred himself for what looked like imminent departure. He abandoned the newspaper, but carefully inserted the purple ticket into his book: you never know, maybe ticket inspectors board Time Machines with the same suspicious frequency as they do that Rarely-on-Time machine, the Corporation Castlemilk-bound No 37.

38

Stop Press
Matthew Lucas of
Caledonia Road,
Hutchestown,
Glasgow, struck
down and injured
by a Bubble Car
in Rutherglen Rd.,
Oatlands, Glasgow.
Condition described
as 'comfortable'.

The almost biblical simplicity of hot-lead prose, the salient facts only, the bones of the matter — fractures all over the shop, including a hairline one in the skull's occipital region. 'The patient was almost certainly saved by his zipless zoot suit,' said a genial surgeon. Tomorrow the media would flesh out the story, develop the human interest angles, which, since the mishap involved a bubble car and a mobile 'cadaver' would, automatically, invite a wacky seasonal treatment. Let's admit it, wouldn't most of us want to scurry into a corner for a yodel if we heard that someone

– even our best pal – had gotten his butt dented by a bubble car?

'It's a terrible business,' sighed Burnett, not for the first time that afternoon, 'terrible . . .'

As our cab came down the Bell o' the Brae and crossed into High Street at its Duke Street/George Street intersection I wondered if by 'terrible' Burnett was thinking of Matt's splintered anatomy or was deliberating more on the possibility of being sued, a threat Mildred Lucas, Matt's wife, had shrieked at him in the hospital waiting-room, although, admittedly, she'd been up to high-doh, at the time. Then, of course, yon big police sergeant hadn't helped Burnett's nerves any either when he muttered something about a bye-law infringement. It'd be typical of the city of St Bungle to be able to flourish some mildewed document, a Dark Age enactment which perversely remained in statute. A constraint on the citizenry from the blasphemous use of shrouds for any other purpose than 'the decent claithing of the deid . . .'

Halfway down High Street we got pinned by a red, which gave us a cabseat view of a pavement squabble that was attracting a sizeable crowd. A wee man and an even tinier woman were wrestling for possession of a nearly bald xmas tree. A custodial dispute, possibly: 'I admit, your Worship, to having committed indecent acts with a randy rowan, and that once I had a knee-trembler with a gallus wee aspen, but that was back in the days when I was still sowing my wild oaks. I've since married and put down roots. I'm fully confident that I can provide the spruce in question with a good home . . .'

What a city was Glasgow! It was really more into vaudeville than it was into violence, a fact seldom appreciated. For instance, while waiting for the ambulance to come, as wee Matt lay groaning on the slushy pavement with authentic slow-welling bloodstains creeping out amongst the spurious red-ink ones, a pair of fat wifies in the Gossip and Grumbles mould had stopped to do a bit of rubbernecking.

'My, would you look at that, Senga!' says one to the other. 'They've got'm wrapped in bandages already. By jings, that was quick, was it no?'

'It's a mummy, missus,' a wee boy tells her.

'D'you hear that, Lizzie?' says her pal. 'It's this poor wee laddies mammy, so it is. S'that no a shame?'

As our cab took the green, the xmas-tree struggle continued to its pine-spilling conclusion. My bread was on the woman but I'd never know the outcome. Never mind, around the next corner, or the one after, there'd be yet another pavement pantomime. And I was proved right, for as the taxi sloshed through the slush-puddles at Glasgow Cross, to be seen fleeing from the Saltmarket into Argyle Street dressed in nothing but his Y's was this beefy looking guy. Hot trottering behind him came a couple of oinks, their strides long and casual, as if to say: 'Don't worry folks, we'll nab'm in our own good time . . .'

'Terrible,' said old Burnett once more. Probably, he was brooding on the prospect of having Paddy Cullen and Archie Killoch working in tandem in the Planet's op-box, an arrangement that was as sensible as hiring Burke'n Hare as mortuary attendants. Not that Burnett had much choice: a fully subscribed member of the show-must-go-on brigade, he'd phoned off a priority telegram to Killoch, inviting him to report for duty at the Planet this very evening. Cullen, himself – I beg your pardon, chief projectionist Cullen, as yet ignorant of the extra stripe sewn by Fate onto his sleeve, would on this bookieless afternoon be at home sat bolt upright on the sofa giving it the big zeez after a liquid lunch of a double-double whisky and a couple of stout screwtops which was his customary chaser after his session in the Dog, of course.

Bewigged with snow, a stream of cars with searching almond headlights whisked past the High Court, carrying our cab onto the Albert Bridge from where a brolly was to be seen soaring into the darkness – a festive falcon carrying aloft the warmth of a woman's hand and maybe just a whiff of her perfume. She stood there by the bridge's snowy parapet, her hand still held in the air as if she entertained the hope that the traffic stream would relent and be persuaded to retreat ten seconds or so. Why not? What're a measly ten seconds? Let's make an xmas pressy of them to her. How rewarding to see that flyaway falcon flapping back, its onxy claw seeking lodgement once more on the familiarity of her gloved hand. In the flux world of Mr Dunne such anachronisms are ten-a-penny.

'Come up to my office for a few ticks, if you don't mind, Thomas,' Burnett said to me after he'd paid off the cab and we were standing beneath the Planet's ice-fanged canopy watching the wind making cones of light with the snow before dashing them to smithereens on the rutted street. As we climbed the frigid stairs up to the lounge somewhere in the dark of the auditorium an object fell.

'That'll be another star falling from heaven,' Burnett said, as if the possibility of further loosening stars falling on a potential client's head was of little immediate concern. 'I asked Patrick to check them out this morning too,' Burnett said as he searched his pocket for the office keys. A fascinating disclosure told quite matter-of-factly, changed my image of the artist O'Toole drastically. Gone for all time was the picture I'd conceived of him working heroically from the platform of perilous trestles, lying on his back, sweat gushing from every pore, and his muscles racked with pain as his brush dipped and tripped, bringing angels and planets to birth on the drab inner lid of the cinema's ceiling. No, none of that – the painting in its entirety had been done on the deck on two-yard square sections of audiotex, a porous, lightweight material designed to retain heat and assist acoustics. O'Toole, having painted a section, would simply haul it by rope ceilingwards and bolt it into position. It was all a matter of keeping the sections in their proper sequence – a sort of hanging-by-numbers, really.

As we padded along the lounge carpet the depressing stink of finito troubled my nostrils again. Arthritic creakings abounded everywhere as the SS *Planet* struggled the last league or so to Demolition, its last port of call. The wind was trying to pre-empt the Sledgehammer as it clouted the northern wall with mighty scudding blows. Burnett's attempts to keep this old wreck afloat was an affectation. Who'd really miss it? Its employees, maybe, though the sums they scraped from the cinema's near-empty coffers were paltry in the extreme. Maybe wee Emily Dodds, the cleaner, had convinced herself by now that the mysterious coin shower this morning had been from the angels, paying some of her overdue back money. No way could she possibly imagine the source to've been a demon smirking at her through a hole in Heaven's floor.

Burnett's office was a damp wee hole. Its desk was littered with papers, receipts, invoices, cups and strips of mummy wrapping. Distributors' publicity material also took up a good part of its space – racy synopses of offered attractions: *Terror From The Tomb* – a mummy stalks the street of a city, a nemesis from the Necropolis, sworn to wreak vengeance on those who have trashed its kingdom . . . And, for your future enjoyment: *Sei Personaggi In Cerca D'Autore* – an Italian tragi-comedy (with English subtitles). On sagging shelves bundles of trade magazines gathered dust. These publications contained photos of sleek grey projectors which starkly underlined the antiquity of the crummy pair of lanterns upstairs in the op-box and through which all movies were to be seen 'as through a glass darkly'.

On Burnett's say-so, I plugged in his electric fire. As I was doing so I noticed three sheets of paper, interleaved with carbons, hanging skew-whiff from Madge Dawkins' typewriter. The pages bore a dramatic, though unfinished message: 'I CAN'T GO ON. THE LONELINESS IS TOO MUCH. I . . .' The sentence seemed to've been stopped in its typewritten tracks by a side-fisted blow on the keys which had produced a manic cluster of letters, figures, and punctuation marks – in much the same way as foul language is sometimes rendered in cartoon captions. The inky bruise seemed to be a warning, the mark left by stoked-up despair. Its hidden message was 'One of these days I'm going to tear a hole in this paper globe and jump through!' Maybe. But it's hard to believe a would-be suicide who writes her farewell note in triplicate.

Wheezily, Burnett fought his way into his chair. Still wearing his hat and topcoat he sat there frowning darkly. From the table he took up a scrap of mummy-cloth. 'Poor Matt,' he murmured. 'What a wretched thing to happen.'

Seated across from him in Madge's seat, I nodded. As I thought about Matt trapped inside his hardening shell, Old Claustro, another of my phobias, began to twitch its feelers and I hastily shut down on the empathising. Sure, I felt sorry for Lucas, yet, I have to admit it – there was a schoolboyish urge to give way to sniggers tickling around my mirth circuits. Guilt-edged concern? Aye, the nasty taste laughing at sick jokes leaves in your mouth.

'What's this I've been hearing about you getting mugged?' I asked'm.

He waved a dismissive hand. Obviously he didn't want to talk about it.

'Got your furry hat snaffled – s'that right?'

He nodded, testily.

'D'you get a gander at'm?'

'If by that you mean – did I see my assailant's face, the answer is no.'

'How no?'

'Because he wore a mask.'

'A nylon stocking, eh?'

'No, a death mask. One of those cheap Halloween things.'

'Did you go to the oinks? I mean, did you inform the polis?'

He shook his head: 'Scarcely worth the bother.'

'Just the same you should – '

'I take it as a sign,' he began, then a soft cough rolled a phlegm-ball into his throat and clotted the sentence. He cleared it. 'I take it to be a sign that my time's about up. It could scarcely be plainer, could it – Death pinching your crown in broad daylight?' The scrap of cloth between his hands gave a weak snap-snapping sound as he jerked at it, then he let it fall limply to the desk. He became a little brisker but still hadn't shrugged off his despondency. 'Mrs Lucas was upset, wasn't she?'

Upset? That just had to be the nuttiest question since the cub reporter asked the newly-widowed Mrs Lincoln if, despite what'd happened to Abe, had she enjoyed what she'd seen of the play? Of course Mrs Lucas'd been upset. Who could blame'r? One minute she's working away there in the wee draper's shop selling nylons and knickers, the next she's being told that her husband while traipsing around in a Cairo onepiece had been struck down and all but dismantled by a speeding bubble car.

'Well,' Burnett sighed, 'at least we can learn from it.'

Sure we could. I'd always keep in mind from now on the hazards which attend the wearing of pyramid tomb-togs while walking abroad in thoroughfares that'r a-buzz with Clockwork Oranges. Those auto-bubble bams, mad they were. Once their go-needles quivered on the quarter-ton they lost all social control and wanted to speed-whip every damned thing on wheels.

'It's never too late to learn,' Burnett informed me. Learn to do what? Drive a bubble car? Take up embroidery? Parachute from a submarine? What was the old duffer on about? Sliding open the desk drawer to his left, Burnett brought out a three-quarter-filled whisky bottle and a couple of tumblers. He unstoppered the bottle and jolted heavy wallops of whisky into each glass. He shoved my drink across the desk to me. After I'd responded to his mumbled toast I took a slug of the neat spirits then lowered my glass. The expected salvo of coughing did not erupt; there were only a few isolated bronchial barks. My lungs had either settled down or were dead. Smashing stuff this whisky. Maybe I should rub some on my elbow.

'You'll be feeling as ashamed as me, I suppose.'

I stared across at Burnett. 'Ashamed?'

'Well, guilty, then?'

'About what?'

'Medical incompetence, Thomas, that's what – first-aid illiteracy. Makes me blush just to think of it, both of us standing there, about as useful as a lecture to a drowning man.' He shook his head. 'I can still see poor Matthew, lying there like a bag of squashed beetroots.' He sipped some more whisky. 'It should be taught in every school in the land.' He meant 'first-aid', not the art of drinking whisky (thirst-aid!). I nodded. He was right of course. Up in the attic with Cullen this morning, if it'd been a genuine emergency then by now the boyo would've been a charred log in the civic icebox.

Burnett, sensing my sympathy with it, went on to expand his idea to everyone in society, from glimmerbrains to genius, being made conversant with at least the fundamentals of first-aid and the rendering thereof. Your average punter usually hadn't the smokiest notion as to the function, let alone the locations, of most of his or her major organs. Yon thick bugger, Toland, for instance, spouting off about some accident he'd seen: 'This guy's erm was laid open fae wrist tae elbow, nae kiddin – you could see aw the liver hinging oot . . .' What a dummy! He'd be a passed fireman by now, able to take the odd driving turn. If the public but knew about some of the brammers they entrusted their lives to, footplate freakos, speed-jockeys without a nerve in their bodies and an equal dearth of brain cells, they wouldn't be sitting back there in their glazed trucks reading the papers and mags with such complacency. Not even if I'd a free pass and Kim Novak to fan me with'r knickers all the way to London, would I board a train if I learned in advance that The Shagger or big Suicide Slattery were at the controls. You would need a helluva lot more than first-aid knowledge to survive a trip with those headcases.

As Burnett droned on about his 'universal first-aid' I thought of some of the drawbacks to his notion. Think of a bus packed from floor to roof with proficient first-aiders, and all of them arguing the toss about the best way to treat this poor guy who's just folded with a cracked pump. Before you knew it they'd be at each other's throats flourishing their competence certificates and their 'First-Class First-Aider' scrolls, a mêlée which would degenerate into a free-for-all in which there'd be much exchanging of highly accurate punches and way-off surmise.

With his 'lecture' completed Burnett delved his hand once more into the drawer to his left and fished out a screwdriver. Wriggling from his chair's embrace he rose and withdrew from the corner a short pair of steps. Equipped with these two mundane items he waddled to the door. 'Won't be a jiffy,' he said, and went out. I suppose if his kit had also included a length of rope I might've got to my feet and followed him to check out his intentions, both from concern for his welfare, and from curiosity for its own sake.

I helped myself to some more Scotch then as I sipped it took an eye-stroll around the office. Gravure prints of vintage racing cars lapped the timber panelled walls. There were signed photographs too, amongst which was featured a much younger-looking Burnett exchanging a handshake with a lugubrious Charles Laughton; in another picture Cary Grant was to be seen with his arm about Burnett's shoulder, the latter grinning at some wisecrack the urbane star had just made, probably at the photographer's expense – real buddy-buddies they looked. Pride of place in the collection was given to a framed picture of Bette Davis who'd mugged a sexy pout for the camera but had ended up looking like she'd just swallowed a stickleback . . .

The photo I liked best was one of Burnett got up in cowboy dude gear, topped off with an outsized Stetson that could've kept the Nevada desert in shade. Bygone goofy days of yore. Now there was a piece of headgear really worth mugging for! Paddy Cullen assured me that most of the photos were fakes. He claimed that the nearest Burnett had ever got to a Hollywood star had been during Roy Rogers' visit to Glasgow when Trigger's stand-in had shat on his brogue shoes.

I soaked up some more booze. Nice stuff – a ten-year-old blend, made before I'd wised up to what a mean old customer John Barleycorn can be, when I'd got to hanging around with'm and fooled myself into believing that a whisky-stain on my shirtfront was a badge of manhood. Right now though it was doing what it was best at, laying a warmth around me as soothing as a woman's arms, perking me up some, excluding my feet, of course. Why'd there never seem to be enough heat going around to spare some for the old tootsies? Go on with that stuff about a woman's arms, said a lulled MacDougall. That was nice that stuff . . .

I kicked off my shoes and thrust my feet towards the electric fire. I was getting to be quite comfy now – except for my nagging elbow. Sitting there on a would-be-suicide's floral-cushioned throne. This was her view of the world, her peculiar vision-slant on its doings. Not much to sustain an optimistic outlook on life, it had to be admitted, but not grim enough either to justify taking the exit-only narco route. They were quite right to call suicide a crime. It was. To seek to induce that stupefying blackness which'll come in its own bad time – it's one of existence's dependables – to flirt with the onset of that forever-in-darkness-floating, that's just got to be criminal, aye, even if it's your fate to be a weeping creature called Madge who's stuck for five days a week in the office of a half-mad film exhibitor typing invoices in duplicate and suicide notes in triplicate.

At that moment I got a déjà-vu nudge in the ribs: 'Hey,' a familiar voice said in my ear: 'this is where we came in!'

39

In their defence of Okinawa, Japanese suicide pilots had little
more than a week to learn how best to make their worst-possible
landing. Then off they went on a wing and a prayer, their doomed
heads swathed in solar head-bands, proud to a man of the honour
bestowed upon them and fully assured of their memorials in the
Yasakuni Shrine.

Me, I don't have the stuff such kamikaze heroes are made from;
I lack their philosophical bottle when the universal Hit Man
happens along. It wasn't then with a martyr's hymn on my lips
that, alongside McQuade, I crunched through the trashed snow
to his car, a Rover 2000, which was parked in front of the steeple-
shorn Bleaker Memorial Church. The building itself had been
stricken from God's payroll so that it lacked the authority now to
grant sanctuary, a privilege it had always lacked as far as I was
concerned. Aye, even when it'd been hooked into the theological
power grid.

Olive green paintwork and clinging swathes of snow loaned
McQuade's Rover a camouflaged appearance and reminded me
of its possible sameness of purpose to the Nakajima ki 115, the Jap
one-trip special plane. An apt comparison, maybe, but with one
major difference – your kamikaze goons couldn't wait to off

themselves, whereas I was definitely leery of this self-immolation lark. I'd need some time to get used to the idea – let's say another forty years or so.

If events in my life continued to take turns for the worse (on the Jeremiah Channel I could see a horned and forktailed weather-man ramming storm-pins into my effigy) then this could be it – I can do without the sarcastic violin, if you please! – my last car ride.

WEAVER: Not for God, not even for me, Tommy, but for the kids from the Scabby, I want you to take this ride like a broken man, let your lasting image be one of cowardice, let those street bronchos remember you as Tommy Clay – the dude who chickened.

For some time now I've been getting the cracked-jorry bounce around Fortune's bent wheel, catching all the downmouth numbers, every pause making me poorer, sorer, and okay, I admit it, scareder. Know what I'd settle for right now? I'll tell you, a simple game of Solitaire. That's right, with a cool lager at my elbow, working those friendly pasteboards on a sunny table at a window that looks onto a quiet little town where all the clocks have stopped.

McQuade began to cuff a snow layer from the car's windscreen: I did likewise to the rear window. Not so long ago the working-class folks had sheeted up their windows to signify a bereavement (the McKinnons up 69 hung out a flag – but that's another story). Playing at the scummy edges of backcourt fever-puddles we kids would keep pitching big-eyed glances up at the blanked-out windows, and we'd whisper to newcomers: 'Somebody's deid in that hoose, so they are.' It was changed days now: out of grudging respect the telly's volume might get lowered a tickle, but that's the only concession you're about to get, 'cepting of course, some completely undisturbed shuteye. I think it was La

365

Rochefoucauld, either him, or Shug Wylie, who said that a cheapened attitude towards death inevitably follows from an impoverished response to life. Aye, the telly with or without commercials, must go on.

We both got into the car; the doors slammed.

Sayonara!

McQuade switched on the ignition then the heater. 'Any ideas?' he asked.

'Oatlands,' I responded with a suspicious alacrity. 'You take the first right, then – '

'It's okay, I know Oatlands.' He released the handbrake. 'That's where the Fast Laundry Service is – right?'

'Laundry Service?'

'Aye, Shawfield greyhound track – where the punters get taken to the cleaners.'

An assassin's laugh alongside a victim's sheepish grin. Like a Russian pause, a solemn wee sitdown before a major journey, we waited while the heater did its work. I gazed at the clotted windscreen, at the melting away of the ice, the ruthless expungement of snowflakes parachuted in to try'n preserve the wintry bridgehead. Outwardly, I suppose I looked calm enough, but in reality my bowels were in that state of nerve-riot which can best be simulated by tossing a live mongoose into a bucket of cobras. The wipers wagged and music came hurling at us from stereo speakers . . . '. . . drinka . . . drinka, drink to Lily the Pink, the pink, the pink – saviour of the human rayhayhace . . .' McQuade reached out and dropped the volume. Who was that group again? The Scaffold? Think so. Aye, build mines high – a long fall for such a wee drop of blood.

The Rover's tyres eased from their snowy sockets then moved from the muffled kerb. Soon we were passing through virgin territory, the white spread of those blank pages upon which housing planners and designers – those licensed vandals – had been naively tendered by the City Blethers to amplify those examples of architectural doodling they'd already jotted into the Projects margins. The concreted concepts that'd been erected so far had a sort of penitentiary glaze to them, a visual smack of censure. What else were high flats but punishment blocks – vertical Barlinnies? Agreed, the amenities available to the new Gorbalsonians were far and away superior to the disgusting dearth of them in the demolished slums, but wasn't having your own toilet and bath too high a price to pay for the privilege of living in a cemetery with traffic lamps?

I'd fixed on Oatlands because I reckoned that Burnett and the mobile Sore Finger would, because of the weather, enact their publicity fantasy closer to home. Now I know Oatlands folk're a hardy breed but I can't see any of them being willing to desert a warm telly, pile on about a half-hundred-weight of Arctic togs, then hit the slush trail to a pesthole called the Planet Cinema where he or she'd be hard put to find a seat with its legs intact, its arms and cushion unripped, and not in the proximity of the gang of horny dossers that groped anything that moved – gender irrelevant – but preferably handy for an exit, an essential safeguard during the cinema's roof-fall season. Who'd endure such hassle just to peer at the ludicrous perambulations of some fusty old sand-stiff – a movie that might, but most likely would not, be shown in sequence because its co-projectionists were a pair of juiceheads who'd be lucky to see the screen, never mind the shadows writhing on it? Only one bod shuffles to mind, a certifiable mummy-freako name of Joe Shovel. Joe, however, is barred from the Planet for swigging 'deathylated spirits' during the screening of The Song of Bernadette. Joe claims to be a reincarnation of King Tut himself. I'll grant'm this much – he's certainly got the skin for it. Another reason I'd picked on

Oatlands was Old Mooney; chances were I might spot'm being transferred to another 'safe house' by the Sooside Maquis.

'You slipped a socket or something?' growls my very own backseat driver.

We drifted onto Caledonia Road, ghosted on past Naeburn Street, kept on rolling alongside the Southern Necropolis. On our right were powdery bursts of snow blown from the tips of obelisks and lofty headstones which could be seen jutting above the icy rim of the graveyard's containing wall. To our left we were bypassing another cemetery, but with a major difference – this one was for the living: bleak assemblages of interlocked concrete, pitted windows . . .

The back-seat driver was in my ear again: 'C'mon Tommy, wise up. This aint no car – it's a fuck'n tumbril! So, let's drop the George Washington crap. No way're you going to tell Godzilla here that you've made the humpbacked monster with his wife. Listen son, we're not talking a busted smile or a dented ribcage, here. We're talking terminal. Have yourself a good look at this guy. If he's not an ice-merchant then Atilla the Hun wore a frock. He'll off you without blinking. Stabbed, slabbed, and tabbed – s'that what you're wanting? Get it together, Tommy. The Planet's going down the tubes, Lucas'll soon be on welfare, just another tired arse mooching around, one more fart in the charity pipeline. But for you Tommy, it's still all there – dazzling days yet to come. You've got prime stocks in the future market, son. Don't go screwing things up with this virtue crap. Who's to know? Nobody. Do nothing, Tommy. Let it ride . . .

We were approaching the junction with Rutherglen Road. As we went through it I got to wondering how I'd handle the fraught situation if I happened to be around when McQuade finally caught up with wee Lucas. Their meeting was unavoidable for obviously diversionary manoeuvres like this one wouldn't always present themselves. What would I really do? What would I say? The script I cobbled together was ludicrous: I give but a sample of its putrid dialogue: 'Listen big man – it's me you're after. He (Lucas) has got nothing to do with it . . .' Desperate stuff. A sharper approach required. 'Big Man, listen to me – your wife is beaverless, hasn't got any hair – there. Clean-shaven, bare as a nun's napper. And she's got a mole on'r left thigh . . .' What drivel.

As we passed the snowed-up rinks of the bowling green a visual puzzle presented itself: at the heart of the green there was a scattering of footprints. Big deal, eh! I could hardly wait to get back home to get it down in my journal: 'Footprints on Rink 1 of bowling green. Blueprints, really, made by children running in a circle. But, something odd: no footprints to show where the gang of merry youngsters had entered the rink nor any sign of those they should've made when they'd exited. How'd it been done? Had they dropped onto it by chopper? Or had they tunnelled their way to – '

A shout was suddenly loosed from McQuade's throat. Simultaneously, he brought the car to a skidding halt in the gutter. I followed his pointing finger. Across the road on the cleared site where McNab's pub had stood a mummy was being harried and baited by a gang of glimmerbrains. As we watched the mummy floundering amongst the mounds of covered bricks and other demolition trash, it tripped over one of its unravelled bandages and almost went down. Recovering, it turned to the converging mob and held up its swathed arms in a gesture of appeal, but there didn't seem to be a mummyphile amongst the vicious little pricks. Snowballs kept on battering the mummy from all angles. Eventually a one-pounder took it full in the wrapped face and with a bright snowburst carried off the specs that'd made the mummy such a figure of ridicule. On the edge of the turmoil Burnett could be seen dithering, but his appeals to the hooligans were about as effective as an optimist trying to piss out a forest fire. Even the so-called adults gathering at the spot were grinning, as if this piece of street theatre had been laid on for their personal amusement.

Poor wee Lucas – his troubles had only just begun, for while he was still down on his knees, scrabbling in the snow for his specs, from stage left there entered at speed a hysterical mongrel with so many teeth glittering in its red mouth you would've thought that its mother'd been humped by a crocodile. As the cur with vicious lunges sought to get a fang-hold on Matt's already tattered rear, two other characters necessary to infuse a further element of farce into the drama were steadily approaching: first of all came the skinniest bloke I'd ever seen (and that includes Sinatra in *Anchors Aweigh*!) Clad in yellow oilskins, and with a bulbous black helmet lodged on his grapefruit-sized head, he looked like a pencil I'd once owned. This skinnymalink was riding an equally emaciated-looking motorbike; so thin was this machine, so one-dimensional, it must've been manufactured during a period of industrial famine. Behind this skeletal rider came an orange bubble car, a real juiced-up wee Jaffa, possibly powered by a hairdryer motor, and blinding along at a speed well into the upper thirties.

When I was a kid I saved matchbox labels. I remember an unswappable favourite which pictured an elephant and a croc having a jungle dust-up. The pachyderm was getting a right good gubbing for the wily croc had managed to get its gnashers around Nelly's trunk and was dragging her into its swamp. Now, as the apocalyptical rider and the bubble car approached and were beginning to edge into the picture, wee Matt was, like the elephant, in deep shit. The dog had'm by the belly-bindings, or at

370

least, by one of them, and was viciously hauling on it. Possibly in an effort to get more purchase from the soles of his skidding wellies, Lucas was dragging his attacker in the direction of the pavement. At that moment a stick, maybe even a crowbar, came whirling through the air. Targeted, no doubt, on Matt, it fell short and stoved in the mongrel's ribs. The impact must've been hellish sore for the bag of fleas, with a loud yelp, leapt about a yard'n the air, landed, started to run off, but after a few hirpling steps it keeled over and lay quivering on the slushy pavement. The kids, their grubby faces puckering in sympathy (such sentimental little sods!), crowded around it.

Lucas, meanwhile, was having spectacular problems of his own. When the taut swathing had suddenly become dogless he'd staggered backwards onto the pavement and only managed to halt at its edge, his arms flailing, his back to the passing traffic. Teetering, it looked an odds-on cert he was going to get messily involved with the traction of a speeding SMT bus. Whether he would've made it – recovered his balance – will never be known for at that moment, the wind, picking up the trailing cloth strip, sneaked it out onto the road and made an impromptu winner's tape for the fast approaching motorbike. Several events happened together, a chord of disaster; the tape got fankled in the motorbike's front wheel; the swathing was snapped taut; wee Matt, like a peerie released from its whip, went birling along the kerb edge before finally spinning out into the path of the oncoming bubble car.

'Holy Shit,' I cried as Lucas, taking the full impact of the autobub, went somersaulting over its roof, seemed to loiter in mid-air for a generous moment – his rags bravely flying – then, abruptly, pitched face-downwards onto the wet tarmac, with the wet schlopping sound of an exploding melon.

Chunks of what happened next shift from fact to fade; the pen croaks mid-sen – another medium must be sought:

Say, how's this grab you? A camera perched shoulder-high, panning left to right to simulate head-movement.

You mean like we're inside the shroudy's head?

Got it in one.

Then we what?

Add heartbeats.

You flipped? Maybe you want heavy breathing as well?

Sure, why not?

I'll tell you why not – coz the fuck'n thing's morgue meat, tomb trash, as dead as your braincells. How come its pump's going badoing-badoing and its breath's making like a hacksaw when it's fit only for carrion and other Gypo jerkoffs. Come again?

'What about some scarabs?'

'Scarabs? The beetle jobs you mean? Yeah, I might buy that: grave bugs scuttling across his non-existent vision. Okay, tell Connie to buy a bagful of scarabs. Oh, and while she's about it; a half-dozen bagels. Now, let's shift some celluloid, okay? Action . . . roll'm . . .

The mummy lies on its back at the bottom of a dry well. Dressed in the waxy folds of its death garb it bears on its forehead and face the bandages of Nekhem and Hathor. It sees faces staring down at it from the well's rim, sees too the blood-red lotuses that are flowering on its delved chest and looted belly. It can delay no longer. Its ka flies up the well's parched throat, goes past the faces with their expressions of spurious concern and goes out, out into the light. Two men are to be seen running from a strange chariot towards the well into which the spectators still morbidly peer. A door opens in a strange spherical machine. Can this be the ferry to the

underworld? From this metal bubble there begins to ooze a
blanched lifeform that looks like a gigantic larva . . .

Cut! Goddamit – CUT!

Burnett re-entered the office minus the steps but bearing in
their place a large framed picture. This he laid before me then he
began his usual set-to with his chair which he won on a throw and
an outright submission. Once he was enthroned, had got himself
tucked in to his satisfaction, he gave the air a critical sniff or two.
'What's that stink? Something crawled in here and died?'

My feet snailed back into their snow-bleached shoes.

Burnett slammed the screwdriver back into the drawer. He
nodded at the picture. 'A promise is a promise, eh?' He tossed a
scrap of mummy-wrapping across the desk. 'Here, it's a bit
stoury. Give it a wipe.' I rubbed the rag across the greasy glass:
Clark Gable's mouldering grin became all the more exposed.
'Something's gotten to'm,' Burnett admitted, 'but you can still
tell who he's about.'

I mumbled my thanks. Useless to point out that I'd been
promised Alan Ladd: a playboy for a cowboy! Ach, so what? A
necrotic hero was in tune with this pisser of a day. Burnett had
decided to buy the hell-ticket to inner calm, that deceptively
short journey it takes a glassful of Scotch to get from hand to
mouth. Having been banned from liquor due to his H.B.P.
condition, Burnett's drink had the added flavour of being a risk-
cocktail. Silly old bugger – his face was already as lit-up as a
Halloween tumshy.

He squinted at the whisky bottle with a knowing eye and
didn't offer to recharge my glass. 'Evaporation, eh,' he said. 'The
very blight of the spirit trade. John Barleycorn having his pocket
dipped, as someone neatly put it!' With his replenished glass
tucked into the meaty folds of his hand, he wriggled himself into a

more comfortable position. 'Tell me,' he said a few whisky sips later, 'that chap with the woolly hat thing and the lumberjacket – y'know, him with the tash who warned us against moving Matthew before he went to phone an ambulance. Who was he – a relative?'

I nodded. 'Matt's nephew.'

'How'd he happen along?'

I shrugged. 'Coincidence, I suppose.'

Synchronicity, old Jung had dubbed what he called the meaningful coincidence, the engine of causality, with its long train of bumper-to-bumper freight-trucks, each of them stuffed with common sense, coming off at the catch-points, making a wreck of the so-carefully-laid plans of those who'd invested in their assured arrivals.

It turned out that the stranger hadn't been McQuade after all. In fact, he'd been who he'd claimed to be: Billy Lucas, Matt's nephew. He'd gone in his car to break the news to Matt's wife then had driven her to the hospital. Burnett and I had ridden there in the ambulance. A surrealistic scene: the groaning mummy; the medic who'd been unable to conceal his smirk, savouring this one – a juicy anecdote to relate over xmas dinner.

After another gulp of Scotch, Burnett settled on me a scrutiny so intense that I admit to've been fazed by it. Eventually, down the tunnel of this gaze I saw, heading my way and fast, the jinking lights of a Rubberland special, a runaway train of thought, its compartments chokeful of cockamamie notions.

'I'm thinking of writing a letter to the Lord Provost,' he announced.

'Oh, aye?'

'Can you guess what about?'

I shook my head.

'I'm going to make a last effort to persuade His Worship to

preserve one of the Gorbals' most famous landmarks, so that it might become a sort of historical reference site, a place where parents can bring their children, and teachers their pupils, a focus for both recreational and cultural pursuits.'

He nodded then removed his hat. Soon a faint haze of steam rose from his bald patch. He placed the hat on the desk. 'You know, of course, to which landmark I'm referring?'

'Shug Wylie's shithoose?'

His eyelids flickered, 'Facetiousness is undoubtedly one of your most annoying traits, Thomas. Well?'

I'd half a notion but I sung dumb.

He raised a hand and gave it a sort of circular flourish. 'This, of course.'

'You want the Provost to preserve your hand?'

'I mean, as you well know, this cinema.'

'I see. A sort of "Save the Planet" campaign?'

He nodded. I put on I was giving the goofy idea some thought. I don't know why – I just did. What a character he was. Last year it'd been battery hens: he'd wanted to install a dozen or so of the clucking things in the boilerhouse. Now this latest equally dumb notion. 'C'mon Oswald,' I said. 'You know the score. Folks've jacked in the movies. It's telly and your bingo, these days.'

'I suppose,' Burnett conceded, 'that the Planet's function as a cinema might cease, but, again, maybe not. It could become a specialised centre, a Film Club, even. Why not even a theatre? Yes, I admit it's a bit dilapidated but the structure's still perfectly sound.'

I shook my head. 'The game's a bogy, Oswald. Why no admit it?'

But once he was in the saddle of an optimistic notion Burnett was a difficult man to dislodge. In fact Burnett's optimism, like Sophie Tucker's corsets, knew no limits.

'Take the People's Palace,' he went on, 'step in there and you're immediately up to your neck'n history.' He leaned both his arms on the desk. 'So, why not something similar, only even more localised, for the Gorbals? After all, we're talking about an area that had its origins in the thirteenth century. It's my opinion that 'The Gorbals House of History' would prove to be a powerful cultural magnet. All sorts of artifacts could be displayed – not just your mugs, jugs and wally dugs, but working models too, living tableaux, people dressed in costumes of the past, maybe a reconstruction of a ward in the Leper Hospital . . .'

Ay'n stairheid rammies and closemouth shirrikens could be enacted by out-of-work thespians, while Tobacco Lords and Snuff Barons, not forgetting lepers, deepsea divers and the odd mummy or two could be seen strolling around. Sundry items of sentimental value to be contemplated; a stank lid from Adelphi Street, a fedora that had once been worn by a likeable petty crook, Babs the Flyman; the last pair of mule shoes to be sold by the High Walk Shoe Company of Cumberland Street; the moothie and bone clappers that'd belonged to popular entertainer, Darkie Marshall; Albert Wheeler's first racing cycle; a fitba jersey once worn by Tommy Ring of Clyde FC (The Bully Wee): A Barber's Chair, made by local craftsman, John Gibson; a pub mirror from The Salty Dog Saloon; a pair of projectors from The Planet Cinema; remains of a fish supper eaten by wife-murderer, Charlie Coutts during his brief incarceration in the Lawmoor Street dub-up; and yet another pair of shoes, shiny ones worn by John Clay of the Scabby, a man who could've rivalled the Great Saphenous for his disappearing acts; a pair of Benny Lynch's boxing gloves . . .

At the Sales Points patrons would be able to purchase wee model slums that tinkled 'I Belang Tae Glesca' when their roofs were raised. But why stop there? You could have 'Pongs from the Past', bottled nostalgia in fog-grey flasks which vile exiles could unstopper, then after a good sniff, say: Gee, hon, don't that take you back – a stapped Gorbals' john!' To which his spouse would rapturously exclaim: 'And sugarallywater, Elmer – is that not megasignificant!'

'What d'you think?' Burnett was asking.

I nodded, 'I think maybe you're on something.'

The sarcasm arising from the omission of 'to' in my reply seemed to've been lost on him. What he took to be my endorsement of his optimistic plan kindled his enthusiasm all the more. Once, back'n the old days, having spilled some sugar, I'd swept it onto a shovel then had thrown it on the fire. Flames had immediately shot up the lum, licking into that blind place where the Sootmonster lived and in whose black throat there had started up this ominous growling which, in turn, fanned shrieked recriminations from Ma Clay: 'You great lummox, you've set the bliddy chimley oan fire!'

There was no doubting that Burnett's 'chimley' had well and truly caught, for his stack began to spit forth sparks, smoke, flame, glowing coals, aye and even fire-bars, as they'd say on the railway to describe an overtaxed loco on a slippery slope. In a very short time, so pervasive was his prodigious gift for optimism that the wreck of the foundered SS *Planet*, through the portholes of which had been projected every human cataclysm from earthquake to heartbreak, began to look rescuable; not intact, of course – no hope of that – but in good enough shape to return to existence in some modified but socially useful form.

On every object he uncovered down there midst the dull corals of ruin he bestowed his uplift, prising them from Gravity's tenacious grasp. In other words, I'd allowed myself to be suckered by the old conman, had let'm take me for a ride in a yellow submarine, the hull rivets of which sprung more readily than did the buttons from a glutton's waistcoat.

Although, so far, he'd fared reasonably well in his foray into the skimpy constructions of the so-called future, it was really in the past that Burnett thrived best. There, he could boldly unwrap mummified memories, safe in the knowledge that they couldn't collapse into dust at the merest touch. The past was a happy hunting ground for him; he never tired of finding new routes into the great Once Was. Steamrollered by his phenomenal powers of recall, I'd often left his company flatter than one of those freaky figures Dunne peopled his duo-dimensional world with. But not today. I was for slinging my hook real soon.

There're fewer fates more grisly than becoming a human shitpan for some boring old asshole, for that's what the nostalgiac's victim becomes, a humble receptacle into which, after a wearying struggle to open history's sphincter, there drops, not the enormously astounding stool all that writhing and grunting had presaged, but instead a tedious procession of memory tollies – plop . . . plop . . . plop . . . plop . . . 'I remember,' Burnett said, 'must've been back in the thirties, when you were just a wrinkle on your Daddy's brow, Thomas, that I . . . plop . . . plop . . . plop . . .'

I left the Planet about twenty minutes or so later. Not long afterwards a movie idol found himself whirling through the snow-filled air to land in a street skip which was already crammed with domestic junk – a sad end for Gable! The snow-machine had been left at max drive, a rate of dispersion that'd soon exhaust its flake-stock and clear the way for the traditional grey xmas. Within a few minutes I was blotted out, invisible except for a pair of eyeballs jerking along, a snow mummy seeking the bleak comforts of its sarcophagus.

I compile a status report: I am hungry; my arm is sore; my

feet're wet; my lungs ache. Ergo, I must be more than a pair of jiving eyeballs. From what source arise these reports on the pangs that beset my corpus crusty? In one of his fascinating, but, alas, flawed books, Dunne had included a droll sketch of an artist at his easel who was painting himself painting himself painting himself, and so on until the multiplying replicas have shrunk to a dot in infinity. Serialism! Watch out for that crafty cousin with his slippery solipsisms.

Once I'm inside my cracked little igloo I'll light the whale-oil lamps then plonk my chilled feet onto a gourd of hot seal blood. The need to tune-out affects the toughest of Eskimos from time to time. Wearied by the sight of the replicating artist he seeks out a wee patch of silence, like an ant creeping under leaf shade, to doze and dream . . . doze and dream . . . in blessed detachment from the terrestrial predators who come seeking for'm but go sniffing on by.

Tranquillity.

There's a jewel of a word. A man could keep warm for weeks on the sparkle of it alone. Tranquillity – a mantra for the closing moment. Tran-kwill-itee. That'll suffice. I leave Nirvana to the prime-leaguers. The mindpeace which I seek is like all cosmic treasures to be found admidst the lowly and is close at hand – Marco's Fish'n Chip Emporium, to be exact. You dig? Aye, a big fish in crackling batter of the deepest gold. Some haddy. Samadhi. Loads of salt'n vinny, please and a pair of tickled bunions.

But Tranquillity is a state denied me.

Marco's Emporium is shut.

Bastard'n Monday!

40

They'd arrived in the library's IN section – Rhona Carlyle and yon right wee horror Sneery Clearie, her with the waxy eyelids and smell of dog bum on'r breath.

Clay dumped the Biggles book, then with all the nonchalance of a one-legged ostrich, he strolled across to the non-fiction area. His heart, a scunnersomely stupid bag of tricks, having decided that he was playing for Scotland and was about to burst the net with a twenty-yarder, turned on all of its taps full bung.

The girls spotted him – it would've been hard not to've seen the watchman's brazier glowing so brightly there in the corner. As they approached, Clay grabbed at a bulky book which, because of its unexpected weight, immediately slipped through his sweaty fingers. It plunged to the floor with a bang that might've been heard as far away as Tradeston, and surely must startle 'Foxy' from his lair. The red-haired fiend seemed to believe that the ears of boys had been provided for him to steer with, rather than for them to hear with: Clay's right appendage began to throb as if in anticipation of the caretaker's pincering grip. Clay saw himself being tugged along in an abject crouching manner, gathering speed as they approached the fateful PUSH-ONLY door through which, having surrendered your library ticket – the hangman's tribute – you were dispatched to the limbo of a bookless universe.

As he bent to lift the book, his nose that'd warned him in a dream that one day it was going to commit suicide without waiting for the rest of his cowardly bits, began to drip. From his trouser pocket – how tight it'd become – he tugged a chunk of floral curtain rag, an action that dragged with it a cascade of jorries; they sped from him in all directions, lodging under tables, below chairs, in darkish corners, even his 'Wizard's Eye', that uncrackable green demon, had fled, but he resisted the urge to pursue it.

Surely now Foxy could come. Clay imagined the caretaker's forbidding door being suddenly whipped open to reveal the terrifying man who'd obviously been disturbed at his dinner for a gore-freckled napkin was loosely tied about his neck and he clutched in his hand the remains of a child's leg . . . Foxy, however, did not appear; it must be his day off.

The girls drew yet nearer.

Frantically, Clay riffled through his mental phrase-book, trying to pluck from it some passable remark. The weather? Was it still raining? No, it was foggy. When the moment came he stuttered out something totally idiotic: 'Hullo, is it still f-fogging?'

'Still f-fogging what?' asked Sneery Clearie.

Rhona Carlyle's pale hand rose to glide through the sleek plum darkness of her hair then she turned her head away, probably to hide a grin.

'What's the book?' Sneery now asked.

'Just a book.'

'An awfy big book.'

'Aye.'

'What's it aboot?'

'Things,' said Clay desperately.

'Let's see, then.' Sneery wrested the book from his grasp then began to flap through its pages. 'Aye,' she nodded as she showed one of the book's illustrations to Rhona Carlyle, 'things awright – UNDER-things!'

It turned out that the book was *A History of the Female Costume Through the Ages*!

'You thinking of taking up dressmaking, Tommy?' asked Sneery.

Clay blushed so hard it was a wonder that his suicidal nose hadn't melted there and then and dropped off.

'Tommy,' said Sneery.

'Whit?'

'You'd better shut your mooth – somebody might post a letter in it!'

With feathery sniggers both lassies moved away.

'I don't remember any of that,' Rhona said. 'You've made it up.'

'No, it's kosher. In one of ma journals. Came across it the other day.'

'That proves it, then.'

'Proves what?'

'A lot of baloney.'

'If it was made up would I ridicule myself?'

'One of your tricks to get sympathy. You blush? A stone would sneeze first.'

'Good, that is. Instead of "bleed" you said . . .'

'For a start, she was never called "Sneery".'

'Aye she was. Definitely.'

'Mary or Merry – that's all.'

'Naw, naw. Mind when you lassies used to play ba'. There was this rhyme that went alang wae it: "One, two, three, alearie, I spied Wallace Beery sittin oan his bumbaleerie, kissin Shirley Temple." Remember?'

'Vaguely. But what's that to do with . . .'

'There was a variation that went . . .'

'Don't . . . they'll think you're drunk. Are you?'

'Listen, it went . . . "I spied Sneery Clearie sitting oan her bumba . . ."'

'Nothing of the kind.'

'There was.'

'Wasn't.'

'Was.'

This was turning out to be one of our better visits. True, it'd begun in familiar style with some lip-sparring, nothing too heavy – feint'n jab stuff, is all. But even when she'd had'r customary go at me over financial shortcomings, sartorial sloppiness, tonsorial neglect, her spleen wasn't really in it, the weight of the glove not there. We seemed a bit closer, somehow, linked by a sunny thread of levity, like in the tale where the dame springs her man from jail by using her bobbin – a right cock'n bull story, yon.

Maybe what'd lightened the atmosphere had been Rhona's decision to take my visit lying down instead of sitting amongst us flat bellies gawping in at the 'Haunted fishtank' or, as I heard a witty medic call it the other day – 'The Electronic Drip-Feed'. Hooked into this apparatus you lie there supine while lulling image on image percolates through your thoughtstream until, after a time, you become so visually corrupted you're incapable of differentiating between real life and the commercials, even of delineating the differences between Ho Chi Minh and Horace the Horse.

Rhona, stretching towards me, lightly rapped her knuckle on my brow.

'Hullo, anybody home?'

I grinned and, perfectly naturally, as if we were lovers, took her hand in mine – and held it – in public for goshsakes!

'Sorry. A thought just crossed my mind.'

'And you'd to give the poor thing your arm's that it?'

Bedside banter. This was good, so very good.

'Eh?'

'What thought?'

'Can't remember now.'

'Course you can.'

'Don't worry, I'll maybe have another one soon.'

'Another?'

'Thought.'

'Idiot!'

And the handclasp going on, those interlaced fingers sustaining the moment beyond embarrassment to that inflowing intimacy of younger, more spontaneous times which proved beyond doubt how thoroughly the tactile sense is embedded in the nervescape of nostalgia; the fierce grieving for a lost smile, voice, or scent. Aye, this comes into it but what's really heavy is the absence of touchability, that mood-flattener when you're unable to simply reach out and stroke or caress a loved one. And what makes such grief even heavier is the haunting regret that you'd been so miserly in doling out the hugs when the chance was still around.

The thought that'd made me link hands with Rhona was lost to me now – gone. Maybe just as well for it'd probably been rooted in malice and self-pity – a poor soil in which to cultivate roses. 'Aye, but jist the stuff tae gar the thistles loup!' as Hugh MacD. might've put it.

When the end-of-visit bell finally rang I paid scant heed. In fact, for the first time since Rhona had been hospitalised I was the last flatbelly to leave the ward. I even turned and gave her a wave when I got to the door. I kid you not.

41

We were discussing our schooldays, Vic Rudge and me, which gave'm a fine excuse for the airing of his expensive dental-repair work (expensive for the molar-howker, that is, for Rudge had probably extracted his cooperation on a 'You-fix-my-mouth-cheap-or-I'll-fix-your-mouth-expensive' deal). Anyway, his mouth fairly winked and sparkled with gold conceits. But having rid itself of the decay and the caries that go along with fangblight, Vic the Viper still retained his gutter markings; the unsloughable skin of a slum upbringing testified to this as did the slangy glitter of his lingo. No way would he seek to have his cold banging speech delivery altered, for in the dark windings of the city which teemed with the defenceless prey he fed on, his voice was a key weapon. 'What was yon PT teacher called, Tam? Mind, him that was podgering the tarts' gym teacher. Eh? Chambers. Aye, you're right – Torture Chambers. A right masochist, eh? Swaggering aboot wae yon leg bone – the humerus, I think they call it, though there was bugger all funny about getting rapped on the nut wae it. "Bone meets solid bone," he used to say, mind? Then, if you were unlucky to cop the period afore the dinner break in his Black Museum; all they white blobby things floating aroon in jars, slices of fag-blitzed lungs, livers that'd been through the booze-grinder. See yon sheep's heart he used to send round. Mind? – bobbing aboot in yon beaker. I can still smell the stink of yon reserving fluid. Aye, a right rotten lump of meat; it was the hairy stuff growing on it that gave me the boke. Wobble-wobble in the beaker and the bone-basher making you haud it right up to your face. Wobble-wobble. Put you right off your chuck. D'you hear about the day I stuck the thing doon yon kid's neck? What was he called again? Cohen. Aye, Ice-cream Cohen. His auld man wanted me crucified in the playground.' He sighed out some cigar smoke. 'Aye, they were the days, eh?'

Oh, aye, they were the days alright, Vic. You strutting around the playground like Mussolini, you'n yon pair, Warty Watson and Knuckles Macleod. 'Pile-on' was your favourite pastime, especially when you found yon Tommy Clay would squeal like a big Jessie just because his ribcage was threatening to splinter beneath the weight of twenty or so bodies. You'd go hunting for'm at playtime, you'n your pack of neanderthals; drag'm from his hidey-hole in the lavvy then haul'm out into the playground and invite half of the school to come'n lie on his screams. 'We've got a lumpa Clay – Pile On!' Aye, they were the days right enough, eh?

In the pub a man babbling nonsense. His head bare as an orphan's plate, the skull blue-badged by an old scar such as a hammer-blow might've left. 'Nazi bastards!' he roared at the barmen. 'And sons of Nazi bastards!' Giving the Nazi salute he goosestepped to the door which wafted him from sight.

'Auld bugger's bomb-happy,' Rudge said. 'Cargo's loose.'

He looked thoughtfully into his drinkless glass. I got the feeling he was loitering in the hope that I'd shove in another round. His stare rose to lock into mines. He shook his head. 'Cannae get away wae it, Tam – you still stuck'n the Scabby. Fuck me, it's like meeting your granny in Argyle Street twenty years efter you've buried'r. I mean chrissake, even auld pigeon's've stopped gawn tae Scobie Street. You'll be telling me next you're still ripping the tables doon the Brandon.'

On a high bracket a TV set dozed in a dream of cowboys and Colorado stone-scapes. Rudge was making me wait for his return round. 'I mean,' he went on, 'nane of us was that bright at school. No expected to be – factory fodder, right? But you, Tam, if I mind right, you were a brainy wee shite, well, wae enough gumption tae get your arse aff the bin when it's on fire. Must've been safter than I thought – hiding behind aw they books.

'Stop that guy – he's got a wean up his jook!'

When Rudge's unmistakable voice had boomed out in the Maternity corridor I had still found it hard to accept that it was really him. But there I'd been, exchanging a hypocritical handshake, mouthin how good it was to see'm again, and updating our respective biographies as we'd picked our way down snow-muffled streets to the boozer. Rudge's wife, so he'd told me, had 'dropped another foal'. The property market was his stamping ground these days. Renting pest-holes to skint newly-weds. Prosperous he looked with it, but still willing, I'd bet, to take the last tanner from a blind dosser.

In the Scabby's backcourt kingdom of rusting railings and midden pits, Vic'd been the undisputed monarch. Nature had rigged him out for leadership, equipping him with a formidable kit of bone'n muscle, not to mention a capacity for survival that outranked Methusela. Vic's philosophy in life was grounded in the need to make his mark. People, he claimed, remembered a wound, bruise, or scar longer than they did a handshake. And in his book that was the prime requirement – to be remembered. His whole purpose for existing at all was to tattoo himself on other people's memories; but to do this you had to get under their skins. And one by one they'd come for him with sleeves rolled up at the ready: gangfighters, schoolteachers, oinks, screws, and social workers, each of them itching to impose his or her authority on'm.

Rudge'd leaned across the table to check out my face.

'You had much in the booze-line the day?' he asked.

'Nothing much. How?'

He rose and crossed to the counter. Almost immediately one of the Maternity Mafia latched onto him, with whiskery smiles and trembly handshake he tried to work Rudge over. For his efforts he received an affable pat on the back and an earful of cigar smoke. Vic eventually returned with the drinks. 'See they pensioners,' he said, 'cannae beat their patter. Great, so it is.' He put the drinks on the table, a double whisky for him and for me –

'What the fuck's this?' I wanted to know.

He flicked some cigar ash from his seat with a hankie then sat down. That sinister event that was intended to be a smile happened to his face. 'It's a tomato juice, Tam,' he said. 'You must've seen one – even in the Dog. It still there, by the way?'

Before I could blow my stack Rudge said, 'I take it, Tam, since I once saw you driving a towel van or something, that you've got that daud of paper that allows you to snuff oot pensioners on the Queens Highway?'

I nodded.

'For somethin more up-to-date than a chariot, I hope.' He smirked apologetically, 'Forget I said that . . .' Puff-puff went the cigar; sip-sip, his greedy lips. 'I want you to dae's a favour, Tam . . .'

The favour was this: for two blue ones I was to drive Vic to a Casino – he felt lucky tonight – then I was to take his car home to Dumbreck and park it in his driveway: keys to be letterboxed. Apart from feeling lucky, Vic also had the inclination to get himself stinko, but was definitely not into blowing into the pig's bladder. Since this was to be his last night on the ran-dan – his wife'd be coming home with the wean tomorrow – he wanted it to be special.

You would've thought that I'd been plugged into the national grid so powerfully did vengeful lightning surge through my bones, shedding on Rudge, I'm sure of this for he clinched his eyes a little from the glare, the raw radiance of long-awaited retribution.

'You've got to be fuck'n joking!'

How I savoured every syllable of that refusal. The vehemence of it was for all the little Clays who'd been strewn behind me, those green-boned, half-toned versions of what I'd become, those snottery-nosed Thomases still back there nursing the hurts visited upon them by Victor the Visigoth. Fate, or whatever you want to call that croupier who shuffled Time with such dexterity, had at last skimmed across that bankrupting table of hers a card of astounding potency – a winner at last. But Rudge didn't seem to think so; he upped the stakes.

'Three quid, then,' he said.

Shrugging, working-class shoulders are good at making this wee gesture of resignation. From the Industrial Revolution onwards we kept getting better'n better at it. 'You'll work an eighteen-hour day, six days a week, and no slacking. Take it or leave it!' (shrug-shrug); 'Right, chaps, when I blow the whistle, up'n at the Hunnish swine. And remember, if you're hit, try to fall face-down on the barbed wire to give the chap behind you a better foothold.' (shrug-shrug): and one day, Thomas, you'll do your chauffeur for the bullying bastard who, when you were a kid, walked all over you with his hobnailed boots! (shrug-shrug) . . .

Rudge fell for it. 'You'll do it then?'

A full-house of hatred as I banged my cards onto the table. 'I'd rather have the pox and five mother-in-laws!'

He laughed at that one – the famous Rudge laugh which was modelled on the chilling giggle of the gangster Richard Widmark'd played in *The Kiss of Death* alongside the reputed-to-be laziest actor in Hollywood (he'd have his stand-in chew his gum for'm), Victor Mature. After the movie'd been to the Planet, Vic could be heard practising the laugh, frightening weans and grannies with it in the putrid backcourts where he casually duffed up kids, or stoned dogs because it'd started to rain or something.

When the manic giggle tapered off Vic lifted his whisky glass and gave his tonsils a good gargling with the spirits; the laugh, as if it'd been refuelled started up again only now there was more edge to it, more threat. A punter who'd been throwing nifty spears until then plonked one about a foot off the dartboard. Even members of the Maternity Mafia ceased their wheedling flattery and turned to glance uneasily in our direction. It was that kind of laugh, and Vic'd been working on it a long time, remember. Around his pulpy mouth some muscle-strips meant to aid the birth of smiles, tried, but failed to simulate an amused expression, but the eyes, those pitiless slum-grey eyes were saying: 'Who the fuck're you to turn me down? I'm Vic Rudge, remember? I wore out shoes kicking your arse up'n doon Scobie Street.' His laughter ceased abruptly. He snapped: 'Three and a half bar. What d'you say?'

I said nothing.

What began as a wheedling tone quickly passed to insult. 'C'mon, Tam, I'm asking as a favour, for auld times' sake. Remember the gang's slogan? – "We're the boys no one can stop – The Scobie Hatchet – chop! chop! chop!"? I mean seventy bob, for fucksake – you widnae make that playin the moothie at Glesca Cross.' This was an obvious crack at my appearance. In other words – 'You look like a bloody busker in that clobber, so don't come the high'n mighty crap wae me!'

His mouth flexed as if he was chomping down his rage. Another wee shot at the wheedling game. 'You'd be doing me a right favour, Tam.' He raised his glass and made a couping motion with it to his mouth. 'A wee drap too much of the auld how's-your-faither the day. Know what I mean, wett'n the wean's heid and that?' He shook his head. 'Cannae be withoot wheels, Tam – no in ma game.'

'Sorry Vic,' I said and felt maliciously pleased with myself. 'Got other plans.'

His face seemed to snap down its few civil features and muscles, surfaced like so many steely components on a ship's war deck, priming it for immediate hostile action. 'Four pounds, then?'

'Not interested.'

'Fuck me, Tam – I could get a run in the Provost's car for that.'

'I'll have to split,' I said, pushing away my untouched tomato juice.

As I rose he caught me by the sleeve, drawing me back onto my seat. 'Awright, forget the Casino. Tell you what, run me ower to my sister'n law's pad – off the Byres Road. I'll give you the cab-fare back. What d'you say?'

I demurred long enough to get his fingers tapping testily on the table. Might not be such a bad idea – a night on the Westend tiles. Ages since I'd been there. I could maybe drop by the Rubaiyat which used to be a favourite pub of mine. I looked across at Rudge then gave'm the nod.

Right away he swung his drink over then smacked the drained glass on the table. 'Right, let's go.' Vic was back in charge once more, the balance restored in his favour. He rose and from his wallet tugged out some banknotes. 'See's a bottle of laughing water, Tam – I've a phone call to make . . .'

Before I'd the chance to touch my forelock he'd crossed the pub to the corner where the phone was being used by a punter in cap'n boiler-suit. One intimidating glare from Rudge and he cringingly surrendered the instrument.

Meanwhile, I was striking back as best I could. 'A bottle of your worst whisky,' I said. 'Make it real rot-gut stuff.'

The barman came back with a smile on his coupon bearing a really fine malt whisky. 'There y'are,' he chirpily said, joining in the joke, 'you canny get worse stuff than this – chew the arse out yer stomach so it will.'

Vic was not chuffed with my driving.

'For chrissake,' he grumbled, 'you're no in your towel-van noo. Take it easy. Watch that bastard.'

I punched the horn as a man weaved from the pavement into our path. The drunky, volleying curses, became a dwindling demon in my rear-view mirror. The car's near-newness fazed me a wee bit, for Rudge in his forthright manner had assured me that I'd have a hinge in my windpipe if I so much as dented an ashtray during the journey. The car was a white Hillman Minx (this year's model), black trim, and with a lean mileage count on its clock: it was obviously well thought of and well cared for. That was about it – there'd be no Sherman-like tour of the dashboard, no jaunty techno-jargon about the magical speed-aids it packed under its bonnet, not even a quick ref to how many secs it took to get from start-to-depart. Rudge was too busy for that kind of crap, too busy, that is, trying to save his pride'n joy from becoming the youngest car in the auto-dump.

The passenger-driver is the worst kind of car sickness there is, about as welcome to a motorist as a raincloud was to Noah. The p/d is the most carping of critics, the Jiminy Cricket of the autoworld, a travelling vote of no-confidence. Sarcastic, too – very.

'I think this bridge has the right of way!'

But even worse than your verbal smartass is your chronic sigher. This gloomster makes evident from the first turn of the wheels his regret for having got himself entombed in your mobile crypt. As I could've remarked to Rudge, who combined grumbles, sarcasm, and sighs, not to mention blind panic, 'There's nac use greeting aboot the quality of the service after they've shut the fuck'n pyramid!' Aye, he was stuck with me until breath did us part, and all the sighing in the world wasn't going to help'm. I think, even as early on as George Square and its Christmas lights where Johnny Mathis was megaphoning his winterland drivel and we were sliding beneath – no, let's be honest, we were juddering beneath – neoned foliage as I, with a regretted grind here'n there, was familiarising myself with the gearbox, I think even then he'd toyed with the idea of dumping me and taking his chances on a drunk-driving charge, either that or grabbing a cab and leaving the Minx as a chrissy present for the auto-vultures of which our city has a no mean amount. But the ejection of an unwilling party from your automobile might possibly be met with resistance of the noisy kind – just the goryless incident a festive oink might want to scribble up some space in his notebook, to give some substance to his flat-footing.

'For fucksake – keep your mind on the road!' bawled Rudge.

He looks rattled. I've never seen a rattled Rudge before. Weird it looks, like Jack Sherman without his Greg's. Barefaced robbery. Denuded of power. I wonder if the crossroads hex I put on'm worked. Don't shake your head at the idea, Jack – it might just drop off. Oops! I turn my indignant face to Rudge: 'D'you see that bass – flinging his anchors oan at the last minute . . .' Rudge was in a flap. He looked like somebody'd opened the window and chucked a fizzing Molotov cocktail into his lap. I scowled at the unseen driver in front. You'll get a crumpled tin arse the next time you try that brink-braking on me, chummy. Now, shouldn't I be on the inside if I'm to take the filter? Aye, so I should be. Here goes. There, nifty bit of steering that, even if Rudge doesn't seem to think so, him and those hornblowing kerb-huggers by the sound of it.

Rudge made me stop, told me to wait, got out, then scurried round a corner. Maybe he was heading for a pub toilet to discard his ruined Y-fronts or had stopped by its courage-refill counter for a big glass of Novocaine. When he came back he was clutching a discreet little package wrapped in confectionary paper and tied with red ribbon. My, he must be fond of that sister-in-law of his: chocs and whisky!

'Eleanor Rigby, she leaves her face in the glass by the door . . .' the lovable Liverpudlians were chanting from Rudge's recently acquired quadrophonic tape-system – the last word on in-car entertainment. I dirged along with the Dab Four, those poor unfortunates who'd wakened up in a cavern to find themselves transmogrified into Beatles, a horrific experience for all concerned, I'm sure. As the Maharishi Yogi didn't tell them (presumably he was too busy laughing into his moneybag), 'Fame is a two-headed adder – one at either end.' A koan worth the considering as they watch their wormlike tunes fleeing their applegreen heads – Mac's too sweet, Lennon too sour. Good to hum along to though, and I did just that while Rudge fussed like an old maiden aunt about my gear changing, my accelerating, my braking, my everything to do with the art of driving. Towel vans, I suppose, can rub off the finer points of negotiating your way through traffic in an over-autofied city. But I wasn't to know that, was I?

Aye, it was really fab, humming about that poor Rigby lassie and about all the lonely people, weaving through the lumpen traffic-flow on those sporty wheels, the very epitomy of dash and freedom, all the more enhanced by my unkempt appearance, the hippie rags, combat-jacket, denims and so on, which my fellow travellers with their envious-looking, lateral glances no doubt took to be the sartorial eccentricity of a social high-flier. But who could that hunched Harris-Tweedy person beside'm be? A hoodlum's jaw on him but all its menace lost by the frantic lip-chewing look of him, the way from time to time he'd fling his hands in the air, his peepers popping. Probably he was the driver's big brother, a manic type being returned to a private clinic where a cure for his class delusions would prove of no avail.

When we arrived at Vic's destination and I'd parked the car amongst a flock of similar beasts huddled as if for warmth near a block of flats – and not a dented bumper or scraped wing to show for it, I said to him: 'I really lapped that up, Vic. No kiddin. Wish noo I'd agreed to drive it hame for you. Nifty job.'

But it seemed that I'd flunked the test. Without a word he passed me the small sheet bearing the Queen's photo and some illiterate's scribbled promise-to-pay, then with a jerking thumb indicated that I should vamoose. I got out and stood in the slush. 'Be seeing you Vic.'

It must've sounded like a threat. He nodded. 'Yeah, yeah, see you Tam.' Sitting there in the car's cockpit he'd the stricken kind of look you'd expect to see on the face of a kamikaze pilot who can't quite figure how he's managed to land his suicide-crate intact.

I slammed the door shut, then went splashing along the thawing pavement.

42

Effie, my personal Harpy – that's right, the one who looked like Nobby Stiles with teeth – has vamoosed. No kidding, she's up'n offed, gone, departed, flown the coop, left without so much as a note scribbled in her green blood, a poisoned chalice, or a dagger through my portrait.

Aye, you're right – I've never mentioned Effie before. And for a very good reason: she warned me (what a ticklesome buzz the past tense gives to the palate!) that any reference to herself, specifically or by innuendo, would result in a triple misfortune coming down on my brainbox. The same conditions applied to her chums: Jonah, Circe, Medusa, and Fred Doakes of Boston. However, she gave me a free hand in my dealings with Fate whom I was at liberty to rubbish and I could bad-mouth that fortune cookie, Kismet, as often and as crudely as I wanted to. Pardon? How'n the hell would I know who Fred Doakes is? D'you think I hang around with that bunch of snake-haired, long-fanged, multi-headed bunch of life-meddling creeps? No way! Anyway, I've never been to Boston, not even to the one in Lincs.

How do I know that Effie's really gone? Well, how do you know whether your head is or is not up a camel's ass? You just know. And what a difference her departure has wrought: hitherto clamped and curtained windows are flung open; light pervades my being; from the cellar arises the sounds of scrubbing, brooming, and hosing; up there on the shingles carpenters' hammers go tick-tock-tick; while through in the mezzanine the brush of a decorator goes slip-slap-slop. (Incidentally, I'm a bit hazy about the purpose or location of the mezza-whatsit, but it sounds like a fine thing to own.)

But maybe I'd better trim back a little on these effusions of elation, just in case another harpy is in the vicinity with her fire-coal eyes on the lookout for a vacant shoulder. Come again? What's the real reason for my sudden upsurge in optimism? Sorry, that's for Rhona to hear first. Aye, you've got it, for her ears only. Right now, I've a sacrifice to make, this being the customary gesture, a way of demonstrating one's thanks for the harpyless future. There's nothing those domestic gods like better than a wee bit buttering up, to be propitiated. Speaking of which, I was well propishiated last night, propishiated clean out of my skull. A lush in the westend slush.

I've decided what my sacrifice should be – to pack in smoking. I'm going to chuck it right now, this very minute, so that when my feet hit the rug they'll be attached to a non-smoker. To mark the occasion, a wee ceremony is called for: 'The Lowering of the Fag'. After I'd had my last draw on my final cigarette I broke the beast's back in the ashtray with my thumb. From the pressure-splits in the tube its amber guts extruded, while around its writhing but rapidly perishing head sparks seethed like a crisis of red ants and, in a twinkling, disappeared. This completed the ritual. I dumped the carcinogenic crap on the bedside table: I was now a non-smoker.

My lungs, a pair of cynical wheezers, hailed the news with a round of coughs, as if saying in response to my pledge of a fresh-air future: 'Aye, we'll believe that when we breathe it!' Cautiously now I lowered my throbbing gourd onto the pillow. A giant woodpecker inside my head was trying to trepan his way to freedom – any minute now his beak would cleave through my forehead. I closed my eyes. For a while, I lay there watching tiny bugs of light swarming in that most personal of darknesses. Wasn't this what the physicists saw when they peered into their dark hives of decaying atoms – the unpatterned awfulness at the root of things? Stability is an illusion – the world's a bag of bees God pokes at with a stick and growls – 'Make honey, damn you!'

C'mon can that stuff. No gloom today. I hereby declare this to be a holiday. Clay Day. I shall disport myself in a carnival manner. I shall seek out laughter and bring cheer to my fellow punters and punteresses. The telling of jokes – a most beneficial social occupation. A cloud on the horizon, though. Don't pay attention – maybe it'll pass over. Talky Sloan's funeral is today. Damn. Maybe I'll skip it. Let the dead bury the dead. Maybe he'll not show. Talk his way out of it.

I rose and flung some clothes about my chittering frame. Crossing to the sink I leaned across it and rubbed a patch in the misty pane. I peered through it: a thaw was underway, albeit a slow one: icicles hanging from the midden roof were grudgingly casting their pearls; here and there holes had melted in the slum snowscape so that there was a warmer, dappled look to the morning.

I soon had a fine fire purring in the hearth. I sat close to the blaze and tried to convince my dead man's bones that a thaw'd been declared to which they were invited.

Outside, on the stairs, someone dropped a grandfather clock.

Well, that's what it sounded like, a pandemonium of chimes, gongs, breaking glass and rupturing clockwork, plus a myriad of tinier dins riding on the backs of these major ones, a cog-busting explosion which, instead of dying away, on the contrary was augmented as the clock went down the stairs with a cracked chime uproar, gathering speed so that when it struck the wall outside my door it smashed itself to instant Time-dross.

I flung the door wide. I'd expected to see a wrecked Grandfather clock laid out on my landing, its casing awry, its brassy guts, all yon complicated gearing which gives the tick its tock, spilled out in shameful exposure – and that's more or less what I did see, but with one major distinction: this was my Grandfather's Grandfather clock!

Looking a whiter shade of pale, auld Wattie Mullens stood crouched on the edge of his half-landing, as if he was trying to psych himself into hurling himself down the stairs. Something that sounded like a bird screech broke from his mouth then, in a creepy, slow-motion parody of the knee-splayed style of the descent adopted by him in his coal-heaving days when, all muck'n muscle, he'd come breenging down the stairs, whistling an Orange Flute tune.

Like an ambulance man examining a road accident victim for signs of life though it was plain to see the head was missing, I knelt alongside the mangled clock and ran my hands over what had undoubtedly been Granda Gibson's finest carpentry piece. As the agitated and trembling greybeard stepped onto the landing beside me, from the tip of the clock's big hand I plucked a piece of notepaper. I smoothed it out and ran my eyes across the cramped handwriting of Eddie Carlyle.

It held no surprises, as snottery as he himself was. Ma Carlyle (hadn't he warned me?) would not have the infested clock in her house. I wasn't to forget that I was to attend xmas dinner at the Carlyles', this year. I was to remember'n be prompt and his mother suggested that I should take the opportunity to get a haircut for it and to wear something more appropriate than that 'old soup-queue jacket' I seemed to favour. I was also to remember to be sober . . . signed: Edward Carlyle, a signature as bleak and devoid of ornamentation as the man himself, the kind you see at the foot of execution lists and Parole refusals. Xmas dinner at the Carlyles', eh? Somehow, I couldn't help but feel that an invite from Eva and Adolf to join them in the Bunker for an 'End to Hostilities' cyanide thrash would sound more inviting.

Wattie gave a wee stagger. I glanced up at'm. He looked like he was about to pop an artery. I rose quickly and placed my arm, my good one, about his shaking shoulders: 'C'mon, auld yin, we'll have a wee swig of tea. What d'you say? A cuppa tea makes you fit as a flea.' I grinned at'm. 'My auld man used to say that a lot. He was a helluva guy for the sayings.'

'Your auld man was the salt of the earth Tommy, so he was,' Wattie said with a fervent ring to his voice. 'And your mither tae . . . great wee wummin. And see your wife . . .'

'C'mon, Wattie, you'll have me blushing.'

I'm still a touch propishiated. Too much jollification. Well, I'd something to celebrate, hadn't I? I'd stuck one away at last into Vic Rudge's net. That made the score about 150-1; no hope of equalising but at least it took the bad look of it away, saved myself from a whitewash. I savoured retro-shots of Vic trying out his facial panic muscles, maybe for the first time; whole nerve chains caught napping. He'd been right, yon towel van had screwed up my driving.

A minor mystery was solved during the tea-drinking session – the identity of the Closet Ghost came out. It'd been Wattie, of course. Who else, when you thought about it. Keeping his head lowered, so that his words were hard to make out, he confessed to using my wc from time to time, either when he'd got 'caught short' or the weather made a visit to Shug Wylie's place difficult, if not dangerous; another thing was the fact that the Bum Boutique was shut during the evenings and, as well I knew, diarrhoea didn't pay no mind to clocks nor watches, and the same went for dysentery. He nodded when I put it to'm that he'd brought the London *Times* to the bog, Friday last. He agreed that it was more than likely, for he was always bringing newspapers and mags, from his rambles. His memory, he claimed, was 'hellish poor', waur even than the auld yin doon in the close. Sometimes he'd go to check his nameplate on his front door to find out who he was. Aye, and afore he'd got back to the kitchen he'd forgotten again. As to the empty carton of Passing Clouds fags, he'd saved ciggy-packets when he was a boy and although his collection had long been scattered to the four winds, auld habits died hard. I considered the other minor puzzles, like who the leather-jacketed snoop had been, also the 'Kelvingrove Kidnap' and came up with prosaic solutions to both. It was more than probable that the Futility Furnishing Co. had stuck a financial agent on my tail and that the 'doppelgänger' incident had been three-quarters imagination on young Jason's part to a quarter of panic on mines. Hadn't the guy taken'm to an artguard as soon as he'd laid eyes on Jason? But they'd played a wee game as they watched me buzzing around like a wonky dalek.

According to the auld rogue, he'd been taking the clock up to his own flat for safe-keeping, and he'd been intending to return it as soon as he'd heard me moving around. Again, I assured him that the ticker was a candidate for the midden and he wasn't to worry himself unduly. I gave'm the fags, about half a carton's worth, and while he was going through his tedious rigmarole about 'good neighbours being the finest treasure to be found on earth', I was kind of shooing him out, muttering gruffly, 'Aye, and may the sun shine on your crops tae, Wattie . . .'

43

I'd missed my last shave at the hands of Joe Fiducci.

He was apologetic, desolated even, but there it was. All the tools of his trade had been packed away. He, himself, would be leaving soon. He awaited the return of Luigi, his son – gone to attend a business matter – then he'd be off. Joe's wife was not too well this morning, he worried about her. He was sorry he couldn't even offer a farewell cuppa, but the water –

I waved aside his apologies. If it was okay I'd have a last wee puff then be on my way. 'Of course, of course . . .' He was double-banking on the apologies and thank-yous this morning, one of his mannerisms when he was uptight about something. These had variations but the most common were: 'Thank you, thanks', 'Definitely, for sure', or 'I'm sorry, so sorry . . .'

It was my turn to look foolish, or maybe even heroic when, having said I was for a smoke and was therefore expected to go through the pre-light-up ritual, the production of cigs for a start, the lighter, and so on, here I was saying instead: 'Ach, I'll no bother – smoking too much these days, anyway.' And to back this up had a fit of coughing which didn't sound in the least theatrical.

Joe nodded his approval. 'Was I in a hurry?' he asked.

'Was I ever?' I replied. We both smiled over a mutual memory.

'You need to get some hurry into your life, Tommy,' he'd said to me one day, 'worry comes later but hurry is now, when you're young, when every way you turn there's another winning-post. The black car days soon creep up on you. Nobody wants to win a black car race, Tommy, but somebody has to lead the procession, eh, somebody gotta be the . . .' He'd hesitated.

'Pall-guy?' I'd suggested, and we'd both had a good laugh.

Well, Joe, old pal, here's another black car day. But maybe I'll chuck funerals as well as fags. I hadn't much respect for Talky when he was alive, so why pay my respects now? Anyway I'm bloody tired looking into the filth-holes of graves, of delivering blood-kin and pub-kin to yon grisly furnace doors. Christ, getting morbid and it's not even opening-time yet. 'Sorry, Joe – what was that?'

He was asking a very droll question: would I mind looking after the shop for a bit. I smiled, convinced he was joking for the two shop-strippers were already to hand and in the very process of robbing it of its assets – both men looked similar in their bunnets and blue boilersuits and in their slow, almost langorous way of going about things. Their problem right now seemed to concern the best method of removing a wall mirror. I would've thought that unscrewing the screws was a logical choice, but then I'm merely an amateur loafer – these guys were real pros. Luigi had obviously hired them; you could tell by the way they were keeping a casual-looking but nevertheless constant scan on the go for his return. The old man they could ignore, for he was obviously loath to see his mirror wall coming down, watch the old familiarity of his place being vandalised in slow-motion. Joe was being serious – he was asking me to mind the shop! He'd a prescription to pick up for his wife, and a few cheerios to say.

I nodded. 'Say all the cheerios you want to, Boss' – a title I bestowed on him on only very special occasions as a mark of my respect. 'I'll see that your shop gets gutted while you're away.' He laughed and the workmen, since it involved the use of only a few facial muscles and could be done without taking their hands from their pockets, laughed too, soft guffaws.

'I won't be long,' Joe said and this was followed by its dutifully edited echo, 'not too long at all … .'

I nodded and tried to look jovial, but privately beneath all that skin rufflement to produce a fake grin, I was saying to myself, 'Yeah, Joe, by the hang of you, you won't be long at all. Black car day soon, Joe, the one when you get to ride with the flowers.'

Whether Joe was going to the chemist or to say his ta-tas, didn't really matter, I guess he just wanted to be absent when the mirrors started to come down. It's all over for a barber-shop when it checks in its mirrors. The sudden loss of the repeated image was a perspective shrinkage hard to bear, I suppose. How could you barber on without the doubled reassurement of a benchful of customers, a nice big healthy crop of hair to be harvested?

With the departure of the old man the pair of workmen got down to some intensive loafing. One of them went to the exertion of planting his behind on the bench. The other one took up a folded-arm stance by the doorway as if keeping an eye on the thaw had been one of his assigned tasks. I'd seated myself in the window-chair for the last time.

His sentence made porous with yawns, the guy on the bench, the *Daily Record* crackling between his mitts, said: 'It's like something oot a cartoon, so it is.' The mirror in front of me just caught his glance and no more. 'D'you see it?' He actually prised himself from the bench and came across to me in his slow lumbering gait. I could've told'm that I'd had a front row seat at the mummy/bubble car drama, but I took a shufty just the same.

Aw jeezuz, look what they've done to wee Lucas – they've turned'm into a bastard'n tree.

BUBBLE TROUBLE FOR MATT, THE MUMMY! ran the headline to a splodge of journocrap, a larky treatment which was in keeping with the photo which depicted this stark white tree with its limbs hoisted on weighted wire-pullies to the ceiling and wee Matt trying to grin chirpily from a hole in its trunk. A nurse was to be seen, lots of her, beaming radiantly as she held a sprig of mistletoe over Matt's bandaged napper.

'What some folk'll do to get their face in the paper, eh?' said workman number two who was still doggedly supervising the thaw. His mate, who'd actually been standing totally unaided for over two minutes, astounded me even more by producing a screwdriver. 'C'mon,' he said, 'we'd best see to getting this lot down.'

Once they'd actually got started the asset-strippers made steady enough progress. Soon they'd unscrewed the mirror at the far end of the shop. It glittered and flashed with some of its old zest as they lowered it to the floor. I could imagine the avalanche of reflected objects which had long roosted there, sense their astonishment at being disturbed so drastically at this late hour of their existence. These now untwinned objects included a dusty coathanger which'd hung on a wallpeg for as long as I can remember. It'd once been the property of someone called Robbie, a name he'd lovingly poker-burned along the hanger's frame. No doubt the conceited Robbie and the clothes this simple object had borne for him on its wooden shoulders had gone the way of all things perishable, as had many of the faces that'd so briefly lodged in that cruellest of inventions – a device that won't spare us from the ravages exacted upon our flesh by the drip-drop-drip of the acid we call Time.

Where the mirror had been, a squatter shadow had already taken up residence. With a sort of tortured care the workmen carried the looking-glass – it was brimming over with novel reflections – to the door. In its passing, the mirror carried off my head (the back of it), and the chair I was lounging in. Reminding each other to have a care, that the underfoot conditions were treacherous, the workmen, with slow crunching steps, made their way towards the van.

About ten minutes later Luigi returned with Joe, whom he'd picked up on the way. Apparently Luigi's 'business matter' had been the delivery to Old Mooney of his P45 and monies due to him. But Mooney still hadn't showed up in the Brannigan household. My heart sank when I heard this for I'd still hoped that there'd be at least a tenner left from my 'winnings'. 'We'll send it Registered Delivery,' said Luigi. He tenderly laid the fingers of both hands on his ears. 'She's a very loud woman, his daughter.'

The last mirror came off the wall and the barber-shop stood steeped in a gloom the overhead lights could do little to dispel; it looked like it'd been shorn of a dimension, and in a way, so it had. I said my farewells to Luigi and Joe, exchanged handshakes and that was that. Joe got a bit teary-eyed while Luigi, in a Cossack hat and sheepskin jacket, very vigorous looking, curtly disassociated himself from a non-profit-making affair like sentiment and began to hustle the workmen. 'No, not that thing – it stays!' he said, as they prepared to uproot the Weans' Chair. All in all it wasn't turning out to be much of a day for Granda Gibson, what with his clock sliding down the stairs to its utter destruction, and now this outright rejection. Joe sighed, humped his shoulders then accompanied me from the shop. Standing in the slush we shook hands again.

'Good luck, Tommy. May your bambino be like you – only faster, eh?'

'Sure Joe,' I laughed. 'I'll send you a postcard from Down Under.'

His wave faltered some and he turned away with a look of puzzlement.

Oops, Rhona, and I promised you'd be the first to know. Never mind, a man may share a secret with his barber but only on the day he retires of course.

Smiling, I made my way across the glassy rubble, heading for the Planet. I was curious to know how the poor mummy had fared in the bungling hands of Cullen and Killoch. There just had to be a few laughs in there.

Was it only Friday last that a deepsea diver was to be seen stepping hesitantly from the auld fleapit? It seems years ago somehow. Maybe it *was* years ago. Maybe it hasn't yet happened. Have a chat with Mr Dunne the next time you see'm doddering along like an amiable old mole in one of his improvised time-warps. You won't fail to recognise him for he always dresses entirely in black, as if in mourning for clockroaches the world over. Other clues? Well, he might have a pencil behind his ear, and he could just be reading aloud from his favourite book: *Nothing Dies!*

I haven't read it myself yet, but one thing's for sure — it provides a dandy excuse for skipping Talky Sloan's funeral!